Index

Preface: Creating a Vibe, with Book Burnings

Book burnings happen frequently for religious reasons. Sometimes a religion is being burned. Other times it's the religion doing the burning. I wonder if a religion has ever been completely wiped from the face of history using book burnings. I wonder if the same could be said for any idea. It can't be enough to destroy the written material. Certainly, you'd have to go after the authors too. A book burning really doesn't harm an author. They already know their religion, their philosophy, their way of politics, or their imaginary world. Book burnings only affect the reader. They're the ones missing out, and quite often, they're the same ones burning the books.

Today, we do not burn books as often as we used to. Rates have dropped again after a sudden peak in 2001 when Harry Potter became associated with Satanism in certain sects of Christianity. We can't find frenzies like that anymore. Perhaps people nowadays are getting far more tolerant of groups like Satanists. Perhaps it's simply the shift to digital. Either way, it is your constitutional right to burn books, and I think the 90's babies are too busy burning government kush to take the time to burn a good book.

I hereby offer this book as a sacrifice. After each story in this collection is a reason to burn the preceding story. After all, burning a book without cause is a careless act of pollution, releasing harmful toluene and xylene into the atmosphere and our lungs. Feel free to use any disagreeable premises outside the ones I suggest. Once you have one, find a patch of gravel away from any vehicles or powerlines; hold the book by its corner and light the opposite corner; then drop the ignited book into the center of your pit. While the book slowly shrivels like a leaf fallen from its branch, remember that you are the breeze that pulled that leaf from its sustenance, cleansing the tree of its rot.

By the time the book is gone, the tree will be just a little closer to your design.

Lucky Girl Noir

I hope you don't think of me as a pessimist just because I believe I'm unlucky. My attitude is completely independent of my fortune. I am still hopeful for tomorrow, even though, more often than not, tomorrow takes a hard swing at my knees. Keep in mind my fortune is also independent of my attitude. No amount of smiling can keep away the hardship.

I've always been cursed, but I really didn't realize it until six years ago when doctors diagnosed me with non-Hodgkin's lymphoma at twenty-nine. As my treatment whittled away my body, I told people how lucky I was that, by the end of all this, I'd be slender and hairless like a teen model. The '90s are back, and I'd be naturally heroin chic.

Little did I know the chemotherapy would give me insulin resistance, so when I reached remission and started putting on weight, I couldn't get it to stop. I'm cancer-free nowadays, but I weigh eighty-five pounds more than I did before treatment. My favorite Le Suit doesn't fit me anymore; the same one in my size only comes in houndstooth. I'd look like op art.

I say I'm cursed, yet by all scientific evidence, bad luck does not exist. I doubt this, however, as do the pessimists for whom I'm unassociated, for the mere fact that scientists ascertained good luck *does* exist sixty years ago.

They're called Lucky Girls—women who are predisposed to flukes. Research on personal chance first began in the 1960s. By 1970, the US and China started mandatory testing on all preschoolers to distinguish high-luck individuals. Bias Probability Testing (BPT) was administered at age three when "whatever makes them happy" could be reduced to a simple confection. A piece of candy was hidden under one of three cups. The examiner told the child to pick up the cup hiding the candy. If the child correctly guessed nine times out of ten, they were deemed fortunate. Once it was clear only girls could possess this attribute, they started to call them Lucky Girls.

Lucky Girls often grew up to enter their dream jobs — doctors and lawyers — propelled to success by biased statistics. A Lucky Girl could guess on every test question and still score every nine out of ten correctly. That's an A- without any effort. So, while the Lucky Girl and I both K2'd our little brains out at the same parties in our high school years, she became an aerospace engineer while I became a beat cop.

I'm proud to say I put in the hard work to bring my rank up to detective, currently working for the San Diego Police Department's Homicide Unit. I'm part of a unique division focused on crimes involving chance manipulation caused by Lucky Girls. Sometimes, people suddenly die from strange accidents or a latent illness when they come near one. The victim's death usually contributes to some fortunate event that ultimately benefits the Girl. Sometimes, it's obvious: a geriatric CEO's heart finally gives out as soon as a Lucky Girl becomes the next in line to replace them. Sometimes, however, a death requires deeper investigation. It's our job to connect the dots.

Like this one: a bus tour at the zoo hit a pothole just as a man leaned over the edge of the railing. He fell over and tumbled under the wheels. The weight crushed his head. Later, we discovered this man worked at In-N-Out and had been stealing credit card information from random patrons. That night, he had planned to charge one of his victims' accounts for a ticket to a foreign country. This victim just happened to be a Lucky Girl.

When we find such a link, the death becomes Manslaughter by Fortune. In these cases, the acting judge always acquits the Lucky Girl, but the government owes the family compensation. Lucky Girls aren't held accountable for these murders as part of a government deal to keep Lucky Girls distinguishable from non-Luckies when in public. In exchange for bearing a blue star tattoo on their cheek, Lucky Girls get certain privileges. The tattoo makes it hard for them to exploit people or businesses in games of chance; that's why you'll never see a Lucky Girl gambling in Vegas.

Because of these slight impedances, no one would ever expect someone outside the Lucky Girl population to bear the same star tattoo. And yet, as I passed my eyes over the dead body on that warm March night, I was convinced a non-Lucky had inked herself to look the part. That mark tied the victim to chance, so my unit was called to the scene. Yet a real Lucky Girl couldn't be a victim of such a heinous crime.

"Must be an imposter," I said, running the ring of my flashlight over the body. The girl was a real beauty—Gen Y with long black hair and a floral shift dress. No pockets meant no ID. I stopped my light on her head, checking our entry wound, half a centimeter, right between the eyes. There was also a contusion on her cheek where a stray bullet had grazed her face. It had split off one of the arms of her star. I knelt and rubbed the tattoo with my thumb, half-expecting it to smear. "It's real."

"I've seen shops offer the design." I turned to see my superior, Sgt. Abelardo Marroquin, looking at her. "It's not illegal, just stupid. Playing dress up like that could piss off a real one. And if you get on their bad side, you know what their luck will do to you."

"Does it even work like that?" I asked.

"They get 'whatever makes them happy,'" replied Abelardo. "Subconsciously, they put out a hit, and Fate's the hired gun."

"This doesn't look like fate, though," I said, continuing to explore every corner of the crime scene. Our Jane Doe was in a back alley between a soup kitchen and an asset management firm. Her left shoulder sat in a gray puddle. I followed the stream of liquid with my flashlight illuminating the source: old tuna noodle casserole leaking from several holes in a bottle-green dumpster—nine holes, to be exact. "This is no random mugging. And this is no imposter. They got her the only way you can kill a Lucky Girl."

Abelardo walked up to where my light fell. He knelt at a safe distance from the dribbling garbage. "Fire ten times, and their luck runs out. Why the Lucky Girl didn't escape with all that time is beyond me, though."

I was shocked. This case wasn't Manslaughter by Fortune. "This was planned assassination."

"Then I guess you can go home," replied Abelardo. His voice was stern. He knew I'd want to stay on the case despite its disconnection from my work.

"What- what are you talking about?" I stammered.

He smiled awkwardly and scratched at the fades of his haircut.. "This is kind of outside your usual investigations, wouldn't you agree?"

"Abby, no…"

"It's been a long time since you've worked a case with an actual culprit. I think we need to talk about it before we make such a leap."

One of the very reasons my superiors assigned me to my current division was that the crimes were accidental, requiring mental work but little in terms of physical activity. This work was deemed appropriate for someone with cancer, but nowadays, I feel stronger. "I'm better than ever. Tempered steel."

"Let's just take it slow, alright?" Abelardo's eyes were darting all over my body. I could feel his gaze measuring me up.

"There's nothing I can do about the weight," I said, disappointed by his judgment. "It's not a sign I'm out of shape."

"I haven't noticed your weight," guarded Abelardo. "This is about the type of work you're used to... the type *we're* used to." He pointed at his abdomen. "I sit in an office most of the day, Penny. I'm not cut out for this either."

I shut off my flashlight and walked to my squad car. I drove into the night, heading towards the center of town. Without a major case, I'd be off tomorrow; I now had the night to blow off steam. The curse had struck me hard, stealing that case away from me. It would have been a much-needed win.

When things go South like this, I often find comfort in playing games with no losing scenario. Practically any drinking game works. The only person who could lose a drinking game is someone who doesn't like drinking. For me, my taste for alcohol has waxed and waned all my life, but two years of separation has built up quite a longing.

I frequent the shuffleboards at Maneki's. The house rule is that your beer can't leave your hand the whole time you play. If it spills, you drink. If you hit an opponent's puck, they drink. If your puck falls into the alley, your entire team drinks.

Currently, my team consisted of myself and a chiseled 50-something in a tight white polo. He was drinking soju alone at the bar, so I asked him to be my partner. He was quick to reply. "If you don't mind a man that's legally blind," he laughed, slipping on a pair of coke-bottle glasses.

"Just my luck." I linked my arm around his and pulled him over to the tables.

I've had close friends ask if eighty-five pounds makes a difference in your dating pool. Honestly, the only thing that's really changed is the age group. Before chemo, I used to easily pass for twenty-three. It helps that I'm short, so I'd hook up with a lot of college guys. Nowadays, I'm clearly the oldest woman at the bar, but I still managed to take home cool dads and silver chads. White-shirt was no exception. After coming in last in our group's round-robin, he took me back to my apartment in Old Town, where we played another game I don't mind losing—strip poker.

I'd gone all-in and somehow lost with a pair of aces. I had my thumbs hooked on the waistband of my briefs when I heard a buzzing sound coming from behind me. My phone was ringing in my discarded jeans. Normally, I'd ignore it, but the accompanying ringtone was "Roxanne," which indicated it was police related.

"Hello, Abby," I answered with frustration. "You called just in time; I came dangerously close to feeling legitimate happiness."

"Well, it certainly can't compare to what I have in mind for you."

"Wait. Are you calling… *with good news*?!"

"John Willomendo's partner caught pneumonia sharing a scorpion bowl with an anti-vaxxer," explained the Sergeant. "He's been assigned as the head of the Lucky Girl murder. He wants you to join him as her replacement."

"He specifically requested me?"

"He requested any female from the Chance Crimes Division with more than four years experience," said Abelardo, clearly bewildered by the specificity. "That would be you, Penny."

"But why female?"

"Because my last partner was female," explained John to me the following day, "and I like to keep my partnership diverse." John and I had agreed to meet the next morning at the scene of the crime. Investigative details were much easier to identify in the sunlight. The body was gone—taken to be autopsied. A white outline was left in its place.

"Why not someone of a different race?" I inquired further.

"I'm already a mix of five races, Penny," replied John, looking eminent, "there's hardly anyone that can divide themselves from me in that regard."

John and I stood next to the dumpster. All the fish fluids had drained out onto the macadam and dried up into a white, dusty film. I cringed as John crouched, drawing his face closer to the residue. He was examining the holes near the bottom of the dumpster. "I need your thoughts on this," he said, gesturing for me to follow him down. "I figured from the angle of these holes that the culprit fired from a window on the second floor of the asset firm."

"Have you confirmed that with forensics?" I queried.

He nodded. "I was right." He pulled out an enlarged photo of the alleyway. "They rendered this image for me. Notice anything unusual?" Our computer had traced the bullet paths digitally in bright yellow, extending from the window in question. Nothing seemed odd to me at first, but on closer inspection, I realized what he was getting at.

"How many holes were in our Jane's body?" I asked.

"Exactly!" exclaimed John. "There was only one complete hole. Plus, one abrasion where she was grazed."

"But there're at least five lines passing through her," I thought aloud, "which means the killer must have fired again *after* she fell down… *after* the headshot… *why?*"

"I was hoping your expertise with luck could answer that question." John straightened up. "Lucky nine out of ten times… does that mean the last bullet should hit? Or is it randomly one of the ten fired?"

I thought back to a case where a Lucky Girl went on a shopping spree, store to store down the Gaslamp Quarter. The first nine of the ten stores she visited claimed to have been "robbed by fortune." Mysteriously, their most expensive item was miscategorized or misplaced in a bargain bin with a discount tag. But as we reached the tenth store in our investigation, they had no such complaint. In fact, they were joyous. They'd just made a fortune upcharging their already most expensive item: a gold Moncler beanie. With all the money saved earlier, the Lucky Girl was happy to pay the inflated price.

"It's always the last one," I explained.

"Well then, what happened here?"

"I can't say for sure," I responded. "It would definitely help if we could get some witness testimony."

"There *are* no witnesses." John sighed.

"They used that office window… you're telling me none of the employees noticed a stranger creeping around their building. I mean, what time was the murder?"

"Forensics says 5 p.m." John looked frustrated. "They were in the building, but I think it's better they explain it to you themselves."

John took me inside the adjacent firm: Adroit Management. We shared the elevator with several gentlemen transporting building supplies, heading towards the roof. One had several bar stools stacked onto a hand truck. Another struggled to carry a variety crate of Belvedere vodka.

We got off at the fourth floor and met with Adroit's founder, Hana Xie, dressed in her own Le Suit, artichoke pinstripe, just like my old one. It looked good on me but even better on her. It was her eyes, big and green; she looked like a sharp blade of grass.

"I'm most interested in getting this investigation solved promptly," encouraged Hana. "I'm actively interviewing, yet our candidates don't feel comfortable with any indication of violent crimes in the area."

"Surely a local would be already familiar with the weaknesses of our East Village," said John.

"Our new capital allows us to search internationally for our recruits," said Hana with a confident smile. "I at least want the facade that we work in a decent part of the country."

"New capital?" I asked.

"It's how they missed our assassin," explained John curtly. "Too busy celebrating their big win to realize an intruder had snuck into their premises."

"Our stock rose 28% and has yet to peak," said Hana defensively. "You can't stop that kind of excitement without a military-grade tranquilizer."

I stared at her.

"Russian Quaaludes," she continued, making a drinking motion followed by a look of illness. "They're delicious, but—we all passed out before closing."

"What a stroke of luck."

"I wouldn't call it luck," said Hana firmly. "Our investment strategy is based on algorithms and tenuous research into the biomedical field. We all share a background in drug development supplemented with online MBAs. We simply calculated our risk expertly."

"Well, it was certainly lucky for the murderer that this all happened a couple hours before they snuck into your office." I pointed out.

"It sounds suspicious, I know, but I assure you there's no one in my office with any motive to kill."

"No, that's not what I'm getting at, Hana. I think we're dealing with an exceptionally fortunate murderer. A Lucky Girl, most likely."

"Penny, what are you saying?" chimed in John, surprised at the thought.

"I worked hard for these opportunities," said Hana lamentably. "I set up a modest operation between a liquor store and a soup kitchen, then stretched my working capital into a team of six renegades, one of which brought me a company researching low cancer rates in capybaras. They transfected their MAGE gene into a mouse and saw tumor sizes shrink by 96 percent. Are you really trying to convince me that human progress jumped ahead roughly five years because it aided in a homicide?"

I raised my eyebrows and flattened my smile.

"Can it, Penny?" asked John, looking almost panicked.

I nodded, thinking about the time my department tied the destruction of the 1858 San Diego hurricane to a Lucky Girl who'd found a gold bar buried under Coronado Beach. "It's shocking how far luck can influence events. It *can* happen, and we have evidence that it happened here. The first shot took that Lucky Girl's life. The only way someone could get them on the first shot is if their luck was canceled out by another Lucky Girl's luck."

"Both the murderer *and* the victim?" exclaimed John. "So, the other nine shots were fired just to hide the fact?"

"Exactly. We can narrow this down pretty easily now." I turned towards Hana, who greeted my excitement with antipathy.

As Hana's strategic mind began questioning everything, she licked her lips nervously. The self-confidence that had once smoldered around her had fizzled out.

"Hana, it's not necessarily that you wouldn't have made money from that company. Luck just might have made it happen earlier. Don't-"

"Put back the fridge!" shouted Hana to a pair of gentlemen behind us. They were moving the fridge from their lunchroom up to the lounge they were adding onto the building. "The rooftop bar is canceled." Her eyes grew wide as she ran past me, heels clicking. "Not until we've really earned it."

John and I promptly left and picked up an envelope waiting for us back at the office before driving to a late-night spot for kebabs and Turkish coffee. The envelope held dossiers on all the known

Lucky Girls in the city. A rare phenomenon, there were only seventeen. Seventeen suspects certainly helped us narrow our search, and around 1 a.m., we managed to narrow it further to sixteen when we matched one of the faces to our victim. "Dolly Parton."

"Dolly Parton is a Lucky Girl?" asked John.

"No. This is Dolly Parton, age 37, born and raised in La Jolla to Jason and George Parton," I read from the dossier.

"But that name can't be coincidence."

"It's a lucky name," I said with a shrug. "You know, people are gonna treat you differently with a name like Dolly Parton. Everyone likes Dolly Parton. The name disarms people. It gets you out of a speeding ticket. It gets you free drinks at a bar."

"Well then, why aren't they all named after celebrities?" questioned John.

"Some get lucky names, others get lucky faces, lucky brains, lucky bodies," I explained. "Luck is as unique as a fingerprint."

"So then, what's our killer's fingerprint?"

"Invisibility," I suggested. "At some point, she decided to be the world's luckiest assassin, and now chance does all it can to render them an unattainable apparition."

"Why isn't this more common?" asked John. "Lucky thieves. Lucky killers."

"These occupations are supposed to be too low class for Lucky Girls. Only the unfortunate are supposed to gravitate toward these desperate operations. Lucky Girls gain their wealth through much cleaner means. I mean, for God's sake, they could simply walk behind a rich guy for long enough, and money might fall out of his pocket."

"So then, she just likes it," mumbled John forlornly.

I liked forlorn John, and, as selfish as this sounds, it's a better look for him. I hated him peri-investigation, reduced to a 'yes man' to my mere intuitions. He's taken me so seriously so far that I thought he was empty, but now I saw the same gritty disdain for Lucky Girls that I had in my own heart. I could see it in John's eyes. It made him look older. His crow's feet stuck out from under his concealer, and his nasal hairs seemed to gray before my eyes.

At some point in your late twenties, caffeine after dark becomes dangerously more intoxicating than a night of drinking. Adulthood wears you down, and that little extra pep feels new and exciting. It makes you do things.

"Oh, Penny." John frowned. "Please remove your hand. I'm not interested in escalating this relationship."

I pulled back, embarrassed. "No interest in a little de-stressing? Doesn't have to get mushy."

"I understand. But no. It's very unprofessional," denounced John. "I mean, don't get me wrong, you're beautiful, and you're clever as well... but I don't like big girls."

"So, you like to fuck *little* girls?"

John's face twisted up. "No..."

"Well, that's a lame excuse not to fuck a lady." The caffeine high bunched up in a spike of anger. "There's some disrespect there."

"No! I clearly respect you, Penny," he said. "I chose you to be my partner, after all. And given how little I've contributed, I'll admit to the fact that you're basically in charge."

"If I remember correctly, you asked for a vague portrait of a woman, and I filled that rather wide margin." I groaned. "Please don't make humor out of that."

"I would never," said John calmly. "I hope this decline doesn't sour our working relationship. I'm really lost without your guidance."

I sighed and tried to put it past me. I picked up the photo of Dolly and slid it on top of a picture of the soup kitchen at the crime scene: Coda's Cookery. "Dolly likely emerged from the exit in the alley coming from the soup kitchen," I explained. "I'd wanna know why a Lucky Girl is in a soup kitchen."

John nodded, happy that I had changed the subject away from my awkward pass at him. "They're completely out of place."

When we got to Coda's Cookery, we met with the titular Coda in the back of the prep area, away from the customers. Coda wasn't just the owner and manager of the establishment, but he also helped to serve the food. We asked if he'd ever seen a Lucky Girl pass through the line, and he scoffed, "We wouldn't have served someone like that."

I showed him a picture of Dolly, just to be sure.

"No one's ever come through our line looking like that."

"Maybe she just comes here to talk?" I questioned.

"It's not unheard of," shrugged Coda. "Unfortunate souls reach out to Lucky Girls all the time. They think if they get close, somehow their luck will rub off on them. The question is what the Lucky Girl gets in return." Coda's face turned bleak. "Just recently, there was Master Juanita out in Texas. A Lucky Girl got a slew of sick and depressed people to start worshiping her. Made a fine cult out of them."

"Do you see much of the crowd in the cafeteria?"

"No," admitted Coda. "I'm too busy serving. She could be leading prayer in my own lunchroom, and I'd never know of it."

"Certainly, your patrons might know?" suggested John.

Coda looked annoyed. "Please don't bother them," he pleaded. "We don't want cops snooping around our soup kitchen. They're gonna think you're looking for their drugs. Then they're not gonna come back. I want them to feel safe here."

"This is a police investigation. We have every right to interview them," said John, too impatient to navigate sensitively around Coda's impedance. "Come on, Penny; I have a plan."

"You want to talk about it first?"

John didn't answer; he walked past the serving trays into the cafeteria. I quickly followed, trying to keep up. As John and I walked towards the big white fold tables, the patrons started to get up and move away from our path. We were like equally charged magnets repelling them from our vicinity.

"John, we should really have a plan."

"Who here knows this woman?" He got up on top of the emptied table and held up a page-long printout of Dolly's face. "I know somebody's seen her!"

There was no immediate answer. A few more people backed away from us. A couple snuck out of the exit. One threw a white bag in his pocket into a nearby compost bin.

"John!"

"Listen up! We're hired to run this case as long as it takes, and I can spend all my time right here if I want to. I'll keep my eyes fixed on your dirty hands as you desperately try to trade pills, arms, and God-only-knows under the tables. Or I can leave now, and you can all eat in peace if just one of you tells me who talks to this girl?"

At first, everyone just kind of looked at each other. Then one guy started pointing, and soon everyone followed his lead. All the fingers began pointing to a single individual reversed into a corner.

"Turn around!" John commanded.

The figure hesitated and hunched over further.

"Now," pressured John.

The gentleman spun around on his heel and lowered his hood, revealing shaggy black hair covering the eyes of a slender face.

"Come. Sit down."

The young man did as we instructed, taking his time to walk over to our lunch table and sit-down face to face with John's ankles.

John bent down and looked at the man from above. "You a cultist, son?"

The man rubbed his face and looked vexed. "I'm a liberal Quaker, does that count?"

"It's certainly not what we're concerned about," I said, glaring at John. He followed my telepathic request and got down off the table. He sat beside me, across from the young man's sunken posture. I kept my gaze locked on his eyes till he stared back. I scanned his face—a short untrimmed beard, and a piercing in the left ear, but nothing to fill the hole. His teeth were impeccable. He looked to be about twenty-nine.

"Can we get a name, son?" asked John.

"Felix Swead," he said in a monotone voice.

"And you want to explain your relationship with Dolly Parton?"

"Old friends."

"Friends? For how long?"

"Since high school," he answered, keeping his replies consistently short. I was certain John's towering earlier had made Felix uncomfortable. "Look, I didn't murder her."

"We know you didn't," I butted in. I thought he'd be more verbal with me leading the conversation. "At this point, we're fairly positive it was another Lucky Girl."

"Then what good can I do for you?" The man shrugged. "I'm just charity work to Dolly. I won't take her money; but she thinks just our little talks, sharing the same air, and our hands brushing, an exchange of cells, could somehow change my life."

"How'd you get like this?" asked John coldly.

"John! That could be incredibly painful for him to recall," I snarled. "How do you lack all basic sensitivity?"

"My parents encouraged raw truth. Leaves less up to coincidence," elucidated John. "I was asking because I wondered if Dolly somehow blamed herself for your current circumstance."

Felix sucked on the patch of whiskers in the center of his lower lip. He shook his head. "I don't find it tough to talk about. Dolly has nothing to do with it. She saw me make a fast transition into oblivion, and she tried all she could to rehabilitate me. She's got a big heart."

"That's shocking to hear," I said with a look of suspicion. "It's a popular opinion that a lot of Lucky Girls are kind of full of themselves. Their luck spoils them from an early age."

"It's true, I agree," nodded Felix, "but *I* also had everything handed to me in my youth. It made me too weak and inexperienced for when things finally got tough. I think Dolly sympathizes with me, afraid someday someone could exploit the same vulnerabilities made from her own upbringing. We're all built so brittle."

"Who do you know that would enjoy breaking something so brittle?" pressed John.

"Well, Lucky Girls are usually quite chummy with one another. Privilege recognizes privilege. I'd say, for them to attack each other, there'd have to be something much larger involved than a petty squabble."

After getting all we could out of the unfortunate soul, we took ourselves back to the diner to recuperate and plan our next course of action. I requested the servers deliver a fresh cezve to our table every half an hour to keep our cups full and our spirits lifted. At this point, we'd been working non-stop for a day and a half.

John and I had begun digging deeper into the social media of our victim. Forensics provided us with Dolly's passwords. They allowed us to see any close social connections we could interrogate for information.

For the first half hour, John kept quiet. He hid his hands tightly behind his keyboard, as if keeping them away from mine. I hated how serious John was taking my earlier offer. It was insulting that he act like I might force myself upon him.

"Her parents?" John suddenly shattered the silence, breaking his gaze at his screen.

"Dead. Natural causes," I said, pointing at a line of text in Dolly's dossier.

"Marital status?"

"Single," I replied.

"Dating anyone?"

"No, no," I continued. "I'm not surprised. Lucky Girls rarely get involved romantically, unless with each other. It's a lot like how celebrities prefer dating other celebrities because they're accustomed to the same things, and their partner won't be just using them."

"Is our victim gay?"

"Tough call," I said, turning around my laptop, "but these two are pretty chummy." The picture I found had Dolly with her hands grasped firmly on her friend's ass, gripping tightly onto the mesh fabric surrounding the shorts. John saw the picture and noticed the star on the cheek of Dolly's friend. He immediately began searching through the snapshots we had of the Lucky Girls in San Diego.

"I think I found her," said John, pulling out a photo. He handed it to me delicately so our hands wouldn't touch.

I rolled my eyes and snatched it roughly from his grip. I read the name at the bottom of the picture. "Prima Zambrano. She lives in Carmel Valley. That's not far from here—or the crime scene."

"We have no motive," John grumbled. "Let's not rush in with too much aggression."

"You're the one standing on tables and threatening the homeless," I reminded him.

"Yes, well, you're the one with a largely negative outlook on Lucky Girls. I urge you to keep that disdain inside while we're interviewing."

I realized quickly that wouldn't be easy. I read through Prima's profile and was disgusted with how easily she acquired a three-story house in the California suburbs. She was originally born to impoverished farmers in Ecuador, but it seemed that wasn't lucky enough for the Universe, so her parents were beheaded in a horrific traffic accident from which she emerged unscathed. She was adopted a month later by Chinese casino tycoons who then raised her in Macao until she was eighteen. At this point, her adoptive parents had bought her a house in San Diego so she could follow her dream of opening a surf shop where she could sell boards made from rare, ultra-hydrophobic balsa wood, which she'd discovered by accident while hiking Alto de Coloane.

"She's a fucking monster," I snarled as we rang her smart bell. The light on the camera turned on as did a small internal speaker.

"Coming!" shouted a cheery voice. Prima opened the door eagerly. She was a tall Latinx minx with full, jagged eyebrows and a confident contour. She initially faced John, then smiled wide as she turned to face me. "How can I help you?"

John and I flashed our badges. "We have a couple questions regarding your acquaintance Dolly Parton."

"The writer or the singer?" she questioned. "I'm close with both."

"Dolly Parton *of San Diego*."

"*Right*, so the writer," confirmed Prima.

"We didn't know she was a writer?" said John.

Prima nodded fast. "Oh yes, yes! She's had many successful exposés. Come inside! I have a whole collection of her work."

We entered her luxurious home. Prima took our drink orders, and then a servant ushered us into a modernist lounge with white bookshelves lining the walls. We sat on a plush white couch and stared at the posters hanging between the shelves: a topographic map of a forest, a painting of a dog in a suit, and a dystopian snow fortress.

Prima sat our drinks down on wood slice coasters. Then, she walked to one of the bookshelves and brought back a handful of Dolly's artworks. "*Begging for Furniture* is my favorite," said Prima, pointing to a cover with a sofa in a cage, "but *Ekon-nomy* is her critical darling."

I flipped over *Ekon-nomy* and read the back text. It summarized a scandal Dolly uncovered in her early twenties while working for Nigerian-born maillot designer Ekon Ibrahim. She had found significant money transfers to close family members back home who used the funds to run conversion therapy camps in Lagos.

"She believed luck led her there to take down a monster," said Prima with a smile. "She was a great example for a new generation of Lucky Girls using their power to bring the whole world positivity."

"Is that how you see it?" I said with a cringe. "I mean, I'm sure this evidence was just sitting there. Dolly was just lucky enough to find it. If she didn't, maybe someone with less opportunity could have."

Prima raised her perfectly shaped eyebrows like guillotines primed for slaughter. She sipped on a dainty glass of mulled wine. "Even though there was plenty of time for someone else to do the digging, it's good that Lucky Girls can speed things up."

John turned his head and glared at me. He didn't want me to push any further. Arguing the good and evil of lucky people wasn't why we were there.

"You seem an admirer, at the least," said John. "Were you and Dolly anything *deeper* when in private?"

"What? *Like lovers?*" Prima smiled shyly. "No! No. She's straight. And she's not my type anyways." Prima matched the bottom of her cup with the wet ring on her coaster. "She's too little. I'm into big girls."

Prima's eyes turned towards me, which left me flattered but uninterested. I never teamed up with girls at Maneki's for a reason. I'm like John in this matter—I like my partnerships to be diverse.

Prima looked down at her empty glass. "Does anyone else need a refill?"

I shook my head right before John did the same. Prima rose from her chair and scurried into her kitchen for more mulled wine.

"So, is that okay?" John asked with a serious expression. It took me a second to realize he was talking to me.

"Is what okay?"

"She only likes big girls."

"It's perfectly fine," I grumbled softly. "She likes who she likes."

"Why's the opposite not okay?" John pressed. His face pinched.

"It's the history of things," I replied sharply, trying to keep this argument short so we could get back to interrogation. "Excluding big girls has kept capable women from social positions and occupations. Excluding thin girls hasn't done jack shit to anyone because, for the most part, the system works in their favor."

Prima suddenly reentered the room. "I couldn't help but overhear," laughed Prima, "If you don't mind me saying, I think both circumstances are wrong."

"How so?" John and I said it at once.

"I mean, ideally, we'd be attracted to only a person's internal features, but we haven't even come close to what could be called body communism. So, our best bet of being fair to ourselves and others is to pursue that which is physically attractive without describing it in too much detail as to exclude others."

"That feels dishonest," said John. "Isn't that just making it seem like all our lives are left up to chance?"

"No?" questioned Prima. "It's just polite."

"Not surprised to hear that coming from someone who has so greatly benefitted from chance already."

Oh gosh. There was salty John again coming out of the woodwork. When John gets bitter, it's like dark chocolate—very tasteful. I shifted internally, trying to forget the thought.

"As a purely platonic friend to Dolly, has she ever confided in you anyone that would ever hurt her or wish her gone?"

Prima curled her lips and looked towards the ceiling. "No, but you see, we aren't as close as the photos may lead you to believe. I've only been her 'friend' for some time in the last year. Before that, as I said, I was a fan. She gave me a chance at something deeper once the position as her right-hand man opened unexpectedly."

"Oh? Who was there before?" I asked.

"Felicia Adorno," said Prima. "Odd times. Lucky Girls don't usually disappear like that, but apparently, she wanted it hard enough."

"She wanted to turn invisible?" I questioned.

"Oh yeah! She hated the fame her luck brought her," Prima nodded. "Luck doesn't need to make you famous if you don't want it to. She wanted to go away, and her luck's so good, it took her somewhere we'd never see her again."

"Do you have a picture?" said John.

"Oh, most certainly. I'm sure I have." Prima got up and picked one of the two books off the table in front of us. She flicked through the pages until she found a photo wedged near the halfway point. "From a book signing," she said. "Felicia was always by her side."

"Oh my gosh," I yanked the photo from Prima's hand. "John, are you seeing this?"

He yanked the photo from me. He stared at Felicia for a second. "I don't share your excitement."

"Cut the hair, add stubble," I instructed, "ignore the star."

"Wait." John's eyes went wide as it dawned on him.

"I guess if you're not a girl, you can't be a Lucky Girl."

We hurried back to Coda's Cookery and waited for Felix to return. Three hours passed. Coda came out from behind the counter and walked towards us.

"Felix isn't coming back here, gentleman. You scared him off."

"Then where does he eat?" John sneered. He'd grown bored two and a half hours ago.

"One of the other kitchens across town."

"And why did you wait three hours to tell us?" I grumbled.

"Cause you messed with my people!" Coda barked. He shut his eyes and quieted his temper. He inhaled and exhaled slowly. "He's camping outback behind the old Ramen Buffet on Third Ave."

We got there as fast as we could. As we made our way to the back of the condemned building, we saw a fort made from old materials foraged from inside. There were rusty chafing dishes stacked into walls and worn uniforms sewn together and stretched into a roof.

"Remember. No dead naming," I snarled at John.

"What makes you think I'd do that?"

"Your weird 'perfectly honest' bullshit."

John glared at me angrily. "Being perfectly honest- he's a man!" He said sternly.

Felix heard our bickering and poked his head out of his encampment. "Oh, please. Won't you leave me alone!"

"Felix, let me make this clear," I said, "I'm not here to question you as to why you chose to become a man."

Felix's head dropped. He sighed, then returned it to an upright position. He looked hesitant to continue listening.

"But there's the question of whether you stopped being a Lucky Girl when you became a man," I continued. "Is that possible? You lost your luck when you identified as a man?"

Felix pulled on his hair and gritted his teeth. "I guess if you know this much, it's too late to protect you." He sat down on the ground and patted the asphalt. "I guess I'll explain."

"Aren't you going to invite us inside?" questioned John.

Felix looked confused; he turned around and looked at his fort. "You'll prefer the fresh air," he explained. He patted the ground again, motioning for us to sit with him.

We sat in a small circle. "I've worked with Lucky Girls for years, and I've never come across this phenomenon. Did you know you'd lose your luck?"

"It's never been considered before. I just wanted to change gender so I could feel more like myself. The further along I transitioned, my life changed for the worse. At first, I thought it was stress, plus pushback from a bigoted society, but then, I realized it was something rooted deeper in the Cosmos."

"How did you get the star removed?" asked John, touching his cheek.

"That's how the government got involved," replied Felix. "At first, the government had no interest in my change. I asked them politely if I could get the star removed to complete my transition. They said 'no'; I'd have to be a man *and* a Lucky Girl. But once my luck started to vanish, they changed their minds. They paid for the surgery and everything if I let them make it look like Felicia had disappeared. They gave me all the necessary documents to start a new life as Felix—identification and birth certificates. The only catch was I could never tell anyone I was once Felicia."

The picture started to come together in my head. "Dolly found out anyway."

"She was, of course, going to investigate the disappearance of her best friend, and her luck led her right to me. She started to visit me in the kitchen and take down my story. She was going to publish it when-" Felix's face strained as he thought about his friend's death.

"Who killed Dolly?"

"A Lucky Girl agent conspiring with the government to keep this secret sealed." Felix stared past me. His eyes widened. "I'm afraid now that you know, their luck has pointed them in your direction. You'll be hunted next."

A shot rang out from a distant building. I had no time to react. The bullet slid past my cheek, cutting it like a blade. My whole head twisted from the force. I screeched and touched my face. John didn't come to my aid; Felix needed his attention. The bullet had pierced Felix's shoulder. He was bleeding far worse than I was.

"Call a medic!" I shouted to John.

"One or two?"

"I'm fine," I called out. "You stay here with Felix. I'm going after her."

"Your blighted ass versus a Lucky Girl?" John scorned.

I looked at him plainly. "That bullet was aimed to *kill* me, John," I said. "If it missed, that means, in a way, Dolly's luck is acting through me. That means the killer and I are evenly matched."

"How is her luck working through you?!"

"I'm solving her murder. I'm a direct tool of her luck," I explained. "Remember what I said about the hurricane acting centuries before a Lucky Girl found her gold? That means their luck exists before birth. Therefore, it might still exist after death."

John's eyes dipped down toward Felix's body. He put some pressure on Felix's wound. "The field is even then," he said. "That doesn't mean she can't shoot you. It just means she'll have to rely on her actual skill."

"Lucky Girls never have to learn actual skills," I scoffed. "I'll be fine."

The building across the street was as blighted as the ramen restaurant, dark and empty. I remembered it used to be an upscale gym misplaced in a lower-income area. There were three floors. Bursting through the front door, I held my flashlight in one hand and my pistol in the other. I scanned the area with my light, illuminating rows of large brown squares where workout equipment used to be. I turned my flashlight towards an elevator. It had no power. Next to it was a doorway to the only staircase in the building. If I wanted to cut off her escape, this was my opportunity.

I quickly pushed through the door and pointed my gun up the steps. She wasn't there. Perhaps she was still hiding on one of the upper floors. I checked the second floor first. The floor was empty, save for an oval indentation where a vulcanized track had been removed. I shut the door and returned to the stairwell. I crept up to the top floor and tried to slide through the doorway without being noticed.

Bang! Bang! She fired two shots at the doorway. One bounced off the wall in front of me, and another lodged in the door's plexiglass window. This Girl's aim was naturally terrible. I rolled inside and crawled to some cover behind the entrance to what used to be a men's steam room. I poked out from behind the corner and saw the Lucky Girl sticking out behind the entrance to the women's counterpart. She was a blonde bombshell covered head to toe in black, form-fitting leather. Her training was horrendous. She kept sticking her head out and making an easy target of herself. I thought about taking the shot right beneath her glistening bangs.

"Don't try to run!" I shouted.

"I wouldn't know how," said the Girl. "I was expecting a cherry picker to crash into one of the windows, offering me escape. Or a misguided helicopter to land on the roof for me to hijack, but here I am with my power gone in your vicinity. It's debilitating being treated like this."

"Like normal?"

"It's not normal for me," she said. She turned the corner and fired two more shots. Neither came close to the sauna entrance. Her body was shaking so badly, making her aim terrible. She was nervous, face to face with someone who could actually hurt her.

"Come peacefully! This doesn't have to end in blood."

"Why do you want it to end at all?" asked the Girl. "Isn't this the best luck you've ever experienced?"

It seemed like this Girl knew more about my life than I expected. I guess if I could find evidence on her, she could easily find evidence on me.

"It's nice getting a few breaks here and there," I answered sincerely, "but all this luck was made so I can find you... I've got to fulfill my end of the bargain."

"Luck might have brought you back from the brink of death just to solve this crime," she suggested. "Maybe if you finish things, it'll let you decay."

It was true that many things could have been altered by Luck to bring me to this moment. It probably made John's partner sick. It probably made the trail so easy to follow. Just as likely, maybe Luck gave me cancer so I could get assigned to a division that works on Lucky Girl cases, making me an asset to solving this crime. We are all at Luck's mercy in this universe of ours, and overthinking it helps nothing.

I turned the corner and fired my weapon—not at her head, but at her knees. She fell to the ground screaming. Her weapon dropped and slid across the floor. I ran to it and kicked it away, then positioned my pistol at her face and stood confidently over her body.

"Why does Felix's transition need to be such a big secret?" I questioned. "Tell me or I'll blow your head in. And knowing my luck lately, I can make everyone believe it's 'self-defense'."

"Since the '60s, it was assumed Luck might be a part of our DNA, but because of Felix, it's now clear it's tied metaphysically to gender identity. The implications of this are huge."

"What's the worst that could happen?" I sneered.

"Theoretical gynopolis," she spouted—like I'd know what that meant.

I moved my gun in circles, suggesting she explain further and quickly.

"The unification of all gender!" she continued. "Why would people choose to be men anymore when they could have the chance of being a Lucky Girl if they transition?"

"But only a handful of those who switch would get powers."

"Some might switch back, but others will stay whether they're Lucky Girls or not. Though not a true gynopolis, even a small shift in gender proportions can mean all sorts of complications for the American machine. Market shifts. Negative population flux."

"People could have easily made these transitions a hundred years ago when only men had the right to vote. It's not as easy to predict as you're suggesting." I reached down and pulled her up. I stuck my gun to her head. "I want to know who you're working for..."

She grinned devilishly. "I won't go that far. I'm just hoping, knowing our mission, you'll empathize enough to let me go."

I shook my head. "No dice."

It wasn't long until backup arrived. They got the bullet out of Felix and brought him to a hospital to recover. Officers placed the Lucky Girl assassin in handcuffs and carted her off to chat with more professional interrogators than me. It seemed unlikely that she'd come out with the truth. She was guarding something too deep to disclose.

"Is it a cult?" asked John. "A government splinter cell?"

"I'm not sure," I frowned.

John and I sat at our usual Ottoman joint and sipped on our demitasses across from each other. He noticed I wasn't in a particularly good mood.

"You think the magic has drained from you?" questioned John.

I nodded. "It's gone. I can feel it."

"Oh, you never were *that* lucky," chuckled John, fighting against my downed spirits. "After all, I still wouldn't fuck you."

I pinned my death stare on John. He wasn't helping, but maybe he knew that. I had a feeling our partnership was nearing its end anyway. Soon, he'd return to his old partner.

"Look here," said John, retrying with a different tactic, "science says we live in a semi-free-willed existence. When luck pulls your strings, it's like being forced to act out somebody else's dreams. Aren't you happy to be free? Perhaps you're free to make mistakes, but at least *you're* making them."

I smiled weakly and excused myself to the restroom. I took my things with me and walked out of the restaurant. I got in my car and left for home, leaving John with the bill. It was small, just a minor annoyance. I felt like he deserved it.

I took a sharp left when I should have taken a right to continue home. I suddenly hankered for soju and sex, a calling best remedied at Maneki's. This feeling was my body returning to its old ways.

I used my check from the last case to buy a bottle of Hwayo to share with a foxy grandpa at the bar. After a few shots, he showed me the tattoo hidden under his fading blonde comb-over—a Star of David right in the center of his bald spot. I told him it was hot and recruited him to my shuffleboard team.

He was fairly good, and I sucked, as usual. Combined, we managed a mediocre performance that the other teams easily defeated. My last push was dramatic and silly, as there was no way we'd win. I gave it way too much force, and it bounced off the frame and flew into the air. It flew backward over my shoulder and headed into the booths.

I followed the noise to where the puck had landed. It seemed to have bruised the forehead of a gentleman sitting all by himself with no beer or soju on the table. He had passed out from the impact. At first, I felt horrible, but then I noticed the phone lying next to his limp hand. The camera app was open, displaying his latest photo: me playing at the table.

I picked up the phone and started swiping, only to discover he'd been taking photos of me all night. Disturbed, I felt up his fallen form and found a gun hidden under his jacket.

It was an agent, likely one from the same sector that had sent the Lucky Girl after Dolly and me. With this phone, I had a lot of digging I could do. Perhaps I could find my way to the next piece of evidence, maybe one of the sector's leaders, maybe a base of operation. Either way, I was happy.

"Why are you smiling?" shouted the old man with the star tattoo. "This guy's gonna press charges when he wakes up."

I was smiling because I was still lucky. The case wasn't completely solved. Luck wanted me to get to the top of this conspiracy. That could take months, maybe even years. I had a lot more time than I thought to bask in Dolly's glorious radiance bestowed upon me.

I left the bar with the phone in my hand and a thrill building in my chest. For a short while, I would know what it's like to be a Lucky Girl.

A Reason to Burn: Lucky Girl Noir

I met Evan Witmer when he was collecting short stories for an anthology series called *Digest*. At the time, I thought it was cool he was highlighting some yet undiscovered voices in literature. Naturally, I was flattered he wanted me to join in the project, considering most of my acquired popularity came via my '80s punk band and my children's series, *Bandmates*. I hadn't written anything for an adult audience before, yet Evan loved my contribution.

I can't say that *Digest* ended up being the commercial smash Evan promised it would be, so I don't think I benefited too much from the project. However, inspired by Evan's response to my work, I have written a couple full-length novels geared towards an older crowd, but an agency has yet to take me seriously.

I don't blame Evan for falling short of his promises. I honestly believe he had done all he could to get my work read. I do feel some animosity towards him, however, with the discovery of one of his newer creations—"Lucky Girl Noir." He had posted it to his blog last March, but I didn't see it until June when I was just checking on how the kid's been progressing. I was flabbergasted at how similar this new short story was to one of the concepts I'd been shopping around since I'd put an end to *Bandmates*. It was supposed to be my new children's series, "The Lucky Ladies of Ft. Lauderdale," about a group of pre-teens on a mother-daughter vacation who discover a magic sea bean that grants them all good luck.

Now I'm not trying to claim any right to the concept of luck; it's Evan's characters that have raised my ire. In my story, there's a non-binary mother who bears a similar backstory to Evan's character, Felix. There's a plus-sized girl that impresses all the others with her courage and strength, like Evan's Penny. There's even a snooty teenager—literally named John—who sells them craft popcorn; he's a socially inept asshole to the girls, just like Evan's John.

Evan's the only other writer I've ever worked with. The major publishing companies rejected me repeatedly, so I shared my notes on my "Lucky Ladies" project with Evan. I wanted his take on what I was doing wrong. He told me the premise was 'dry and cliche,' suggesting that I change the setting to 'anywhere but Ft. Lauderdale." Well, it seems San Diego was more what he had in mind.

I don't think I need to craft an argument about why plagiarism is wrong. Suffice to say, if you've ever had the experience of missing out on opportunities because someone stole your work, you know how I feel right now. I want Evan's story to be burned, and so should you.

- Pirated Penman, Bonny Bride

Three Days West

As Quinten Hare left town on the back of his horse, Jump Rope, he could smell his wheel of chèvre cooking in his saddle bag. The flames had spread to consume every building on the south side of the only road in Woodrose. This inferno was unbeatable with the limited options of Gay 90s Colorado; pail after pail of well water would not slow this blaze. Soon it would make its northern expansion to the other half of town once the evening breeze inevitably picked up. Quinten was not welcome to stay and watch manifest destiny. He left his homestead behind him and slowly galloped towards the mountain that towered over the town to the west—a piney fourteener with a gray gendarme shaped like a coyote. Mt. Triduum, they called it.

Quinten knew the next nearest town was just on the other side of Mt. Triduum. He'd seen traders leave in that direction when they finished business in Woodrose. While these traders circumnavigated the elevation, Quinten didn't shy away from taking the direct path over the top. It was a difficult path with an uneasy texture and stones that would collapse, but Quinten and Jump Rope had extraordinary coordination when paired. They'd gained remarkable agility working in the Hare family's pea fields. Mice in the pea fields attracted snakes that were best untrodden lest Jump Rope be bitten. This trained set of eyes made crossing a mountain easy, picking the right boulders to weigh on.

Quinten made the trek in just under a day. The way down was a lot easier than the climb. He slid his horse gracefully down the western face of Mt. Triduum, skidding lip to lip like a set of stairs. After one particularly perilous scuttle, his horse needed a second to rest, having almost sent them into a barrel roll.

"You're better off taking the slow way down," came a xyloid drawl from the cloud of dust they'd ascended. "You just might miss out on something valuable…." The old man stepped into view. He was wearing a pair of black waders that took up most of his bottom half. A green woolsey and a matching gibus covered the rest of his top. His arm was outstretched, and in his hand was an angle made of thin copper wire. He held it loosely in his palm so it would twist, pointing every which way. Suddenly, it stopped on a pile of rubble to their right. The old man gasped with excitement. He quickly attacked the rock pile, rummaging around the stones until he shouted, "Yellow cake!" He pulled out his hand and stuck it out before Quinten's stirrup.

Quinten looked down at the little golden speck in the old man's palm. "You a prospector, dotard?"

"You should mind who you're calling a dotard," said the old man. "The gold in these hills is my strongly guarded secret, or else those celestials out in Pike's Peak will come and steal it all. I don't share this type of information with just anyone!"

"I take it the only way to find the aforementioned gold is with one of that there compasses you're holding?" asked Quinten.

"It's not a compass… it's a doodlebug!" said the man enthusiastically. "It's formed from a special vein of copper found only in the Orient. It's drawn to gold's scent like a truffle hog."

"And you'd be happy to part with it?"

"Mine? No!" said the old man stuffing the doodlebug into his boot. "I have one more… but it's back at my camp."

Quinten patted his stomach. "I'd be more than happy to discuss this matter over some chuck," he reached into his pouch and pulled out his wheel. It had lost most of its shape, having melted in the fire. "I got some cheese to share… if you got some chili?"

"Yes. Yes, please! Follow me!" said the old man. He led Quinten down a modest slope of grass and weeds to a log cabin just a few more minutes west. The house was very rudimentary: a doorway, but no door, no windows, and little furniture. Inside was a bed roll resting on a pile of leaves and two barrels. On one barrel was a chest with a steel padlock; on the other was a pile of gold. "The fruits of my labor," said the old man proudly. He then walked over to his bedding and brushed aside the leaves near the bottom. He unveiled a loose floorboard that revealed a holding area for his food when displaced. He picked out two cans of pinto beans and took them outside to a cauldron over his fire pit. "Come and sit!"

Quentin tied Jump Rope to a tree, sat on a log around the fire, and pulled out a knife. He started stripping his cheese, throwing chunks into the pot of beans. A spurtle was lying on the ground. Quentin brushed it off with his sleeve and stirred the chili.

"How much would you be willing to part with for one of these?" said the old man with a sly grin. He picked up another doodlebug from behind his seat and waved it around like a magic wand. "It can practically make gold appear… out of thin air!"

"Sounds like you'd want a whole lot for it."

The old man shrugged. "How much is eight dollars?"

"A *whole* lot." Quentin chuckled.

"Seven dollars," countered the old man. He teetered the doodlebug between his fingers.

"What does a man with all that gold need with seven dollars?" questioned Quentin. "Sounds mighty greedy."

"Well, I can't use the gold yet!" shouted the old man. "Once it's cashed in, there's no stopping 'em from finding out where I got it. This place will be swarming. No, no, it's better to lie low for now; I keep all my transactions to paper money."

"I see." Quentin pulled out the spurtle and watched the bright white cheese stretch from the bottom of the pot. "You don't like dotard. How about a real name?"

"Stot," said the old man plainly. "Everyone calls me Stot."

"And you live alone, Stot?"

Stot rubbed his whiskers. "That's the type of question you might ask before you rob someone of their gold…" cautioned Stot.

Quentin laughed. "Oh no, Stot. I'm not a thief; I'm a pea farmer. Even if I were… there's nothing in that fort worth stealing."

Stot stared through the fire with a look of confusion. "Just a year's worth of digging..."

Quentin stood up and walked slowly into the cabin. Stot came chasing after him. "Hey! Hey! Where are you going? What are you doing?"

"Look, I know your trick, mister," said Quentin, stomping up to the pile of gold. "My friend on the other side of this here hill does the same damn trick." He picked a nugget off the top.

"There's no trick! These tools just don't work for two out of three people. It's all about mental glint. Some people lack it."

"I'll show you lacking glint." Quentin sighed. He rubbed the nugget against the black lock on the chest. "What color is that streak there?"

The old man squinted. He shook his head. He couldn't make words; his lips just quivered.

"It's dark green… this is fool's gold!" He chucked the nugget over his shoulder. It fell in the crack between two of the wall's planks. "I reckon there's a whole stash of doodlebugs here in this box." He tugged on the lock. "You must get them from the same guy as Ox back in Woodrose!"

"I don't know any Ox! I'm the sole conspirator in this here activity." Stot looked worried; his eyes traveled to the gun in Quentin's holster. "Iffin you're willing to leave peacefully, I'll let you take the rest of the chili with you. That's about all I got to grovel with in full honesty." The old man's head turned to the empty compartment by his bed.

Quentin shook his head, then patted the man on the shoulder. He left the cabin and motioned for Stot to join him around the cauldron. "Come get some grub," said Quentin, taking a seat. "You got any bowls?"

Stot shook his head.

Quentin snickered. "How about a couple big leaves, so we don't burn our hands eating this?"

Stot nodded and rummaged through his leaf pile until he found two hand-sized catalpa leaves, then brought them out to the fire. They filled their leaves with chili as though they were little plates. They held the leaves up to their mouths and let the chili slide into their lips.

"I'm not looking to ruin your business, mister," explained Quentin. "Hell, Ox and I got along just fine; and I'm certain the two of us could too. That is if you're willing to call me your nephew."

"You humiliate me, then ask to be my family?"

"My old town was tight-knit. We didn't take kindly to strangers, and I doubt your home is any different. You're the devil they know. I'm the devil they don't. But, if I say I'm your kin, they'll take to me much faster, agreed?"

Stot slurped down a fat wad of cheese from the tip of his leaf. He wiped his chin with his sleeve and nodded. "You're my son."

"Nephew."

"My brother was a monk. He never had children. I, on the other hand—" the old man cackled "—I had my fair share of ladies."

"Fine," said Quentin. "You must have laid with a girl with a hell of a chin, though, because we look nothing alike." Stot set down his leaf and rubbed his round, receding cleft. Meanwhile, the top of Quentin's neck met with a sharp V-shaped jaw.

When the two finished their meals, they descended the mountain on Jump Rope. There was too much weight on Jump Rope to keep sliding, so they took a slow path plotted out by Stot. As they reached the bottom of the mountain, the pines cleared from sight to reveal gorgeous fields of green cultivated with rural life. It was so much like Quentin's old town; his first thoughts were, *how am I so blessed to have returned home?*

They galloped past a pair of ranch houses at the start of the road, then moved inwards towards a farmstead with rows of tall steaks stuck in the earth. Stripes of copper wire ran between the stakes, offering a rudimentary trellis for which the crops could climb.

"Where are you taking me?" asked Quentin.

"A farm. Blu Leveret's farm. You'll like him a lot. He reminds me of you."

"He grows peas?" Quentin stared at the pea plants creeping up the wires.

"Peas and short ribs are the preferred meal here in Rosebud."

"How traditional," replied Quentin. It was the same in Woodrose.

Stot directed Quentin past the pea fields towards a tiny blue barn in the distance. Someone had decorated the outside with colorful flowers and thick, black quotes: "Till this moment I never knew myself" painted across a field of columbine; "To be the idol of one's idol" beneath a row of fireweed. Quentin didn't recognize the materials these stemmed from. He didn't do much reading.

Stot took Quentin to the structure's back wall, where three sunflowers had been repurposed into targets. Stot stopped them from walking into the line of fire. He pointed at his friend several yards away from the targets, standing in front of a two-room horse stall. The horse inside had a towel wrapped around his ears to protect his hearing.

Quentin stared in bewilderment at the man aiming his pistol at the makeshift galley. He had long hair, lighter than Quentin's, but parted at the same point over the right eye. It was combed all the way back, curling towards the nape of his neck. He was dressed similarly to Quentin, too, the only difference being the color scheme: a brown vest swapped for a blue and a white long sleeve swapped for a red. However, the two faces could not be more dissimilar. Blu's face held none of Quentin's sharpness, instead sporting a box under his teeth.

Quentin watched this man's firing technique. He cut the top layer off a cheese lying on a barstool to his left. He made sure to get a little rind mixed in with the creamy center, then lapped the cheese off his knife. When he drew his gun, it was two-handed, one thumb resting on the knuckle of the other. He swallowed the cheese like a pill, then pulled the trigger firmly.

A loud bang sounded off. The horse behind Blu stood motionless. A tight hole formed in the center of the brown spot representing the flower's disc.

Quentin felt like he was looking at an impressionist with an impossible amount of insight into his history and personality. "Is that Kunik?" He pointed to the wedge laid out on the barstool.

"Have you a slice, stranger," offered Blu. "Given you're a friend of our town's faithful psychic." He said it with a slight sarcasm, something only Stot would pick up on.

"He's my boy!" Stot feigned enthusiasm. "A relic from my days with Sprout. Finally, he's come back to his daddy."

"Where's your mother been raising you, boy?" asked Blu. "Miss Sprout used to teach me and my brothers when we were real little."

"Woodrose," said Quentin. "Just over the hill."

Blu nodded, then handed him a slice of cheese. Quentin took it into his mouth like communion, then took a second to savor it.

Once it melted down his throat, he whipped out his pistol and made a hole just above Blu's.

"Remarkable," he said with a nod. "You know, I know the cheese helps because—"

"—when I was a young man, I was the only one of my brothers who wasn't lactose intolerant," interrupted Quentin. "I was the only one who could shoot the pit out of a palisade peach from our kitchen window."

Blu stared at Quentin strangely. A crumb of rind hung from his bottom lip. As he perked up into a smile, it fell onto his brogans. "You're a new part of his act, aren't you?" Blu snickered. "So, your son's a psychic too... Hell, I know it's all a trick and you almost got me. You're gonna sell a hell of a lot more of that wire, Stot!"

"I never told him about that, Blu," said Stot, matching Blu's level of amazement. "This kid just pulled that shit out of thin air! No kidding…"

"Well then, how'd you know that, son?"

"I'm no son; I'm twenty-five, same age as you," replied Quentin.

The boy's talent amused Blu. He nodded with a look of excitement. For a second, he thought he was talking to a genuine magic man. "I am… Hmph, not even the old man knew that, and he's known me for years."

"I've never bothered with remembering birthdays." Stot snorted.

"And the reason you're turning your barn here into Emmental is because you're tearing it down," continued Quentin, "on account of your wife…"

"Wait, hold on now!" Blu suddenly turned red. "The trick's not funny anymore. Not when you bring up a missing person. Makes me think you know something about her disappearance."

Quentin shook his head and motioned for Blu to calm down. "Sandy, *my* wife, went missing three weeks ago. And the sight of her old writing studio was making it hard to accept she was gone for good."

Blu swallowed his anger. He just winced, holding his breath. He didn't know what this meant, and he hoped Quentin would just come out and say it.

"I think we're connected somehow," said Quentin. He turned to Stot and pictured his friend Ox. Both scheming old men, living in the woods, roughly the same age, and having laid with their schoolteachers. "It might not just be us. Take me into town, and we'll see how far this thing extends."

Blu offered Quentin a place to tie up Jump Rope next to his own horse, Hopscotch. They then strolled down the only road into Rosebud. Soon the fields vanished, and, in their place, rose modest structures built from blue spruce and iron spikes. Every building seemed familiar by the shapes of their roofs and their placement in town. Looking closer, Quentin felt the cool touch of deja vu in the center of his face. He'd walked this road two days prior in Woodrose on his way to drown his sorrows at Pal's Saloon.

He remembered the songs sounding from behind the church doors, trying to lure him into a better choice for his morning activities. *"Somewhere, somewhere, beautiful isle of somewhere, Land of the truth where we live anew, beautiful isle of somewhere..."* Their pitch was off, but differently than Woodrose. It sounded worse, but it might be a tolerance he built up to his own choir.

Quentin saw Blu eyeing the church doors. He knew what he was thinking. Maybe the Lord could offer better medicine than his days at the bar. Right on cue, though, a distraction pulled him away from the light.

"Bluford, come and help me with your uncle!" called an aggravated voice from the barbershop. If Blu's uncle was anything like Quentin's, he had court today for drunken harassment. "I caught him before he crawled into the courthouse without a pair of pants."

Sitting in the barber's chair was a frail man thrashing about in his seat. He pounded a bottle of laudanum on the leather arms like a gavel. He was wearing nothing but a baby blue coat, oversized enough to cover his genitals. The barber had wrapped a belt around the man's belly and the back of the seat, tightening the man in place.

"Hold him down while I give 'em a shave!" said the barber. "We must make him look professional. Less wasted. Maybe your friends can go fetch him a pair of pants from the tailor."

"There's no point." Quentin sighed. "You sober him up, you get him there, but he's still found guilty. Judge hates him, remember?"

Blu looked displeased with Quentin's projection. "So, you've gone from mind-reading to fortune-telling?"

"This all already happened to me," replied Quentin with a jaded frown. "Now it's all happening to you." Quentin undid the strap around the old man's waist and set him free. "Might as well bring him with you. Today's the last day you'll see him before they take him to Territorial."

"Fine," conceded Blu, "but this stays here." He pried the laudanum from his uncle's vice and put it next to the jars of disinfectant in front of the barber's mirror. "No outside drinks at Stranger's."

The Stranger's Saloon was a tent fortress with a piebald cloth tied around a tobacco-stained frame that creaked in the wind. Inside there were three stools at the bar and three round tables. One table was nearly full, seating four men dressed from head to toe in crimson furs playing cards. A barkeep delivered fresh drinks to these red fae, homemade whiskey from a golden-steel distillery kit in the back.

The barkeep's name was Dawn, a stranger to Quentin but a pal to Blu. He wore clothes yellow as the sun: a blinding bowler hat and a matching vest. For a man dressed so joyously, his expression was rather gloomy. Dawn glared at the sight of Blu's uncle as they dragged him inside. "Oh, that cannon's about to blow!" shouted Dawn, pointing towards the exit. "You can bring him back when he's sober!"

"I know where the sawdust is," replied Blu, setting his uncle in a seat. He stared at Quentin, then back at Dawn. "He stays drunk till the sheriff picks him up, you hear?"

"He gets beer then!" Dawn picked out a blue glass bottle from a dusty cabinet. People rarely went for beer with his whiskey so renowned, but if Uncle was going to stay alive, he needed something with less burn.

Dawn popped the top on the bottle and plopped it on the table. Suds spewed from the top and landed in Uncle's lap. The drunk suddenly sprang awake and began binging on his new treat. He took a few big swigs, then took a second to speak. "Could use a little poppy!" Uncle began fishing around his pockets.

"Uncle, no!" Blu slapped the man's wrist. "Stick with booze."

"Thank you." Dawn sighed. "What will the rest of you be having?"

"What's the latest experiment?" asked Blu.

"Plums," answered Quentin. Blu glared at him. Quentin was already a stranger in this town; he didn't need to be showing off any strange powers. Quentin explained away his foresight, "It smells like plums."

"Prune juice base," explained Dawn, looking complimented by the man's perception. "Then I added the rye and some Belgian yeast. Two weeks later, and it distills just under 90."

"Three of that," ordered Blu. Dawn was quick to deliver. Once the drinks were flowing, their imaginations began to speculate on the parallel lives of Quentin and Blu.

"It's not just me and Blu. You each have a counterpart back in Woodrose," summarized Quentin.

"It's like Rosebud and Woodrose are living out the same story but not at the same time. Rosebud is in the past."

"By how many days?" questioned Stot.

"It took me a day to get here, and now it's two days before the day I left," counted Quentin. "That means it's three days in the past."

"Why three days?" pondered Blu, pairing his whiskey with a fitting cheese. The smoky sweetness stirred well with some brie. "There's something to that detail…"

"Come to think of it, that's how long the trip here took," called out Stot.

"Which trip?" questioned Blu.

"You were too young to remember… Hell, were you even born before your mother moved here?" questioned Stot.

Blu shook his head. "I was born in town."

"Well, the journey was perilous. We were pioneers. Columbia was overcrowded, and the land was expensive. We sought greener pastures. Identical twin brothers, Otis and Alan Yoke— outspoken Free Soilers—assisted in a treaty with the Native Americans. They freed up some land in northern Colorado. Otis and Alan volunteered to lead a group of ten families to start a settlement as long as they should be elected mayor and deputy mayor, respectively."

"Otis Yoke was still the mayor when I was born," interrupted Blu.

"And Alan Yoke was ours when *I* was born," said Quentin.

"Well, the brothers split up when they reached Mt. Triduum. Alan saw the coyote on its east side and said, 'this must be the place.' A coyote had saved him as a child—bit a scorpion off his face while he was sleeping. But Otis saw the coyote differently, having made friends with the Indian chiefs. He adopted their belief that the coyote was an omen." Stot sipped his drink and cringed as it burned his throat. He looked over at Quentin. "It may have only taken *you* a day to cross on your horse, but the caravan was slow and had to go all the way around the mountain. There were many stops, many delays. It took three days."

"So, these twins had the same vision for the same town," replied Quentin. "It just started three days apart."

"They split their followers evenly, so they each had the essentials," continued Stot. "Each took a farmer. Each took a rancher. Each took a trapper."

Quentin gazed over Blu's shoulder at the trappers in question. In both towns, these men made their fortune primarily on fox skins, and they wore these treasures proudly on their bodies. Red papakhas. Red strollers. Red fluffies. Red carriage boots. Quentin could tell which of these men was the leader just by how he played poker. Barrow, his oldest friend, was the leader back in Woodrose. This man and Barrow both wore their hats backward so that the tail covered their tell—a pair of winks whenever they lied.

Blu caught Quentin gazing at the gentleman behind him. He widened his eyes and turned his attention to Blu. "If I weren't here, you'd be over there betting your lunch money with the Cracklings."

Blu felt around his pocket. It was true; he'd packed his pants for some gambling that day. He turned to the men in red, staring at his best friend with the tail over his face. His name was Farrow. Blu shook his head. "Don't call them Cracklings. Sounds like they're weak and dying. We call 'em Punks. The start of the flame. They bring in most of the money from outside the city, then trade it with the rest of us."

Quentin reached into his pocket and handed Blu enough money to double his in. "Go *trade* with 'em."

"You really don't mind waiting here with, uh…" Blu looked over at his uncle, his eyes turning frantically, following the ghosts hidden in the walls.

Quentin smiled devilishly. "Actually, I'm gonna be by your side, offering you advice. After all, I know how this game turns out."

"What are you suggesting?" asked Blu.

"I can't remember every hand, but I remember when they're bluffing."

"You want to cheat our best friend." Blu grimaced.

"Like Barrow's never done anything disrespectful to you."

"It's *Farrow*," corrected Blu, "and everything's square last time I checked. No reason to gouge."

"You'll need the money," pressured Quentin.

Blu looked surprised. "For what?"

"The Silver Baron finds you, Blu, and he wants interest," explained Quentin with a look of despair.

Suddenly Blu looked horrified. "Damn… those seeds were supposed to pay for themselves…."

Quentin turned his eyes down toward his drink. "Well, we've been putting a whole lot of our profits into drowning our sorrows…"

Blu looked down at the bare ice in the bottom of his glass.

"Farrow makes plenty of money, Blu," pushed Quentin. "He can handle the hit."

Bluford sighed, capitulating. "Be honest. Did you come here just to screw with people in the past? Or did you *really* not know things were like this?"

Quentin shook his head rapidly. "I came here…" He frowned. "I just came here looking for my wife, Pearl."

Bluford stared for a moment and saw the despair in the man's eyes. He nodded and reluctantly agreed to play along. He took his glass to the bar for a refill, then settled at the poker table, where the Punks excitedly greeted him.

"Cool Blu!" Everyone shouted at once; they raised their whiskies and clinked their tumblers.

"The sky! The sea!" shouted one with a beard.

"The ol' spruce tree!" shouted another with his front teeth missing.

"A friend to you and me?" said a third with hunched shoulders.

"The man who brings us peas!" Farrow laughed, bringing the cheer to a close. He punched Blu in the arm and dealt him a hand. "How goes the peas, farmer?"

Blu, feeling guilty, found it hard to look his friend in the face. He turned his head upwards and forced a grin. "It's a hell of a lot easier than fox hunting."

Farrow stared back. He could tell something was off. He had a feeling he knew what it was.

"You know, Blu, I wanted to tell if my wife was a real princess," said the man with the hunch, "so I stuck one of your peas under her pillow to see if it'd leave a bruise. The next morning, she wakes up, and she's got green stuck in her teeth. Turns out she's Princess Mary Adelaide!" The man started laughing so hard his head kept dipping lower until his neck grew out of his chest.

Nobody else seemed to share in the laughter.

"Now's not a good time to talk about wives," murmured Farrow, drawing the flop to push the game forward. He snuck a look at Blu, whose sunken expression hid behind his cards. Suddenly, Farrow watched Quentin drop a barstool to Blu's side and squeeze his face in front of Blu's hand. Farrow looked annoyed. "You mind not barging in on my friend's business?"

"It's alright, Farrow, he's with me." Blu shoved Quentin's face back behind him. "He's the spawn of the prospector."

"He sells magic wands too?" Farrow laughed.

"No, I'm a humble pea man myself!" Blu nodded. "Nothing compared to a Farrow like yourself. You've got a tomb picked out yet?"

"Yeah, well…" Farrow chuckled. He'd heard plenty of jokes about his name.

"They gonna bury you with your slaves here?" Quentin pointed to the other Punks.

"Calm down!" Blu swatted at Quentin. "Too much drink in you…."

"Gosh." Farrow laughed. "Remind me not to make fun of this guy's daddy again." Farrow laid the turn. Two sixes were now on the table: hearts and spades. Quentin could see that Blu had the six of diamonds, and if he remembered correctly, Farrow should have the six of clubs. What he didn't have, however, was the high card.

Farrow smiled smugly and pushed ten silver dollars into the center of the table. The man with the hunch folded. The man with the beard folded too. The man missing his teeth raised a dollar. Blu hesitated to make a move. Quentin pinched his leg; that was their signal. Blu would push through to the end.

Betting was completed. Farrow drew the river—a three of hearts.

"Two pair!" shouted the man with missing teeth.

"Three of a kind!" said Farrow, overtaking his opponent. His high card was a king. Blu had him beat.

"Three of a kind… aces high," said Blu stoically. He scraped in the winnings and hesitated to look at Farrow's reaction. Quentin nudged him to stop acting so stiff. It would seem suspicious. Blu looked up and stared at Farrow, who was smiling wide.

"Bested again!" Farrow chuckled. He began collecting everyone's cards to shuffle for the next round.

Farrow slid two cards in front of his fellow trappers. Then, he held out two cards, snipped between his fingers in front of Blu's face. "You in or out, bud?" asked Farrow, wiggling the cards.

"I'm in," conceded Blu, plucking his cards from Farrow's hand.

Suddenly the turns started to go by more quickly as the pleasantries tapered off and competition began to take over. Blu never won enough hands in a row to look suspicious, but he sure did take home the trophy whenever it came down to Farrow's bluff. Farrow didn't seem particularly angry at Blu for having good fortune for a change but was mad at himself for playing so sloppily. He kept fiddling with the tail on the front of his hat, wondering if he'd accidentally covered the wrong eye.

Soon the competition tapered off as well, and what was left was four drunken players keeping the game alive for the sole purpose of legitimizing their drinking. Although not playing per se, Quentin kept up well with the competitors. He drank until it didn't matter anymore if he'd lived the day once already; he couldn't see a damn thing coming.

Soon the men were all singing. The bartender watched in horror as Uncle joined the boys and sang the loudest. *"Somewhere, somewhere, beautiful isle of somewhere!"* They went out into the streets and shouted into the night. *"Land of the truth where we live anew, beautiful isle of somewhere!"*

Once outside, everyone's instinct was to head home. Quentin and Blu said goodnight to the Punks and leaned on one another as they returned to the farm. As they reached the pea field, both their heads had the same idea simultaneously, and they ran off in separate directions. Blu ran inside his home and fetched himself a piece of cheese. Quentin ran to his horse outside to do just the same. But as Quentin lifted the wheel out of his pack, he was surprised to see a pair of words he'd carved into the wax: *DONT SLEEP.*

Quentin couldn't remember why he had to stay up at the time, but he knew he had given himself that note for a good reason. He also knew he'd hunt for cheese if the drinking got out of hand.

Quentin followed Blu into his house and found him lying on his dining room table. "Quentin! Quentin," said Blu. "Quentin, tonight was a good idea."

"What was tonight?"

"The con we played during poker," grumbled Blu; he didn't have the energy to explain this to him. *"Somewhere, hmm-hmmmm, beautiful isle of somewhere..."* He sang instead, reducing some of the words to mere hums. "Quentin, don't you see this here *is* your beautiful isle of somewhere. Isn't this Heaven, knowing everything before it happens?"

"I guess so," replied Quentin. He was rummaging through the kitchen, looking for some water to sober up.

"Quentin! Quentin," snarled Blu. "Heaven is two days ago. You can fix all your problems if you could just go back two days ago," he said longingly. "What if you found this place two days before my wife disappeared… You could have told me not to let her leave my sight—"

Quentin wasn't listening; he was gulping water out of a pail.

Blu was exhausted. He stared upwards and saw the Jerusalem crickets crawling in and out of the cracks in his ceiling. He followed the black specks around in circles until he grew dizzy. He blacked out.

An hour passed until one of those crickets above him stepped on dew and lost its grip. It fell from the ceiling and lodged itself in Blu's throat. He suddenly sprang to life, gagging on the free dinner. "Jesus—*huk*—Christ." He swallowed the insect and hopped off his table. He quickly rested his palm on the wall before he completely collapsed. He was still very intoxicated. He was curious if Quentin had fallen asleep inside the house. He couldn't remember where he last saw him. He checked the kitchen, then the parlor, then he went upstairs. He checked the guest room, then *his* bedroom. He pulled back his sheets—no one was there. He pulled back his wife's sheets—no one was there. That last part slowed Blu down a little. He paused and sighed sullenly. Then it hit him—perhaps Quentin fell asleep in his wife's studio; Jump Rope was hitched up beside it.

Blu ran out of his house and headed towards the shed. In the dark, reading the words on the walls was impossible.

"Wha—uh." Blu stared in confusion as a pattern of Quentins spun around his vision. They were all emerging from the studio door with a book tucked under their arms. It was his wife's book, the one she'd been writing before her disappearance.

Quentin looked terrified seeing Blu; he was certain the man would have been out cold after their adventurous night. Quentin took a few steps in the direction of his horse. Blu predicted the trajectory and chased right behind him, following him to the stable and tackling him before he could wake Jump Rope from rest.

The book came flying out of Quentin's grasp onto the dirt. Desperate, Quentin began tearing at it and throwing dirt and mud onto its pages. He was trying to make it illegible.

"No! No!" shrieked Blu, grabbing Quentin's wrists. He fought hard to remove the crumpled pages from Quentin's palms. He needed to protect his wife's memory; that book was all she left behind. "Why are you destroying her?"

"Because you read the book!" shouted Quentin, giving in to Blu's vice. He lowered his arms to the ground and tried his best to explain.

"I'd never break my promise," growled Blu, sticking his knees onto Quentin's back to pin him. He picked up the book and slid the crumpled pages back inside. He tried to flatten them out with his hand. "Maybe we aren't so much the same…."

"It's the drink!" shouted Quentin. "If I wasn't here, all that losing, all that whiskey, you think about the last time you were happy. And you read the book…."

Blu's wife had made it explicitly clear to Blu, just as Quentin's wife had made it clear to him, she was embarrassed by her writing, and she'd prefer if no one read it till she was sure it was decent. She wrote for children, and the childish imagination could be easily ridiculed if not done tactfully. Blu knew little about the story from all she told him; she wrote with characters consisting of mainly anthropomorphized animals, just like the ones they had around the farm.

"So, you've been keeping me from temptation," grumbled Blu, sticking the book under his arm. He slowly rose from Quentin's back. "I suppose you're only trying to keep me an honest man." He reached down and helped Quentin onto his feet. "I might have reacted too strongly. There's still a lot of whiskey in me."

Quentin brushed the dirt and horse shit off his clothes. He waved his hand about in front of him. "I'm just trying to give you a better life than me." Quentin sighed and stared at the tattered book. "We should light a fire and finish destroying it."

"You're telling me that two days makes all the difference," pondered Blu, "between knowing she'll come back and losing all hope."

Quentin shook his head. "She won't."

"But Quentin, you said you left your Woodrose to find her..." grilled Blu. "Then have you really lost hope?"

"Yes!"

"... Or is there more to this story?" questioned Blu, pulling the book out from under his arm.

"No, Blu!"

He flipped open the book to crumpled pages and began to skim. The main characters were mice, facing off against rival snakes that live in the pea fields. The girl mouse was married to a rotund boy mouse addicted to cheese. She's caught in a love triangle between her timid yet jovial husband and a brave warrior fox that wins her heart by eating the snakes in the garden.

Blu closed his jaw and made a wince. "It's not bad." He cringed. "It makes you wonder why she wouldn't let us read it."

"Blu, no. It's a mistake. You're reading too much into it!"

"I'm reading too much into the book you were desperate to destroy?"

Quentin rubbed his face.

"Why... Why did you leave your home?"

"It takes only a few hours before the story spoils inside your head, leaving you with very unhealthy anger," explained

Quentin, urging his counterpart to remain calm. "If you let those thoughts in, they will destroy this town and the lives of all the people within it."

Blu twitched, his body unsure of what move to make next. "Is there something I don't know yet that makes Farrow not the fox?"

Quentin looked at his horse and then down at the dirt. "He's not…." He looked at Blu, his eyes welling up with tears. He knew he couldn't lie. "He's the fox, but that's not to say he did it."

Blu looked at the sunrise peeking up from behind Mt. Triduum. The sky burned bright orange. "Stranger's makes a good breakfast."

"I hate him too, but we got his money," pleaded Quentin. "Just leave it at that."

Bluford left to go into his house. He was off to clean and load the proper arms. If he were to hunt a fox, it would be with his Sharps rifle.

Quentin shook his head and quickly mounted Jump Rope. He dashed away from Bluford's farm, trying to reach the only other means he could think of to stop the coming inferno. It takes two to start a war; perhaps the other side might retreat if adequately convinced. He wasn't positive who warned Barrow before their fight back in Woodrose—his bet was on Ox, the only other person he'd told what was in his wife's book. Hopefully, he could do a better job than Ox to stop the confrontation before it began.

He rode back into the hills and found the trappers' tents just as he would have found Barrow's. The Punk with missing teeth was up early cleaning his horse. He stopped his brushing and stared strangely at Quentin.

"Get your boss," growled Quentin.

"He's still asleep, Sonny," said the Punk.

"No, I'm not!" Farrow grumbled and climbed out from behind his tent flaps. He rubbed his eyes and sported a scowl. "What are you selling, boy? Can't it wait till after breakfast? Or is that the new strategy: get 'em while they're groggy?"

"I'm just here to warn you, Farrow," called out Quentin, staying atop his horse. "Stay the fuck out of town, and don't go to Stranger's this morning!"

Farrow looked aggravated at first by the demand, but then he smiled. "You must have had one Hell of a premonition." He sneered. "Did you dream about me?"

"I just heard a rumor."

"What rumor?"

"A rumor that Blu's out for your blood."

"Blu's my oldest friend. We were raised together."

"You killed his wife."

Farrow's teeth gritted. "Did you tell him that?"

"No," snarled Quentin. "He found some record of it in his wife's writing."

"*She* wrote that I killed her?" Farrow chuckled.

The man with missing teeth started laughing.

"Are there ghosts involved?" Farrow sneered.

Quentin was losing his patience. He pulled out his gun and pointed it at Farrow. "Now you listen here. The notes mentioned the affair, Farrow. You're found out!"

Suddenly, two clicks sounded off behind Quentin's back. He turned to look over his shoulder and saw the remaining two Punks emerging from the woods with their rifles drawn. They had bear traps at their feet filled with dead foxes caught in their teeth.

"Sandy and I had a special connection." Farrow sighed. "I would not call it inappropriate." He gestured for Quentin to lower his weapon. "I'll talk to him, boy. Straighten this all out."

"He won't believe you. I know he won't because I didn't," said Quentin softly. "I could shoot you right now and save this town."

"But then you'll die," said Farrow, squinting dubiously. "Would you die for a town you don't belong to?"

Quentin's hand shook. He hadn't had any cheese that morning. His aim was shit, and his grip was moist. He took a long breath, then lowered his weapon.

"You're going to stay here with my men," said Farrow, motioning for the Punks to surround Quentin. The man with missing teeth pulled out his pistol and completed a triangle of loaded guns that encircled Quentin. "You're just going to have to trust that I can talk my friend down."

Farrow walked into town on foot and arrived at Stranger's just in time for Dawn to finish his first stack of pancakes. Hot cakes were free if you got there before nine. You only had to pay for the whiskey to pour on top; it was a unique variety Dawn brewed up with blackstrap molasses mixed in.

Farrow poured his shot over a thin square of butter and watched the two combine into a blonde puddle on top. He licked his lips, then swallowed his pancakes in three large gulps. He wiped his hands off so he wouldn't get anything sticky on his gun. Once they were immaculate, he pulled out his pistol and shot behind the bar. Dawn ducked and shrieked, but the bullet wasn't for him. Dawn stood up and stared at the tubing atop his pot still. A little hissing noise sounded from a small abrasion.

"I'll pay for it," promised Farrow, gesturing for Dawn to leave it alone.

Dawn looked unpleasantly surprised by the random assault on his equipment, but Farrow had also paid for a sizable percentage of the saloon's drinks over the years. He gave the man a break and let the pipes hiss.

It was just a few minutes before nine when Blu arrived with his rifle lying in his hands beneath his chest. His face was crooked; his jaw tensed on one side. His eyes peered around before landing on Farrow. The rest of the crowd took the hint from the rifle that they best be leaving.

"You're just in time to catch the special," said Farrow, gleaming positively. "Drinks are free." Farrow pointed to the hissing pipe atop the distillery.

Blu sniffed hard through his nose. He could smell the ethanol vaporized into the air.

"I'm just trying to create a safe environment so we can chat," continued Farrow. "No guns, okay?"

"What makes you think I'm going to need a gun?" questioned Blu. "Am I not gonna like your answers?"

"Your herald has prepared me to explain my relationship with Sandy." Farrow smirked. "It's just a similar taste in authors, Blu!"

"What the fuck does that mean?"

"She likes William H. Brewer; I like William H. Brewer!" exclaimed Farrow. "It's a book club, Blu. Nothing but a book club."

"A book club I knew nothing about."

"What do you know about books, Blu?" questioned Farrow. "You don't read!"

"I read plenty," snarled Blu, tossing Sandy's book on the bar's counter.

Farrow stared in confusion, then opened the book to where the torn-out pages had been hastily reinserted. He began to read. "It's about talking mice…" snickered Farrow. "This is fantasy — you can't believe fantasy, Blu!"

"God dammit," growled Blu. He pointed his rifle forwards. "Keep reading."

"So, she loves the husband…. and she loves this fox…." Farrow continued to read as his eyes bounced back and forth over the words. He flipped the page. The next one was blank. "It doesn't finish."

"I can guess the ending," said Blu. "The fox eats the lady mouse."

"Why would I kill your wife, Blu?"

"Why would you sleep with her, Farrow?"

"I've done neither!"

"You covered the wrong eye," droned Blu. He pointed his gun just under Farrow's brow. Farrow's face looked horrified for a second. His lower lip shook. He grabbed the tail of his hat and yanked on the tip slowly. He flipped it over to the other side. He'd flipped it back and forth so many times during the poker match he'd forgotten which side the twitch was on.

Blu stood up and kicked his chair under the table. He turned away from Farrow and approached the saloon's tent fly. He lifted the flap with his forearm and stepped outside.

Farrow took off his hat and held it under his arm. He reached for his pistol.

Bang! Blu fired the rifle through the frail cloth of the saloon's front wall. The bullet struck Farrow's neck and sent him to the floor. He refused to choke on his own blood, choosing instead to hold his breath and raise his pistol high up in the air. He pulled the trigger out of pure spite.

Kaboom! Blu flew backward as the tent popped like a balloon, sending flaming gas in all directions. It scorched the doctor's office to the left. It lit the courthouse to the right. Then it slowly worked its way onto the barbershop, then the tailor's store. Everyone had time to escape their businesses with what money and merchandise they could carry. Soon the street was filled with hats and suits, deli meats, and guns and ammo. The stores were turned inside-out before they each burned.

The town tried its best to douse the flames with buckets of water, but it was spreading too fast for them to fight it. With every splash they threw, it reached across another curtain or charred another door. Everyone's tireless efforts lasted a mere thirty minutes before their racing hearts couldn't beat any faster. Their legs wore out, and their arms couldn't lift another bucket. Collectively as a town, they fell to their knees and watched their village fall into ruin, acceding to destiny. Among the collective surrender were the rest of the Punks, having stripped off their warm pelts to counteract the combined heat of the fire mixed with running to and from the well. Dressed down into white union suits, they blended in among the crowd.

Quentin was there too. He was probably one of the last folks keeping the water coming long after most others sat and watched. The other townsfolk thought it was funny watching Quentin continue to pour barrel after barrel. He seemed to be working the hardest for a town he never belonged to.

Quentin didn't stop until Blu stepped in his way. He put his hands on the brim of the barrel and weighed it down until it touched the gravel. Blu let go and stared at Quentin's big, red eyes, flooding with tears in an attempt to remove the ash on his face. Quentin let go too. He rubbed his eyes and gave Blu a stare. Blu expected disappointment, but it just looked like self-defeat.

Quentin joined the rest of the town on the ground. Blu stood up in front of him and took off his hat.

"You're welcome to stay," said Blu to Quinten. "You're not responsible after all… you're not—*really me.*"

Quinten nodded. "Where will you go?"

"Wisconsin," said Blu with a look of optimism. "I heard the cheese curds are extravagant." He bowed one more time to Quentin and the town before climbing atop Hopscotch and heading north.

Blu stood in the ashes of Rosebud. If there were any minute differences between Woodrose and here, place names and roof colors, they were all burned away. The black skeleton that remained could be rebuilt into something unlike either town before it; it just needed months and months of hard labor to regenerate.

Over these months, Quentin would help the townsfolk in any way he could. He'd go with the Punks into the forest to gather wood. He'd go with Stot to Denver for nails. He'd join Dawn till sunset putting it all together. They rebuilt the barbershop and the church; they even rebuilt Stranger's, turning what was once a tent into four solid walls with a false front.

In the evenings, Quentin would retire to a small encampment he made in Blu's pea field. The fire had burned the barns to the ground, including Sandy's shack. However, the fields remained fertile, and the peas still vined, so Quentin took over. He wondered if anyone in town would stop him; it wasn't really his property after all, but overall, the town just sort of accepted him as a replacement.

Hearing how the others talked about Blu, Quentin almost felt like he should return home to Woodrose. Some people blamed Blu, but just as many blamed Farrow, and the vast majority called it Sandy's fault. It's interesting what the people were willing to tell Quentin that they could never tell Blu.

Farrow was just the tip of the iceberg compared to the vast network of men she slept with behind Blu's back. Apparently, she was a bit of a joke, 'the tart of the town.' By extension, Blu was a bit of a joke too. Knowing what he did now, Quentin doubted he could ever know what man she was with the night she disappeared.

Even if Quentin could relinquish responsibility for its destruction, he wasn't sure he could go back to Woodrose ever again. They might forgive Quentin, but *he* could never forgive *them*.

A Reason to Burn: Three Days West

A cowboy rescued me during my third tour of Afghanistan. I was on road clearance—flagging IEDs from Rūdbār to Landay—which would later be swept by a D9 operating a few days behind us. Taliban presence had been eliminated from the area years back, so we were relatively low-staffed and reduced to tactical weapon sets combined with heavy-duty body armor in case of shrapnel.

At one point, my team was a simple two-man operation, myself using a Minehound for sensing the explosives, while my partner, Private First-Class Tom Baker, wore the signal jammer. As we reached Dahmarda, we followed the pattern from previous explosives and found that these sites had already been cleared. It wasn't necessarily mysterious; locals or other coalition forces could have done it. Little did we know, it was Iranian opium smugglers stealing the IEDs to guard their drug caches.

Once they got word of our interference, they cornered Tom and me outside a remote mutton farm in Khanesin. They arrived on horseback and sprayed at us from atop a small hill to our east. We took cover behind a concrete shed on the southern half of the farm. It was two versus six. We had a knife and a pistol each; they all had HKs. We surrendered our equipment to them, hoping they wanted our sensors to find more bombs, but their orders were specifically to kill us.

Tom suggested we run for it, hoping our blast suits would shield us from the bullets. I urged him to stay, but he made his choice and ran out into the line of fire. A short rattle sounded off. The dust rose, and Tom fell. Everything went quiet, and I began to pray.

Suddenly I heard the buzz of a cylinder spinning, then another one layered overtop of it. *Click. Click.* Two cylinders entered their frames. I stuck my head out to see a Pashtun rancher, the property owner, come out on a chestnut Qatgani with dual M1895s drawn from his holsters. A red shemagh covered his face, and a white pakol kept the sun from his eyes.

I at once felt like I had entered a world of black and white I'd read about when I was a child gobbling up the legends in my Uncle Eli's *Western Story* collection. He had every issue of the magazine's thirty-year run, separated semi-decadal into six safes in his basement. This Afghani cowboy was the typical white hat coming to rescue me from the bandits.

He fired seven shots, taking down two and injuring three. Before the enemy could return fire, he bolted away on his horse and scooped me onto his back. He turned around and smiled confidently. He tipped his hat and winked at me. Then he pulled out his gun again and fired another seven shots, killing two of the injured and injuring the one unscathed. Before they could chase us down, the farmer kicked his stirrups and sent his horse flying back toward Dahmarda. Here he dropped me off with the D9 crew and tried to tell me something in Pashto. I can't translate it directly, but it roughly means, "I keep my honor under Pashtunwali."

Pashtunwali was like a cowboy code of ethics: a set of rules for an otherwise lawless land followed by the Pashtuns. It says to show the utmost hospitality to your guests, and when I hid on his property, it was his duty to protect me. Cowboys like him are the modern knight-errant all the way down to the loyal steed between their legs. We should preserve their glory and teach it to the next generation by continuing the works of dime westerns and cowboy pulp. The Golden Age of Western cinema did an excellent job of continuing their tradition, but it ended too quickly with the rise of Spaghetti Westerns in the 60s.

Those Italians brought an unwanted shade to the once clear conscience of our heroic cowboy. It used to be that the cowboy's turmoil stemmed from his unshakeable honor system; he had to do the right thing even when it put his life at stake. But Eastwood and Bronson brought monsters to life, cowboys only by the way they dressed. These men sought vengeance, vices, and treasure. Cowboys used to be synonymous with Superman, the lawful good, but Spaghetti Westerns acted like a drain pulling them into the center of true neutral.

Modern returns to the western genre have widely ignored the films before the Spaghetti Westerns and have therefore normalized the darker interpretation. I can't say I've seen anything pay homage to the dime novels of my youth, except maybe Brokeback Mountain, which is a grand return to the white knights of the west. It just so happened that these two white knights loved each other very much. There's nothing wrong with that. It's only natural for two men to recognize the hero in one another.

However, Spaghetti Westerns aren't solely responsible; it's been a largely international conspiracy that includes Sauerkraut Westerns, Goulash Westerns, Meat Pie Westerns, Ramen Westerns, and Evan Witmer's newest creation, the Avocado

Western. Witmer has succeeded in further removing the cowboy from his former glory, which I did not think was possible. Witmer hasn't fixed the broken morale of the cowboy but instead grafted it to a soft layer of Millennial pomposity.

The archetypal saloon has changed into a microbrewery. The damsel is an artist with a she-shed. The main character has advanced preferences for cheese. Even the scenery lost its modesty: painting bright, pretty colors and patterns over the traditional beige. Not only have my heroes lost their gallantry, but now, they've lost their reserve. I'm truly livid reading Witmer's material. By burning *Three Days West,* we are cutting out the heart of the Avocado Western before it can root.

- Daanesh's Damsel, Sebastian Smith

Zantar

The Albionians are a race of aliens that settled into most of the Milky Way galaxy. Their terraforming technology allows them to inhabit any terrestrial planet with equatorial temperatures under 500°C. Only the law could protect other worlds from their occupation. The Natural Deed came into effect during the early days of Albionian space exploration. It guaranteed that Albionians would not settle onto planets belonging to a star system having at least one native sentient species. Under Albionian law, a native species not only has land rights to its own world but all planets in its system. Because of this, despite their inoccupancy, Mars, Venus, and Mercury were off-limits to the Albionians.

For these reasons, the only space travel through the Solar system is under government-approved exceptions, such as military espionage, non-contact human study, and time-sensitive deliveries. One such delivery included sixteen mothers on their way from the Sirius system to Barnard's Star. The ectopic birth specialist on Nyan Tolo had suddenly passed away, leaving several high-class socialites with high-risk deliveries in the hands of lesser doctors. The government agreed to send them to the next leading expert on GJ 699 b, saving time by cutting through the pocket of space between Earth and Mars.

The mothers-to-be funded this expedition themselves, meaning there was little vetting of the crew. Cheap personnel were favored over experience, and the experience presented to them wasn't verified. This allowed several shady members of the Green Moon crime syndicate to become trusted personnel. When the ship drifted somewhere in the space between Earth and Mars, they became so remote from any colony that they disappeared from radar. In this fog, the mutiny began.

The crew instantly killed any mothers who fought back. Those who surrendered peacefully were given a more merciful death sentence—being shot into space indiscriminately in cigar-shaped escape pods. While these pods were fitted with amenities and a modest food supply, the women all died in labor. If their children survived the birth, they drifted into nothingness alone before dying from neglect. Only one infant survived as Earth's gravity captured his cigar. It floundered in our atmosphere briefly before sticking like a dart to the forest floor in the Noanet Woodlands of Dover, Massachusetts.

Exceptional safety features kept the baby inside alive and well during this perilous plummet. Explosives were stored in the hinges of the spaceship's doors in case damage sealed the passengers inside. A loud pop rang out; the crinkled aperture shot forward, leaving a gaping hole in the side of the pod. The baby slipped out and crawled into the wilderness.

The child's solid black eyes absorbed the world around him. White pines towered over and covered the sky with their beryl needles. Bright pink may flowers dangled just over his brow. The Albionian infant can stand just hours after birth; an evolutionary quirk picked up from the need to outrun predatory amphibians on their ancient home world. The little boy gathered his strength and picked himself up onto his hind legs. He reached his hand out and touched the flower's petals.

The boy laughed, utterly unaware of the terrible events that had placed him in ecological peril. The chaos of his first moments was too much for his young mind to process; his memories were cleared, beginning anew at the emergence from the space pod.

Alien laughter is not like our own. It sounded eerily like a wild turkey riddled with a venereal disease calling out in pain. The call of a weakened animal, of course, attracted hungry predators looking for an easy meal. Luckily for the alien, these weren't our usual associations with carnivores; bears and bobcats were too far off to hear. Only the raccoons arrived to investigate the noise. Seven of them circled the infant as he giggled among the Rhodora.

The raccoons began communicating by flicking certain portions of their striped tails to the left or the right, faster or slower. Their eyes worked like scanners picking up a barcode.

"A baby. Our baby?" The raccoons noticed a resemblance. The baby was gray, just like them, with large black eyes. He could stand up like they could and seemed to have a matching dexterity.

Curdtar, the raccoon's leader, came up close to the boy and examined him up and down. He noted the similar face and coloration, yet this baby was hairless and sinewy like humans. "Not raccoon. But not man. Somewhere in-between."

"Zantar!" shouted the youngest of the nursery. *Zan* was their word for man, and *tar* was the word for their own species. The baby now had a name. "Protect it?"

Curdtar took another look at the baby's anatomy. Its alien physiology is fit and agile, perfect for hunting all types of prey. Then he noticed the opposable thumbs. "Useful," said Curdtar. "Protect, protect."

As the sun set on that eventful day, Zantar followed the pack of animals into the dark woods. Zantar's baser instincts encouraged him to accept the raccoons' protection. He could sense their good intentions, either from the gentle subtleties in their behavior or from the budding extraterrestrial powers in Zantar's brain. Because of his species' enlarged parietal lobules, he could communicate telepathically with all other lifeforms with a centralized nervous system.

On the first night of their nocturnal adventures, the raccoons led Zantar on a quest for acorns to test his skills at climbing. He needed to be nimble on tree trunks and quick in the branches if he would keep up with them. Curdtar led them to the tree with the tastiest nuts—the white oak, where the creeks converge. It's far away from the dens of carnivores and well hidden from rival nurseries.

One by one, the raccoons stood at the base of the tree and scurried up its bark, disappearing into the dark cloud of verdure above. Curdtar was first, then his brides, then his children from oldest to youngest. Then it was Zantar's turn; he was last in line. The raccoons flashed their tails above him. He could hear their thoughts telling him to "climb, climb!".

The attention made Zantar shy and nervous. His skin began to sweat, a sticky substance usually associated with his species' propagation—an adhesive to bond partners during their acrobatic mating rituals. Zantar used the bonding agent to quickly climb the tree's bark, joining his raccoon brethren in the branches above the forest. Up there, the rest of the nursery gathered acorns from the branches' ends.

Zantar's stomach growled. The only thing he'd eaten after his conception was a small amount of protein mixture dispensed from a metallic teat built into the walls of the escape pod. Zantar picked the nearest acorn and stuck it in his mouth. Suddenly, a shriek sounded behind Zantar's back, followed by a strong punch to his head. A ring of claws pricked his neck. Zantar spat the nut back out into his hand.

Curdtar leaped onto the branch before Zantar and began flailing his tail rapidly. "Reckless! Foolish!" Zantar didn't understand. Curdtar's severe response shocked him so that his hands started to shake and the kernel in his palm bounced around. "Danger! Danger!" flagged Curdtar.

Zantar stared back at him with wide, sad eyes. His child-like instincts were still present even in this mature ordeal. Tears ran down his cheeks; he didn't like being scolded.

Curdtar sighed. He wiped the sweat from his angry brow, then grabbed the boy's wrist. He lowered the acorn away from Zantar's mouth. Then he pointed at the other raccoons. In a narrow line, they descended from the canopy with their arms full of forage.

Zantar followed the troops down to the tributary, where they sat their nuts to the side, beginning to wash their paws in the stream. Zantar took his one acorn, brought it down the tree, and placed it beside the others. He, too, dunked his hands in the water. He took them out and stared at the shimmering water dripping over his slick spongy skin.

Curdtar suddenly appeared to his left with an acorn outstretched in his hand. He placed it in Zantar's palm. He then grabbed Zantar's hands and cupped them over the acorn. "Water helps us feel," explained Curdtar. "Bad eyes. Good hands." Curdtar let Zantar touch all the little crevices of the acorn. "Important. Touch before eat."

Curdtar picked up the acorn Zantar had picked off the branches. He replaced the one in Zantar's hands. "Touch, touch," he encouraged. Zantar followed the instruction. The water made things more tactile; he could feel the difference Curdtar hinted at. The nut Zantar picked had subtle peaks and valleys over its skin. Its shell had scales.

"Pupae," signaled Curdtar. "Pupae is not nut. Pupae poison."

Zantar dropped the chrysalis to the ground. It belonged to a toxic family of brown-tailed moths.

Curdtar picked up the good acorn again and put it in Zantar's hands. Curdtar instructed him to feel it closer. Zantar could now tell the difference; he recognized the unique pressure against the fingertips. The real acorn was smooth and far less rubbery. It felt like a knob of wood.

Zantar understood the leader's earlier warning. He wanted to show his appreciation. Subconsciously, Zantar's head had associated the sights of their tails with the sound of the words in his head. Language slowly snowballed inside Zantar's head. He reflected his vocabulary skills at Curdtar, projecting the image of a tail into his eyes. "Thank you," said Zantar with his mind.

Curdtar rotated his face and smiled. "Protect, protect."

Zantar smiled back. He looked down at the acorn in his hands.

"Eat! Eat!" insisted Curdtar.

Zantar was excited to fill his stomach finally. He held the nut by its stem and bit at the caramel-colored pericarp. His smirk suddenly faded. He crunched down a few more times and then swallowed with a wince. "Hard. Bitter," said Zantar.

Curdtar chuckled. He took Zantar by the shoulder and directed his attention to the thick layer of leaves and pines at their feet. "Tastier food." He pointed down at the ground. Curdtar began pushing away the foliage and then made his way into the soft soil beneath it. He'd scratch at one spot, find nothing, and move on to the next. "Lots of work for larvae," said Curdtar. "Nuts much easier."

Zantar joined the leader in his hunt. Zantar could see the image of these "larvae" in Curdtar's mind. It was alive, and it had a brain. Zantar scanned the undersoil for tiny thoughts emanating from the ground. He heard the dreams of a grub calling out from just under his left foot. "Flying," thought the grub. "Flying and growing."

Zantar punched a deep hole in the earth with almost superhuman strength. He went wrist-deep, then yanked a fat pink grub out of the ground. He blew the dirt off it and then looked at Curdtar.

Curdtar encouraged him to indulge. "Grub always safe."

Zantar bit down on the nymph's head. The texture was slightly better. It was less demanding on the teeth but now strangely gooey. Gooey can be okay when paired with sweet, but this bite was still bitter. Zantar forced it down. Curdtar could see the disgust again on the boy's face.

Curdtar took a moment to explain one of the many lessons of a young raccoon: the Hierarchy of Meals. "The easier to get, the worse it tastes," said Curdtar. "Tree nuts at the bottom. Then bugs. Then bird eggs. Then birds. Then the zannite," listed Curdtar. "The fall is here, so the eggs aren't laid, and the birds are leaving fast. That leaves nuts and bugs."

"What about the zannite?" questioned Zantar. He recognized the affixes in the word; it translated to man-food. "You've never taken me for zannite..."

"Not prepared," said Curdtar. "Zannite needs strategy. Strategy needs skill." Curdtar looked at the hole the boy had made in the ground. A record time for catching grubs. "Though, you *are* getting better. You *can* speak like us, now. You *can* move like us, now."

"Then... zannite?" Zantar's body craved something far beyond the selections he'd been shown so far. His mouth watered as his imagination conjured up the many possibilities of zannite. He saw golden fruits that melted into warm honey with each bite.

"Two weeks," conceded Curdtar. "You need time to appreciate the other parts of our culture, so you know what you will leave behind if zannite goes wrong."

Half a month passed by quickly as Zantar absorbed the raccoons' warm nature; by contrast, the cold climate of New England took effect. The raccoons showed Zantar their dances in the moonlight. As a flurry came down, their footprints decorated the snow with circles of tracks. Then they showed him their favorite game; to grab their ankles and roll their chubby bodies like snowballs down the sides of hills. When they were all tuckered out, they showed Zantar the beautiful nests they built around the forest deep inside the tree hollows. They stuffed their homes with hay, cattails, and the discarded clothes of men to battle the coming chill.

"It's time," said Curdtar, on the morning of Zantar's fifteenth day among the raccoons. The first layer of winter had made the larvae even harder to find, and the panicked squirrels were depleting their nut reserves. Even a small supply of zannite could recharge the hopes of the nursery. "It's time, my son."

Curdtar led his nursery to the forest's edge, where the trees began to dwindle, and strange footprints appeared in the snow. They had no toes, and they were striped along the width. Then the trees completely stopped, and a broad black river separated the raccoons from an otherworldly cave that glowed in the dark through little squares of ice along the walls.

"Human den," explained Curdtar. Then, he pointed at the river. "Street," he explained. "Always run fast across the street. Or the lights will hit you."

"The lights?"

"The least of our worries," frowned Curdtar. He motioned to Lozan, the lookout hidden just beneath the home's windows. He kept signaling something from afar. All the raccoons on their side of the street began repeating the signal.

"Familiars, familiars." They all began to repeat with panicked inflections. They all pointed to a creature with his paws now pressed against the window. Its fur was blonde, but its body looked lupine. It was like a wolf with the sharper features removed.

"They're not quite animals. They're not quite humans," explained Curdtar.

"Then they are also zantar?"

"No!" Curdtar corrected him passionately. He placed his hand on Zantar's shoulder. "There is only *one* Zantar."

Zantar nodded.

The dog disappeared from the window. The lookout peaked inside and gave the rest of the raccoons a thumbs up.

"Look there," said Idcurd, one of Curdtar's brides. "It's what you were made for." She pointed to a polymer barrel along the path leading up to the human den. One by one, the raccoons were running toward the container. They tried to lift the seal on top, but the handle didn't work with their less-developed hands.

Curdtar stared at Zantar's thumbs just as on the day they'd met. Curdtar frowned. He was displeased with his bride's sentiment. There was much more to Zantar now. However, this *was* an obstacle that only Zantar could conquer. He waved for Zantar to cross the road. Zantar hurried over. The other raccoons stepped aside and allowed Zantar to get up close to the lock on the barrel. He tried pulling up on the plastic knob. It wouldn't move, so he twisted it side to side. That worked; he freed its x-axis. He shoved the knob to the right, and the lid popped. The other raccoons heard the latch come free, and they tackled the barrel with excitement, toppling it over. The cover banged open and beautiful zannite spilled out down the driveway.

Zantar was surprised at the form of the ambrosia. Its colors and shapes were so vast and miscellaneous. There were white shards in protein-covered slime and mounds of wet gravel that smelled like the sweetest acorns he'd ever encountered. Then a large black bag slid out from the very bottom of the barrel, making everyone's eyes widen and mouths drool. This bag was oozing red blood; it was a mound of carnivorous delights.

Eek! Eek! Before anyone could indulge, the lookout sounded out. *Eek! Eek!* Curdtar looked worried. This was bad. Lozan wouldn't give away his position unless the situation required immediate withdrawal. This was something worse than a familiar. "A fire-breather," signaled Lozan.

Without hesitation, the brides and the babies left in a panic. Only three remained: Curdtar, Zantar, and Lozan. Curdtar flailed his tail. "Provide distraction," he said to Lozan.

The door to the house opened, and a man came out with a long cylinder clutched in his hands. Lozan jumped from the windowsill and charged the man. The "fire-breather" was lowered to the ground, and the man pulled the trigger. Lozan closed his eyes before being blasted to pieces.

Zantar heard the blast and leaped out of the container, his arms clenched around the sides of the trash bag. "Run!" said Zantar to his father. Curdtar hesitated, watching his son run faster than any creature he'd witnessed. Zantar sped down the driveway and bolted across the street. Curdtar didn't leave until his son was by his side. Then the two dashed forward into the woods together.

Two more shots rang out. Flashes lit the world behind them, casting shadows in front of their path. The bark of the trees beside them disintegrated, leaving what looked like claw marks from the bullet.

Bark! Bark! As the forest got denser, the man got desperate and released his familiar. It could duck and crawl under the thickets just like the raccoons could. The rapid fire of the familiar's paws replaced the thumping two-step of the human.

As he ran, Zantar used his powers to hear the familiar's thoughts. "Make dad proud. Kill poof. Make poof killed. Dad proud." Zantar couldn't find much use for these ramblings, but then he realized if he could hear the familiar, the familiar could "hear" him. Zantar projected a fake tail in the familiar's eyes, just like he would do to communicate. He kept flashing the tail in one direction, swinging it to the right, to the right, to the right. Suddenly, the familiar was certain he was seeing the raccoons veer East, despite his nose's insistence. The familiar dashed off in the wrong direction, giving Zantar and Curdtar time to escape.

Crawling on their hands and knees, ducking under roots and thorns, they eventually found themselves in a sparsity in the woods. Here, Zantar could use the pause in the excitement to find the rest of the nursery by sensing the direction of their thoughts. "Worried. Worried. Leader? Leader?" It echoed through the forest. Zantar and Curdtar followed the signal until gray patches appeared through the breaks in the brush. They'd found the others.

Zantar surprised them all by dumping the bag onto the ground in front of his family. It was full of venison viscera, scraps tossed out by a hunter who had processed his latest kill. Zantar impressed his family with his strength, carrying the bag in his mouth throughout the escape.

"Love." "Love." "Love." All the raccoons, including Curdtar, circled Zantar, lightly pressing the tips of their tails against him. They brushed the sweat off his skin with their soft fur as they gently lifted and lowered their tails in soft peaks. This was their word for affection. "Love." "Love." "Love."

After the feast, the raccoons were too full to do their usual jigs, so they simply lay in the moonlight. Some sprawled out in the snow, cooling off their bodies, hot from digestion. Zantar felt nutritionally satisfied for the first time since joining the raccoons;

soft, warm chemicals graced his brain as a reward for filling his veins with solid fats and complete proteins. Curdtar, lying next to him, braced his fingers around Zantar's. Lying on his tail, he couldn't speak physically, but Zantar heard the secrets in his father's mind. "Proud. Prouder than any son before."

Suddenly, the snow clouds above them began flashing strange colors. Zantar thought he might just be dizzy from eating too fast. He got up on his elbows and stared forward. The clouds refracted a dozen red and blue lights glowing in the distance. They were coming from the streets at the edge of the forest.

Two loud honks blared through the trees, sending the wildlife rushing past their nursery's siesta on the ground. Squirrels darted around their bodies. Bats fluttered overhead.

"Should we follow them?" asked one of Curdtar's other sons.

Curdtar stood up calmly and felt the contents of his stomach shift with gravity. He belched, then listened closely. The horn blared again, longer this time. A doe and her buck scuttled forward with tired expressions on their faces.

Curdtar shrugged. Then he waved his arm, giving the signal for everyone to follow. Slowly, everyone got off the ground and wandered away from the lights and sounds. Little did they know, the cops had already taken aim behind them. It was a trap.

Red lines crossed over one another in thin air. The raccoons froze still, having never seen this atmospheric event before. The red lines ended in tiny dots over their hearts. Everyone but Zantar was selected. Pops filled the air.

Zantar looked to his left. Idcurd and one of her daughters rocketed backward, propelled by bullets boring through their chests. Zantar looked to his right. Pieces of Curdtar's oldest son, Losnik, splashed onto the ground. Zantar locked eyes with his father, who placed his tail on Zantar's shoulder. "Love. Love." Curdtar's nose was struck, sheering his face clean off.

Zantar turned around to run, but a wall of officers descended upon him from behind. Another wall appeared at his front. They converged upon him with their guns lowered and nets outstretched.

"Not necessary!" screamed a feminine voice from behind the wall of troops. "I said… *not… necessary!*"

One officer stepped out, breaking the circle surrounding Zantar. A woman in black plaid pants and a lavender sweater took his place. She signaled for the officers to lower their nets. She put a hand on Zantar's shoulder and smiled. The woman could feel Zantar's body shivering. She thought he was just cold, but this was shock and mourning. His family had just been gunned down in an instant.

The woman uncoiled a scarf around her neck and tied it around Zantar's. "Do you speak?" she asked.

Everyone abruptly dropped to their knees and covered their ears as Zantar stood silently. He unknowingly projected the horrors he felt inside onto everyone else's brains in the surrounding area. The cops and the woman cried out in agony as a high-pitched *eek! eek!* circled in their heads.

"What's screaming?" called out one of the officers. He saw the boy standing peacefully, his mouth shut. "What's doing this?"

The woman with the scarf returned to her feet and pulled a sedative from her pocket. She bit off the cap and lunged the needle into Zantar's left buttock.

Zantar fell to the ground, unconscious.

This woman in lavender was Dr. Alecia Staight. She was a leading developmental psychologist teaching at nearby Harvard. Word had reached her lab earlier that they may have another Genie on their hands. A hunter in Dover had spotted a feral child rummaging through his garbage for food, surrounded by raccoons. He assumed the raccoons to be rabid after one tried to assault his leg upon discovery.

Alecia was paired with a SWAT team to retrieve the boy from the unhinged predators safely. Now that Zantar was in her custody, fast asleep in the passenger seat of her minivan, she realized she was in far deeper than she initially imagined. She couldn't stop staring at his discolored skin. Alecia needed to get Zantar to a doctor at once.

"Aniridia and mild ichthyosis," said Dr. O'Sullivan. "A product of inbreeding."

"Are you sure that's all it is?" asked Alecia.

"We can't be sure of anything until DNA testing returns," explained the doctor. "If it's as bad as it looks, he might not be easy to assimilate back into society."

"It was the same with Genie, Oxana, and Madina. They never are easy."

"But your boy might be particularly impossible," warned Dr. O'Sullivan, "if we add on an intellectual disability."

"I've worked with the handicapped for years," sneered Alecia. "I find your outlook pessimistic."

"Well, where will he be living? Foster care?"

"Hell no," snarled Alecia. "He lives with me on Francis Avenue."

"That's a better environment? Boston?"

"It's not Boston," sighed Alecia, "it's Cambridge."

There was so much Zantar needed to learn, but given his fit of screaming upon extraction, Alecia knew they should first focus on building his vocabulary. The pain of being abandoned in the woods and desperately clinging to survival left the boy with many emotions he needed to express verbally.

She dressed the woozy Zantar in some clothes she'd planned on gifting to her nephew for Christmas; this was far more important. She then sat Zantar down at the kitchen table and tested what words he could recall from pre-trauma. The doctor estimated Zantar's age to be between four and seven, so there should be some simple words and phrases he could recognize. Alecia needed a baseline before they could begin learning anything new.

She opened a picture book full of animals, which the boy should be accustomed to. She pointed at a picture of a dog. "This is a…"

No response. She tapped the image again. "Bark! Bark!" she said. "I am a…"

Zantar's brain suddenly came alive. "Familiar, familiar!" He projected into the woman's brain but used his tail signals as usual, so all Alecia saw was a series of black and white flashes suddenly appearing before her eyes. She panicked and dropped the book into her lap.

She pinched the crease between her eyebrows. She thought she was having a migraine. She excused herself from her dining room table and threw a few pills down her throat to help. When she returned, the book was unfolded on the table before Zantar. He was tearing furiously through the pages until he found what he was looking for.

He jammed his finger against the page, pointing to a picture of a raccoon. His eyes welled up with tears, and he began to sob.

"The raccoon?" she spoke. Zantar's mind connected the word to the page.

Zantar repeated it back with a sad inflection. "Raccoon. Raccoon."

"Did the raccoon hurt you?" As each word was spoken, Zantar saw its meaning in his head.

He mixed up the words and made his point. "You… hurt… raccoon."

Alecia was shocked. "We… We did hurt the raccoons. We had to. They were dangerous."

"Dangerous?" Zantar saw Alecia's idea of danger behind her eyes. He saw a raccoon leaping into the air, foam on its lips. It sunk its teeth into an officer's neck. Zantar didn't know the word "no," but he certainly knew the raccoons were not this word "dangerous."

"Dangerous!" he repeated angrily, pounding his fists on the table. *Bang! Bang!* "Dangerous!" he repeated. *Bang! Bang!* "Dangerous!" He was trying to say they weren't.

Alecia could tell this was a moment of disagreement between her and the boy. She realized she'd started education too fast and that verbalization wasn't the boy's problem—it was trust. She had to backtrack and try again.

"Can you remember your name?" she asked the boy.

He took a deep breath and pulled his fists off the table. He looked down into his lap and frowned. "Zantar," he pouted.

"Well, Zantar," sighed Alecia, "let's get you some food."

Alecia had accidentally stumbled across the best means of reaching young Zantar. It seemed like such an obvious suggestion, bridging the gap with comestibles. Zantar was especially suggestable to its charm, given the culinary adventures he once shared with Curdtar.

Zantar imagined Alecia would bring him to something akin to the grubs or the acorns. He was shocked when a plate slid before him with a paddy full of protein stuffed between what looked like a pair of mushroom heads. The top head was sprinkled with seeds, while the paddy was topped with plants and a golden layer of melted ooze.

"Zannite!" said Zantar, his eyes wide and mouth watering.

"It's a burger," chuckled Alecia. "Craigie on Main makes one of the best."

Zantar started chowing down like crazy. Alecia figured he had never seen a burger before, or there had been quite some time between occurrences. She could only imagine how long he was out there in the wild.

"Zantar..." said Alecia softly.

Zantar just kept on eating.

"Zantar, I want to ask you some more questions," said Alecia, putting on a friendly face. "Can you take just a small break from eating?"

Zantar finished his latest bite, then took a deep breath. He resisted the urge to continue and slowly lowered the sandwich.

"It's nothing too hard. I just want to know about your family."

"Raccoons were family," said Zantar bluntly.

"But what about your family before the raccoons?"

Zantar shook his head. "There was no 'before the raccoons'."

"Then what was there?"

Zantar racked his brain, trying to recall. He strained so hard he transmitted the half-memories into the surrounding airspace, where Alecia's brain picked it up.

"Egh!" she whimpered. She thought she was having another migraine, but it was different this time. There weren't any flashes of light, just sounds—a roar like from the bottom of a missile. Then she felt something. Her body rapidly shook like she was stuck in some large malfunctioning machine. It felt almost like experiencing a car crash. "How do you do that?" she said with agitation.

Suddenly the pain stopped. The noises and shaking all went away as Zantar perked up across from her.

"How do you make all this noise?" she asked.

Zantar cocked his head to the side. "Talking. Head to head."

"Telepathy?" asked Alecia.

Zantar nodded. He supposed.

Alecia started to consider the possibility that there was much more to Zantar than the doctor suggested. Psychic abilities have always proven false in the past, but there was a chance this child was some next-level human; gifted by the same genetics that resulted in his cinereal skin. Or, less likely, this boy wasn't human at all.

The flashbacks Zantar sent Alecia gave her an idea. She could perhaps trigger more from this vestigial memory if she could apply the correct stimulus.

Alecia took him to the Mary Baker Eddy Library, which is normally an unusual place to bring a child, given that Mary Baker Eddy was the founder of a now-dying cult that started in the 1880s. But in the center of this nuthouse is a priceless work of art—The Mapparium—a forty-two-foot glass globe with a pathway running through the middle. Three hundred LEDs illuminated the map of the world from the outside, depicting all the nations' borders from 1935.

As Zantar stepped inside, he was suddenly immersed in the image of our planet. The blue from the oceans reflected off the sheen of his eyes. This catalyst lit his neurons aflame, just as Alecia had predicted. Alecia and the rest of the tour suddenly got a glimpse at Zantar's first few hours of life floating above Earth. Then they saw it all come crashing down.

Suddenly everyone inside the Mapparium started screaming as they felt like they were diving headfirst toward Earth. Because of the weird acoustics inside the glass ball, the screams were bouncing around from all directions. Alecia snapped herself out of the transmission and quickly grabbed the boy. She ran him out of the exhibit before the rest of the group could recover.

Alecia returned Zantar to Dr. O'Sullivan with word of her progress.

"An alien could make sense," said Dr. O'Sullivan. "Our enzymes aren't capable of fragmenting his genetic material for testing. That could be because it's chemically independent of our own DNA."

Dr. O'Sullivan turned away from Alecia and looked at Zantar. "Where. Are. You. From?" he enunciated.

"The forest," replied Zantar.

O'Sullivan nodded. "But before that?"

"Let me show you."

Dr. O'Sullivan's eyes suddenly rolled back in his head. His stomach flipped like he was riding a rollercoaster as Zantar's crash landing played out in his mind. He placed his hands on his bulbous belly.

"Zantar, look out!" Alecia shielded the boy with her body as O'Sullivan let out a loud belch followed by a flow of white liquid. It splashed onto the floor and projected forward until it sprayed all over Alecia's back.

"Miraculous!" shouted Dr. O'Sullivan, snapping out of the illusion. He wiped the vomit from his chin and quickly pulled a towel from the sink in his office. He tossed it to Alecia to clean up. "This link between minds. It could allow for rapid transfer of information."

O'Sullivan spun around and started searching through the upper cabinets. He chose a book he was familiar with and put Zantar's abilities to the test. "Tell me, child, how much do you know of human biology?"

"Absolutely nothing," frowned Zantar. "I don't even know my own biology."

"We'll get to that later… for now, listen here…." Dr. O'Sullivan opened the textbook to a chapter on diagnosing skin conditions. "A punch biopsy is a minimally invasive procedure in which a millimeter radius hole is made in the patient's skin where there is a suspicious growth or lesion…." The doctor slammed the book shut and stared into Zantar's eyes. "Describe the tool being used."

"A circular blade attached to something that looks kind of like a pencil…"

"Fascinating," said the doctor, "and what diseases might this be used to diagnose?"

"Lentigo melanoma… nummu- nummular dermatitis?"

"Even more interesting," continued the doctor. "Those were the precise cases for the last two patients I used the procedure on… Ms. Staight, do you know what this means?"

Alecia nodded. "Instantaneous learning."

"Precisely!" exclaimed Dr. O'Sullivan. "As long as the person speaking fully grasps the concept, Zantar gains the entire breadth of their knowledge on the subject. Well, at least their most recent knowledge. I tell him I have three kids, for example, and he immediately knows their names."

"Margaret, Jessie, and Sullie," called out Zantar.

"It's remarkable," replied Alecia. "He could advance much faster than an average child, let alone a feral child."

"We need to be reading Plato and Paine," exclaimed O'Sullivan. "Maybe even Machiavelli."

"Isn't that too political for a child?"

"That's up for him to decide!" shouted the doctor. "He doesn't absorb our opinions from our minds, just all the proximal facts. I'm curious how his innate biology will organize all this new information. He could see patterns completely invisible to our mere human understanding!"

"Boston is the mouth of America," concluded Zantar after a long day exploring the city's historical sights. They'd marched the Freedom Trail and watched some reenactments of the events leading up to the Revolutionary War. Alecia and Dr. O'Sullivan decided that an excellent way to begin Zantar's philosophical education should start with the birth of American politics. Zantar had absorbed so much from the tour guides and actors they'd met that O'Sullivan begged his alien mind to craft his own opinion of it all.

"The mouth?" questioned O'Sullivan; it was not his expected answer. "Now, why would Boston be the mouth?"

"Well, if Kansas City is the heart of America," replied Zantar, "then St. Augustine is the asshole."

"Wait, what do *you* have against St. Augustine?"

"Nothing, it's just been here the longest." Zantar smirked.

"Very clever," grinned Alecia. "So, then, what makes Boston the mouth?"

"It's always spilling tea."

Alecia laughed. O'Sullivan restrained. He was trying to get Zantar to take this seriously. He doubted the alien brain's capacity for rhetoric stopped at jokes.

"Why not the *brain* of America?" asked Dr. O'Sullivan. "We're the center of biotechnology in the US."

"I mean, sure," said Zantar with a sarcastic grin, "but there's several of these so-called centers throughout the country. The list includes Durham."

"Where's Durham?"

"Exactly," snorted Zantar.

"Is he shitting on Boston, now?" Alecia chuckled. "I guess he's a real Bostonian, then."

Zantar shook his head. "There might be something of an initiation missing from what I've scanned of everyone else. It's a common memory. Something that binds you all together into a single cell."

"Really? Well, where would you like to go?"

Zantar smiled. "Fenway."

Of course, the wintry weather prevented any baseball from going on, but that hadn't stopped the town from setting up a winter wonderland for the young and young at heart in the center of the field. There were two structures: an ice rink for skating and a three-story luge for downhill games. The suggested games were either sledding or tubing, but Zantar had his own activity in mind: grabbing his ankles and rolling down like a snowball.

As Zantar tumbled down the hill, he felt the snow slowly building up on his back. He opened his eyes and saw the world flipping over and over. The dizziness took away all his sensations and made him laugh uncontrollably, sending these feelings into the air. The whole crowd on the mound felt a sudden rush of warmth under their hats. Zantar imagined

Curdtar rolling beside him, causing the kids atop the hill to stare in confusion as the illusion of a rolling raccoon appeared on the slope.

Alecia met Zantar at the bottom. She helped the boy wipe the frost off his clothes. "I got you something to warm up," she said, handing the boy a hot chocolate and a Fenway frank.

"Thank you," said Zantar. Zantar lifted the hotdog up to the foam cup and dunked the tip into the cocoa.

"Those don't usually go together," warned Alecia.

Zantar bit down anyway. A tad soggy, but overall, he liked it. Zannite was zannite.

Suddenly, Zantar's chewing slowed to a halt as his attention hung up on strange colors appearing in the clouds overhead. A thin black rod pierced through the stratus layer, blinking bicolored; two slow, solid beeps of yellow followed by four rapid flashes of green.

Zantar turned to face Alecia. She was staring at the lights with bewilderment. She turned her head and stared back at Zantar. It seemed neither of them had any quick answers about what they saw.

"It's a ship," murmured O'Sullivan. He pointed towards the sky as the needle threaded further through the clouds, revealing a sizeable funnel-like structure attached to its base. It looked like a metallic Solo cup, spinning on its y-axis.

Screaming sounded off in the distance, followed by strange metallic chirps. The people on the slopes began running towards the exits to the stadium but were blocked off by what looked like astronauts with salmon-colored bodysuits and steel-colored orbs encasing their heads.

In the hands of these spacemen were rifles just as silvery as their headgear. When they pulled the trigger, a flash of yellow light expelled from the gun's tip. Anyone hit by the beams splattered like they'd been hit by a bus. Parents tried throwing their children over the stadium walls into the bleachers. Barely anyone could escape, and the assailants seemed to be killing indiscriminately.

Zantar was quickly scooped up by Dr. O'Sullivan, who was now running across the snowy field, trying not to slip on the slush. Zantar peered over O'Sullivan's side to see Alecia take a blast to the shoulder, caving in the top-right corner of her body. She fell to the ground with a lifeless gaze.

O'Sullivan kept charging forward. He had no time to waste, and he couldn't look back, not even for Alecia. He knew in his head that these men were here for Zantar and that Zantar was most likely never supposed to have been on Earth. That left Zantar's fate up to chance, which was not a reliable condition for a child.

O'Sullivan got Zantar to a row of small, brave hands reaching down from the bleachers trying to help the other kids up. They latched onto Zantar just as a blast knocked the doctor's head off his shoulders. Zantar heard the blast strike but couldn't bear to see another friend torn to shreds. He kept his glimpse forward and took the doctor's silence as a sign he did not survive.

Zantar began dashing up the stairs between the stands with the other kids. They dashed out into the stadium halls and spread out in all directions. Shrieks rang out as more spacemen appeared, trekking through the sea of kids, ignoring them mostly. Occasionally, a child would attack their legs with their fists and kicks, but then the spacemen would just fling them away with a brisk push.

These spacemen were different from the ones outside. These had their blasters holstered on their backs. Their hands held blue tarps instead. These blankets had a second layer on the bottom of what looked like bronze webbing.

Zantar tried to keep his head low as he wandered through the crowd. Despite his hiding, he soon found himself wedged between two walls of militia. The nearest spaceman grabbed Zantar's head and shoved him back into an empty corner. Then another spaceman dropped the blue curtain over Zantar's head. As the webbing touched Zantar's skin, a little zap sent him unconscious.

He awoke three hours later in a padded cell. He felt no pain, and he didn't seem to be confined to any chains or restraints. The cushions on the wall were made from black sponges. Zantar rested his hands against them, pushing the fabric in and out. Then he looked upwards at the room's only light source on the ceiling. The whole top was a glass window with the stars glowing through. Zantar looked up at the sky and saw a tiny blue dot where Earth was. Zantar sat back in his cell and coiled his legs to his chest. He was back in space.

A whirring sound whistled along the edge of the cell's only door. It slid open, revealing an older man that looked a lot like Zantar but was taller and had a large hump on the top of his head. The man squinted and read through Zantar's recent memories.

"Concerning," he said. "After learning conversation, you might have difficulty transitioning back."

"Excuse me?"

"Conversation has become redundant, child. A vast majority of your kind simply shares memories," explained the tall man. "It saves time. It conveys all the information in a single instant."

Zantar shook his head. He didn't understand. The tall man twitched his eyes. Suddenly, Zantar *did* understand.

Zantar could recall numerous instances of the tall man sharing memories in the past. He did it to buy groceries. He did it to catch up with friends. He did it to spice up the bedroom.

Zantar also saw the man's name.

"Xux-596," muttered Zantar.

"But who are *you*?" replied Xux. "I don't think Zantar will be culturally acceptable." Xux addressed the walls. "Computer!" he shouted. "Run a biographical assembly for the boy."

"LNA matching… maternal parent found: Hoh-2755 of Nyan Tolo."

"Contact close connections. Inquire on names," commanded Xux.

"Contacting relatives," replied the feminine voice of the computer. "Asking for input. No interest. Contacting recent mates. Asking for input. No interest. Contacting close personal friends. Asking for input. Sax-1080 says, 'After a night of drinking, Hoh-9100 was the top choice. If it's stolen, Jix-180.'"

In Albionian culture, their preference towards minimalism has led to most names being formed of a single syllable. There were countless of these, yet some were more popular than others. Given the size of their population, this syllable was followed by numbers to act as a unique identifier. It's considered good luck for the number to end in a zero; even better if it ends in multiple. It's also a recent trend to name boys after their mothers.

"Is Hoh-9100 taken?" asked Xux.

"It was taken twenty-one days ago," droned the computer, "but Jix is free."

"Then Jix-180 it is."

"Affirmative. Creating an official record."

"I'm Zantar..." said Zantar.

"Perhaps today, but we *will* reassimilate you," sneered Xux, "you, too, will realize it sounds like a pet's name and will crave your mother's name. Just the same, you will talk less and less, only speaking to address your hardware. And then, you will begin to dress in the proper colors to diminish the odd looks. And you will take alcohol baths twice daily to avoid rude comments. Your ferality will slowly recede, and you will prefer the civilized ways of Albionians."

"Civilized?" questioned Zantar. "You blew away my friends."

"Humans are not a negotiating species, Jix. They kill their own race one whole city at a time. Their films depict us as unreasonable invaders who need to be slaughtered. We couldn't risk our lives. We performed an appropriate extraction."

Zantar began kicking at the padded walls; he shrieked out loud. His anger boiled over, but unlike the humans, it didn't seem to faze fellow Albionians. Being around mind readers their whole lives, they've learned to keep others out if they wish.

"I bet you're hungry," said Xux. "I can prepare you dinner."

Zantar stopped his tantrum and turned to face Xux. "I've been through enough peace offerings to know when I'm being manipulated."

"So, you'll never eat again?"

"Not across from you."

Xux shrugged. "Fine, I'll stand; *you* will eat. And if you do, I'll share with you something of interest."

Zantar snarled. He couldn't imagine being persuaded, but Xux had come prepared.

"Your mother's death, Jix, I know it's intimate details," explained Xux," and you won't hear them from anyone else. They're military secrets."

"You're military?" questioned Zantar. "They sent the military for a rescue mission?"

"In an advanced society, that's all a military is facilitated to do...."

Zantar walked up to Xux, ducked under his arm, and walked past him. "Show me to your kitchen."

Once there, Zantar was presented with three photos on the dining table. "Cip-4444, San-34201, and Mik-3," said Xux, standing at the table's edge. "These are the men who killed your mother in an attempt to establish an illegal weapons cache on Mars."

Zantar examined their features. They all looked like him, and they all looked like Xux. They were gray, and their eyes were big, black, and soulless. Zantar missed the eyes of humans. They had touches of color.

"So, this society is advanced and civilized, but it creates men like this," huffed Zantar.

"Every society has its detractors," defended Xux. "It's how we deal with them that makes us enlightened."

"...which is."

"It's *your* decision," he said with a tight grin. "At least, it should be... there are some who believe a feral child should not have a say in punishment; that it would be like asking a wild animal to play judge and jury."

"What even makes something an animal?" questioned Zantar.

"A lack of subtlety," replied Xux.

"Do you think *I'm* an animal?"

"Of course, you're not. There is no reason to judge your decision as primal without first hearing what you propose." Xux bent his head down towards the table. "So, if you have any initial thoughts, now would be the time to share."

"Blast them to pieces," said Zantar with a laugh, "like you did to the humans."

"Oh, Jix," said Xux, displaying a frown. He returned to a straight posture. "I'm afraid we don't kill our prisoners. We minimize death whenever possible. Discipline included."

Zantar growled. "Then what do you expect me to say? What other option is there?!"

"You could make them wear black."

"Black?!"

"For the rest of their lives."

Zantar clenched his fists, and the internal agony became unbearable.

"It's the color of surrender," explained Xux. "It would be very embarrassing for a soldier of the Green Moon."

Zantar stayed silent. He pulsated with anger.

"Right," sighed Xux, having waited too long for a response. "You need more time. The bloodlust of the humans is still inside you. When it fades, you'll know the answer."

Xux went into the fridge to pull out some food for Zantar. He slid it onto the kitchen table in front of his face. Then Xux walked away. "I promised I wouldn't bother you while you ate," he called out from down the hall, "but use this time to think wisely."

Xux had given Zantar what looked like a glass baby bottle with a bright orange rubber nipple. The fluid inside was thick and completely transparent.

Zantar cringed. This was no zannite. He popped off the top and smelled the liquid. It was odorless. He gagged, then hurled it at the wall. The glass smashed and left a colorless smear.

"I want them set free," called out Zantar, his fist pressed against the table. "I want them set free on Mars, on whatever shanty base they've made on the surface. I want you to supply them with that minimalist slime you served me in a bottle. And that's it. You take away their vehicles and all lines of communication. What you leave is three men and their den in the woods. And they'll be left there until they're not the same."

Xux came back into the room with a peaceful expression. "It will be arranged."

"And *I* will decide when they're not the same!"

A Reason to Burn: Zantar

There are four named raccoons in "Zantar," but the story alludes to more being present. In nature, a nursery can grow up to seven, so we can estimate that Evan kills between four and seven raccoons during the first climax of his story. As a lone incident, I wouldn't call for a book burning on behalf of a little animal decimation, but I'm afraid this is just the latest in a long, shameful pattern.

Let's return to Evan's first collection: *Pages from the Pizza Crows* where he spears a horse, shoots up a dog, drugs a bear, and separates a monkey from its paw. Then follows *Digest,* where he takes out an indeterminate number of deer, a wolf, a leopard, a couple of goats, and another dog.

I know how it must sound; tallying up every dead animal makes me look eco-friendly. I'm not a vegan or a vegetarian; I'm an occasional litterer and drive an old Jeep. I'm not really concerned about the state of our planet. I'm more worried about the safety of the citizens in Buffalo, NY.

I've been plotting Evan's location over the last few years. He grew up in Reading, PA. He moved to State College, PA, for college, then recently shifted to Buffalo for a new job. Reading's unsolved cases statistic has dropped significantly since Evan left in 2011. During his ten years at State College, we see five serial murders committed with the same mushroom-shaped blunt object. The killer has never been found.

I believe Evan is responsible for these killings, and in-between dissociations, he enacts his twisted fantasies on imaginary animals. He has unintentionally let his delusions run into his material. As people read his sociopathic descriptions of animal mutilation, it normalizes the destruction and encourages Evan to continue his mindless rampage. Burning "Zantar " may be our best bet to break Evan's ego and get him to turn himself in. Otherwise, the police have been no help at all. Without anything connecting Evan to a six-to-eight-inch mushroom-shaped weapon, I can't prove anything. The closest I've come to finding a link has been hacking into his Grubhub account and finding orders for mushroom toppings on pizza, cheesesteaks, and artisan hamburgers.

If this investigation isn't taken more seriously, I predict a series of strange disappearances at Buffalo's nearby tourist destination of Niagara Falls. Large international crowds are the perfect prey for types like Evan. It takes much longer for foreign countries to realize their citizens have gone missing overseas.

My latest forensic experiment has been releasing raccoons into the garbage bins outside Evan's apartment. I can use the fantasies in his stories to stimulate his killing response in reality. By getting him close to the animals he mutilates, he may try to release tension by slaughtering them. So far, interactions between Evan and the raccoons have been plentiful, but nothing has evolved into violence. Evan has taken up feeding the raccoons small scraps of grilled cheese, chicken wings, and ravioli stuffed with, you guessed it, mushrooms. He's named the more distinct-looking raccoons; one is Bowie, and the other is Antonio. By no coincidence, these are *human* names so that he may simulate something as close to homicide as possible.

Rest assured, Evan *will* strike again, and I'll be there this time to capture it on camera. If you live in Western New York or plan on visiting, I encourage you to practice basic safety procedures. Lock your doors, check your back seats, and keep a romantic partner or close friend tethered to your body via a reinforced strap.

- Self-employed Sleuth, Tyler Woodchute

Sea Creatures

The Saronic Gulf is the only way to and from the Mediterranean's most celebrated wharf, Port of Piraeus, on the edge of Athens. Most traders will go their whole lives without thinking twice about their safety along this prevalent route. However, dangerous winds can even occur on the most peaceful tides when the Anemoi, gods of the wind, are feeling particularly ill-tempered.

Zephyrus, god of the western wind, would sometimes get sick eating his favorite meal of mussels and feta; and when he did, the ships in the Saronic would have to battle against his unpredictable gales. Most ships would be fine with the proper adjustments, but sometimes the wind would take a ship too close to the northeast corner of the island Aegina. Here, mainland Greeks know to cork their ears with beeswax and wool; but the importers are not as well-trained. Less versed in proper mythology, these Seljuqs, Carthaginians, and Sicilians come within earshot of the siren that's perched along this coast.

"Euaí! The horizon's my promenstria! This vessel is ambrosia for the heart," sings the siren, Molpe, *"Join me on this rock upon the ocean, Our Aphrodisia holiday will start!"*

One such unfortunate vessel, a Libyan barge carrying papyrus, turned its course at the sound of the song. Before their captain even had to say it, the oars doubled their speed and rammed their bow into the limestone stacks where Molpe had perched. As the seas drowned their cargo, the shipmates bobbed peacefully on the surface of the waves, stuck in a deep trance. This gave Molpe time to visit each sailor individually.

Molpe flapped the gull wings on her back and hovered over her prey. She then carefully lowered her legs and wrapped her yellow, webbed toes around the victim's shoulders. Molpe's weight sunk her victim just down to their collar.

"Do you speak Greek?" she asked in her native tongue. Most men did if they traded in Athens, and it certainly made her work easier when they did.

"Yes, my swain," affirmed the Libyan, in the proper speak.

"Then raise your chin for me, dear," she said avidly.

Completely enamored, the mariner did as he was instructed. He looked upwards between Molpe's legs and smiled at the sight of her cloaca, gifted to look like the human counterpart.

Molpe licked her lips, then buckled her knees. A sharp yellow beak slid out from between her human lips like an alien proboscis. She dove her head down with a swift arc, slamming its tip into the center of the sailor's neck. The beak then chewed away at the sailor's tendons, digging and dragging until she freed the esophagus from the rest of the body. Then she bit the top end of the esophagus and slurped it up like a bird does a fat, juicy earthworm.

A ship of this size usually satiates Molpe for about a month, two months if it's a slave ship. In that time, she just needed to wait for Zephyrus to poison himself again, and given his ravenous appetite for shellfish, it always came soon enough. But the next time it would, Molpe found herself in a strange predicament. The winds were present, but they did not deliver a lost vessel. Molpe spent half the day waiting impatiently as the moist air ruffled her feathers and the winds blew salt into her eyes.

Molpe considered the possibility that a sailor had been caught in the squall but simply escaped with proper luck. Still, her hunger made her too agitated to accept this fact peacefully. She flew to the top of nearby Mt. Oros to get a broader view of the surrounding sea. To her surprise, she saw a ship *had* crashed into Aegina, but it was lower down the shore. It had collided with an empty dock in an abandoned marina south of her nest. Bewildered, she flew down to investigate.

"Euaí! The waves are my promenstria! These sailors are ambrosia for the heart," sang an alto voice a few octaves lower than her, *"Join me on this rock upon the ocean, We shouldn't spend this holiday apart!"*

Every siren has its own version of more or less the same song. Humans only think their music is unique because they're killed before they hear it twice. No one siren's song is the correct version. They sound similar because every sailor likes to hear the same thing – love has come to break the monotony. However, Molpe hadn't heard *this* version, and she'd met her other six sisters numerous times before.

Molpe landed beside this mysterious, new siren, perched on one of the sunken Sicilians wading in the water. As her feet balanced on his crown, the weight wetted the end of the man's beard.

The strange siren was fairer than Molpe, and her body was far slimmer. It looked as though she hadn't been eating as much as a monster should. The siren slurped half the length of an esophagus before lifting her head to see Molpe staring at her. She finished her meal with a hard suck, then retreated her beak back into her human lips. "Have we a problem?" she said shyly.

"I've never seen you before," explained Molpe. "What is your name?"

"Teles," they said.

"Well, I understand you need a place to feed, Teles; we all certainly do," droned Molpe, keeping calm despite her growing stomach pangs, "but it can't be right upstream to my nest."

Teles turned away from Molpe and looked up the shore, trying to spot the nest she was talking about. "Oh, I knew this place seemed too good to be true," she said with a defeated expression, "already taken it seems."

"For quite some time, too," replied Molpe, "but there's plenty of room on Antipsata; I've considered moving there myself for the triremes coming out of Old Smyrna. It's the tannins in their wine; it sticks to their gullets and adds a nice oakiness."

"Someone's beaten me there too, I'm afraid," sighed Teles. "Raidne *has* boasted about the flavor."

"Raidne?" questioned Molpe. "I'm sorry, but just how far does my family extend nowadays? Last I checked, Achelous had grown too old and impotent to foster any more monsters?"

"An accidental aphrodisiac has recovered his vigor, I'm afraid," explained Teles. "A herd of sacred bulls was to be delivered to Alyzeia for sacrifice to Heracles. The cowherd had inherited the position from his father and thought he could deliver twice as fast if he cut across the Achelous River before it widened in the north. The narrow flow proved too strong. The herd was drowned, sacrificing all that precious bovine to Achelous."

"Foolish boy," huffed Molpe, "so then how many of you are there?"

"Well, my mother is Sterope, and I have five sisters," listed Teles, "but then there were six born before us from Thalia. And now there are four born after us from Erato. And then there's a new batch of three on the way from *your* old mother, Melpomene."

Molpe stood in shock. Her mouth hung open at the thought of her father in such an orgy. Teles could see her half-sister's beak shivering in the back of her throat. "What a disgusting old man..." cringed Molpe, "but thank you for the information. Feel free to stay where you are, little sister. I think it will be me who makes her leave."

Molpe realized that with her father's new sexual power, sirens would soon fill the Mediterranean to the brim, and there was nothing she could do to stop it. It didn't matter where she went; some sister nearby would be culling her supply. Not to mention, this rise in siren attacks would surely attract a new hero to see to their elimination. Only lowkey monsters lived as long as she.

Molpe decided it was time to haunt the seas somewhere far away, without her father's influence, so that he could not fill it with his hungry offspring. However, Molpe's human proportions made flying long distances difficult without somewhere to rest in between. The open ocean proved a problem for her. She wondered if she wouldn't need to fly if she found the proper alternative. She could, instead, sail.

The world is mainly water, so there are many places for Molpe to go; she just needed to hitchhike with the right crew. She began venturing away from the shores of her home and hovered over the Aegean Sea, looking for someone from a land far enough out. She could tell each sailor's level of exoticism by how they dressed.

She did laps around a horse transport until she saw the leopard pelts and pointed helmets on the warriors. These were Numidian cavalry, legendary fighters from just south of her original nest. That's nowhere near far enough, so she moved on to the next vessel. This one had flags with foreign writing on them, and the men sang songs she couldn't understand; but as she swooped over their heads, she noticed their long flowing locks and realized these men were merely Lycians. Their colony was just a short trip to the east.

She flew up high once again for a bird's eye view, looking at the ships themselves for anything outlandish. From above, she noticed all the ships seemed to be following the trend set by Zephyrus' distress. All their sails were angled to a beam reach to combat the western wind's influence over their route—all except one—there was a strange long boat that seemed utterly unaffected. Only a few miles from departing Piraeus, this boat seemed to follow a flow all its own. Upon closer inspection, its sails did not interact with the winds above but seemed to face whatever direction the sailors wished to travel. This spell had never been cast by any Greek before—the Anemoi would protest—and so Molpe figured this was magic from a foreign tome.

Molpe flew close and caught sight of the voyagers; they were Varagians, warriors from Scandinavia hired by Greek nobles for their ferocity to act as bodyguards. These men seemed to have carried out their contracts and were headed back to their homeland to share their rewards.

The Nordic lands would all be sufficiently removed from the Mediterranean. All Molpe needed to do, then, was catch a ride clandestinely. She couldn't come straight at them from above without being seen, so she dove under the sea like a pelican does to catch its food. She entered the water a hundred meters in front of their ship, then reemerged just as their hull passed overhead. She hugged the stem between her arms and climbed the front of the vessel until she was just under their bowsprit. Here, she flipped around and used her wings like a clamp to fix herself to the front of the boat. Holding still, she was perfectly disguised as an ornate figurehead, wholly camouflaged from other ships passing by.

A week and a half of smooth sailing were all it took before they reached the shores of Scandinavia. The crew would spend another three days making their way to Aarhus, the most popular port in the Baltics, but Molpe saw no need to wait. She hopped off when they reached the North Sea. She'd caught sight of a beautiful island with marengo rauks along its east side and realized that was an ideal spot. She could prey on any ships that took the path between this island and the mainland, which should be just enough to keep full but not too much that she should attract a hero, that is if they had such things as heroes in Scandinavia. There was so much she still needed to learn.

"Euaí! The horizon's my promenstria! This vessel is ambrosia for the heart. Join me on this rock upon the ocean, Our Aphrodisia holiday will start!" Molpe sang to a fishing boat as it passed by just a few miles from her new nest. Ships like this were caught in a strange current that only appeared once or twice a month with no regular pattern. Molpe could tell when the current was active as the ocean would turn brown like shepherd's tea. The strong flow would kick up beige sugar kelp off the seafloor. At the sight, Molpe would immediately cast her line, so to speak, towards any ship caught in this tide. Her first few attempts, however, proved fruitless.

Molpe was astonished as the boats would sail right by her without so much as a sailor turning their head in her direction. She figured the air in this sea didn't carry sound as well, so she took larger breaths between her lines and increased her amplitude, but the ships continued to pass with indifference.

Molpe's stomach growled with hunger; it'd been three months since she'd eaten back on Aegina. She was becoming desperate. Her skin felt clammy, and her eyes darted about the ocean in a panic. That's when she saw a strange patch of red among the blue and brown on the surface. She squinted and saw tendrils of hair, merlot locks, floating just under the water.

Her instincts told her not to prey on dead things; they could carry disease, but it was three months since her last meal, and she wondered if she could keep carcass meat down if she tried hard enough. It might tide her over till she figures out the cause of her voice's sudden impotence.

Molpe flew over the red mark in the ocean and stuck her feet beneath the waves till her talons coiled around a pair of soft shoulders. Molpe flapped her wings and dragged the body upwards out of the sea.

"*Agh! Kors i røven!*" The maiden screamed in Nordic tongue as she was yanked into the open air. "*Hvad laver du mod mig, kærlig?*"

Molpe was shocked but ultimately grateful that the body was alive. Live prey should pass through her so much easier. She kept tugging upwards, bringing the body out inch by inch. She looked down at the body and saw the lady's hands were full: a chisel in her left hand, thin as a nail, and a strophion with shells ornamenting the cups.

"*Sæt mig ned, elskede,*" continued the sea woman. She didn't seem scared, just slightly curious about where she was being taken. "*Jeg kan ikke forlade havet.*"

Molpe was surprised at how heavy this woman was until her waist left the water, and it all became clear. While the top half of this woman was a frail human, the bottom half was thick and scaly. This woman had the long, cobalt tail of a wolffish growing down from her hips.

Molpe immediately gagged and released the woman from her feet. Molpe didn't eat fish; she had a horrible allergy.

The red-headed woman slid back down into the water with a loud *bloop*. Her head reemerged and stared up at Molpe, fluttering above. She caught sight of the siren's cloaca and blushed. She looked back down at the water.

"What are you?" asked Molpe with a look of aggravation. She was feeling impatient as her first dinner in forever was suddenly ruined. She almost sounded like it was the woman's fault for choosing to be half-chum.

"Vhat do you speak… *Greeg*?" said the redhead; she was trying to say Greek through a thick accent.

Molpe flew back up to perch on a stone, then glared angrily down at the girl. "I'm Greek, yes," she said shortly. "Can you understand me?"

"I speak… a little," she said choppily, "but I understand very well!"

"How's that?"

"I'm friends with kraken," replied the mermaid. "They do jobs for Poseidon… smiting mainly, but their home is here."

"I see," sighed Molpe. She felt bad for giving such a rude introduction earlier. "I'm in pain; otherwise, I swear I'd be more talkative. I apologize for the attitude- and the sudden liftoff."

The mermaid lifted her eyes and stared at Molpe's hunched posture atop her rauk. Her wings shuddered, half-extended. Her face was flat, and she held her stomach. "You're sick?" asked the mermaid.

"Hungry," cringed Molpe. "My song doesn't attract any sailors to my rock... I need those sailors to eat, but they don't hear me. Or maybe they just don't care."

"They don't care," replied the mermaid, "because they don't understand..." The mermaid opened her mouth and bit the top of the sea, gathering a thin pool of salt water in her lower jaw. She threw back her head and gargled the seawater until it cleared her throat and sinuses. She spat out the mixture of saline and phlegm and suddenly began to sing. *"Hurra! Horisonten er min fastnandhi! Dette fartøj er Idunn for hjertet."* The pitch was all over the place, and the rhythm fluctuated wildly. *"Deltag i mig på denne klippe på havet, vores Ostara starter!"*

Molpe glared strangely at the mermaid. The mermaid stopped her singing and blushed. "It's okay? Or it needs to rhyme?"

"No, no," said Molpe. "It's... it's fantastic."

"I can sing?"

"No… no, you can't, dear, but the translation is just what I need!" exclaimed Molpe with a look of joy, "but I noticed there's no mention of ambrosia."

"Replaced with Idunn, food of *our* gods," replied the mermaid.

"And Aphrodisia?" questioned Molpe.

"Ostara," said the mermaid.

"And when is Ostara?"

"Today is Ostara," said the mermaid with a sly smile. "I love you."

"Really?"

"I'm kidding… it's not today," she said with an awkward laugh, "but still…."

Molpe pointed her lips to the sky and started to sing. "*Hurra! Horisonten er min fastnandhi! Dette fartøj er Idunn for hjertet. Deltag i mig på denne klippe på havet, vores Ostara starter!*"

Suddenly the fishing boat that had passed by earlier unaffected paused on the horizon. The row boats on the sides of the ship were quickly untethered. They splashed as they each hit the water. The craft's passengers abandoned the ship all at once, piling on top of each other to squeeze fifty men into two small faerings.

The men then began to row backward against the stream of water. They used an almost supernatural strength bewitched from the depths of their beings to backtrack to Molpe's new island. Here, they flipped their boats and waded in the water, waiting for Molpe to take her piece. Molpe's stomach growled at the sight of all this thick, veiny neck.

Molpe flew up into the air, then landed on the shoulders of the nearest sailor. "Excuse me, darling, but can I get another translation," she said to the mermaid at her side. "*Raise your chin….*"

There was no response.

"Fish woman," she called, "translation, please!"

Still, she heard no answer. Instead, the air was filled with an irritating scratching noise, like metal grinding against stone. She looked over her shoulder and again saw the mermaid working at her strophion. She seemed to do it every time Molpe tried to lure in some fresh meat.

"Do you…. *craft* to my music?" asked Molpe with a look of confusion. "Is this why you come with the tide?"

"*Ja,*" affirmed the mermaid. "My best work..." She held up the ancient brassiere in her fingers. An image of an angel was carved into the left breast. The detail was captivating; delicate feathers were rendered into the aragonite. The right breast was just as intricate, with bearded Vikings praying to the angel, each of them waist-deep in the ocean with waves crashing behind them. "Because of you!" she said, staring at Molpe with glistening sheep's eyes. "You are a muse."

"Not quite," replied Molpe dryly. She reached down to the man under her feet and grabbed his beard. She yanked upward, cocking the man's face towards the sky. Then she did her usual dive and bit the sailor's throat. She yanked out his esophagus like the cord on the back of a toy doll. Once it slithered down her throat, she turned to face the mermaid. "Can I have a proper name to address you?"

"Annegrete", said the mermaid, beaming. "Please, call me Anne."

From then on, Anne would always appear with the arrival of the beige current. She'd come prepared with a fresh strophion with unsculpted cockles. As Molpe projected her new ditty, the many faces of the North Sea became Molpe's dinner and Anne's next artistic subjects. Each new work was part of the same series; an angel on the left boob and congregates on the right. Sometimes the angel was alone. Sometimes there was a scene behind her—either the sun at one of many altitudes or the moon at one of its phases. Sometimes clouds, sometimes stars, sometimes both. The congregation also changed depending on how the men dressed when Molpe tore out their piping.

For one such meal, half the men were dressed in layers upon layers of tunics. The other half was topless and wore black sheaths over their heads. The dusky sky added a wonderful background to the scenery. Anne was excited to show Molpe the finished work. This coaxed her into speeding up the process, adding the last carving just before Molpe could feed.

"Behold!" said Anne. "Close to masterpiece."

"Miraculous," said Molpe, landing on a half-naked body a few feet in front of Anne. With Molpe's pressure, the edge of the man's sheath dunked into the water. "Your artwork is beautiful, but I must reemphasize... your skill is completely independent of my music."

Anne shook her head vehemently; she gave the shell in her hand a quick stab. She was fixing a small defect she found near the bottom. A curly chip of umbo flew from the tip of her chisel. It whizzed past Molpe's left eye.

"My voice *clears* minds," continued Molpe. She reached down to the head between her feet and shook it with her palm. There was no resistance from the sailor.

"Not mine," said Anne, scanning her creation one last time. "I hear music; I see shapes and lines."

"...but then what about what follows?" pushed back Molpe. "Doesn't my vermivoration appall you?"

"It's mostly fishermen and vhalers," shrugged Anne; with a tilted smirk. "The vhales are my friends. It's nice to see the vhalers eaten for a change."

"Sometimes it's whalers. Not all the time," cautioned Molpe. "Sometimes it's traders. Sometimes it's warriors…" Molpe's eyes dropped toward the sea, "and sometimes it's slaves." Molpe gripped the hood of the sailor between her toes. She yanked the veil upwards to reveal the osseous face of an unkempt man with a scold's bridle clamping his mouth shut.

"Pokker ta deg, there's no need to make this part any more gruesome," Anne gestured to all the bodies without bags and gags. "There's plenty to eat without them."

"You see, that's the thing; there's no good men and bad," pushed Molpe. "It's all food to me. Because I'm an amoral monster, not a muse," she said dramatically.

"*Pfft*," said Anne dismissively. "There are no *monsters*. You're childish."

"What do you mean?" Molpe scoffed. "What do you call me?"

"Well… what is your farther?" asked Anne.

"...a god."

"And your morther?"

"A muse," sighed Molpe, "but that doesn't mean…"

"Two birds make bird. Two fish make fish," said Anne with a smile. "A god and a muse. Makes a goddess and a muse."

"A goddess?" said Molpe with a look of shock. The compliment was difficult to process. Years of negative self-image made her resistant to its absorption. She just wanted to tear the word apart in her hands. This feeling manifested in her reaching down to the slave's throat and piercing his neck with her sharp fingernails. She ripped open the visceral compartment and revealed the amaranth mucosa beneath the surface. Furiously, she crunched the tissue between her mandibles and tore the throat out sideways. The esophagus hung from her beak like a long sausage.

Anne looked closely at the slave as he lost a vital part of his anatomy. The expression on his face was like a herring yanked from the sea. His eyes didn't blink, but the pupil in its center occasionally jerked. It seemed to dance as each ring of his esophagus stretched out the hole in his neck before sliding out. He didn't scream, but then again, how could he? His vocal cords now hung in the air, separated from his neck.

"They feel no pain?" questioned Anne with a worried expression.

Molpe swallowed her food and laughed. "I can't say that for sure," she chortled. "I know they can't express it."

"The slaves," sighed Anne. "It's too far. You will stop."

"Excuse me?" exclaimed Molpe. "You can't tell me to stop!"

"Stop grossing me out," threatened Anne, "or I can't kiss you."

Molpe's reaction was stiff and unsure. She let her beak disappear back into the depths of her oral cavity. Slowly, she raised her wing to her mouth and wiped the blood away from her lips. When the wing left her face, her bumptious expression was gone, replaced by faint curiosity. "I get a kiss?"

Anne dropped her work on the water's surface, letting her tools sink to the ocean floor. She submerged her anterior and kicked her tail, shooting herself across the sea. Once she was at the slave's dead body, she placed her hands over Molpe's talons, then pushed herself upwards, reaching her face as far up as she could.

Molpe stared down and gazed at Anne's fluorescent pink lips. She froze for a second, then shut her eyes. She buckled her knees and arced her head downward like she would to feed, but she kept her beak inside. She allowed her human lips to press to Anne's, forming a tight pucker.

The kiss was brief, and soon Anne detached. She sank back into the ocean, lowering her body bashfully until only a pair of eyes poked out of the water. She stared straight ahead.

Molpe stood up straight. She kept her eyes down on Anne. "Your lips are cold," said Molpe delicately.

Anne rose upwards a bit until her top lip broke the surface. "You didn't like it?"

"No, no!" Molpe waved her left talon in the air. "I… I really liked it. I even loved it. It's not like *fishy* cold; more like ice cold. Our lips kept sticking together."

"It's what I was," replied Anne. "Iceberg."

"You were... an iceberg?"

"I was carved from a lost iceberg that strayed into the North Sea. My sisters, too, all at once. The artist freed seven of us from the block, then the sea god Njord brought us to life."

"So then, by your logic, you're a goddess too," said Molpe, with a crooked-looking aura.

"Ja," affirmed Anne with rosy cheeks, "and an artist."

After that day, Anne stopped appearing when the brown tide rolled in. Instead, she appeared every day. And every day, she and Molpe would talk and flirt until their emotions bubbled over. They entered into their Reniorian model—Anne lifting upwards, Molpe leaning downwards, their lips connecting the air and the sea.

During one such passionate session, Molpe left the early stages of physical affection and began to explore more alternative means. She let her puckering lips guide her beyond Anne's central features and ventured down below her chin. She tasted Anne's neck, mixing her lust and gluttony into a single cardinal desire. She turned the corner and began to circumvent beneath the jawline. She moved some of Anne's hair to the side to proceed, only to catch a strange glimpse of dark skin when she fluttered her eyes.

"What…" Molpe looked oddly at the black feature. "Why are you branded?"

"It's not a brand," chuckled Anne, pulling away. "Have you never seen a tattoo?"

"I've seen ink like that," said Molpe. "The Greeks distinguished their criminals with them. Otherwise, the skin stays pure and untouched."

"It means nothing like that," defended Anne, letting her hair down to shield the markings. "It's a Viking rune. All my sisters' each have their own. Mine grants protection."

"Well, you no longer need protection," proclaimed Molpe. "I'm the osprey on your gauntlet, ready for your word."

"Oh, my little elskede," said Anne sweetly, "you're more of a hungry sea mew."

"Well, I don't know what to do," grumbled Molpe. "Now, I can't associate you with anything but vagrants and adulterers. The worst of the worse."

"I disgust you?" Anne frowned. "You disgusted me."

"And *I* changed," argued Molpe. "I haven't eaten slaves in months."

"Okay," said Anne with a defeated expression. "I am only ice, so if you really need it gone. It should only take the warmth of your breath to melt it away."

Molpe thought about the offer. Anne turned around and presented the back of her neck, and nodded. Molpe was surprised it was all so simple. "You'd let me take it away."

"I'd let you do anything to me, I'm afraid," admitted Anne.

Molpe's eyes wandered around the empty ocean. It was nighttime, and the stars lit the waves with white specks. Moonlight dimmed and glowed as a thin layer of clouds ran overhead. A moonbeam blinked on the rune. Molpe took a deep breath inward, then leaned down towards Anne's neck. She opened her mouth wide and breathed slowly. The warm heat worked its magic.

All the discrepancies between them slowly began to vanish. Over the necfu7xt week, the goddesses acted out something like a marriage—a mashup of traditions from both cultures. They exchanged locks of hair, bathed together, then sacrificed some livestock they stole from a trade ship. They then consummated their relationship on a Friday. This consummation was to the extent that a bird and a fish *could* physically consummate. Fingers did most of the stimulation. Lips put in some of the work, tasting the bestial cocktails made by cloacae and papillae.

The morning after their tireless lovemaking, Molpe felt the sudden urge to reinvigorate them with some breakfast. The daylight revealed they'd been blessed with a brown sea, and a small ship could be seen eclipsing the dawn.

A symbol of becoming an official pair, Anne agreed to try some of Molpe's food selection, if just once. She wanted to understand her lover in every way possible. In return, Molpe agreed to eat kelp for the following week.

"Hurra! Horisonten er min fastnandhi! Dette fartøj er Idunn for hjertet. Deltag i mig på denne klippe på havet, vores Ostara starter!" sang Molpe. Her voice was more feathery than usual, sounding almost like a lullaby. She wanted the sound to be special, something charming for which Anne could be brought out of sleep.

Anne had slept with her head resting on Molpe's rock. As Molpe's song hit her ears, beautiful dreams filled her head. She saw something like a child that could fly with its wings, then swim with its tailfin. It played in the space between its two mothers. Anne felt a warmth envelop her body; then she opened her eyes to her wife.

Immediately, the fuzzy feeling left her chest as the sight of her lover's worried face came into focus. She was gazing up at the bireme that had stopped before her rock. Instead of jumping into the sea, the ship's captain stood alone, at starboard, his hands holding a jar over the taffrail.

"What's the look for, elskede?" asked Anne, swimming up close to her wife. She came to her side, then stared up at the captain. He had placed the ceramic right on the edge of the railing and began to fling his hands about in a series of specific patterns.

"I think he's deaf," said Molpe.

"And that worries you?"

"Well, he's wearing Greek armor," she pointed out, "and notice the column of wings nailed to the mast. Pretty much the same size as my own."

"Hold on," said Anne, blocking the sunrise from her eyes with her hand. "I should be able to make out what he's saying…."

"Why would you speak sign language?" asked Molpe.

"Jellyfish," said Anne firmly. "No ears."

"Right… but also no hands?"

"Tentacles," explained Anne. "Now, let's concentrate." Anne squinted and slowly deciphered the Greek's words. "I am Dysophone, hero of Piraeus. I come for the wings of the one called Molpe. That's you, love…."

"Can you tell him to 'fuck off,' or I'll peck his eyes out?"

"I wouldn't do that," warned Anne. "He also says that he has a jar full of sun rays straight from Helios. He's threatening to drop them into the ocean and melt me like a snowman."

"And what are the, uh, stipulations to prevent that terrible idea?"

"The wings come off," said Anne softly. She looked horrified. Tears were building up in her eyes. "You don't have to do that for me."

Molpe shook her head. "How did he find me?"

"A legend changed," frowned Anne, "legend reaching all the way back to Athens of a bronze road that appears in the waves and leads sailors to a magic seamstress that lives in the sea. Gift the clothes to the woman you love, and she's guaranteed to love you back. At least, that was the tale a year ago. Now the road's changed from bronze to mud, and the maiden at its end eats you alive…."

"I never knew I had such an effect on your reputation," grimaced Molpe.

"It's perfectly fine," said Anne with a look of defeat. "I didn't start crafting to be anybody's legend. I only gave my art away to make room for more. The best reward has never been in exchange for my effort; it's been the effort itself. I wanted to improve my work; therefore, I met you…."

"Oh, Anne," whimpered Molpe. Her eyes were tearing up too. "Just know, when I do this, I do this for you."

Molpe flew onto Dysophone's ship, bent over, and spread her wings. Dysophone turned ecstatic and whipped out an ornate xiphos. He made the surgery quick, but that didn't make it less painful. Molpe shrieked in agony as the blade cut into her wing pit, then kept sawing through until it severed the patagium. This occurred twice, the second time worse than the first, as Dysophone's strength faded with the second chop, and he had to slice slower and less gracefully.

Molpe felt an odd shift in her center of gravity as she noticed all the weight missing from her back. The stinging sensation brought her to a near mental shutdown. The world became blurry as she was picked up and violently thrown overboard into the sea.

"Elskede!" cried out Anne; she dove under the water and bolted forward like a torpedo. She landed her outstretched arms under Molpe's backside and swam her back up to the surface.

As soon as she broke the water, Anne flipped Molpe onto her stomach and beat the patch of skin between the stumps of her wings. She patted hard until the water drained from Molpe's lungs. Anne stuck her ear close to Molpe's lips and could hear the breath rolling in and out. It was faint, but it was present.

"You didn't kill her," signed Anne up towards the captain. The glossy wetness over her face highlighted the curves of her despair.

Dysophone shrugged, then signed back with an oddly genial gaze. "Sirens have wings. Her wings are gone. She's no longer my problem," he signed. "She can't return to Greece, and that's all my destiny requires. The rest is all Varagian myth. Let them restore their bronze road to glory if they choose- but I didn't come here to end agape."

Anne stared back in disbelief. Her lover would be spared.

Dysophone disappeared from the edge of the ship. He returned to his crew on the bottom deck and allowed the boat to continue. Soon Dysophone's vessel was well-off in the distance, and Anne was left alone with her wife bleeding profusely in her hands.

Anne doused the feathered nubs with saltwater, clearing the blood off the contusions and disinfecting the wounds. Anne grabbed her most recent works and wrapped three strophions around Molpe's torso, bandaging the wounds. "Euaí, the- the horizon's my promenstria," sobbed Anne. "This vessel is ambrosia for the h-heart." She sang quietly, only loud enough for the woman cradled in her arms to hear. "Join me on this rock upon the ocean," she sighed. "Our Aphrodisia holiday will start..."

Molpe's body was growing thinner each day. Molpe was physically weak and emotionally fractured from her mutilation. She didn't have the energy to feed herself, but Anne knew a good meal could be just what she needed to recover from her amputation.

Anne couldn't attract sailors like Molpe could, but she refused to let that stop her. Sidestepping a few of her earlier boundaries, she did what had to be done to get her lover back in order.

"Two strophions for six of your slaves," she said to the merchants atop a passing ship. She stopped them on the bronze route and offered them her wares, but for a price.

The merchants stared down at Anne with flat expressions. They turned away from her and formed a huddle in the center of their ship. Anne heard one laugh at a particularly hushed sentence. Anne knew slavers were conniving bastards. The last thing they would do is give up their precious cargo easily, especially when their buyer seemed so meek and pretty.

"Legends said these were gifts," said the merchant captain. "There was no price mentioned."

"Five slaves," bartered Anne. She feared dipping any lower, but it was tempting. She couldn't appear too desperate, or they might fall prey to their wiles.

"The slaves bring us money—money we need to survive."

"What's surviving without love?" Anne retorted, appeasing to the lonely hearts of sailors.

"But five slaves?!"

"Two loves. At the same time," she continued, appeasing to the lonely *groins* of sailors.

The merchant showed a smile buried under a bushy yellow beard. Then, he noticed the strange mass of bloody bandages floating at her back.

"What's that?" said the captain. "A friend of yours?"

Anne reached behind herself and laid her hand on Molpe's midriff. "It's food. Another slave."

"We could use another slave," said a merchant behind the captain. He grabbed the captain's shoulder and pointed to a raft tied to their port.

The captain smiled at the man. "Another slave *and* mermaid clothes."

"Don't ruin this," said Anne. "Do you really want to be the men who ruin the bronze road?" She gave the toughest expression she could muster. "The Greeks will have your head."

The captain patted his underling on the back, then sent him below deck. "Four slaves – and we let you keep yours."

Anne hesitated. Then, she nodded.

The slaves were tossed overboard, where they paddled in the water, trying to keep afloat with their atrophied legs. Anne wouldn't force them to suffer too long; she grabbed her carving pick and got to work on each slave's neck. "*Stå stille!*" she screamed, instructing the slave in her hands to stop his squirming. "Let's make this quick." She dove her pick into his Plender gap and tore upwards, cutting a long slit in the front of their neck. She forced her hand inside the cavity like prying open a clam for its pearl. She pulled out the esophagus and held it in the air like a trophy. She chased after the remaining slaves trying to swim away but with nowhere to escape. She excised all their esophagi and let their hollowed-out bodies sink to the bottom of the ocean. Anne then delivered the worms to her sick bird and helped guide them down her throat.

It wasn't as much as Molpe usually ate, but it was enough to get her out of her unmoving state. Within a day of her feeding, Molpe showed signs of returning to normal. She hummed weakly, then slowly worked up to whispering. "Are we okay?" she asked. "Have I been too much?"

Anne kissed her wife's dry, flakey lips. "No one gets tired of their muse."

From this point on, Molpe's recovery went exponentially quicker. Soon, she was back in working condition, and the two found the strength to make love again. With time and plenty of help from her beloved, Molpe learned to feed again without her wings. It's somewhat the same; only she'd gouge at their necks from low instead of high. Either way, Molpe's song returned to the air, and Anne's imagination was graced by its magic. She started a new collection of strophions, where her angel's wings were clipped; but the men on the right were all the same.

A Reason to Burn: Sea Creatures

My stage name is Y. Heidem, and I have been a professional drag queen for the last thirteen years. I've been the most requested host for drag events in Santa Fe since 2006. I am well-known for my signature braless look, where I keep my neckline extremely low and contour my chest to create some A-cup cleavage. My character is obviously inspired by classic braless icons like Gloria Steinem, Kate Moss, and Debbie Harry, and I share in their perspective that a bra simultaneously hypersexualizes the female nipple while sexually oppressing the well-endowed.

Evan Witmer's "Sea Creatures" contrarily treats bras as a form of artistic expression. They're Annegrete's only creative outlet. He suggests that strophions, the period's equivalent to a bra, are a positive, liberating force for his feminine character. However, all of *my* connection to the feminine energy has shown the exact opposite. Considering Evan's never worn a dress, I think it's clear which one of our perspectives is based on real-world experience.

The bra is a clear symbol of vesture conformity for the feminine shape. It's practically redundant for women with my physique, and it can be a source of pain and discomfort for those with larger breasts. Scientific benefits have never been proven, and, in fact, there's evidence to the hypothesis that losing bras helps to keep breast shape in old age.

There's a million different art forms Evan could have given Anne besides crafting artisanal undergarments. I mean, I get that origami is out of the question because the paper gets wet and painting wouldn't work 'cause the colors would run, but what about dancing? Or acting? What about martial arts? Evan focused his women's artistic force on building the very shackles that bind her, and I think that's very antiquated. For that, this story should be burned.

Now I, for one, am not going near an open fire wearing this much silk, so while I encourage the *symbolic destruction* of his story, it doesn't necessarily have to involve flame. Bra-burning itself is just a myth stemming from the Ms. America Protests of the 1960s, where bras, along with a multitude of feminine products were thrown into a trash can, a trash can most witnesses remember as *not* going up in flames. Similarly, there's no need to be so extravagant with Evan's work. Simply tear out the pages and throw them in the trash.

- Second-wave Side Bitch, Nicolás Lopez

Lizard People Take Orlando

JK Rowling's fast decline into blatant transphobia worried Bill Davis, president of Universal Orlando. Her comments could affect the number of guests they'd see at the Wizarding World of Harry Potter's annual Christmas celebration. This decline in sales led to a series of confidential conversations between Bill and then acting mayor of Orlando, Buddy Dyer. Bill asked Buddy to remove protections on the wetlands surrounding the theme park so Universal could begin construction on the Forbidden Forest, a brand-new interactive attraction to counteract JK Rowling's bad press.

Two years later, a jury convicted Buddy of corruption, forcing him to step down. The FBI found irrefutable evidence he'd accepted bribes in return for hastily removing those wildlife protections.

A special election was called, and four candidates came to the forefront of the race. The last mayoral election only saw Democrat affiliates, but this time two Republican candidates rose to the occasion, splitting the options equally between the parties.

The conservatives were trying to piggyback off Florida's overwhelming support for then-President Trump. Bob Behr, one of the Republicans, was the acting CEO of Florida Natural Orange Juice. His platform borrowed a similar ethos as Trump—an excellent businessman capable of "running the town like a business."

Then there was war veteran and two-term city councilman Kerry James. His experience building affordable condos for retirees in Kissimmee had already won him a large part of the 50-and-older crowd.

On the Dems' side was Aiden Gleason, a former televangelist pastor turned fiery politician promising to instate participatory budgeting and set up a cooperative economy to combat the city's extraordinary poverty rate. Compared to Aiden's audacious character and plan of action, the other Democrat looked like a rather dull moderate.

Zaffre Davis was a doctoral candidate at the University of Central Florida, getting his degree in Public Administration. Years of research helped him craft a list of reasonably attainable goals dealing with small civic matters like lowering penalties for marijuana possession and raising sales taxes to renovate public transportation. While the meek platform painted Zaffre as the most vanilla candidate, a secret double life made him the most interesting choice of the four.

Zaffre was in a lull between his campaign appearances—a carefully planned break between his open forum hosted by the political clubs at UCF and the first real debate. In these nine days, he would slip away to Miami and hop on a cruise where every passenger dressed as an anthropomorphic character, including himself.

While most of the voyagers aboard the Norwegian Joy were furries, Zaffre was a scalie. They were more or less the same community, with a key distinction between their classes of vertebrate—mammals or reptiles. The unique terminology first came with the popularity of dragon costumes, but Zaffre's imagination rarely went to mythology.

Zaffre's fursona was a Floridian caricature in the form of the official state reptile, Alligator mississippiensis. His name was Mason Miller the Concrete Filler—a single father of three, operating a ready-mix cement truck for small residential projects. He was an old-line Protestant and a conservative liberalist racking in about 50k per year.

When Zaffre puts on the mask—he becomes Mason. Mason can befriend just about anybody but prefers big meetups like this, looking for like-minded folk. There's an automatic connection between two people when they have similar fursonas. Our favorite species is an indicator of what traits we most identify with in the animal. Is it their bloodthirsty behavior or their natural shyness? Is it their cold-bloodedness or their ecstasy in the sunlight?

Scalies were a minority among the furries but were growing. As Zaffre made his way to the pool area for brunch, he was happy to see what looked to be an iguana judging by the spiny dewlap under her chin. She just pulled a fresh stack out of the waffle bar and placed it under the soft-serve dispenser. A ribbon of chocolate-vanilla swirl oozed out of the nozzle and curled onto the top waffle.

"Fantastic idea," Zaffre cheered.

The iguana girl turned to face Zaffre. He looked at the back of her costume's mouth and saw her real mouth smiling.

"It's just an ice cream sandwich," she laughed.

"No, I'm talking about the spines on your back… those are tips from foam swords. You did amazing with the spray paint," Zaffre explained. "You do that yourself?"

The iguana girl nodded and said, "You can get fake swords at the dollar store, two dollars each. Cost me maybe like fifty dollars total. I'm Rachel, by the way."

She held out her hand.

"Mason," Zaffre replied as the gloves of their costumes curled together. "I'm jealous, really. I'm not creative enough to make my own costume… or rich enough to get one customized. I found this old mascot uniform on Craigslist. I at least cut off the felt shirt it was wearing. It had a big LOL on it."

"Was it trying to be funny?"

"I think it was from *Land O' Lakes* High School."

"Never heard of Land O' Lakes, except for the butter."

"Well, Florida's a big state. You local?"

"Just moved here, actually."

"From where?"

"Cuba."

"Green card or work visa?"

"...uh," Rachel chuckled softly. "Am I being interrogated?"

"No! I don't... I'm not judging; I'm really deep into studying migration. I'm legitimately curious as to where we come from and why we came."

"I really can't say."

"Well... if it's so much of a big secret. Why don't I tell you a secret of mine first?"

Rachel shrugged and gave a slight nod. It sounded like a fair trade.

Zaffre looked to his left, then to his right. Everyone was busy scooping food into the mouth holes of their costumes. No one was looking at them. Zaffre quickly slid the head of his costume off, then placed it back on.

"Okay?" Rachel snorted.

"I'm actually Zaffre Davis."

Rachel shook her head in confusion.

"I'm running for Mayor of Orlando," explained Zaffre.

"I don't know you," replied Rachel sternly.

"I'm running to replace Buddy Dyer...."

"I don't think people care about mayoral elections as much as you think they do."

"Well, every level of government is important, Rachel," sighed Zaffre. "This is an important election, and I'm an important guy."

"So?"

"So… I don't normally take off my mask. Ever. I'd lose voters if they knew I lived such a… *fringe* lifestyle."

"And I'm supposed to reciprocate, now?"

Zaffre nodded.

"Your secret was weak. You haven't even broken the law."

"And you have?"

"Yes!" Rachel said shrewdly. Her eyes widened with a serious expression. She looked around for eavesdroppers, then lowered her voice. "I came to Florida on a raft."

Zaffre leaned in close and whispered. "So, you're undocumented?"

"Yes."

"I didn't know people still did the raft thing?"

"Wet feet, dry feet policy is gone, but the main incentive is still there. My family was poor. I had no time for school, and I needed to work. I told them I'd come to America and send them money back home."

"Well… are you happier here?"

"I live as a housekeeper in Key Biscayne," Rachel answered. "This hasn't been everyone's experience, but in my case, things worked out really nicely. I'm on a cruise, aren't I?"

"Right…" replied Zaffre sullenly, "but it must be weird living with this constant threat of being discovered."

"Yeah… it's almost like the undocumented could use a strong voice in politics."

"Yeah?" Zaffre replied bashfully. "How about Aiden Gleason?"

"The weird minister lady? She's running for Mayor now? Zaffre, people can't take her seriously. *You* need to advocate for us."

"It's not that simple. I'm supposed to be the moderate. I only make little splashes; big splashes scare away the older voters. They're like ducks lying on a pond."

"The middle's moving inch by inch to the left every election cycle. Don't tell me you can't make people care about people like me. It's not like we're new here."

Zaffre looked down at Rachel's breakfast. Her ice cream had melted into an ecru puddle soaking into her waffle's pores—its crisp yellow darkened and became something like a bread pudding.

"Look at all the trouble my flirting caused you," Zaffre griped. "Allow me to get you a fresh stack."

"This is flirting?" Rachel asked, staring at him in disbelief. "Aren't we rambling about politics?"

"It's not rambling," Zaffre assured her. "Tune into the debate next Saturday, and you'll see I'm taking this quite seriously."

***

The first debate was held on stage at the Walt Disney Theater, down the street from Orlando City Hall. Tickets sold out, filling the seats with roughly 2,700 people. Normally a crowd this big could intimidate a first-time runner like Zaffre, but while Miller was good with one-on-ones, Zaffre found a sea of eager listeners comforting. Falling on deaf ears was like claustrophobia.

Zaffre, Aiden Gleason, Bob Behr, and Kerry James assembled on stage at 2 p.m. They smiled and waved to constituents invested (and rich) enough to buy a ticket. The audience wasn't exactly filtered down to the elite, but there was certainly an unnatural percentage of gynecologists and obstetricians among the crowd.

Local celebrity AJ McLean opened the night, aiming to warm up the candidates with some straightforward questions and general fanfare.

"How do you feel about transportation options in our city... If you could change one thing in our zoning code, what would it be and why... Go Orlando Magic?"

Once AJ's softballs were finished conjuring up humdrum one-liners, local news personality Matt Austin followed up with the real sticklers.

"Hate groups such as Proud Boys, Patriot Front, and NSM are well documented in Orlando and greater central Florida. How are you going to take the steps to not only disavow these groups but actively dismantle them?"

"Simply put," began Kerry James, "nobody on either side is above the law. Whether you're Proud Boys or one of the many Black Hebrew Israelite organizations, if you attack the citizens of the City Beautiful, their schools, their churches, or their businesses, you will face criminal charges."

"Well..." chimed in Bob Behr. "As someone in the orange juice business, I'll tell you what, *simply* doesn't cut it." A forced laugh was suddenly squeezed out of the overly polite audience. "In all seriousness folks, I've mitigated potential bias in all forms at my bottling plants with monthly sensitivity seminars, a practice that can be mirrored politically through outreach programs which can lead our most vulnerable youths away from the influence of hate groups."

"I just want to say," Aiden Gleason interjected, "am I the only one that feels like everything Bob Behr says is, ironically, *un*natural?" A more organic laughter rose from the audience. "There's a phoniness there that I think is fairly noticeable to our proud Orlandoans. You can't treat them like their idiots, Robert."

"Well…" Bob Behr smiled nervously and leaned into his microphone to say something, but Aiden wasn't finished. She hushed her opponent and continued her attacks.

"Kerry James, on the other hand, is all honesty, but I think it's interesting he can't talk about hate groups without bringing up the Black Israelites. He loves turning any question into a way of appealing to frightened white people. It's all very manipulative and very sad."

"You're one to talk about hate groups," Kerry responded, "with so many links to Liberty Council."

"Mr. James, those are right-wing conspiracy theories. We're here to discuss serious matters." Aiden was staring him down with a tall, confident posture. "Matters too serious for someone so young and naive as my fellow Democrat, Zaffre Davis. He's barely legal, and he wants to take on the responsibilities of mayor."

"Wait…" Zaffre mumbled. "I, uh, I actually haven't spoken yet."

"It makes very little difference whether you do or don't because I've seen your platform, and it seems better suited for a spring break destination like Daytona or Panama than one of the most visited cities *in the world*. People don't need more marijuana reform, Mr. Davis—leave that to the governors—let's focus on fixing the raw moral fiber of this city."

The crowd roared with applause while Zaffre panicked looking to the Republicans to see their responses. They looked relatively unphased, their phony smiles barely wavering. They knew they could take some light beatings from the Democrats without it affecting their mainly Republican voter base, but Zaffre would be losing direct support. He needed to rebel against his timid nature or else be trampled.

"I strongly object to these claims that I'm some sort of babe in the woods. I've studied public service for eight years, while I believe your credentials are more suited for running a televised mass or a church bake sale."

"A pastor has leadership experience, oration skills, a sense of right and wrong," Aiden sneered. "An elitist's education has made you small and earthly. These people are looking for bigger plans than yours!"

"Oh, I've got… bigger plans," Zaffre stammered. "I've got plans to… wage war."

"A war!" Aiden laughed menacingly. "A war on what?"

"The incarceration and deportation of undocumented workers."

"Oh, okay…" snorted Aiden. "And what exactly does this war entail?"

"Easy…" Zaffre took a moment to consider what he was about to say. Sticking his neck out like this was the first time he'd ever made huge waves. He could see all the ducks spreading their wings to lift off. "I'm gonna... make Orlando into a sanctuary city."

The crowd was silent. So was Aiden. There was this long awkward pause. Everyone was looking at Zaffre, and Zaffre looked at the moderators.

"Maybe you could provide a little *depth*?" asked Matt Austin. "That's quite a departure from your usual platform."

"This isn't a platform; this is an obvious attempt at usurping me," sneered Aiden.

"We do find it incredibly jarring," called out AJ McLean.

"It's not jarring at all," replied Zaffre. "It's as middle ground as it comes. Undocumented citizens want our basic human rights. Those don't exist on a political compass. They're caught dead in the center with me. If anything, the Trump administration has pushed things too far right with overpowering ICE. I'm trying to get things back to the status quo we're all comfortable with. Every immigrant has a chance—a slim chance—but a chance even if they're here illegally."

"Governor DeSantis has put bills in place to ban sanctuary cities," Matt Austin said confusedly. "Is this a coup?"

"The Supreme Court is clear: the federal government *cannot* commandeer state and local officials to help them enforce federal law. Banning sanctuary cities is forcing local law enforcement to follow the orders of ICE. That's the overstep. I'm taking a step back and bringing us back to the sweet, satisfying neutral position," continued Zaffre. "Nobody has yet to challenge this sanctuary ban but doing so would result in its immediate nullification."

"This gives me hope, Jon. This gives me a lot of hope." The next day Zaffre was in his car on a road trip south to Key Biscayne. He was playing any podcast that mentioned his name in their episode description. Until then, he'd only heard himself speak on 538, but that day he found himself on something more progressive-left—Pod Save America. Co-host Tommy Vietor was raving about Zaffre's speech. "Tell me, Jon, are we finally winning over the Reagan democrats?"

"You know, relatively speaking; he's actually kind of an early bloomer," replied fellow co-host Jon Favreau. "Nancy Pelosi, Kamala Harris, and even Ruth Bater Ginsberg all started out relatively centrist only to really polarize in the later stages of their career. Zaffre might just be hitting this pubescence faster than others due to our day and age. Everything's instantaneous... even our opinions."

Zaffre's fear of making waves waned as he listened to the progressives laud his decision, but then it returned full force as he realized he'd also made headlines on the opposite end. Any of his balloters willing to consider conservative opinion for balance would wonder if they could still trust him.

"He's bringing illegal immigrants—violent criminals so bad their own countries don't want them, and he's bringing these criminals around young children to visit theme parks," raged podcast personality Matt Walsh. "Maybe it's naivety, or more likely reckless rhetoric trying to outdo the craziness of his current opponent Pastor Aiden Gleason."

Blink. Zaffre shut off the podcasts entirely. He slipped on his gator mask and switched over to a playlist full of Whitesnake, Mason's confidence music. He wanted a little mood boost before seeing his latest romantic fixation for the first time since the cruise. They were meeting in Key Biscayne; she was allowed a room on the property she worked at to house herself.

The house itself was a gorgeous two-story Mediterranean with enough space to fit two families, but outside of Rachel, there were only the two owners: Cobey and Albi Mansouri. The couple opened the door, standing side by side. They were both handsome and young and dressed in dragon kigurumis modified so the wings were ripped off. Cobey's was green; Albi's was blue.

The couple welcomed Zaffre into their living room with a pair of unblinking, flat faces. They then sat him down on a wingback accent chair that must have been custom-made; there was a hole in the butt made specifically to fit the tail of a fur suit. Cobey and Albi took a seat across from him on a leather couch. It, too, had tail holes; one for each in the couple, sewn relatively close together so that the two would be in contact as they sat.

Zaffre looked down at the coffee table between them. The surface was transparent, and under the glass was a pile of sand with the symbol "乱" drawn into the grains. Zaffre looked back up. The homeowners were staring him down. "Is Rachel coming?"

"I mean, she's here, in the house," said Cobey coldly. "But she's not coming out. Not until we talk."

"Oh."

"Zaffre, are you aware *we* could get in trouble for harboring an undocumented immigrant?" Cobey questioned him. "And that's, of course, in addition to putting poor Rachel into harm's way."

"You probably should switch the order of your concerns next time," said Albi. "Otherwise, it makes you sound selfish."

Cobey glared at his husband, then turned his attention back to Zaffre.

"I'm… I'm not going to tell anyone." Zaffre stuttered.

"You see, how do we know that and, even more importantly, how do we know you're not going to hold these facts over our baby's head to get her to… *do things*," sneered Cobey.

"Zaffre, we don't trust you." Albi sighed. "I mean, first and foremost, you're a politician."

"…a politician who openly praised support for the undocumented."

"That makes us trust you less," chuckled Cobey. "You're fucking erratic, man. We don't know what you'll do next. You took campaign advice from a stranger you met on a boat."

"What can I say? I'm a moderate. We're relatively shallow," shrugged Zaffre. "One of the key features of being shallow is our propensity to listen to beautiful women. Let's thank the lord that Rachel had something progressive to say."

Albi turned to Cobey. His serious face broke. "He seems honest, at least."

"I know… I *want* to like him," Cobey replied. "What did your outburst cost you?"

"A few white votes, not as many as I thought. In return, I've officially gained a market share of the Hispanic population."

"That's got to be nearly half of the voters," replied Albi.

"In Orlando, it's closer to a third… still can't complain," Zaffre said with a few short nods. "Well, actually, I can. I'm still lacking in some important areas. Gleason's still got most of the gay vote, which seems ripe for the picking. I need a good approach. Maybe you two can help me?"

"What makes you think we're gay?" Cobey asked.

Albi elbowed Cobey in the side.

"Okay, yes, we're gay." Cobey shrugged. "In fact, I'm so gay that when I was bullied for being gay, I wished I was gayer just to spite them."

Albi leaned over and kissed Cobey on his cheek. "His dreams came true."

"How important *is* the gay vote in Orlando?" asked Cobey.

"Well, there's plenty of gay men working in costume at theme parks…" explained Zaffre, "and then the Pulse night club shooting provoked a lot more to come out in support."

"But I don't understand. How do *you* not have the gay vote in Orlando?"

"I'm not gay, guys."

"We know you're not… but you do have a similar sexual situation…" said Cobey pointing at Zaffre's costume.

"I don't see the equivalencies."

"You're part of a sexual minority, and you certainly keep that fact closeted," replied Cobey.

"But are gay people okay with such a parity?"

"We're gay! We're telling you it is!"

"But you're also furries, so you're biased."

Cobey sighed. "Regardless of whether *the world* thinks the two are the same, you need to find the similarities *yourself* and use them to speak to the LGBTA heart-to-heart."

Bzzz. Bzzz.

"Rachel's texting me from upstairs," Albi said. "She wants to know what's taking so long?"

"Just go up there," insisted Cobey, gesturing to the stairs. "I think we've toyed with you long enough. You're no threat to us. As you said, you're moderate—you're no threat to anyone."

Zaffre took some slight offense from this vague denigration, even if it were something he'd say so himself. At the sight of Rachel, however, any animosity faded, and she had his full attention. Rachel was wearing nothing but a tracksuit, which may, in fact, seem like quite a lot outside of the furry community. But now, Zaffre could see her body shape unmasked by the jagged shape of an iguana suit.

"You want to see my terrace?" asked Rachel.

Zaffre nodded as he walked into her room and was led to the sliding door on the sidewall. He stepped through and entered out onto a small balcony, just big enough to fit two people.

"You know, I realize it's an awful lot for someone in my position," Rachel said, "that doesn't mean I don't deserve it. I clean *really* well."

Zaffre frowned. "I'm sorry if my recent fame might have… freaked you out?"

"I can't be mad at you. I chose to tell you," replied Rachel. "I was finding it hard to contemplate that I'd just met you, and now you're on my television and in my headphones."

"You weren't expecting me to say anything?"

"I expected you to say something along the lines of a symbolic gesture; I never intended for you to go to war with the governor of Florida."

"Admittedly, I've never been afraid of Ron DeSantis. He's worse than a moderate. He's a tool, like a weathervane. He points in whatever direction blows hardest."

"You know, I can't say it doesn't slightly attract me, though."

"What exactly?"

"The fact that you're 'making waves.' The birds might fly away... but it attracts the predators."

"Iguanas aren't predators, Rachel."

"Yes, I know Zaffre, but I'm not dressed as the iguana right now," she laughed. She reached her hands up to Zaffre's shoulders. Then she placed her hands on the sides of his mask. Zaffre quickly grasped her hands and pulled them back down.

"You don't want me to kiss you?"

"It's not that."

Rachel cocked her head and pointed to Zaffre's mask. "You don't want me to take it off?"

Zaffre nodded. "Mason handles the one-on-ones. I have problems with intimacy."

"Fine," conceited Rachel, "but you're going to have to show me what's possible with this suit on."

Zaffre smiled. "Everything."

***

The next debate was held at Orange County Convention Center so they could fit twice as large an audience as the last time. Tickets to the second debate were far more sought after than the last, given the added media attention.

Matt Austin stayed on to host alongside distinguished moderator Martha Raddatz. This time they both played hardball. It almost seemed the two were competing to see who could break the debaters first.

"What are Orlando's top priorities regarding public education?" asked Matt.

"How would you implement restorative justice in prisons and social work?" rose Martha.

"Should the Johnny Reb statue even be displayed in so much as a cemetery?" countered Matt.

"What makes you a good representative for the LGBTQ+ community?" topped Martha.

Bob Behr began spouting off some bullshit about oranges.

"Some of us have thick skin like the timeless navel orange, while others have thin skin like the youthful tangerine. It's the responsibility of we thick skins to protect you sweet, little clementines… I mean tangerines. Tangerines."

"I think the gay community has done a great job representing itself," followed Kerry James. "I won't stand in their way."

"But will you lift them up, Kerry?" blurted out Aiden Gleason.

"Because Evangelists are known for lifting up gays..." replied Kerry, sarcastically.

"You're a Christian too, Kerry; you know there's been progress in every faith."

Zaffre knew this was his time to strike. Both his opponents were stuck fighting the weight of their faiths. Zaffre, on the other hand, was agnostic, the most moderate religion. He could reach the gay population with his spotless record. He just had to word it correctly.

"A lot of baggage comes with siding with a church. The unassociated, such as myself, can promise the gay community a truly open-minded perspective."

"You're not exempt because you don't pray," Aiden critiqued. "You're still identified as straight, white, and male. You don't have a damn clue what these people have gone through."

Zaffre begged to differ. He'd gone through some excruciatingly wild shit that he could bust out, but then he'd be comparing the scalies to the gays, and if he did that, he was no better than Bob Behr comparing gay people to fruit.

Zaffre suddenly shouted, "I mean, personally, I was force-fed excrement-" His opponents all went silent. The crowd followed, and the hosts' mouths gaped.

"Zaffre, are you just saying wild stuff now 'cause you know it'll get you on the news," sneered Aiden.

"I'm trying to relate," explained Zaffre. "People could sense I was a little different, and they did a horrible thing to me."

"What? What did they do?" begged Martha Raddatz.

"So, me and a friend thought it'd be hokey to spend Christmas in Christmas, Florida. We were convinced the little village would certainly do something special due to its namesake. We were disappointed to find that actually the lights and decorations seemed to taper off as you entered the town. My friend convinced me to get a drink to make the trip worthwhile. We asked for two hot toddies. They came served with half a urinal cake slid onto the rim like a lemon wedge. Naturally, we wouldn't pay for what was certainly hot piss served in Nick & Norahs, but they wouldn't let us leave unless one of us finished our drink."

"But why were they targeting you?" pushed Martha.

"Because…" Zaffre stalled. He couldn't tell the truth, but he'd said too much not to follow through. He had to say something.

"I'm gay?"

The crowd stared at him in confusion.

"Yeah… because I'm gay."

"Oh?" Aiden was surprised. "You've never specified that before."

"What can I say? I'm a moderate; we don't lean on identity politics."

"So did you drink the piss?" asked Matt Austin, topping his opponent's prying with, by far, the most invasive question of all.

Zaffre nodded. "And if you elect me, no one else ever will."

The crowd began to applaud. First, a few snaps and pops, then the whole thing began to roar. Zaffre smiled; he took a moment to bask in his well-deserved praise.

***

"But did you really deserve it?" asked Rachel. "It's kind of a lie."

A few days later, Zaffre met with Rachel, Cobey, and Albi to pick up a new fursuit. Rachel and Zaffre sat in the back of the Alfa Romeo while the Mansouris sat up front.

"It wasn't dishonest," Zaffre explained to his friends. "It all happened, but it happened because I dressed like this—not 'cause I'm gay—but the latter's more palatable."

"Right, but then it's still a lie," rebutted Albi.

"If the two are equivalent, why is it not okay to substitute one for the other?" asked Zaffre. "You're the one that said they're the same..."

"You're taking what I said too far," sighed Albi.

"Your story made me so sad, Zaffre!" consoled Cobey. "I grew up in Redneck Riviera. I promise you we're not all like that. There're so many backwoods bartenders who would die for the chance to serve an alligator some whiskey. Your costume is so cute!"

"Thank you." Zaffre would have complimented their costumes back, but it turns out what he thought were their costumes earlier were their pajamas. Cobey and Albi were having their real costumes custom-made. Renowned artist, Shinji Higuchi, was designing Albi's in a special effects lab in Japan. Cobey's, however, was ready for pickup right there in Florida, back in Zaffre's domain of Orlando.

The car stopped in the parking lot outside the Costume Department of the happiest place on Earth. The group emerged from the vehicle and wandered inside a warehouse with mouse ears on the front door. Once the Imagineers saw Cobey had arrived, they wheeled out an impressive suit for a cartoonish-looking monitor lizard that could stand on its hind legs. They asked him to try it on, so they may take a few pictures for their portfolio.

The suit's eyes could move and follow people around the room. An articulated tail could wave like a robotic tendril at the wearer's whim, and the mouth automatically moved to match the wearer's words.

"How do you guys have so much money?" asked Zaffre.

"Well, Cobey's a coder, and I'm a patent attorney," answered Albi. "We met when Oracle infringed on Cobey's method for managing failovers."

"And you both just happened to be scalies?"

"Honestly, a lot of my interests were all drug-related," explained Cobey as he began trying on his suit piece by piece. "But I was approaching thirty, so I needed to try new things. Albi taught me all about his lizard character and the stories he wrote about him, and it all sounded fun, so together, we made *me* one on GIMP. I'm a perentie!"

"What's that?"

"It's like Joanna the Goanna; she's the evil lizard in The Rescuers."

"I've never heard of The Rescuers."

"Well, it's a Disney movie, Zaffre. That's why it made sense for them to make my costume." Cobey slid on the head of the costume and began posing for a scrawny cameraman taking pictures in the corner.

Click. Click. Click. Three flashes went off, capturing Cobey in a playful prone position, a sassy genuflection, and a jovial star posture.

"Does anyone else want to try it on?" Cobey asked. "It's really fun to operate."

"I'd feel weird wearing out your new toy," replied Zaffre.

"Oh, have some fun!" cheered Cobey. "You were kind enough to accompany me. And if you like it, maybe we could pay them to make one for you that looks like the alligator from Peter Pan!"

"I think that was a crocodile?"

"Close enough, Zaffre." Cobey slipped off the helmet and undid the zipper on the back of the suit. "Come here and try it on."

Rachel shoved Zaffre forward. "I wanna see you in it."

Zaffre sighed and decided to give in. He took the bottom of the suit from Cobey's hands and slipped it over his pants. Then he took the torso and put it on like a jacket. He bent over and had Rachel zip him up. Once she finished, he brought his head back up.

Click. Click. Click. Suddenly, three camera flashes blinded Zaffre. "Woah, hey there, cameraman," chuckled Zaffre. "Wait till I get the mask on first, okay?"

The cameraman didn't respond. He moved the lens off his eye and began examining the pictures he'd taken on the little screen on the back of his camera.

"Excuse me, camera dude, can you actually delete that last one?" called out Zaffre.

The cameraman kept spinning the dial in the camera's corner, scrolling through the pictures he shot.

"Hey! I only want them taken with the mask on…" griped Zaffre, growing frustrated.

"Well, I want one with the mask off…" droned the cameraman. A sinister smile appeared across his face as he eyed the money-making shot.

"Hey, tell your camera guy to delete his photos!" shouted Zaffre at one of the costume designers.

"He's not our camera guy," answered the designer. "We thought he was with you?"

"He's not!"

"Well, he came in right behind you."

The cameraman let go of his camera and bolted for the nearest door. As he dashed forward, the camera swung violently around his neck by the strap.

"What's going on?" cried out Cobey, looking stunned.

Albi stepped forward with a grim expression. "I think Zaffre's in deep water."

***

Zaffre was positive it was Aiden Gleason's spy who'd captured him engaging in scalie acts. He figured—of all his opponents to take the race so personally, it would be his fellow Dem. He wasn't sure where or when she'd leak the photograph to the media, but Zaffre felt it might be during the next debate.

"A soda tax... in Orlando?!" Bob Behr sneered. "Would that include Butterbeer? You want to tax mouse ears next?"

"Why am I not surprised that the guy that sells orange juice is scared of pushback on sugary drinks?" Aiden turned to the crowd and prepared for a small laugh or modest cheer, but the people were silent, despite her best work. Aiden kept her smile from fading and returned to lock eyes with Kerry. She saw Zaffre, the man behind her fading audience, standing awkwardly behind him.

"I'm shocked there's been no response from our well of surprises," snarled Aiden, leaning past Kerry into Zaffre's direction.

Zaffre didn't respond. He gave a soft shrug.

"Zaffre?" repeated Aiden. "Zaffre, you're awfully quiet."

"Just… letting Bob take his swing at you," said Zaffre. "It's rare when he doesn't speak in tangy metaphors."

In reality, Zaffre was too afraid to talk. The excitement he once felt standing up to his opponents could not outweigh his fear of being exposed. The thought of the world knowing his secret filled his mouth with the taste of piss.

***

A day later, Zaffre received a bronze envelope carrying a picture of him in costume. There was also a letter with a time, date, and meeting place. The address said Tallahassee. Zaffre shook his head—he was expecting Tampa, where Aiden's church was located. He typed it into Google, and suddenly it dawned on him. It was a Tijuana Flats a few blocks away from the capitol building.

The restaurant was cleared out when he arrived. The only person inside was Governor Ron De Santis sitting in the back with two megajuana burrito bowls. The governor got up and pulled out a seat for Zaffre. Ron grinned.

"I had my best men tracking the wrong candidate," said Ron between bites. "Aiden seemed like the most trouble till you called me out on live tv." A piece of lettuce fell from his mouth into his lap. "Then I realized you were the real danger all along. Starting out moderate, then slowly leaning left as debates continue. It's like boiling a frog, raising the temperature one small step at a time. We don't even realize we're dissolving into broth."

"It was never my intention to pick a fight with you. Haven't you kept up with the news? I say crazy shit to get acknowledgement."

"You took things too far, Zaffre. I had no choice but to expose you. I wanted to catch you with a woman and prove you lied, but this is far better. You're part of a cult full of lizard people."

"It's not a cult. It's a fandom."

"And do you trust the public to make that distinction?" asked Ron devilishly. He sucked the low-fat queso off his fingertips.

"No. I don't," Zaffre's head dropped, "so I don't know what you're waiting for."

"I'm waiting to see how extreme you are." Ron wiped the spit off his hands. "I wanted to see if we could reach an agreement."

Zaffre pulled his gaze up from the bottom of his cardboard bowl.

"I allow you to win. Then, you renounce your plans to attack my ban on sanctuary cities. Publicly, you say you flip-flopped with the realization that Governor DeSantis is a better ally than an enemy. It's for the good of Orlando that we cooperate."

"That sounds fairly reasonable," said Zaffre with surprise. "Surely you need me to do something far more nefarious."

"No?"

"You don't want… Muslims banned from Disney World? Von Braun added to the Kennedy Space Center?"

"God no, Mr. Davis. I'm a very simple man. Simple like you," sighed Ron. "We're very much the same. You're the moderate liberal; I'm the moderate conservative. That middle ground spans miles."

Zaffre stared vacantly at Ron. He swallowed a mouthful of rice and beans, then threw out the rest of his burrito bowl. He left Ron at the table without thanking him for the meal.

Zaffre drove back to the mansion in Key Biscayne. He had plans to spend the night with Rachel. They sat down together for dinner with Corey and Albi. Zaffre explained the details of Ron's agreement.

"He doesn't see our views as necessarily opposing," said Zaffre. "We're more the same than I initially realized."

"What are you saying? You're nothing like him!" shouted Rachel. "There's no way you can take that."

"No, Rach, I'm definitely taking it. This is a good thing," assured Zaffre. "Everything works out!"

Rachel looked confused. "If you get elected this way, you'll have helped nobody but yourself."

Zaffre tilted his head and frowned. "I have tons of other plans for this city besides making it a sanctuary."

"Protections for stoners and a new bus."

"And… free parking downtown. On the weekends."

Rachel's lips sucked inwards. Her eyes shut. Without another word, she picked herself up from the table and left the kitchen. Corey and Albi sat in silence, staring at the tense exchange from the other corner of the table.

"Personally, we're not surprised at you at all," explained Corey. "You made it clear to us from the beginning you have the integrity of a horny teenager."

"It's a shame, though," said Albi. "Rachel thought there was some substance to you. She believed in you so much she asked me to take her last paycheck and put it towards something special."

"Espionage!" exclaimed Corey. "We bought our own team of spies."

Albi pushed three folders forward, each one containing dirt on a respective candidate.

"Zaffre, in the past, you've blindly followed strangers' advice to unexpected notoriety."

"That's a good way to put it."

"Well, I implore you to do it again. Come clean. Then make *everyone* come clean. It won't guarantee you'll win, but it keeps the status quo. And that status is your element, Zaffre."

***

The final debate was held at the Amway Center for the biggest attendance yet. Zaffre didn't waste any time getting to the point, beginning with the uncomfortable truth about himself.

"So, I'm not gay," began Zaffre. "I never was."

Aiden suddenly broke out into an uncontrollable smile. A fog of bullshit lifted from the debate floor.

"I was using their plight to cover up my association with a particular subculture that cosplays as anthropomorphic reptiles. Mainly for fun. Sometimes for sex."

Aiden's face fell back into a scowl.

"If you're lying about your sexual identity, how can we be sure you're not lying now?" asked Matt Austin.

Zaffre pulled out his first photo, the one of him in costume, and held it up to the nearest camera lens beneath the stage. Everyone saw the image appear on the screens behind the candidates.

"There's no question. I'm a scalie. And I'm sorry for lying."

The crowd murmured amongst themselves. It wasn't the type of chatter that precedes an angry mob, but it certainly wasn't the voice of approval.

"These are unclean to you among the swarming things that swarm on the ground: the mole rat, the mouse... the great lizard of any kind!"

said Aiden quoting from the Bible. The crowd finally reacted to her again, returning with triumphant applause. "I hope you don't think this admission of guilt somehow absolves you."

"No," sighed Zaffre. "No one's getting absolved today."

Zaffre held up the next photo in his hands. Kerry James was shown shouting at two topless men grappling with each other and what looked like somebody's unfurnished basement.

"Kerry James has been betting on blood sports in Orlando's Little Saigon."

The audience began to gasp. Some seemed agitated. Others seem disgusted.

"If I tell you the sight of battered men arouses me, do I get the gay vote?" asked Kerry.

"And Bob Behr regularly walks around his house in a D-size bra stuffed with pomelos." Zaffre held up the next photo.

The crowd seemed less irate with this one. There was more of a snicker.

"Well, I, uh, I uh…" Bob stuttered as his cheeks blushed. "You see, the pomelo represents maternity in the island culture of Luzon, and I, too, identify as a family man."

"Zaffre, please get it over with," interrupted Aiden with a look of despair. She knew what was coming. "We all know which of us you actually needed to take down."

"Aiden, I hated finding this one out," said Zaffre holding up a picture of Aiden attending a mass. "What the fuck are you doing attending meetings for Liberty Council?"

"I needed the Christian votes from Kerry James," admitted Aiden. "*I knew I could get* the votes from Kerry James. We're both Christ-loving, but only one of us can lead."

"Don't you see? We can all lead, Aiden. Even with our secrets out there. We need to trust the Orlandoans to recognize the imperfections of their leaders and choose the shiniest turd of the bunch."

***

"This is the worst turnout in Florida history since Boca voted during Hurricane Michael." The night after the election, Pod Save America analyzed the surprising results. "Nobody voted."

"This will be the first mayoral election decided by sortition in the history of Orlando," said Tommy Vietor.

"Wouldn't it be more logical to choose four new candidates?" asked Jon Favreau.

"It's the rules!" replied Tommy. "The winner is decided by random through means of alectryomancy… Florida style!"

A professional reptile handler placed a blindfolded alligator in the center of the room. His interns placed four bowls of bullfrog legs in the surrounding corners. The alligator was spun around ten times, then let off his chain.

Zaffre watched the dizzied reptile stumbling around the court. Zaffre sat next to Corey in the manor in Key Biscayne, watching the show on a large flat screen. Rachel hadn't talked to Zaffre since he revealed himself on stage. Albi took her with him on a trip to Japan to see his new costume. Corey assured Zaffre she wasn't mad anymore; she just needed time to think.

On-screen, the alligator dipped its head into a yellow food dish in the top left corner. He began to swallow the raw meat inside. Matt Austin stood up out of his chair. He lifted the microphone up out of its stand. "And the winner is…"

A Reason to Burn: Lizard People Take Orlando

Zaffre Davis is clearly Evan Witmer's amalgamation of the furry fandom, as he is the centerpiece for this story, while the other scalies act as props. Zaffre is highly problematic not because of his ignorance, his shyness, or his cowardice; but because the "average furry" is portrayed as slightly left-leaning. I take offense.

On the contrary, the furries I interact with daily are some of the most profound examples of traditionalist paleoconservativism. As active members of the Christian Furry Fellowship, we find our lifestyles easily compatible with the teachings of our Lord and Savior, Jesus Christ. I met my wife at Monday night Bible club, both of us attending in costume—myself a lion and her an Awassi lamb. We were married after a brisk three months of dating and made our first physical contact on our wedding night. Prior, we would only hug, hold hands, and kiss through our costumes, separated by a respectable inch of foam and felt.

If you think about it, fursuits are inherently conservative; they cover just as much as a burqa would, completely desexualizing the wearer. It may be true fursuits themselves sometimes depict animals in the buff, but even this trend has begun to die out as creators want to add more and more character to their fursonas. I personally accessorized my koala suit with a Dope Faith hoodie and a burgundy nail bracelet. My wife dresses in a gray bonnet.

I know what really runs through Mr. Witmer's mind, though, to lead him to believe we're all a bunch of granola heads. It's porn, our subculture's undeniable ties to cartoon fetishism. Indeed, we must all then have some assumed level of open-mindedness regarding sexuality. I'm afraid not—current statistics indicate that only 25% of furries indulge in these erotic arts; they seem more prominent because these works come from our loudest members. But even then, when we dissect this sexual side of our community, it still turns out to be more red than blue. Jay Naylor, our most prominent erotic artist, is a right-of-center gun nut. There's no escaping us, no matter where you look.

Portraying furries as gays, immigrants, and liberal politicians insults a diverse community. People don't appreciate stereotypes regarding races and religions, genders and sexualities, and I think they're just as harmful to fandoms. I recommend that you burn this book and, in doing so, acknowledge the full spectrum of a community. If we've embraced any axiom in this turbulent decade, it's that we should not ignore diversity

- Zooish Zealot, Roy Bania

The Spirit Realm

New Orleans is far from the only city celebrating Mardi Gras in the two weeks leading up to Fat Tuesday. An hour's drive to the west will lead you to Baton Rouge, the state capital, where festivities take on a tamer form. The parades, the jazz, and the king cake are all still present, but the beads won't cost you public nudity, and drinking in the street is strictly prohibited.

Intoxication is still widely celebrated at the local college, Louisiana State University, but these Mardi Gras festivities have become a more interiorized affair taking place in the many house parties just south of Tigerland. Skamingo House on Lake Breeze Drive always held loud revelries on Saturday nights, but the second weekend in February was their official Mardi Gras celebration, capped to "invitation only" so that the cops wouldn't charge them for overcapacity.

Skamingo House was unique in that it didn't belong to any sole sport, club, or fraternal organization. Instead, there was a mix of students stemming from the original three homeowners: Sohan, Theodule, and Dark Web Dave. This trio's connection began in Spring 2011's PHYS 237: Introduction to Modern Physics, where they combatted a weed-out course that filtered for three majors: Astrophysics, Philosophy, and Biochemistry. It took a real team effort to conquer that class: Sohan contributed his notes; Theodule contributed his homework answers; and Dark Web Dave contributed his dad, an editor for Scientific American. Their resources evened the playing field against a class that was fundamentally altered by the chancellor to begin gatekeeping for certain majors they aimed to be 'known for' in an attempt to build a stronger identity than their rival Tulane.

The boys' tests were online, so they took them together in the same room, thereby ending up with identical scores. They all passed the class with a B+, which is, of course, the college A. Sohan, Theodule, and Dark Web Dave took such a liking to one another they decided to ditch their assigned freshman roommates to rent a house together at the start of sophomore year.

The three students would introduce their previous alliances into the mix of partygoers that would then frequent their house. Sohan brought his brothers, sisters, and themsters from Phi Sigma Pi, Theodule brought the logging team, and Dark Web Dave brought Paranormal Investigation Club.

"Every semester we do shrooms and go on the city's Haunted History tour," explained Dave to a timber bucker from the logging team. She had beautiful hair and an inquisitive mind. "Other than that, we get together every Tuesday and watch horror movies in one of the auditoriums."

"You do shrooms for the movies, too?" asked the timber bucker.

"Not really. They're expensive, even online. Kind of a special occasion sorta thing."

"The logging team is great friends with the foraging team," said the timber bucker with a tantalizing gaze. "I can get them for you at just $40 an ounce."

Dave smiled devilishly. "I'm a little atypical in that a good drug deal can really turn me on." Dave planted a quick kiss on the girl's lips. "Wanna come smoke with me?" He grabbed a bottle of whiskey off the bar with one hand and the girl's pocket with the other. He led her over to the staircase down the hall.

The house's activities were divided among the three floors—the basement level had beer and power hours, the ground floor had cup games and liquor, and the top floor was reserved for poking and smoking. The latter was only for those fortunate enough to receive a special escort from one of the three homeowners. This is where Dave took the bewitching timber bucker.

Dave brought her into his room and was shocked not to find his prized bong in its usual place. It was an oversized pipe, five feet tall, and shaped along its length to look like an ECG signal. Dave had smaller pipes, but with a girl present, he wanted to show off the big one as a sort of phallic ritual.

Dave set the whiskey down on his dresser, then ran out into the hallway, where he saw Sohan's door was shut. Dave rapped on the wood a few times and asked politely, "Are you using Heartthrob?"

Sohan inserted a key into the knob and turned. The door creaked open a bit, and Sohan stuck his neck out. The sweet notes of Durban poison wafted out of the room and sucked up Dave's nostrils. It smelled like Fruity Pebbles. Sohan disappeared again for a second, then returned with the big glass instrument for which Dave sought. Heartthrob was so heavy it had to be passed off with two hands; as a requirement of such, the door to Sohan's room had to become fully open.

Dave smiled at Heartthrob as the heft shifted to his grasp. Then he frowned at the sight of Sohan's empty room. "It's you alone in there, buddy?"

Sohan looked surprised by the question. He shut his eyes and shook his head. "I've got Banhmi." He pointed to a slow loris latched onto his back. It was the house pet, but technically Dave's purchase since he contacted the seller.

"I'm taking him too," said Dave, plucking Banhmi off Sohan's back and letting him hang from his arm. "Need all the tricks in the book to impress a girl like that," he pointed with his thumb at the timber bucker standing patiently in his doorway. "You should go downstairs. You don't wanna catch the noise, do you?"

Sohan shook his head, but that was a lie. In fact, after getting high, one of his favorite things to do was masturbate, especially to amateurs. The sounds of their coitus could make for an excellent ambiance to help him along. Some people pay for that sort of thing.

Dave scurried to the side and gave Sohan a path to the stairs. "Well, go on, now. You have friends down there."

"I'm scared to get drunk," admitted Sohan.

"Really," Dave glared at him judgmentally. "What's changed?"

"Well, it's just the last three weekends have been sort of regrettable," admitted Sohan with a look of self-pity. "I flashed the party, Dave."

Dave shrugged. "I can't remember."

"I'm sure some people did, and it only takes one to label me a sex criminal."

"I don't know… everyone was of age," hummed Dave. "Look, the dark web's got plenty of sex criminals, and you're not like them. You can be naked in your own home, Sohan; just don't force yourself on anyone."

"Well, then what about last Saturday," asked Sohan, "when I started chanting the n-word?"

Dave chuckled a little. "You're probably fine in most people's eyes. You could easily pass for black. I mean, let's be honest, our parties are primarily white people, and they can't tell the difference."

"I'm just scared I'm on the edge of being the next frat boy disgrace dragged across the internet," scowled Sohan.

"I mean *good*," said Dave, patting his friend on the shoulder. "I'm honestly happy to hear you don't want to be a supremacist or a rapist. The fact that you care about that shows you're not one of those psychopaths."

Dave paused.

"Look, Sohan, there are men with questionable behavior, and there are men who question their behavior," Dave said. "Right now, you're the latter."

Sohan looked up and wiped at his big red eyes. "You think I'm gonna be okay?"

"Yes!" laughed Dave, leading Sohan out of the doorway to his room. He took him over to the staircase and patted him forward. "Social isolation is certainly not the cure to apathy, to begin with. Solitary practically breeds social maladaptation. The key is to resocialize, considering what you've learned from previous failures. In other words, drink *re-spect-ful-ly*," enunciated Dave. He shoved Sohan down to the second step. "Only sip when the game calls for it. Stick to beer. And check yourself in the bathroom every so often so you can proceed accordingly…." Dave left Sohan on the staircase and left for his bedroom. Sohan heard the door shut, then heard bed springs compressing.

Sohan traveled down the steps to the first floor, where the party had assembled all the beer pong tables into a single island in the center of the room. He recognized a few of his frat members standing around the circle. They were playing a massive game of chandelier. He saw Theodule standing in a sparse outer ring surrounding the actual players. Theodule cheered on one of Sohan's sisters every time her turn passed; then, the two would strike up a small conversation between playing.

Theodule caught sight of Sohan staring and gave him a polite wave. Sohan waved back with a weak smile. He liked Dave better as a friend, but Theodule had more of his respect. He was a huge help around the house, especially after parties when the rest of them were hungover. Theodule didn't drink; it was on account of some religious pact he had with the rest of his family. They were strict French Catholics.

When they first met, Sohan thought Theodule could never fully enjoy a party like he and Dave could. Nowadays, Sohan just envies his sense of control. The way he could strike up a conversation with a girl was astounding. Without nary a sip of alcohol, his every word was a well-calculated craft.

Sohan took his eyes off the game and passed through to the basement. Here, the rooms were dark, lit up only by the UV lamps hanging in the corners of the ceiling. Besides that, a projector lit up one of the walls and played YouTube videos.

Sohan continued down the steps and was encouraged by the crowd to join in on the power hour just about to begin. For each hour, they chose a different genre of music and found a respective playlist explicitly created for this game. The playlist would play one minute of each track. When the song switched, it signaled everyone to take a shot of beer.

The last power hour from 8-9 was sixty minutes of 80s pop, as chosen by the Paranormal Investigation Club. The Logging Team chose the genre from 9-10, and they went with Straw House, a type of EDM with country influences.

Sohan, who needed a beer to join in, walked over to the black plastic tub in the corner. The tub was filled with tap water and topped with ice. It was unusually empty, with an oddly thin canister floating around its north edge. "It's a mini keg?" questioned Sohan.

"It's the only size they have if you want a *good* beer," said a tall man wearing an electric blue zombie on his shirt that glowed in the dark. The UVs reacted with the material, giving it a menacing triple aura. Judging by the morbid attire, Sohan guessed this fellow was from Dave's film club. "It's a *Rye*-PA," said the man, sporting a charming smile. "It's called Mississippi Mudwater."

Sohan filled up his cup with the brown fluids and took a sip. The brew tasted like it was served on a slice of burnt toast. Some people enjoy those notes, but Sohan found it a cacophony. In the end, though, beer was beer. The song switched from banjo looped over a pounding bass to a build-up made from a synth board and an autoharp. Sohan drank.

The structure of the game was congruent with Dave's earlier advice. Sohan felt as long as he was following the rules, he was pacing himself. Sohan found the thought relaxing, and he managed to bring out his true self for a bit. He saw two women beside him staring at a phone screen that was Shazaming the latest song.

"Are you two fans?" questioned Sohan, trying to be friendly.

"Actually, it's morbid curiosity," one said. "We're curious what a Straw House artist looks like. I was thinking like a Deadmau5-style mask, but it's a giant cowboy hat that covers his entire head."

Sohan laughed and took it further. "It's a pair of DJs. Disco Biscuits & Gravy."

"Sharp," said the girl holding the phone. She looked up at Sohan and smiled. Sohan couldn't tell any of her colors with the UVs painting the world plum, but he noticed her hair and her lipstick definitely matched. They were either both black or some other color darkened to near nothing.

"Oh, that's a bummer," said the dark-haired girl's friend. She was shorter and blonder. She was pointing to the resulting match on the phone screen. "He's just Svensson… and he looks like every other Swedish DJ."

"A Swede, huh?" Sohan smiled wide. "It oddly makes sense. Country's kind of conservative and EDM is kind of liberal… and Sweden's historically neutral."

"Oh! Getting political?" asked the girl with the dark hair. "I didn't know we reached that point in the night…."

Sohan laughed at first until it sank in how right she was. He *was* getting political, which meant he had reached a certain level of intoxication more normally associated with hours of drinking. He swore he'd only started a few minutes ago; he was astonished at how loose he was feeling.

"Never mind. Last thing I wanna do is get political."

"Well, that's not the Sohan I know," said the short blonde friend with a faint chuckle.

"I'm sorry. We've been introduced?"

The girls looked at one another and laughed. "Yes, Sohan," said the dark-haired girl. "Last weekend, you explained your *controversial* theory on linguistic discrimination."

Sohan felt embarrassed. His drunken persona preceded the real thing, ruining the main event with an abysmal opening act.

"I've certainly given the n-word more respect lately," continued the dark-haired girl. "Not sure I feel the same about you…"

Sohan braced into an apologetic stance. His drink pressed to his chest. His eyes shut, and he touched his brow.

"Oh my gosh, you look so worried," said the dark-haired girl. "Look, I'm sure you're a completely different Sohan than the one we remember," she said with a genuine smile.

"I'm better than that, I swear."

"Then let's change the subject," suggested the blonde friend. "Something as far from politics as we can possibly go."

"What's something completely one-sided?" asked the dark-haired girl.

"Banhmi's pretty great," said Sohan assuredly.

"You mean the food or your pet?" said the dark-haired girl with a smirk. "Either way, it is pretty great."

"Well…" frowned the blonde girl, "That kind of depends on how you feel about illegal animal trade, doesn't it?"

Sohan realized the day he got Banhmi that there would always be some mild criticism given his procurement through illicit means. As long as no one turned him in for his exotic friend, he wouldn't usually care, which made the aggravation growing behind his eyes unexpected. He looked down at his drink and was shocked to see the cup was still half-full. Whatever was aiding his anger wasn't the alcohol. Regardless, the emotions boiled over.

Sohan's attachment to his pet suddenly outweighed his interest in staying apolitical. Despite their best efforts, the conversation quickly picked up pace as Sohan came to his pet's defense. It wasn't long until the screaming started. First, it was just Sohan excitedly expressing his love for his creature's monkey-cat morphology. Then the blonde girl took it as a challenge and raised her voice as well, nailing him with the ethical repercussions of extorting wildlife for personal entertainment.

Sohan heard certain words flying out of his mouth, meaning he was losing his shit again. "Classist!" was his classic aggression, especially towards particularly attractive women that opposed his ideas. "Naive!" was largely a criticism of himself, which he then projected onto others. "Bush-Licker!" was new, but it was certainly in line with his recent string of hate slurs that came loose when his mind deteriorated to a certain stupor.

A cool, logical intelligence deep inside this roaring beast heard the language coming out of his mouth and tried its hardest to steer him away. The drunken rant was alluring; however, it rewarded every outburst with a shot of dopamine through Sohan's core. Sohan's inner sanity saw only one choice left and turned to an old adversary for help. Sohan could feel the faint seed of a black-out building at the bottom of his mind. It was ordinarily slow to consume his consciousness, but if he concentrated on its woozy numbness, he could encourage it to flow upwards like a black slime rising from the drain to devour its prey.

"Classle… nive…" he heard his speech beginning to slur as he directed the blackout over every last neuron. "Shplicker!"

Sohan had coaxed his body into a free fall. He landed on his back, hard on the floor. His beer spilled out onto his chest. There was enough left over to cover his entire shirt. His once glistening white polo browned and darkened, a mixture of his skin showing through the fabric and the amber suds soaked into the material. Sohan lost consciousness and entered into a deep rest.

By the time Sohan resuscitated himself the next morning, the shirt had dried, and the color had settled on a dentin yellow. Unable to recall the events leading up to his demise, he wondered if the stain had come from a torrent of vomit. Sohan tasted his mouth. There was nothing acidic about it, and his throat didn't feel like there was any recent erosion.

Any pain above the neck was directed toward his ears. There was a strange mechanical noise blaring in his face. Every beat caused his head to throb harder, and the beats were coming so fast it sounded like a buzz. His body begged for relief. He opened his eyes to see his tormentor. The projector flashed above him; out of its speakers came static.

Throughout the night, YouTube's playlist received no human input, so it selected its power hours using an algorithm. At first, it played as many Straw House playlists as it could find, but as time went on, this limited supply dwindled, and its contingency decayed. It began to go on wild tangents, seeking out other fringe sub-genres of dance music. It eventually landed on a power hour for speedcore and extratone, the fastest genres in existence. The beats were so rapid it sounded like a jar of washers being poured into a garbage disposal. The pitch of the steel crunching rose and fell as a backing bass beat pounded at the pace of a rabbit scratching its ear.

Sohan's perception felt fuzzy, like he was either hungover or still drunk from the night before. He tried to check the time on his phone, but it wasn't there. Oddly enough, neither was his wallet nor his keys. He looked up at the large novelty clock hanging under one of the UVs. "It's Miller Time" glowed in the center of the dial. The hands said 10:30 am.

Sohan scanned the rest of the room and suddenly felt crowded. He thought it was strange so many of his guests had stayed the night. Most of his friends lived within walking distance of his house; he always offered safe bedding to those who blacked out, but never has he had so many cases that all the couches were layered with multiple people. The surplus then spread out onto the floor.

Sohan focused on the blue zombie staring at him through the darkness. The boy with the shirt was passed out while sitting up; his back rested against a black support beam with chargers hanging out of its sockets. Sohan tried to walk over to the boy but discovered it was too difficult to stand. His body felt weak and half-numb, like he hurt himself when he fell. He had to inch his body forward until he could raise his hand and give the boy's face a soft pat. There was no response. He pinched the boy's chin and shook it a little. Still, the boy lay motionless, his mouth now wrenched open. Sohan crept his fingers forward onto the boy's neck. It was cold and damp, like a frost had come and gone overnight. He pressed hard on the vein but felt no pulse.

Sohan blamed the numbness in his fingertips and tried to wake someone else. He saw the blonde-haired girl lying with her head over the couch's armrest. The memory of their fight suddenly hit Sohan and made him cringe, but certainly, his current agony was punishment enough. Sohan tried calling out to her, but his jaw jiggled uncontrollably. He continued to squirm forward, then grabbed the girl's shoulder. He pulled on her too hard, and her whole torso came tumbling down over the arm. Her head hung upside down, her eyes wide and motionless. Then gravity yanked her shirt down over her face.

Sohan stared in bewilderment at the strange pattern over her midriff. Either her veins had risen, or the skin around them had shriveled. It looked like the underside of a leaf.

Sohan took notice of all the arms and legs of the bodies surrounding him. He realized they all sported the same markings, meaning they all suffered the same fate. For a moment, Sohan thought he was all alone. Then, a voice suddenly echoed in the dark. "Hop in, chief, the water's fine." Sohan turned his gaze upwards and aimed his eyes at the corner of the room. It was masked in shade; the UV light atop it was shattered.

Sohan drew closer, squinting at the dark spot, trying to make out a person but failing to find the matching shape. Instead, he saw the hollow tub holding the beer and ice. He got up closer and looked inside.

"Don't be shy. The water's crisp..." The sound seemed to be calling out from the steel of the keg; it was either that or the speaker was invisible. In Sohan's current state of mind, neither possibility seemed implausible. "I'm serious, chief," continued the keg, "we might wanna put you on some ice with the fever you've got going on."

Sohan looked surprised by the suggestion. His puzzled expression faded as he touched his face and felt a sharp pain. He could almost singe himself on his own skin. He started nodding, stuck in a highly suggestible state. He removed his shoes and socks, then took off his shirt and pants.

"Underwear too, man," said the keg. "You'll need something to change into when you're done."

Sohan just kept nodding. He pulled down his gray tights and inched his naked body across the floor. He hurried up to the edge of the tank and hoisted himself up and over the edge. He fell in face first. The sudden temperature change made his eyes bulge. He lifted his head above the surface and exhaled loudly. No one in the room reacted. Then, Sohan flipped his body over and found a nice seat in the tub with his legs over the side and his head laid intimately beside the mini keg.

"Well, hey there, Sohan," laughed the keg boyishly. "You know, that's actually a really sweet body you got there..."

Sohan was still getting adjusted to the pool and ignored the compliment. Instead, he shivered and felt at the goosebumps building up on his forearms.

"Do you fast?" continued the keg.

Sohan opened his mouth but still couldn't speak. He shook his head weakly.

"Well, then, I've got to know your secret."

The keg brought Sohan's attention to his own body. He stared down at his supple form and discovered the horrific circulatory webbing was just under his skin too. He was so frightened he tried again to speak, gasping and stuttering interchangeably.

"I'm on a pretty great meal schedule myself. I eat a whole salmon every twelve hours. It's very high in nootropics."

Sohan could feel a vice in his chest as he succumbed to the panic. He sunk his torso deeper into the water to try and relax. On the other side of the container, his feet slid up the wall and hung over the rim.

"I think some 'trops would do you good," suggested the keg. "I don't know if it can restore the damage... but it can certainly reinforce what's still there."

"D-d-damage," finally, Sohan was speaking. "D-d-d-d-... amage?"

"Surely you've noticed the social barriers that once divided us have evaporated," explained the keg, "this coincides with the disintegration of the temporal sulcus, the social center of your brain."

"Damaged," repeated Sohan. "Damage..."

"And from your limp, I'd say it's also done some work on your cerebellum."

"...damaged."

"Hey, I'm sort of talking to a caveman here," chuckled the keg eagerly. "How about you dip your head in the water, so I can understand you?"

Sohan's head fidgeted.

"No, seriously. Dip it," urged the keg. "It should really, really help with the swelling."

Desperate to understand, Sohan shut his eyes and braced himself for another sudden chill. He did exactly as he was instructed. He slid his legs and butt further over the edge so his head dropped under the water's surface. He lay there for a moment until the numbness began to fight against the pain stinging in his temples. He quickly realized how relaxing the freezing temperatures were when encompassing his skull. He let the waters work their magic on the tension in his head, then slipped back up when his breath required it.

As water dripped off his nose and chin, Sohan felt like someone had removed a football helmet squeezed tightly onto his head. He tried to speak and was happily surprised. "My brain's not alright." He was making complete sentences again. "Nobody's brain is alright." He looked around the room with his senses feeling restored. All the bodies were still lying in place. He realized his basement had been turned into a mausoleum.

"Well, I'd say you were poisoned," said the keg sullenly. "Can't say why though; you all seemed like such a nice bunch."

Sohan pressed his hands against his face and groaned into his open palms. He certainly felt like he'd been poisoned, but this suggestion required accusation, something he couldn't muster in his current state.

"Who?" he murmured behind his hands. "Who… poisoned…?"

"I didn't see anything suspicious, although my sight's limited to the basement," explained the keg. "You did get involved in a series of altercations. I wonder if you made an enemy who'd be willing to kill."

"Blonde girl's dead," grumbled Sohan.

"Well, it wasn't just the blonde," said the keg, chuckling softly. "Round 1 was a knock-out, but then you returned for Round 2 with a vengeance."

"I kept going?" said Sohan with a look of shock.

"Yes! Yes… yes, you did," explained the keg. "Fought the poor boy with the ghoul on his chest. Took a piece of me with him."

"A piece of you?"

"Well, he was making fun of you for taking a dive after just a few sips of his favorite drink. He recommended you stick to Millers. That really hurt you for some reason," detailed the keg. "So, you called him a pretentious necro; then you called me 'RaceTrac runoff.'"

"Sorry for the insult… I lose control sometimes."

"It's okay, I got my revenge," replied the keg. "There's a bunch of glass at the bottom of this tub."

Sohan looked up at the broken UV light and then down at the water. He didn't feel anything sharp when he got in.

"You mustn't have much feeling left in your ass," laughed the keg.

Sohan reached under his body and could feel little points dug into the back of his thighs. He started to yank them out with ease. There wasn't even a pinch. Sohan brought one of the shards to his eye and examined the blood on its tip. "Zombie Boy's dead too," mumbled Sohan. "Who else got in my way?"

"Can't say," sighed the keg. "You went upstairs for a few hours. Whatever went on, it's out of my jurisdiction. Why not check with the liquor?"

Sohan looked over at the staircase. Given his condition, it would be a tough climb up the stairs, but he didn't have much of a choice. If he wanted answers, he'd have to investigate further, and any more witnesses would be at the bar.

Sohan plucked a few more glass pieces from his bottom, then tried to wriggle his way out of the tub. He managed to get the top half of his body over the lip. He relaxed and let gravity pull the rest of him downwards onto the floor. He flipped over onto his stomach and then crawled over to his clothes. He needed to dry off first, but there weren't any blankets in the basement. He thought about the towels he kept next to his shower, but those were on the top floor. He would have to crawl up the steps wet and naked.

"You're not just leaving, are you?" called out the keg as Sohan wormed his way over to the bottom of the staircase.

Sohan ignored the keg and began to ascend, throwing his body onto each step with a violent lunge.

"Bring them back down with you, will you?" called out the keg as Sohan disappeared behind a wall. "It's lonely down here with everyone dead."

Sohan pushed open the door to the basement with his fingerprints, then made the final plop onto the plane of the first floor. Sohan hoped that he'd come across some more survivors—possibly Theodule, given he wouldn't have drunk anything. When he heard a conversation at the top of the steps, he thought he just might be rescued. Tired from the climb, he sprawled out on the floor and listened.

One voice was shouting from the counter in the kitchen. "Bianca! It can't be, another boy, another chance at happiness." The voice was that of an old British man. "But will this one listen? Oh, can he hear us?"

"Oh, Winston!" called out a voice from the living room. "Mia fresca brezza, may I dream with you?" This voice was that of a young Italian woman. Its melodramatic tone sounded almost insincere.

"Yes, dream! Dream, my buttercup. I think he hears us…." continued the old man. "He's looking right at me!"

Sohan had turned his head to face the "bar" on the kitchen countertop. Most of the bottles had been displaced, but the one that remained was a clear glass bottle with a tall square body and stubby round neck. At the top was a red-steel cap, and on the front was a long white label with a rounded edge at the top reading: "Westminster Dry Gin."

"Yes, young man, come here, young man!" called out the gin. "Grab a seat, ol' chap!"

Sohan looked at the two seats tucked under the edge of the marble countertop. The nearest seat was filled with a dead body: a short, bearded gentleman in a flannel and jeans. Sohan grabbed the man's arm and yanked him down to the floor. Sohan looked at the empty seat, then looked down at the body. The dark no longer masked the colors of the dead. The man's skin was sallowed and glistening with sweat, resulting in a hideous gold sheen. The veins that pressed against this flesh were dark purple, as though long, thin bruises threaded throughout the body. Sohan stared the man in the face, seeing if he could recognize him. He only knew him as a player from the lumber team. The man's sclerae were murky green.

Sohan breathed deeply, then gained the courage to look down at his own body. The skin had definitely yellowed on the backs of his arms, but the veins weren't quite purple. Most were still pale, and the few that had been colored were light blue.

Sohan swallowed his disgust and crawled his way up onto the chair. He grabbed the bottle of gin and pulled it in close.

"Easy now, boy!" called out the gin. "I'm not a toy, though you younkers certainly act like it. I thought the professors back at Imperial were wild animals, but the American student is plainly worse."

"What exactly did you see?" begged Sohan.

"A couple of tonks grabbing at each other's willies. A shot glass stuffed in a mug's arsehole. All types of rude dance… you included."

"Oh God, I danced?" groaned Sohan, stuffing his face into his palm. "Did I fight anyone?"

"I wouldn't call it a fight."

Sohan winced. "Then what would you call it?"

"Well, you climbed on the table in the middle of flip-cup. They tried to get you to come down so they could finish… and you really wouldn't listen. They just kind of let you go. No harm done, though; most people thought you were hilarious. The fella you threw to the floor there even took some pictures."

"Really?" questioned Sohan. He dropped out of the seat and landed with a thud next to the man in plaid.

"Oh… be careful," called out the gin sincerely.

Sohan reached into the man's chest pocket and found an old flip phone. He pulled it out and checked for service, but the SIM card was missing. He pressed a few more keys to get to the camera app. Once he was there, he scrolled through the most recent photos. There was a picture of two gentlemen touching the tips of their chainsaws over a large gold trophy. Then there were a few nudes, two of himself, one of a woman with her face cropped out. Then the photos from the party followed: A keg stand in the basement, a chummy portrait with an old friend, then Sohan, dancing on a plastic beer-pong table, sagging at the fold in its center. There was a red cup in his hand. Sohan couldn't recall what he was drinking.

Sohan examined himself and the other people standing in the shot. It was an old phone, so the resolution was fuzzy, but he swore he could make out a few vaguely purple markings around their wrists and ankles. "When did we first show symptoms?" called Sohan to the gin.

"Behaviorally, there wasn't much of a difference. As your brains melted, you all just acted drunk, which you all expected from one another, so no one noticed when things got bad."

"But the coloration…"

"By the time it showed, you were all too gone to care," said the gin with the sound of disappointment. "Even as people fell to the floor, the party had to go on."

"Did you see who poisoned them?"

"Young man, I am sharper than the rest," explained the gin. "I used to be a scholar. A mathematician at Imperial! Nothing gets by me. I'm practically a sleuth… I know exactly who's responsible, but you must do me a favor in exchange."

Sohan nodded.

"You'll bring my lover to me. She's in the room adjacent. Thin girl, green eyes."

Sohan grabbed the gin's neck. "I could just bring you to her."

"No, no!" scolded the gin. "Hands off! I thought I made that clear. I want *her* in *here* with *me*. This is the bar… the living room is Vladimir's domain."

"Okay?"

"I want him to be left all alone." The gin lowered his voice. "He's the one you want…."

Sohan shut the boy's phone and stuck it in his pocket. He crawled away from the kitchen into the living room where the cup games had been played. He found himself circumventing several fallen friends he recognized from his frat. Their mouths were slightly ajar, and a smell like old honeydew leaked from their lips. Sohan crawled past them to the rows of pong tables in the back of the room. He recognized the one he danced on, with dark shoe prints pressed onto its surface. A green glass bottle was in its corner with ornate curves and a cork on the top. Sohan pulled himself up so his chin rested on the table. He read the letters molded into the glass: "Signora Sweet Vermouth."

"Avvicinati," whispered a woman's voice with a subtle Piedmontese accent. "Come in close, so he can't hear us."

Sohan stared at the bottle strangely. Suspicious, he complied. "Is the old man dangerous?"

"Oh, no… not at all," she said faintly. "He just bruises easily."

"I take it this romance is one-sided."

"We've shared a few martinis in the past," sighed the wine, "we're certainly compatible… but he's not alone."

"There's Vladimir?"

"Sì, the Spetsnaz," said the wine sweetly. "One compares me to infinities; the other compares me to a snowflake. I am both everything and wholly unique."

"Where is Vladimir, anyways?"

"He's been taken…" said the vermouth sullenly. "A girl took him into the bathroom with her."

"Are you jealous?"

"Terrified," she murmured. "She drinks from the bottle." She hesitated, then, breaking her own silence, whispered, "Please, take me to Vladimir."

"I promised the gin I'd take you to him."

"You don't owe Winston anything. He's lied to you," explained the wine. "Vladimir is a poet, not a murderer."

"I'll decide that for myself." Sohan snatched the vermouth off the table and crawled with her in his hand. He inched into the hallway dividing the kitchen and the living room and turned the corner. At one end of this hall was the front door, and at the other end was the bathroom.

Sohan didn't bother knocking and slid his body inside. The light was still on, and the room was very crowded. He had to curl his body into a tight space between the sink and the lifeless girl on the floor. A colorful streak of liquified king cake trailed over the lip of the toilet seat and down the front. The trail ended at the girl's lips. Sohan recognized her; she was from his frat, Melody, the girl Theodule was flirting with early on in the night.

It was natural for Sohan to reach out and check for life, but he wasn't surprised when he didn't find a pulse. His hand traveled down her body as he returned it to his side. It brushed against the girl's hand, its knuckles still clenched around a liquor bottle. It was a liter of vodka made of thick, cheap plastic. Its body was broad and round with indentations on its back to make an easy-to-use handle.

Sohan grabbed it from her hand and brought it closer. The liquid was all gone; it was entirely empty.

"He's dead," sighed the vermouth. She sounded heartbroken. "Arrivederci, amore mio".

"Comrades..."

Suddenly, a muffled voice of a broad Russian male emanated from inside the toilet. "Comrades, I'm in here."

"Vladimir!" shrieked the vermouth. "Vladimir, are you alive?!"

"They stuffed me in a can, Bianca," echoed the toilet. Sohan opened the top lid so they could hear better. Inside were more colorful crumbs soaked in bile and what were apparently the remains of Vladimir. "My mission is a long one, and we submerge within the hour."

"Vladimir... take me with you!" called out the vermouth. "Sohan, you must do the right thing and pour me in with him."

"Sohan, you will not!" growled the toilet. "You will protect this woman, yes?"

"No," grumbled Sohan. "I have no reason to protect any of you. Sweet as you may seem, you could be laced with poison. One of you is. Might even be the old man."

"Winston?" questioned the vodka.

"Don't bring him up!" cried the vermouth. "Not in front of Vlad!"

"It's too late. I know I'm leaving you with him," admitted Vlad, "but I can't stop what comes."

"*I* can keep them separated," suggested Sohan. "If you're honest with me, that is."

"You have to believe me, then. I am *not* the assassin!" called out Vlad. "Neither is Bianca. Neither is Winston! Look how little they've been drunk… certainly not enough for everybody to have had a taste. And me, most of me, was turned into aldehydes deep in the liver of that body on the floor."

"So, then whoever it is, is almost empty," muttered Sohan. He was thinking of that mixed drink he had in the photograph. If he could just remember the taste, he could remember what was poured inside it, but these memories were lobbed off and incinerated by the toxin inside his body. Somebody poured that drink for him. "It's possible they're not acting alone."

"Do you know anyone who can buy poison?" questioned Vlad. "Without thinking of motive… just who has the means?"

Sohan shook his head until the obvious hit him. Then he froze and began to wonder. It was tough to disregard a good motive; otherwise, he'd be sure it was Dark Web Dave.

Suddenly, the sounds of thumping and scraping gurgled from the ceiling. Something was happening above them, separated by a thin membrane of wallboards and plumbing. Everyone kept silent, listening to the strange sounds. A faint shriek concluded the noise.

"I think someone's alive up there..." said Sohan softly. "I have to investigate."

"Then sound the diving alarm," grumbled the vodka in the toilet. "It's time."

Sohan nodded. He didn't know how, but he understood precisely what the vodka was asking of him. He didn't question it too deeply, as it was already a mystery how he could hear vodka at all.

Sohan flicked the handle on the toilet seat and sent the dirty water into a spiral.

"Caro Dio," prayed Bianca, loud enough to fight with the rushing of the water, "brilla una luce per il mio angelo."

In a matter of seconds, Vlad disappeared completely into the dark of the drain. "Perdonaci," she paused for the gurgle at the end, then continued over the soft hiss of the plumbing, "perché abbiamo... amato nel peccato."

"Now that he's gone, be honest," said Sohan sternly. "Do you really want to be left alone?"

"I'm so young," said Bianca weakly. "It's tough to have a head full of young people's thoughts without anyone to share them with."

"You don't need to give me excuses," sighed Sohan. "I will do what you request of me."

"Bring me…" Bianca seemed to be crying now. Her words paused to sniffle. "Bring me to the old man."

Sohan nodded and did as she proposed. Sohan crawled out of the bathroom and sat at the kitchen table. He gracefully stuck the vermouth beside the gin.

"If you spent a minute more in that bathroom, I would have lost my mind," grimaced the gin. He seemed irate by Sohan's tardiness. "I didn't tell you to take any detours!"

"I flushed Vlad down the toilet," argued Sohan. "You'll never see him again. You don't think that deserves praise?"

"You didn't have to bring her to watch," groaned the gin, "but I only expect so much from a young *paki*."

Sohan snickered a little under his breath. *Paki.* White people really couldn't tell what brand of brown he was. Being on the other end of such a nasty slur was certainly interesting. Sohan took a moment to weigh his feelings. He didn't feel necessarily broken from the insult, but it seemed the type of thing he shouldn't let go. He figured others felt the same about him.

Sohan crawled down the hallway between the kitchen and the living room, this time toward the front door. He managed to get up close and reach the doorknob. He jiggled it but was not surprised to see it was locked. He used to have a key, but he had no idea what he'd done with it.

He climbed down from the door, then turned around. He inched over to the bottom step of the staircase, then looked up at the dark hallway at the top.

"Hello!" shouted Sohan. He swore he had heard someone earlier. If he could just summon them, they might be less incapacitated, and they could help him search for his keys. "Hey! Hello up there! Are you there? Hello!"

Suddenly, Sohan sucked in his breath as a loud stomping erupted upstairs. Seven loud bangs were followed by the noise of a door unlocked. It creaked as it opened. More loud bangs followed. Then there was the sudden appearance of a head. It peaked out from behind the corner.

Sohan recognized the top of their head: the pinkish-white forehead, the shaved red hair.

"Dave?" called out Sohan. "Dave, I'm fucking tripping. Everyone's dead, and the booze is alive. I'm pretty sure I want out of here, but I don't know how…."

Dave came out from behind the corner. His clothes from the night before were missing, now replaced with a toga made from his bed sheets. The sheets were black with faint, white stains blotched here and there. One long gray oval on his arm looked like an elbow patch. Underneath it hung Bahnmi, still alive and unaware of what horrors ensued.

Dave whispered something in Bahnmi's ear. Then he picked up the pet and held him close to his head. Dave kept nodding like somebody was speaking to him. Dave started whispering again; Sohan could make out a few words this time. "...kill him too."

Dave quickly disappeared behind the wall. Sounds echoed down the staircase. Glass clinking against wood. The crack of plastic. Fabric tearing. Three soft clicks. A whoosh. Suddenly, the dark hallway was lit up with whites and yellows. Dave turned the corner again; this time, his hand was filled with a bottle of amber liqueur stuffed with a flaming black cloth.

Sohan could hear the bottle screaming gruffly, "Got' dang coot lit me up like a cow chip!"

Dave threw his arm back to full extension, then swung forward. He released the bottle, causing it to spiral through the air down the stairway.

"Catch me, compadre!" screeched the bottle. "Don't let me shatter!"

Sohan's reflexes were never exceptional, and now that his brain had eroded, he was far worse. The bottle collided long before he raised his hand over his head. Luckily, it hit Sohan's soft face and was kept in one piece. It bounced off his nose, then rolled along the floor.

Sohan's nose started to bleed, but he barely felt it. He didn't have time to care for the injury; instead, he selflessly went to aid the flaming bottle. He crawled over to the burning wick and blew on it with all his might. It was a highly ineffective tactic. Flaming liquor was beginning to leak from the overturned bottle. Sohan burned his hand at the touch of the bottle, but this, too, he couldn't feel. He powered through and crawled into the kitchen. Winston was too distracted to notice his return, focusing all his energy on re-wooing the fine wine.

"I shall count your wine diamonds like freckles on your face," swooned Winston.

"You mustn't do that," replied Bianca shyly or perhaps reluctantly.

"But you're vast and endless... like stars in the night sky!"

Bianca sighed, almost inaudibly. "Sometimes a woman likes to feel small."

Sohan reached by their awkward tension and grabbed a red cup from atop the bar. He trudged it over to the sink and filled it to the brim. Then he carried it in his mouth, his teeth chewing the rim till he reached the flaming bottle down the hall. Here, he slowly spilled the drink over the flame.

"Hang on, buckaroo, don't water me down!" hollered the whiskey. "You're gonna dilute my personality..."

"Oh, sorry," apologized Sohan, stopping his dripping. "So, so sorry." Sohan noticed that as the water passed through the membrane of the flaming fabric, it gathered inside the bottle, displacing the whiskey inside and sending it over the finish.

"There's no need to apologize, Sohan," said the whiskey with a dry, neutral tone. Its gruffness disappeared, and it went up in pitch. Then his accent suddenly returned. "Ya' damn well saved my cowhide!"

"Oh, God," winced Sohan. He realized he'd watered the alcohol like a teenager refilling his parent's bottles after a secret house party.

"Your acquaintance upstairs seems to be acting irrationally," droned the whiskey in his neutral tone; it almost sounded like Sohan. "Gringo's gone loco!" He then shouted bombastically.

"Did you *see* him poison the party?"

"Worse than that, Sohan," he said dryly. "He damn near girdled that yellow belly's neck!"

"He killed a guy?!"

"He had a pair of hostages, but it's been reduced to one... His painted lady's still kickin'!"

"Okay..." grumbled Sohan; he was distracted, catching sight of the burns on his hand. "I guess we've got to rescue her."

"Don't make me relive that traumatic experience," he said plainly; but as his cowboy personality suddenly swung back in place, he reappraised, "Let's lasso this bull!"

Sohan nodded, then licked his thumb. He plugged the top of the open bottle, wearing it on his hand as he ascended the stairs. "A bit invasive there, aren't we?" droned the bottle.

"I'm just trying to keep your bodily fluids intact," said Sohan.

"Sheeeoooot! Just be sure to leave the money on the highboy."

Sohan crawled up the stairs quietly to not alert Dave and his captive to his presence. When he reached the top step, the door to Dave's room was just around the corner. Sohan didn't have a weapon, and the door was shut and most likely locked. Sohan couldn't just knock and hope things turned out okay. He needed a distraction.

Sohan crept into the upstairs bathroom across the hall from Dave's room. He saw a peach-colored towel hung on a rack next to the showers. He grabbed it and wiped off what remained of the moisture from his bath in the basement. Then he wrapped the towel around his naked waist. It felt particularly good to be slightly clothed again. He hoped to shield his private area from whatever horrible ill will Dave had hidden inside him.

"Did you help Dave poison the party?" asked Sohan to the whiskey. He popped his thumb out the top and held the finish to his nose. He inhaled hard, trying to see if the scent seemed familiar. Was this the liquor in his cup?

"I consented to nothing," said the normal voice. "Fellar musta spiked me when I had my eyes closed," came the Western draw.

Sohan held the whiskey up to his eye and measured the level inside. It was still half-full, or was it half-empty?

"Can I trust you?"

"There isn't much I can do to you."

"How do I distract Dave?" continued Sohan.

"I'm willing to sacrifice a little piece of myself if it means saving that poor girl… stuff me in the soap dispenser, hombre!"

Sohan looked towards the sink. He crawled over to it and climbed up onto the counter. He grabbed the soap dispenser and poured out the viscous fluid inside. Then he poured about half of the remaining whiskey into the empty vial.

"It smells like wild apricots in here," came the whiskey's dry, normal voice; it was now emanating from the soap dispenser while the Western accent stuck around in the original bottle. Splitting him in two seemed to separate the personalities into their own vessels.

"Now grab some bleach under the sink!" called out the whiskey bottle. Sohan did as he was told. He unscrewed the top and positioned the lip over the open soap dispenser.

"W-wait," stuttered the soap dispenser. "I'm… scared."

"No need to hesitate!" called out the whiskey bottle. "He's me, and I'm him, and I'm givin' you permission."

Sohan tilted the bleach.

"My eyes! My eyes!" screeched the soap dispenser. Its eerie likeness to Sohan made him stop his pour.

"Don't stop now!" commanded the whiskey bottle. "Just a little bit more!"

Sohan closed his eyes and cringed. He continued to dribble the bleach into the vial. Slowly, the screams vanished as the alcohol inside the dispenser changed chemically. Soon the whiskey inside was no more.

"So how long do we have till it explodes?" questioned Sohan.

"It ain't gonna explode, partner," chuckled the cowboy. "We done made chloroform."

"I thought we were going to distract Dave…"

"That can be done with a simple slam of the door," explained the whiskey, "but now we got something to take him out when he comes inside."

Sohan stared down at the soap dispenser bubbling over its brim like a man foaming at the mouth.

"Pour it on the face towel," continued the whiskey, "and once he rushes in… shove it right in his bazoo!"

Bang!

Sohan slammed the bathroom door and laid the bait. Suddenly, he heard the jostling of a key in the door across the hall. A few soft clicks sounded, then a creak as the door slowly opened. Dave masked his steps up to the bathroom door, keeping quiet, but when he reached the knob, he went berserk.

The door burst open, followed by Dave charging in with his face red as a cosmo. Sohan tried to splat the towel in the center of his face, but the rush was too disorienting. He missed his target. The towel and his hand flew past Dave's head and over his right shoulder. Dave took advantage of the error and tackled Sohan to the ground.

Dave was far heavier than Sohan, much more built. He had Sohan firmly pinned to the floor. Sohan struggled with all his might as he stared Dave in the eye. Sohan could see the subtle green building up in his sclerae.

"Why would you poison *yourself,* too, Dave?" questioned Sohan. "Are we all in some kind of suicide cult that I didn't know about? Is that what Ghost Club really is? All those fuckin' shrooms drove you all insane…."

Dave's glare didn't waver. Suddenly, a second head appeared in Sohan's line of sight. It was Bahnmi still clinging onto Dave's back. His head popped up over his shoulder. He nudged Dave's neck with his cheek.

"Spare him?" questioned Dave, staring into the animal's eyes. "After all he's done." Silence filled the room. Dave nodded as he stared intensely at the primate's timid expression. "He does owe us an explanation."

Dave turned his head away from Bahnmi over his other shoulder. He saw the towel meant to smother him. With one hand pinning Sohan by the neck, he reached backward and grabbed the cloth. Then he applied it tightly over Sohan's face.

"Fight it, hombre!" shouted the whiskey from somewhere out of sight. Sohan had blacked out so many times in the last day he figured he just might stand a chance against the chemicals fluttering around his brain. Soon they coated his consciousness thicker than any artsy beer. This blackout was not a slow, warm envelopment like with booze; this one came on strong and cold, like being thrown into a deep freeze.

When Sohan awoke, he was surprised to see he wasn't in Dave's room. He was in his own bedroom. Dave was there, kneeling on his bed. He had Bahnmi on his back and a piece of glass pipe in his hand—a shattered chunk of Heartthrob with dried blood on its edge.

Sohan turned to his left and, to his dismay, he saw Theodule with his throat slit lying against the wall. An arm was tossed over the body's back. It belonged to a young girl with an athletic build, dressed in a tight black sweater that accentuated her muscles. Sohan recognized her; it was the timber bucker Dave had taken upstairs to smoke.

"The painted lady," grumbled Sohan through his haze.

The gash under Theodule's chin was dry and black. The girl kept sticking her head to the wound like she was listening to its sound. Every couple of moments, she'd laugh, then reply. "I think it's cute you care."

"He's dead…" mumbled Sohan to the girl. She shot him a glance. She looked offended. "He's dead!" said Sohan louder, trying to hurt the woman.

"Let her talk!" growled Dave with a frightening glance. "*You* can't hear him, but *she* can." Dave removed Bahnmi from his back and held him up close to Sohan's face. Sohan could feel the creature's breath on his nose.

Dave pulled him away. "You're sure it's him?" He brought Bahnmi up to his ear. Dave nodded; his face looked disappointed. Dave then sat Bahnmi daintily on the sheetless mattress.

"Kings and philosophers," whispered Dave before turning around. "That's who gets poisoned." Dave got up in Sohan's face. "So, did you poison me because I'm smart or 'cause I'm royalty?"

"So- you think I'm the killer?" Sohan sneered.

Dave snickered. "You weren't expecting Bahnmi to tell me, were you?"

"Bahnmi isn't talking to you, Dave."

"You can't hear everything, Sohan!" he snarled. "It's like when we talked to our toys when we were kids. Our parents couldn't hear them talk back, but *we* did."

"Bahnmi is saying it was me…?"

"You took the poison from his teeth," explained Dave, putting a finger in the primate's mouth.

"I didn't even know they were poisonous."

"Liar!" screeched Dave. He grabbed something off the shelf and tossed it onto the floor. It looked like a translucent rubber bladder with tubing attached, the type a biker straps to their back for water. This one, however, was almost empty, and the liquid left inside was molasses brown.

"Whiskey?"

"Arrr… a l-little further South."

"Rum?"

"A-admiral Nelson…" he said in a woozy pirate-speak. "Last we spoke, we was pilfering below deck."

"Are you drunk?" sneered Sohan. "We've never spoken before…"

"Ay… three sheets to the wind."

"Listen to your friend, Sohan," cautioned Dave.

"Can you hear him?" questioned Sohan.

Dave shook his head. "Doesn't make it any less true."

Sohan turned back to the pouch. "How can a drink be drunk?"

"Arr, every drink gets drunk!" laughed the bladder. "I've been drunk so much; I'm down to the last few drops."

"What are you talking about?"

"You fed the whole crew the ol' skull and crossbones…" explained the rum. "One mate at a time."

"Maybe *you* poisoned everyone."

"Argh! *You* cracked the bottle," snarled the rum. "That's me ol' vessel in the corner." Sohan turned and saw an empty bottle of rum sticking out from under his bed. "You mixed me in with kisses from the imp." Sohan turned upwards and saw Bahnmi on the bed.

"I don't remember that."

"Arrgh…" the pirate's voice wheezed softly. "You don't remember a lot of things about yesterday."

"I'd remember killing everybody," shouted Sohan.

"Why'd you do it, Sohan?!" growled Dave.

"You're the ones killing people!" Sohan sniffled. He was starting to weep. "Why did you kill Theodule?"

Dave rolled his eyes. "Surely, he's in on it too. It's just too coincidental he never drinks, then we all get poisoned."

"You're paranoid."

Dave nodded. "Severely!" he agreed. "My brain's been physically altered by monkey spit. The only thing keeping it from melting away completely seems to be the weed we smoked." He pointed to his chest with the glass piece, then to the timber bucker, then to Sohan. "All three of us smoked and turned out a little less scathed than the others."

"It's the antioxidants," said the timber bucker with a smile.

Dave walked forward and held the glass piece up to Sohan's throat.

"Open his mouth," whispered the timber bucker.

Dave dove the serrated edge of the glass pipe into the center of Sohan's trachea. Sohan gasped for air as the glass slid out from his throat, leaving a large hole in its place. "Prepare the bag," said Dave to the timber bucker. "He dies appropriately."

The timber bucker poured together a concoction mixed with the remains of the rum in the bag. She poured in the gin, she poured in the vermouth, and she poured in the whiskey. Then they took Bahnmi, reached into his mouth, and squeezed his tongue from the base to the tip. A wad of venomous saliva landed in the bag.

The timber bucker shook it up; then Dave stuck the tube into the hole in Sohan's throat.

Sohan heard the inhabitants talking inside the bag like a gaggle of ghosts sharing the same body.

"Keep your gloves off her, seppo!" cried out the gin. "And don't get any ideas, chav!"

"Arr, I don't fancy ladies," growled the rum. "I'm coconut flavored if you know what I'm saying."

"Isn't this what you wanted, vecchio?" questioned the vermouth. "We're completely untwined."

"Too many knobs, not enough twats!" shrieked the gin. "And they're packing us into a paki!"

"I reckon the boy's a vaquero…" suggested the whiskey.

"I'm f-kah." With the tubing hooked up through his throat, Sohan could only gag his response. "I'm a f-kehn, fucking Bengali!"

Dave held the bag up high while the timber bucker squeezed. The ultimate mixed drink drained into Sohan's neck. He gurgled and choked as his airway became clogged with burning liquor. Some of it flowed down into his chest and scorched his innards. Some of it floated upwards and trickled out his mouth. The voices in the bag now shouted in his head.

"Davy Jones welcomes us!" cried out the rum. "I hear the shrieks of his sirens!"

"No sailor," grimaced the whiskey. "That there's the sound of the sheriff ridin' in."

Skamingo House has been on the FBI's watch list for quite some time due to the nature of Dark Web Dave's numerous internet dealings. When word got out about several missing persons, all last present at Skamingo House, the authorities quickly put a raid into action, especially after the stink of death wafted over to neighboring houses.

A team of ten police officers armed with rifles stormed the front lawn trampling the pink flamingo next to their walkway dressed in a checkered trilby and dark sunglasses, the very mascot that gave the house its name. They kicked open the front door and spread out among the floors. The team of four that took the top floor began screaming for the inhabitants of Dave's room to drop their weapons. Dave did no such thing and charged with his chunk of glass. The officers opened fire and sent a bullet through what remained of Dave's brains.

The timber bucker shrieked and latched onto Theodule's body, hugging him closely like a stuffed animal. "Protect me!" she hollered. "Save me!" Cops quickly surrounded her and separated her from the body. They pinned her to the ground.

Finally, there was Sohan, whom they had to rescue from the vices around his wrists and ankles. They couldn't get him to stand up straight. He was hobbling around drunk and poisoned for the second time in twenty-four hours. They decided to let him sit on the floor and tried to counsel some answers out of him.

Sohan's towel fell off as he wriggled around the floor. He began rambling, naked and drunk. The officers couldn't get any straight answers from him. His words were just long strings of slurs.

"Fucking chav!" murmured Sohan. "Fucking chav, fucking Yank!" Suddenly, Sohan changed his vernacular and yelled back at himself. "Argh, mind your manners, baron!" His dialect changed again. "Shut pan, you got' dang limeys!"

Unfortunately, even after a stomach pump, Sohan's condition would not change, and he'd be diagnosed with schizophrenia induced by neurotoxins. While the investigation initially suspected using slow loris venom in the crime, analyzing every drink at the party would reveal an unusual fungus growing in the beer.

A closer look into the supply chain of one Galvez Brewery, a local microbrew in Spanish Town, revealed they'd been importing the rye for their Rye-PA from small growers in Israel to capture the flavor of authentic Jewish bread. An international investigation ensued, revealing an undiscovered race of ergot growing on their imports.

It was an ergot unlike any other they'd seen, interacting with nanoparticulates in the brain too small to measure. Its mechanism remains unclear, but what's certain from the only two survivors of that night in February is that while the ergot stimulates the union between man and object, it compensates by tearing the links between man and man far apart.

Sohan received long hours of rehabilitation to try and retrain his brain for human socialization. No matter how much his therapists tried with him, they couldn't encourage him to leave his room for anything outside his basic needs.

On a typical Saturday night, Sohan would finally emerge to bring a "pick-six" home from the grocery store. He'd pop his selection open all at once. He lays them all out on the desk beside his computer monitor and asks them each to introduce themselves.

"Ay, top of the morning to you," said the cheery voice of an Irishman emanating from the stout.

"Next," sneered Sohan.

"Pleased to meet you, señor," came the surly voice of the Corona.

"Next," Sohan repeated.

"How do you do, mein durstiger freund?" came a bubbly Bavarian accent from the pilsner. It was that of a luscious German Valkyrie.

"Stop," called out Sohan. He had no need to hear the others. He picked up the pilsner and held the bottle up to his ear. He felt the cool glass on his face; it was soothing. With his other hand, he began to click on his mouse, bringing up a screen full of amateur porn. He took his hand off the mouse and unzipped his pants.

"Just keep talking to me…."

A Reason to Burn: The Spirit Realm

I'm sure there's somebody out there who must have noticed my unusual absence from a story about iconic liquors. Somebody who snacks on black jellybeans must be missing their favorite nocturnal beverage. Multiple beers and a wine have appeared, and they're not even really spirits, so I ask, where's the 'green fairy'?

Well, Evan strung me along for quite a bit. He built my character early in the planning stages of "The Spirit Realm" but then never used me. He molded me into a centenarian caretaker for a funeral home, something to fit the beverage's morbid, even occult, aesthetic. I was written to be dramatic but right about everything, but he never got far along enough to fit that attitude into the plot. Not that there weren't plenty of spaces for it. But once Evan introduced that damn gin, Winston, he hesitated to use another old man in the story.

Eventually, Evan realized he couldn't use me as a senior-citizen and decided to age me down, but this just made things worse. He went halfway through turning me into a leather queen goth girl before dropping the idea altogether and leaving me that way. Now I've got this horrifying stitched-together personality where I stalk the long narrow hallways of a mausoleum while simultaneously keeping up with a vast TikTok following.

When Evan reached the end of the story without finding a place for me, I felt like an actress who'd been edited out of her starring role. I mean, how could you do a story set in New Orleans without including a bottle of absinthe? Absinthe is French as fuck and lets you see ghosts, a perfect fit for a tale called "The Spirit Realm".

It's not so much negligence as it is disdain. Evan openly admits he hates anything anise-flavored. Every time he has tried to drink me in the past, he's loathed the experience. He's tried me poured over a flaming sugar cube; he's tried me with cake on the side; he's tried me stirred into a slushy. He abhors me, not just for the taste but for the very feeling I leave in his head and stomach. He describes it as a "licorice-flavored flu."

Any flu-like symptoms Evan might have experienced would be from my exceptionally high alcohol content. I'm sure I won't have to defend my proof to anyone. Those who enjoy a good burn give me due respect. But for Evan's clear *dis*respect, I suggest we use my inherent flammability as a symbolic device and dip the pages of "The Spirit Realm" into a shallow pool of me before lighting it aflame.

I hope Evan enjoys the smell.

- Stunted Stock-character, Absinthe

The Pimp Who Slapped the Ripper

I'm not sure when the concept of pimps and madams became distinct. At some point, they were both just known as procurers. But like actors and actresses, the role was divided along lines of sex, and each half was delivered a part. The pimps were the merciless beaters, while the madams were the empathetic manipulators. You must understand then why I call myself a lady, but I also call myself a pimp.

I've always seen my girls for what they were to me: a means to amenities outside the reach of an East Ender. They were my fancy clothes, my Banting diet, and my coach service. Each trollop was the embodiment of a luxury. If she was bruised, I saw my clothes shredded, my food rotted, or my carriage in flames. Therefore, it was in my best interest to keep their bruises covered and punish those responsible.

I punished myself accordingly for what I did to Zadie. There was no dinner for me that night. I missed her cheek and swatted her square in the eye. Gave her a shiner and a mean scratch. I spent the rest of the evening applying cover-up by gaslight. I started by using a thin layer of cold cream over the bruise so the rest of the makeup sticks. Then I added the powder.

"Good as new, gigglemug," I said, putting my puff into my trunk. It was a compact receptacle where I kept my office supplies. Each side was upholstered with leather, dyed mauveine like the rest of my wardrobe.

I looked up from my case and examined my work on Zadie from a different angle. It was perfect. My shredded clothes were magically stitched back together. It helped that Zadie's long-wearing smile sold the illusion of placidity. It was an eerie thing. Not just to me; her clients were aware of it, too. It never vanished, no matter what was done to her. I had the back of my ring stuck under her eyelid, and it never wavered. "Are you okay?" I asked for the hundredth time. "I must work on my aim, dear. I'm ashamed."

Zadie nodded hurriedly like she hadn't heard the question.

"Zadie, it's tough to know when you're really absorbing things." I sighed. "Are you going to come late to your shift ever again?"

Zadie shut her eyes and shook her head frantically.

"I trust that's to be taken seriously." I stepped behind her, then patted her back till she was out in the street. "Get to it."

Zadie began to hum and waddle off into the dark. My bottom girl, Melita, quickly took her place in front of me. If Zadie was my clothes, Melita was my diet. I see all the finest delicacies in the curves of her body: pink hams for her feet, bright carpaccio for her rosy thighs, and her middle was red like flank steak. It was a shame some men couldn't appreciate her strangely rosy complexion, but those who did were obsessed. That's why Melita is the bottom girl; she was my first girl and remains my best.

"Fannie." Her voice was lowered so no one in the streets would hear her. She put her lips up close to my ear. "The Celt's putting girls on Baker's Row."

The Celt's invasion was not shocking. The other territories in East End were constantly in flux as pimps and madams butted heads in the streets. The Celt had never quarreled before, but it only takes a bit of greed before pimps push boundaries.

I found the Celt outside his favorite bar on Buck's Row — the Round Dog Tavern. He's an easy person to spot. His hair was coral red, extending halfway down his back and woven into a fishtail braid. The silk vest he wore over his bare chest matched blue tattoos inked down his naked arms: images of crosses and bears, triskeles and trinities connected by spiraling Celtic knots.

"Celt." I came up straight to his chest.

"Purpleback," murmured the Celt with a Cockney cadence.

"You're too far West."

"But I'm not in *your* West."

"We agreed upon a no-man's-land," I said, holding out my arms, gesturing to the ends of Baker's Row. "I have witnesses saying you've intruded."

"I won't deny it, but I've got to make transactions." He pointed over his shoulder with his thumb. "I've got bluebottles on Buck's Row, so I moved where it's safe."

"Pay the inspector; they just want bribes."

"They're not just looking for a ponce. They're out for a murderer."

"A murder? Who'd you kill?"

"It's not me."

"Then *who died?*"

"Young fing named Polly, no minder, used to whore around sunup. I just let Polly do 'er thing. Only seemed to attract the barmies. Kept them away from my girls. Guess one really snapped, minced up her middles. Now she's brown bread."

"*Your* brown bread if I catch more girls on Baker's."

"Or what?" said the Celt, stepping forward. An inch separated our torsos.

I stood firm, keeping my eyes locked on his. I squeezed my thumb till the knuckle cracked loudly.

"One day, us should just join forces." The Celt raised his hand, landing his palm on my elbow. "We could rule New Town if you'd just… take a step back down." He ran his hand up my arm to my shoulder. "A pimp's only good as his bottom."

My hand was eager to rise as well. I had to actively fight its levitation. "I was never a bottom."

"Then it's a promotion."

If I let my hand move freely, I could do some real damage to his boney face. It was an ugly mug that tapered at the chin. It looked like a dog's canine. I could shred it to pieces, and women would pay him just as little attention. What my backhand lacked in strength, it made up for in feminine armory. I had nine cocktail rings distributed across five fingers, studded with sharply faceted violet sapphires. When my hand met a face, these jewels serrated flesh like the edge of a steel whip.

The only downside to cutting the Celt's cheek would be his merciless retaliation, which I would not survive. It'd be like a honeybee using its one and only sting before its organs come tumbling out of its bottom. There's no point in keeping my dignity if I'm dead, so I took a step back.

"If I see your girl cross onto Hanbury, I'll take her face off." I swatted the air in front of the Celt's nose. He blinked and crinkled his upper lip.

I felt I'd given the Celt enough grievance to keep him out of my territory. I didn't like how close he pushed me to swatting him. I was beginning to suspect he wanted me to hit him just so he could strike back. He wouldn't hit a woman first.

I retreated to my usual street just before sunup. My deal with the constables said we'd be gone before the children could see us, roughly 6 a.m. That's when the young chimney sweeps began their shifts.

I decided to use the last working hour to collect weekly dues from my girls. I only charged ten shillings—a small wage for small services. I could sting, but I couldn't kill, which was good enough for *my* girls. Honestly, they couldn't afford better protection. There was something a little off about each of them, so they brought in less than the usual prostitute. I was their only choice, the discount pimp.

When 6 a.m. rolled around, I returned to my carriage to drive home. I took a piece of my earnings and gave my driver, Hughie, his monthly dues, plus a little extra to afford food for Hare, my horse. Hare was named Hare because he walked with a hop due to a pocket of fluid in his knee. I couldn't afford a good horse, but Hare did the job just fine. I liked to play music in the carriage that matched the beat of his limp. That way, he looked to be dancing.

The windup gramophone in my lap was playing "Hand Me Down My Walking Cane" when we reached the West end of Hanbury Street. The horse and carriage bobbed up and down to the beat, attracting the delighted eyes of passersby. "A nice night, Purpleback?" a young street sweeper called out, cleaning the shit left behind Hare.

"Lovely, yes!" I said.

"Was it really, Miss Hill?" asked my driver in his soft, childish voice. Hughie was a sweet boy, only twelve years old. Despite his age, he was an immaculate driver and a useful shot. He would guard my carriage at night, sleeping inside it with the rifle I'd given him. Since the day we met, he has done exactly as I told him without question. His freckled face reminded me of a childhood friend I had in my somber youth—we suffered through a lot together. Hughie was a wonderful boy, and he deserved respectful answers.

"It was an awful night, Hughie." I laughed, "Murderers on the loose, pimps at odds with each other. Zadie got a black eye. It was all messy, but the company must show strength in these challenging times. And so… the night was lovely."

"Of course, Miss Hill," said the child. "A lovely evening tomorrow, too."

Hughie parked the carriage outside our home on White Lion Street. I share an apartment with Hughie's parents, the Davies. That was how we met. I hadn't made the necessary funds to live independently, and I'd promised myself the next girl I brought in would pay for more lavish living conditions. Maybe a flat on China Row if she was a real winner. I had a candidate in mind. I often found myself in Shoreditch, in the front row of a dingy playhouse, cheering her on.

Elizabeth Stride, the voluptuous Swedish actress famous for playing Louka in *Arms and the Man*, was on my procurement list. She had long, blonde, tousled hair that hung over her chest and those dainty ankles men desired. Her popularity waning from the natural progression of age, she'd been reduced to playing pantomime at The Frolic—perhaps the cheapest entertainment in all of London.

It was cheap enough for the Davies to join me. I paid their son, and their son paid them, and that money went to the shows. So in a way, it was like I paid for their seats. They treated me quite nicely, almost like family—especially Hughie. He looked up at me with this big smile, wide as Zadie's but earnest with all the innocence still intact.

"Why did the witch steal away the princess?" whispered Hughie during the play. Without spoken words, the finer details of these plots were lost on children.

"To make her dreams come true," I said with a grin.

"Then why does the prince look so angry?"

"Because she took the princess before he could," I said. Then I held my finger to my lips. We shouldn't annoy the rest of the paupers; the show was their one escape from exiguity.

Afterward, I had no problems getting backstage to the narrow outhouses they called changing rooms. The women's room had enough space to fit two dresses, a mirror, myself, and Elizabeth.

"I can get you the attention you deserve," I told Elizabeth. She kept her eyes fixed on the mirror. This wasn't the first time I'd tried to recruit her. "Your crowds are all women and children. Grown men pay twice as much... but they come to *me*."

"Men or no men, it makes no difference," said Elizabeth, dabbing a wet sponge to erode her makeup. "There's no such thing as a more quality audience. All eyes are the same to me."

"Well, some are blue, some are brown, and some are *green*," I said with a long inflection. "Don't you miss the days of higher pay? I told you I'd match whatever you make here, plus ten pence. That offer still stands."

"Ten pence for the cost of vagrancy?"

"*Authorized* vagrancy," I countered. "Vagrants work shorter hours and work half as hard. Just stand against a wall for six hours. You can sing while you do it if you like."

"Maybe I *wouldn't* mind the life of a vagrant," said Elizabeth, "but not one of *your* vagrants."

"There's something wrong with *my* vagrants?"

"I refuse to believe you're so naive," sneered Elizabeth. "The harlequin, the rosebush, and the pirate. Now you want to add the world's oldest whore to your freakshow."

"Worst of all, the ringmaster trains her freaks with a whip!" A third voice sounded from the dressing room door. I turned and was surprised to see the renowned Madam in White. "*I* can offer a sound business to beautiful women such as yourself." She leaned close and checked herself in the mirror, adjusting her neckline to tilt the ratio of skin to dress.

Madam Jane Cook was rumored to be a former Dahomey Amazon assimilated into the grime of Eastern London. She ran a team of ball gazers who told fortunes in a subterranean parlor under Canning Town. Her women were undeniably more in vogue than my own.

"If you want top-shelf women, you give them top-shelf respect, not a backhand like this." Jane grabbed my hand and raised it so my jeweled hand glistened in the mirror. Elizabeth's eyes fixed on the diamond on my pinky, where an eyelash connected to a speck of flesh stuck beneath the girdle.

I snarled and yanked my hand away, chipping the glass and scratching the mirror's silver bezel. Jane looked pleased with herself for eliciting such a reaction.

I was a woman doing a man's job. If I didn't use my hand, I would never get respected. And if I wasn't respected, how could my girls attain their own top-shelf respect?

Elizabeth turned to Jane and smiled. "Now, *we* should talk."

A wild feeling filled my chest. I felt so slighted, but it was different from the Celt. The Celt had me wondering if I was too soft. Jane had somehow done the opposite. I used the same strategies as any other pimp on the street to keep my girls in line. I had to use my hand if I was going to appear scary. The only way I even got my women was to seem just as frightening as the boys. Prostitutes needed a dangerous pimp to ward off the psychos. It was always for their benefit.

Jane was an old bottom-bitch who spun off into her own enterprise. I wanted to reach right into the center of her and smack that young bottom girl in the face, but things had changed. She was a madam making pimp money, and that amount of power could have been enough weight to crush my fledgling operation. I backed off once again, taking my fury with me into the night.

I clobbered the cobblestone beneath my heels and rushed to check on my girls. Fueled like this, I tended to put that energy into micro-management. Melita was the least of my concerns, so I always checked her last. Zadie always found me; I never found her. That left Annie.

Annie was my Hughie and Hare. Her eyes were like a child, but she limped like my horse. Her wooden leg affected her stride. She claimed she was born without it, but the stitch marks said it was lost.

Annie waddled up and presented me with my weekly pay, one day late and a shilling short.

"I needed an extra day just to get this much," she said. "Can you forgive the debt?"

"Let's assume for a second you're not just stealing from me." I scanned her body up and down, checking for new purchases. Her ribs were showing through her shirt. "You're not pulling your weight. Try harder."

Annie looked frustrated. "There's legs that look more like legs, you know. You pay for one, and I guarantee sales will go up."

"There's no negotiation. You will give ten shillings, not nine. Do what it takes to make the difference and hand it to me before sunrise." I reached for the nine shillings in her palm, but she pulled it away in a panic. That crossed a line.

I raised my hand to her. It went a lot better than last time. My fingers met her cheek right on target. Instead of knocking her head backward, it twisted with an elegant flow. A torrent of saliva shot over her right shoulder. A perfect slap sounded like a tree branch snapping in the wind.

As soon as the hit landed, Annie turned and ran in fear of further injury, but there was no need. I could stop myself quite easily once things got physical. Some of the steam was gone, so I could calm down.

"Annie," I called out. "Annie, come back. We're all even now." I'd find her some other time.

I spotted Zadie in a nearby alley. I wanted to check in on her before I lost her again. As I approached her, she started scratching incessantly at her behind.

"You've got fleas, have you?" I laughed as I walked past her to look at her back. Zadie flailed about.

"Those dots on Wilhelmina. They jumped onto me! *Eck! Eck!*" Suddenly, Zadie bent over and vomited up a black torrent.

"Those aren't dots, young lady; those are rat hills! Black omen!" I screeched. "You've gone and murdered yourself, you fool."

Zadie's smile shivered but kept its form, even under dire circumstances.

"How did you get rat hills?"

"Wilhelmina!" she repeated. "Wihelmina's one of Celt's girls."

"That Neanderthal again!"

"She moved onto my corner and started selling us as a combo package."

I punched the nearby brick wall over and over until my hand went numb. The Celt's intrusion had not only begun; it had already maimed one of my girls. I watched Zadie collapsing against the wall and saw my purple derby hat pummeled out of shape; my speckled ostrich feather snapped beneath the Celt's heel.

I cut through the avenues and dashed through the doors of the Round Dog, hoping to catch the Celt while he's wankered, but he wasn't there. I only knew of one other spot to see him, but barging into a pimp's lair was dangerous. His makeshift office was in the alley between the shoe shop and the rundown terrace houses on Raven Row. The Celt didn't check on his workers. Instead, they were to visit him at the office three times a day to evaluate their night's effort.

As I crossed the street on the other side of the alley, there was an eerie calmness about the area. The shoe store looked to be abandoned. The only people I saw were crawling along the ground. These were the Celt's girls, their limp bodies lining the pavement.

I wrapped a purple scarf around my face before entering and stepped over half-undressed trollops scratching their many pustules. One girl in a blonde wig with a harelip wiped the blood off her face and smeared it along the ground. Another girl cupped her mouth and clung to the wall as her pretty little pencil legs jiggled underneath her.

"The Celt! The Celt!" I shouted through my scarf. "Take me to him!"

The arm of a woman lying face down in some garbage suddenly rose. It pointed as though it were the only living tissue left on her body. I followed its directions to a Morris chair against the alley's back wall. Lying fully reclined was the Celt. His shirt was unbuttoned, exposing a bare chest full of rat hills. His head was hanging over the backrest. I stood on my toes and peered at his face from above. His eyes were yellow and red; they clung open, motionless.

I screeched like a train forced to halt. My hate-fueled assault could no longer happen. This left me with unresolved animosity. My right hand clenched. The bones in my knuckles cracked. I looked at all the girls dying around me and shivered. What a waste of life. This is what happens when a pimp fails their women. If the Celt were still alive, I would have laid a blow on his face for every dead girl I could see.

The Celt died like he lived: a desperate man who fucked his own girls. A little abstinence and I wouldn't have been left with so much tension.

I left Raven Row expecting that to be the worst part of my night, but as I returned to Hanbury, I realized just how bad things could get. The streets were swarming with top hats and blue tailcoats. For a moment, I was afraid my contact in the police department had betrayed me, but no one seemed to be searching me out. No, they were standing still in small groups of four and three. They were all discussing something clustered around a backyard.

"*Ms.* Purpleback." Inspector Neil suddenly stepped before me, his sizeable blonde mustache giving me a start. "*Ms.* Purpleback, your cooperation in this matter will be greatly appreciated." Inspector Neil had been graciously accepting my bribes in return for leniency. He was my point of contact with the world of law enforcement.

"Please," I said. "Just call me Fannie, Inspector."

"Oh, I thought she might be yours." He grabbed my hand firmly with his gloved claw. He wrenched me into the backyard to hover over the girl in question. Her parts had been plucked out and distributed across the grass, and her face was swollen from a beating. It was hard to recognize her initially, but I looked harder and found the welts on her cheek.

"I knew your rings would match!" The Inspector laughed. He kept looking at my hand clutched in his and the marks on the girl's face.

"Neil, listen to me. I didn't do this!" I shouted in panic. I finally yanked my hand out of his grip and backed away slowly.

"Ms-" He caught himself. "Fannie… we know who did this." He stepped forward, beckoning me to join him back at the body. "Of course, it wasn't you. This here's a loss."

I nodded and imagined my horse and carriage driving off a cliff.

"I've read about madams and their girls," continued the Inspector. "Basically, mothers and daughters."

I hadn't the focus to correct him. "Who done it, Neil?"

"The Whitechapel Murderer," said the Inspector, looking nervously at his feet. "He signs his name 'Jack the Ripper'."

"Signs his name?"

"He leaves us notes."

***

Dear Boss,

I'm down on whores, and I shan't quit ripping them till I get buckled. Grand work, the last job was. I gave the lady no time to squeal. How can they catch me? I love my work.

The next job I do, I shall clip the lady's ears off and send them to the police just for jollies. Keep this letter back till I do a bit more work, then give it out straight. My knife's so sharp, I want to get to work right away if I get a chance. Good Luck.

Yours truly,
Jack the Ripper

P.S. They say I'm a doctor now. ha ha

***

"I don't get the joke," I said.

"Some journal published that we're looking for a culprit with medical skills. His anatomical knowledge *is* above average. One theory says doctor. The other says butcher."

"*Right*… but why is that funny? Him being a doctor?"

"Because we're probably calling a street bum a degree-holder, which has to be the highest compliment they've gotten in their life."

"I was a street bum," I said quietly, "and I turned out alright." With that, I walked off into the night. I ventured home and crawled into bed.

I returned my purple dress first thing in the morning. It was only ever a rental. Instead, I chose a more modest wear: a tattered tea gown with a brown mark on the stomach. I bought it off the pickers. It wasn't exactly purple, but it was a dark pink, which was as close as I would get.

For the next few days, I kept the news from the Davie family, unable to look their son in the eyes, but eventually, the boy tracked me down, drinking my troubles away at the Round Dog. I'd been chatting with one of the Celt's old ladies as she'd recently become unemployed. The only thing holding her back from joining the other pimps was the horrible facial scars left by the rat hills. I could see past her skin to the shiny new dress the girl could earn me. I tried to seal the deal, but I was distracted by

Hughie pulling on my dress, trying to force me to come home. I was an inebriated mess, so I felt bad and went along with the child.

When the Davie family woke me in the morning, they told me the news spreading through town: Purpleback was broke. I had no choice but to confess. They weren't happy when I couldn't pay them for their son's services any longer. Their faces strained, and their stomachs growled. Hughie broke down into tears.

"I can still be your driver," he hollered. His collar was soaking wet. "I don't need the pay!"

"Quiet," shrieked Mrs. Davie. "We need quid, and you're getting a new job."

Hughie sniffled, "Can I still please sleep in the carriage?"

"Sleep where you like," groaned Mr. Davie. "More space for your mother and I."

"It's dangerous outside," said Mrs. Davie. "More dangerous than it's ever been. You haven't heard? Bastard killed two more last night."

"The Ripper did?"

Mrs. Davie ignored my question at first. Then she sighed angrily and answered. "Yes," she said. "Elizabeth Stride... Catherine Eddowes."

"Elizabeth," I whispered under my breath. The actress had been slain only a few days into her new life. All the promises of returned acclaim had come true, but certainly not in the way she'd hoped.

With my inability to pay rent exposed and the Davies angered, I got up and walked out the door. As night fell, I caught sight of myself in a puddle building up under a horse. By moonlight, I looked like the very women I managed. My robes could no longer shield my honor. Royal colors intimidated the likes of Zadie and Annie, but they were gone now. All I had left was Melita, and she didn't require such showmanship. Melita has always known her place. I brought her back from the brink of starvation. She relied on me.

When I caught Melita between suitors, she smiled and ran up to me. She stretched out her hand and produced a large mound of change.

"I can spare you twice the shillings as usual," she said. She held out my hand for me and began spilling the coins into my palm.

"It's not even payday," I said, feeling pitiful. "That's *your* money."

"I'm only as good as my pimp," said Melita, dropping the last shilling. "It's for the good of the company."

"Well, the company thanks you." I let the coins fall from my fingers into my breast pocket. "I want you to come with me tonight."

"I best pick up the slack from the other girls."

"Please," I said earnestly. "This is more important."

I took Melita by the hand and pulled her forward. She dragged behind me at first, then picked up the pace. She didn't ask where we were going, so she either figured it out herself or trusted me even in my dire state. I led her to a little shop along the River Thames: The Eye of Mawu.

We clanked the brass knocker out front. A little slider pulled left and revealed a thin slot at the top of the door. Dainty, gray eyes peered through, quickly replaced by pitch black. Footsteps receded. Footsteps returned. A new pair of eyes appeared, less dressy and chestnut brown.

"What a surprise." The door creaked open, revealing Jane Cook. "I wasn't expecting you."

"He got your girl," I said.

"Lizzie was also a dear friend," said Jane.

I rolled my eyes. "I know you didn't take it lying down."

Jane poked her head out the doorway and saw Melita standing behind me. "You've shut down shop just to come see me." Jane's eyes softened. "Come inside. Take a seat in my office."

As we walked through the halls of Jane's magic shop, we saw into the open rooms where the men were serviced. At the entrance was the table with the crystal ball and the two chairs, behind it was a curtain, and behind this curtain came the sounds of sensuality. Men called out as they made contact with the spirit world. The women made coos as though they enjoyed it. I'd never encouraged my girls to do such favors, but these men were paying much higher prices.

At the end of the hall was a red door with a padlock on it. Jane undid the steel and turned the knob. She hurried us all inside, where we found comfortable seating arrangements placed in front of a roll top. Melita and I sat on soft stools while Jane laid back in her recliner on the opposite side of the desk.

I peered around the room. Stuffed birds hung from the ceiling, exotic species I'd never seen before. Behind Jane was a fireplace with a long, gold-tipped spear mounted over it.

"Did you use that spear… for combat?" I questioned, gazing at the magnificent weapon.

"Oh, it's not really mine," said Jane with a restrained laugh. "I bought it at an auction. Those rumors work well for intimidation, but *I* grew up an orphan right here in Limehouse."

"Ditto," I replied enthusiastically. "Of course, I was in White Chapel."

"Look at that. So much the same." Jane reached into her drawer and pulled out a photograph. "I was fostered in a special academy for etiquette. Methodists who believed they could reform the streets of London through charity. Good people. They were good to me."

I looked around uncomfortably. "Sounds like a dream out of a painting book." Melita glared at my fidgeting. "We should all be so lucky… I found myself working under the merciless control of a whore. By day, she ran our business, washing carriages for pennies. She'd slam our little hands in the doors if we weren't quick enough." I pulled off a few of my rings which hid the strange bends in my knuckles. "With nowhere to go home to, I followed her into the night. I thought she might have a home I could sneak into, but she just kept working. Sleeping with the same men we serviced in the day. She'd spend the night in their warm beds while I froze out in the snow. I *hated* her."

Jane smiled. "You seemed like the type."

"The type?" I cringed.

"It happens all the time. Men take their childhood trauma out on my girls. You're just like that." Jane tucked her photo away in a folder and shut her drawer. She folded her arms on her desk and sighed. "Now there's a Ripper out there killing our workers, and I'm sure his childhood bears some resemblance to your own."

"You think I want them dead?"

Jane looked at Melita sitting quietly; her eyes fixated on her lap. She looked nervous, scared even. "No, but your feelings towards them are just as bizarre."

"I only want the Ripper dead," I said assuredly. "The Ripper and the Celt, but I came too late to catch the Celt. Now I'm left with all this rage and no one to strike."

"Yes, the young man with the rat pimples," said Jane. "That's reason enough not to live in a gutter."

"How do we catch the Ripper, Jane?"

"We use what we know to cast the appropriate line," she suggested, "then we let you loose to dispense hot vengeance."

"You won't join me?"

"I don't do violence." Jane closed her eyes peacefully and tapped her nails on the table. "I trust your vision of justice will suit us both."

"We could leave Melita as a lure. Keep her isolated somewhere no one would hear her scream."

Melita kept silent. Her eyes had risen from her lap to stare at the edge of Jane's desk. She looked uncomfortable with the suggestion.

"She wouldn't be in any real danger, of course," I continued. "I would hide nearby and corner him before he strikes."

"It'll be better if you, yourself, are the bait," suggested Jane.

"But I'm not..." I shook at the suggestion. "I'm not selling."

"Not really, but we can make it seem like it," Jane said. "Sweetie, your empire is gone. It's public knowledge. Now, we all expect to see you on the street to make up for those losses."

"I would never," I said. "But if that's how they see me… I suppose I can play the part—as long as it doesn't kill me."

"You can strike before he does," continued Jane. "You just need to see him coming."

"How will I know it's him?"

"His letters have leaked to the newspapers. The Ripper scoffs at the title of doctor. It's possible he knows doctors or that they took something from him, something they can't make right." She stood and led us out to the hall. "I've seen a man like that outside my shop. He never has the courage to come in. I've seen the stitches through the peephole, a botched effort to reshape the disaster he was born with."

"Are you sure it's him?"

Jane shrugged. "I'm not certain, but I've got my girls tailing him. He's been skulking around Spitalfields since the last murder. All we must do is get you close. And get you alone. If it's him, he'll take the bait."

Spitalfields was the dilapidated dream of a silk industry in England, completely outdone by cheap French imports. Now this part of town has lost its grace and become a foul-smelling rookery, where droppings drip from windowsills and famished children lay half-conscious in the mud.

Some might've thought it difficult to find isolation in such an overcrowded slum, but Jane's trollops were well-accustomed to the area. There were scarecrows that kept the rooks away from certain cavities—girls stationed at corners to keep watch. I was situated in an empty cul-de-sac which often serves as an arena for the Wild Boys. The girl that brought me there assured me they'd be preoccupied. That was a promise she'd keep personally as the Eye of Mawu opened wide for a wild orgy.

I felt foolish waiting there in the streets, a common hooker. The veil between my status and theirs was gone now as the cobblestone clacked beneath my heels. It would be boring if it weren't so humiliating. Something about the embarrassment made time seem to pass faster; my every other thought was blank, so only half of every second seemed to exist.

Every time someone passed by the entrance to the cul-de-sac, I felt shame, as though this was some punishment. It was easy to forget that this was for my benefit. Not only mine Melita's too, and every prostitute in this city. As someone turned the corner and walked my way, my body flushed. I wanted them to turn around before they saw my face and knew my name.

"Oh, Purpleback," called out the shadow approaching. He caught sight of the faded rags covering my fair skin. "You're no longer purple." He was a short man-made average by the tall hat atop his head. A long black cape flowed behind him. "I'd been eyeing your girl Annie from the shadows for quite some time. Something about her face just did it for me. But there was always this richly colored procurer too close by. So, I ask one victim at knifepoint who is that eggplant standing in my way. Purpleback, they named you. But what are you now?"

"I'm still Purpleback."

"But the colors of twilight have passed. So… has the sun set… or has it risen?"

"I've never been more ashamed," I told the phantom. "This is surely the end of day."

The dim gaslights overhead cast a shadow off the brim of his hat. I couldn't see his face until he removed the headgear and introduced himself as Jack. He huffed through his blistered lips. His face was a hideous mess; the right side sunk like a bag of mush. Threads and twine kept it from falling off the good half. "I heard you've been through Hell," said the Ripper.

"It wasn't my first visit. Every time I come back, it loses some of its novelty. It's just a bunch of steep hills to me." The Ripper's comment boiled my blood. He acted so distantly, but he was the one who put me through that Hell. He killed Annie, and for that, I wanted him to suffer.

"You must be tired," he hissed. He reached under his cape and pulled out a knife. It was a special-looking blade, six inches in length, the first four inches bent into a serpentine. The tip was straight and marked with dried blood.

I stood firm and cracked my knuckles: the rattle of my tail. "You certainly know hardship," I said, touching my face. I wondered how much like me he was. I wondered what made a man like this inside and out. "Were you born ruined?"

"My face was crushed beneath a knee-high leather boot," he grumbled. His face grimaced. "Nothing saucy. I was just a boy."

"I wonder if I could recognize you without the stitches," I told him. "I can't tell your age."

"Where did you live?" he asked me earnestly.

"Nowhere."

The Ripper nodded. "In the night, I hid in Poplar, but the injury made me forget… most else."

"Could you have been a cab washer?"

The Ripper shrugged. "Does it matter?"

"We have similar lusts," I said. "I wonder if it stems from the same woman."

"It's a big city with tons of terrible people," said the Ripper. "You really think we're similar?"

"To an extent. I get my vengeance as a lady. You get yours as an animal."

"A pimp isn't *like a lady*," said the Ripper. "You've always been playing dress-up as a man."

"So have you…" I said between gritted teeth. "You wilted ape."

The Ripper howled in anger. The healthy parts of his face suddenly grew as ugly as the mutilated half. His good eye became bulgy and bloodshot. The corner of his mouth scowled and hung open, revealing jagged yellow teeth. His knife went straight for my guts with an underhanded swing. I grabbed the rounded edges near the base and held it there with my left hand. I felt it cutting into the flesh on my fingers. I shouted and shoved forward. He took half a step back and raised his dagger over his shoulder, aiming to plunge it into my neck or face.

I twisted my upper body and swung my hand at his face with all my power. The Ripper ducked down and dodged the blow. He then slashed his knife to the side. I cried out in pain as the blade slid through the back of my hand just under the middle knuckle. The Ripper let go of the handle.

The blade was now stuck in my hand. I gagged at the sight. The reddened tip was now dripping with my blood. The final three inches were sticking out from my palm.

"Mommy took the toys away," the Ripper taunted in a strange voice. It was like the air left his lungs. There were dry heaves after every word. "Don't lock them away!" He reached for the handle sticking out of the back of my hand. I backed up before he could touch it. I held my hand up high. His short arms couldn't reach me, so he ran forward and shoved me over.

I fell, my arms flying out to my sides. The back of the handle hit the cobblestone, sending the knife in deeper. I clenched my teeth and shut my eyes, and, in that second, the Ripper pounced on me. The weight was modest, but he balanced it all on my throat, wrapping his hands around my neck.

I gazed at him, eye to eye. He wept like a little street orphan hungry for food. I'd seen those eyes in street puddles, and I'd seen those eyes in Melita and Annie, Elizabeth, too.

I shut my eyes. I concentrated on my right hand, willing the knife's pain to disappear. All I needed was a second. I found my anger and let it flow, and I swung hard at the crumpled side of the Ripper's face. The slap carried a glorious smacking sound, made louder by the wet blood on my hand.

I had forced the knife through the Ripper's cheeks; a torrent of blood spilled from his face. The grip on my neck let up. I coughed furiously, trying to gather oxygen back into my chest. A piece of his severed tongue fell out of his mouth onto my eye. I brushed it off with my free hand. I tried to force my eyes open as I wheezed.

Those teary, childlike eyes began to rain on my face. "Oh-" he whimpered, "cruel... whore."

I removed the blade from his cheeks. The edge was still stuck in my palm. I used my other hand to shove him off me, then stood up. He was still lying down in the center of the cul-de-sac. I ran before I saw him die. The fight had made a lot of noise, and soon, people would come to investigate. I took the opportunity to run away before more people could see me dressed so lowly.

"Dead or alive, it doesn't matter." Jane coddled me after seeing the wound to my hand. Her girls carried me into the Eye of Mawu and injected me with a healthy dose of opioids before covering my eyes and ripping out the blade. The sensation was strange, like a mix of butterfly wings and pointy things. "You're a good girl, and you've done a good job." Her voice was sweet and stoic. Jane brushed my hair with her fingers like a mother would her daughter. Under the spell of the drugs, I let it happen, leaning into every stroke and eventually falling asleep in her office.

I woke up in my apartment with the Davies. Mr. and Mrs. Davie were peeking inside a wrapped present. Hughie was posted by the front door with his rifle. "If he comes for you, I'll take him out."

"The Amazon says he could still be alive," said Mrs. Davie. She knelt at my bed and leaned close to my face, "To think you… assaulted a man like that… well—"

"You've certainly earned this," Mr. Davie supplied. He brought the beautifully wrapped box to me and dropped it on my bed. "It's payment from Jane."

"I'm not a working girl," I said. "I don't need payment."

"It's a thank-you," said Hughie. "Come on, Ms. Hill! You have to see it, at least."

I stared at him with a blank expression. Then I looked at the box, untied the bow, and lifted the lid. I tore through the sheet of white paper on top. I saw my beautiful purple dress folded up inside. I touched the fabric and shouted at the boy. "Did you sell the horse and carriage?"

Hughie hollered. "Hare couldn't go anywhere even if he tried!"

"Grab the record player." I stood up. "Let's go for a ride."

With my dress returned, I thought I could jump back into work like nothing had happened. However, as I bobbed up and down in my carriage, I could not feel the same joy I did before. The music passed through me without drawing out any sort of emotion. A chimney sweep yelled my name. I ignored him and kept my eyes directed at my feet.

I felt weird. I survived a brush with death, and somehow that changed me. That night, I voiced my concerns to Melita.

"You're scared he's still out there," she said. She put a hand on my arm. I brushed it away.

"I can't be scared. I have to be the one that's scary."

"You're plenty scary."

I looked down at my hand, covered in gauze. "My stingers broken."

"It will heal."

I stared into Melita's bright red appearance. I'd never seen one of my girls stare at me this way. It was rich with empathy. For a moment, the face of my orphan mother flashed in my head. Melita was nothing like her. Annie and Zadie—they were nothing like her.

"Do you ever worry I'll kill you?" I asked.

"What? No!"

"I've hurt you before."

Melita's eyes left mine. She touched her cheek. "I always thought it was part of the job."

"Maybe I could be more like Jane Cook," I continued. I raised my bandaged hand. "I could still be scary. I could still get respect. I just need to make sure I'm slapping the bad guys."

A Reason to Burn: The Pimp Who Slapped the Ripper

I've been a fan of Evan Witmer's writing since he started taking commissions for foot-fetish fiction to pay his way through grad school. I never put in any requests myself, I swear, but "Sandy Toes" was trending on Literotica for six straight months, so I had to check it out. It's remarkable the detail he'll go into describing a tongue's journey across a freshly shaved callous. It's remarkable because Evan doesn't have any interest in podophilia himself. In fact, he's admitted to finding the genre so disgusting he can only write it on an empty stomach.

Imagine my surprise at reading "The Pimp Who Slapped the Ripper" and finding the details of the Ripper's infamous genital mutilations completely ignored. There was no mention of Annie's uterus being completely removed or the stab marks in Catherine's groin. Mary Kelly goes entirely unmentioned, including the details of her amateur mastectomy. I was looking forward to the flaying of the areola.

My first thought was that Evan had gone soft. Now, I think he's collapsed under the pressure to appeal to a wider audience that wants him to focus less on the gory details and more on the emotional core. That leaves us gorehounds high and dry, and we were the first ones to embrace Evan's abrasive style. It feels unfair. I made a delicious, rare steak to pair with this reading, and now I fear I've wasted it.

What does Evan gain from ditching the edge and going full-on pop? A higher Goodreads score? Is that what writing's boiled down to nowadays? It seems, with the massive volume of self-published works, mainstream appeal has become the highest honor.

Upon further meditation, I think Evan should have quit after *Digest,* and every story in this new collection should be thrown into a fire. Something dry and heavily controlled seems appropriate. Maybe a pile of dead leaves in a Big Green Egg. "The Pimp that Slapped the Ripper" is so watered down I'm afraid it might not burn. Splash a little brake fluid on there just to be safe. The other works in this collection just reinforce that point. There's a salty Western, a cutesy romance, and a political satire—each one step further from his origins in graphic horror and dark fantasy.

If we're going to Keep Witmer Weird, it only starts with book burnings. We've got to bring Evan back to his roots by reminding him of what inspired him to write in the first place: his depression. Devoted fans should humiliate him physically, mentally, and spiritually. Substantiate his deep-seated fears of a blank, meaningless afterlife. Refer to him as "skinny boy" on social media. Poke fun at his floundering love life. If we make him sad again, he'll express his agony through his writing, and we'll see a return to vivisections, eye gouging, and bodily explosions.

- Bloodbath Bibliophile, Michael David Simmons

Washed

Zander Xenarthra woke up naked in the shower, hot water stinging his face. His first reaction was to stand up, but his body kept slipping around the bottom of the tub. He looked down at his skin; it was foamy and glistening. He checked for injuries but couldn't see any cuts or swelling.

Zander threw his body over the edge of the tub. He slipped out with a soft thud. He found himself lying on his bathmat, the memory foam cradling his face. He stared at his towel rack; a bright white linen had gathered a layer of dust in its threads. He pulled it down and wiped himself off.

Zander stood up tall and walked up to the bathroom mirror. He wiped off the steam with his towel, then checked his face; he couldn't see any bruises. He spun around and checked his back in the reflection. The only blemishes were red and purple pimples deep under his skin. They ran down his back, over his ass, and onto the backs of his thighs. Some adults might find acne shocking, but the only strange thing to him was that the bumps and hills were missing their usual sheen.

Within that missing layer of grease, bound to its skin flakes and sebum, were Zander's memories. Now that he'd been cleaned, his memories had been erased. The last thing he could remember was a campout in his backyard two decades ago on his thirteenth birthday. A day later, puberty would begin. After that point, he started storing his memories exclusively on his skin.

Zander wouldn't bathe himself unless under extraordinary circumstances. The process of restarting after having everything wiped clean is extremely intensive. Zander kept checking himself for injuries because he was convinced somebody else was responsible.

Zander left the bathroom and checked the apartment. None of the furniture was toppled or turned. The front door was still in one piece, and the lock was bolted. Zander checked the windows; the one beside the fire escape was left open.

Zander spun around, and the sight of bright red caught his attention. He walked into his entry hallway and stared at the three red picture frames along the wall. They seemed intentionally attention-seeking. The one furthest to the left was a doctor's note dating to his childhood. It exempted him from showers after gym class; the official diagnosis read, "involuntary dermacoding." The frame beside this one held his first paycheck from work. The company's name and address were printed along the top: Lily's Pads, IT Department, 8383 NE Sandy Blvd. Finally, he looked at the picture all the way to the right. If he hung it on the wall, it must mean something. But what was important about a map of Senegal?

Zander, searching for answers, took a bus to the offices of Lily's Pads, where he assumed he must be working. A tent was out front with a couple of young faces tossing free sanitary wipes to passersby. Lily's Pads was a non-profit that got period products into the hands of the homeless, and getting their name out there helped reel in donations. Zander squeezed past the interns and went through the front door.

Once inside, the first floor was a maze of cubicles. Having repeated the labyrinth for several years, he naturally knew which directions to follow like a laboratory mouse. Zander found himself standing in front of an office with a bowl of sugar to the left of its keyboard and a bag of grapefruits behind the monitor. This was undoubtedly Zander's setup; citrus was known for flushing out smells, and Zander needed all the help he could get.

Zander sat down at his desk and picked out a grapefruit. He dug his thumb under the peel. Just out of sight, somebody flashed across the entrance to his cubicle. They seemed busy at first, but then they suddenly returned. Zander didn't see their face, but he heard them sniffing at the air. Then they spoke, "Hey Zanny, I walked past here, and my eyes aren't watering," said the lady. "I think your cleanse is working."

"I'm- sure we work together, but we… are going to need a reacquaintance," explained Zander. "How long have we worked together?" Zander turned his seat to face the woman in his doorway. She was mid-forties, with a black bob. Behind her red glasses, her aged eyes looked concerned.

"Two years," said the woman. "You saw someone die, didn't you?"

"Now, why would you ask that?"

"Well, if you can't remember me… I guess you've washed yourself?" questioned the lady. "I thought maybe you saw something you wanted to forget… but I suppose you wouldn't remember if you did." The woman's serious expression broke, and she smiled politely. She held out her hand very formally. "I'm your HR Director, Cheryl McShaun, and *you're* my greatest project."

"A project?"

"A pet, really," said Cheryl. "I ended up in an organization of all straight white girls, never saw much adversity, and then you suddenly come along and stink up the place."

"They can't fire me for that, can they?" questioned Zander.

"They spun it as a dress-code violation," explained Cheryl. "I fought tooth and nail for you, Zanny."

"Well," Zander nodded earnestly. "I hope I've shown my appreciation…"

"No thanks needed," said Cheryl with a look of confidence. "I used my work with you to secure my position as Director. If anything, *I* owe *you*."

"Then maybe you can help me, Cheryl," inquired Zander. He leaned in close and said it softly. "I think someone I know did this to me…"

"Oh," Cheryl frowned.

"What all do you know about me?"

 "Well, I know you're not married…" listed off Cheryl. "Although I might have assumed you were single due to your condition."

Zander nodded. "So would I."

"Have you checked your phone?" Cheryl stared at Zander's pockets.

"I did on the bus," replied Zander. "There're only six contacts. My landlord, a pizza place, three tech support agents, and the courier guy who delivers my… Kowloon squab."

"That's expensive food, Zanny." Cheryl looked surprised. "You make that much money doing IT?"

Zander shrugged, "Apparently."

"Do you not have a family?"

"I definitely don't have any siblings. Unless my parents had a baby after I was thirteen, but that never was the plan," explained

Zander. "As for my parents, I'm fairly certain they've both expired."

"How do you know?"

"Well, I'd think I'd have them in my phone," answered Zander. "Plus, I have a memory of a family funeral, and neither parent is beside me."

"How would you remember that?"

"Well, sometimes my grime gets trapped *under* my skin… and that doesn't wash away." He turned around and prepared to lift his shirt.

"Zanny, no! Shirts stay on at work," scolded Cheryl. "Use your words…"

"Right, no, right- it's just pimples. They hold onto little blips of disconnected memory. Lots of details are missing."

"That feels like our best bet of getting you some answers," said Cheryl. "What do you see in your blemishes?"

"I see myself at Vital Elements, that organic store downtown," recalled Zander.

"Well, there's nothing really telling about a grocery store," said Cheryl sullenly.

"Right, but I'm in the shampoo aisle…"

"Preparing to clean your brains out, perhaps?"

Zander frowned. "But why?"

"What else can you see?"

"Sometimes I find myself at Bacon Strip... buying *two* BLT burritos."

"I guess there's no point watching your weight if you already look greasy."

Zander glowered. "Cheryl, the other burrito is probably for someone else."

"But you have no friends."

"Maybe I do," pondered Zander. "Maybe I have a friend who doesn't have a cell phone." Zander dropped his grapefruit and stood up. "I'll go to the Bacon Strip and see if it reminds me of anything."

"You can't just leave work…" pointed out Cheryl. She thought for a moment, then shrugged. "…unless I come with? That way, we can call it some form of sensitivity exercise."

"You'd really come with me?" questioned Zander. His head raised; he looked surprised.

"I like helping you, Zander," she said warmly. "I've been defending you so long I've developed a bit of a maternal instinct."

Zander happily accepted Cheryl's company, and the two of them found themselves, an unusual pair, on their way to a strip club in the middle of the day. Bacon Strip wasn't just any eatery; it was one of Portland's most prestigious gourmet strip clubs where the food was just as good, if not better, than the naked dancers.

"Can I see some IDs?" said the girl at the front counter.

Zander pointed to the food app on his phone screen. "Uh, no entrance needed," replied Zander. "We're here for pick-up…"

"What name was on the order?"

"Xenarthra."

"I'll have that ready for you in a minute, sir," the girl behind the counter replied. "We just finished frying your bits."

As the smell of bacon entered his nostrils, Zander felt a slight strain in his legs, as if they were ready to take him somewhere. He had to hold himself back from taking off out the front door. He grabbed onto the edge of the counter and held on tightly. He caught sight of a woman staring at him curiously from inside the club. She began to approach but, surprisingly, walked right past him.

"Cheryl!" hollered the stripper. A tattoo of a pig showed on the woman's tit. It was turned around and bent over, showing off its rump. She had a pasty with a corkscrew on the end of it right over where the pig's tail should be. "Cheryl, it's too good to see you."

"Oh, hey, Madonna!" said Cheryl, reaching for a hug. She saw the corkscrew and lowered her arms. She went in for a handshake instead.

Madonna grabbed it with both hands and shook it wildly. "Cheryl, you're dressed like a CEO."

"Oh, I'm only HR, Madonna," she said modestly, "but it's all I ever wanted."

"Same, girl, same!" Madonna put her hands on her hips and laughed. "Look at us, making it out and thriving. Well, I just wanted to say 'hello'. There's a big tipper who just bought a bottle of Zinfandel." The stripper shook her tooled-up tit. "I feel my services would be appreciated." She waved with her fingertips, then got back to work.

"Pick up for Mr. X!" called out the girl at the front counter. She held up a plastic baggie with the business' logo on the side: A pig in a suit throwing dollar bills into the air. Zander grabbed the bag and pulled out one of the two tinfoil bricks inside.

"I may not have memories, but I still have instincts, especially for things I repeat over and over," he explained to Cheryl. "I just need to initiate them with the proper stimulus." Zander unwrapped the tin foil and unfolded the lip of his tortilla. He held it up under his nose and breathed deeply. Suddenly, his feet were moving again, and he did nothing to stop them this time. Cheryl followed close behind.

Zander's feet led him outside, then surprised him with a sharp turn to the left. Then they made another left; then they took him across the street. Zander's feet were leading them to a yellow tent at a dead end on the other side of the road.

"You feed the homeless?" Cheryl said as she caught up with Zander at the tent. "Zander, I'm proud of you."

Zander reached down and undid the zipper on the front of the tent. The flap flopped over, revealing the cluttered mess inside. Suddenly, a middle finger rose from the opening. It shivered in the air, then retracted. A man's eyes took its place.

"Zander," said the old man. "Zander, why do you look so matte?"

"Well, you see, sir-"

"Sir? You never call me sir!" The old man undid the rest of the flap and climbed out. "Are you Big Zander or Baby Zander?"

This old man had long, grizzled hair with matting at the roots. His hot breath rose upwards into Zander's nostrils. Zander recoiled, "Why do you smell like taro?"

"Ah, so it's *Baby* Zander," said the old man; he nodded slowly. "*I'm* Stink Bird."

"I'm sorry, bud, I'm sure that's a cool, ironic nickname, but I'm gonna need a *real* name," Cheryl said. "HR ladies can't call homeless men stink birds."

"Then call me Bird, lady."

"Oh… alright."

"Zander and I have known each other over several cycles," explained Stink Bird. "He loses his memory every four or five years."

"Wait, you're saying I've been friends with a homeless man for over a decade?"

"Well of course… we're kindred spirits, Zander! We have so much in common: left-handedness, Hyperborean ancestry, and of course… *intertrigo!*" Stink Bird raised his arms and gestured to the dirt coating his body. Stink Bird wore a vintage Blazers sweatshirt; the white stripe across the chest was stained with a hundred shades of brown. On his bottom were a pair of pajamas spotted with Dalmatian faces. The pajamas were riddled with holes and held in so much filth they looked tough as leather.

"I actually know a shelter that would let you shower!" Cheryl interjected.

"So do I!" sneered Stink Bird with an angry expression. He waved about his middle finger. "I'm not dirty 'cause I'm homeless; I'm homeless 'cause I'm dirty!"

"Then why on Earth do you stay dirty?" questioned Cheryl.

"I'm an ablutophobic. I'm afraid to bathe," explained Stink Bird.

"What's there to be afraid of?"

"Norman Bates."

"Oh, honey." Cheryl shook her head. "There's no Norman Bates."

"Trust me… there is." Stink Bird's head dropped.

"Stink Bird," interrupted Zander, "how did I lose my memory in the past?"

Stink Bird raised his head. He seemed stoic. "Well, one time, back in college, you got so black-out drunk you shit your pants at a house party. A bunch of strangers pitied you, took you upstairs, and bathed you. Another time you fell in a pool, and the chlorine took a good chunk of your memory away. More recently, however, you straight up did it to yourself."

"Intentionally?" Zander couldn't believe it. "That doesn't sound like me… or at least the parts of me I can remember."

Stink Bird nodded, completely sure of himself. "You *really* wanted to forget something."

"And what was that?"

Stink Bird appeared shocked by the question. "Zander, I reminded you a few weeks ago, and look how that's turned out… It honestly seems like you might have erased yourself again. You just can't handle this memory."

"Zanny, maybe you should let the memory go," Cheryl suggested.

"Was it a woman?" asked Zander with bright eyes. "Does the sheer mention of her name send me into heartbreak?"

Cheryl snickered a little but tried to hold herself back.

"Cheryl?" questioned Zander. "What's so funny?"

"Zander, I'm sorry… that was adorably optimistic." Cheryl's smile was bleeding through. "I think your condition would make finding a girlfriend incredibly difficult."

"Are you kidding?" Stink Bird scoffed. "Women crave us! We're practically dripping with androstenone. Most people wash theirs off before it reaches effective levels."

"Then why don't I have any girls in my phone?" Zander frowned.

"Well, that's 'cause of *Big* Zander," sighed Stink Bird. "I'm afraid, once your memories build up again, you tend to fall into this pattern where you become a bitter asshole… Y'know, women like a sunny disposition."

"Like you?" scoffed Cheryl.

"Yes, like me!" called out Stink Bird. "Someone in my position either finds his peace or we, well, we… shove off."

Cheryl turned to Zander, who was stuck in a long pause. He was sad to hear that his inner stink was holding him back from relationships far more than his outer stink. He thought about what Stink Bird had said and wondered if that's why he kept cleaning himself voluntarily. Was that his way of trying to *shove off*? Every time he cleaned, it was basically like killing his identity and starting anew.

Suddenly, a low gurgle emanating from Stink Bird's stomach filled the silence. Zander shook himself out of his funk and came to the aid of his friend. He reached into the doggy bag and pulled out Stink Bird's burrito. He pushed it into Stink Bird's hand.

Bird looked disappointed. "Where's my drink?"

"What drink?" questioned Zander.

"You always bring me a burrito *and* my milk tea!" exclaimed Stink Bird.

"Oh," Zander was sad again. He felt like he had left his friend underwhelmed. "I can go get it! Just… where do I go?"

"Boba Queers," Stink Bird pointed to the right of the alley. "Only two blocks that way."

Zander nodded and hurried off to fetch the drink. Meanwhile, Cheryl stayed behind with Stink Bird. At first, they ignored each other, but then Stink Bird coughed loudly and broke the silence. "Say!" he exclaimed. "You work in HR… that's like government work, right?"

"No. It's- it's not."

"So, you would have no idea how to get me a passport?" Stink Bird inched closer. Cheryl could smell the taro.

"You want a… passport?" she asked.

"Yes, yes, a passport," repeated Stink Bird.

"Well, where are you flying, Bird?" asked Cheryl.

"Senegal." He said it so assuredly.

"West Africa?" questioned Cheryl. "Mr. Bird, that's quite different from the streets of Portland…" Cheryl considered it for a second. "It might be much nicer." Cheryl turned around and pointed to the left of the alley. "Go to the shelter on Burnside, and they'll help you get your birth certificate. Then take that to the library, and they can help you get the passport."

"Thank you," said Stink Bird with an earnest nod.

Suddenly, Zander reappeared in the alleyway with a bright purple drink in his hands. He ran it over to Stink Bird, who grabbed the beverage, ripped off the lid with his teeth, and sipped delicately on the brim. "Taro helps with weight loss… no need to be dirty *and* fat."

"Hmm…" Cheryl cocked her head. "I thought you'd lose hope." She turned to Zander, who was polishing off the last few bites of his burrito. A drop of chipotle mayo fell from the emptied wrapping and landed on his shirt. Zander grabbed the bottom hem, then raised the sauce stain to his tongue. Then he paused and let it go before he could lick. He realized if he wanted to remember such a delicious lunch, he'd have to let the residue stay.

Cheryl saw the whole disgusting incident and was suddenly inspired. "Zander, when you woke up naked in the tub, where did you find your clothes?"

"I got new ones out of the closet," Zander answered.

"The ones you had on before your bath; if you found those and tried them on, wouldn't you be wearing your dirt from the day of?" questioned Cheryl. "Wouldn't that let you remember what happened that day?"

Zander crinkled up his tin foil wrap into a little ball, then tossed it into the opening in Stink Bird's tent.

"Hey!" He raised his finger.

"Come on, Cheryl, let's see if we can find those clothes back at my place." He turned to Stink Bird. "I know you say it was me, but I gotta be sure."

Cheryl and Zander hurried back to Zander's apartment across town. Zander led the way in, rushing inside to get started; meanwhile, Cheryl strolled in more slowly. Her eyes were scanning the place in disbelief. She was expecting their search to be more difficult.

"Your home is so pristine!" exclaimed Cheryl. "It's… so unlike you."

"Cheryl, if I could, I would be just like this room," argued Zander. "The dirt doesn't define me; I'm just stuck with it."

Zander passed quickly over his living room furniture. He turned over the cushions and checked beside the legs. Then he searched the bathroom and promptly found it empty besides his used towel. All that was left was his bedroom. He threw open the closet door and saw everything folded and hung neatly in place. Then, he turned to his hamper. He stepped on the pedal at the bottom and flipped open the lid.

"It's empty." He seemed aggravated. "Everything's washed… doesn't that seem suspicious?"

"Maybe you washed them before you showered?" suggested Cheryl. "That way, you wouldn't find them and remember something."

"Right…" sighed Zander. "*Something.*" Zander rummaged through the end table drawer. He didn't find any clothes, but he found a flashlight. He got down on the floor and began shining the beam under his bed. "Oh, what have we here!" Zander threw his arm far under the mattress and reached for the wall at the other end. His hand grasped around something small and fabric. He yanked it out and held it up in front of his face.

Cheryl cocked her head to the side. She was staring at a felt green beanie. "You think that was on your head before you showered?" she asked. "Zander, that's probably been under there far longer."

"Perhaps," said Zander, "but a lead's a lead." He opened the hat like a pocket and stuck the flashlight over the opening. He stared into its illuminated depths. The inside was coated in loose hairs and yellow scales. He clicked off the flashlight and tossed it onto his bed. Then he grabbed the brim with both hands and stretched it wide. He closed his eyes and pulled it snugly over his head.

Suddenly, flashes of a trailer park appeared in the back of his head. He saw a wife with an enormous red afro in a pair of beat-up overalls. He felt a deep feeling of admiration for her as she beat eggs into a creamy, blonde omelet. She looked up and smiled at him. Then Zander saw a pair of kids waiting for their food beside him. There was an older boy and his sister. They looked nothing like him, but they had the woman's red hair. They were laughing over an activity book full of crosswords. Zander felt overwhelmingly proud for a moment. The happiness peaked with a shot of them sharing breakfast, then quickly, the feeling twisted into guilt. The bright, colorful scenery faded. He saw a back alley lit by a shadowy moon. He made deals in the dark with burly men dressed in all black. They followed him inside a rundown bar where they cut lines of cocaine in the bathroom. Then the scenery changed; this time it blurred. His surroundings were rushing past him. He saw himself driving a truck down the highway. Bright orange barrels filled with hazardous chemicals bounced around in the back. It was raining on the road; the wheels of his vehicle splashed in the potholes. Zander felt a sick thrill in his chest. One of the barrels in the back stuck out. He saw the inside of it. The chemicals were swapped for stacks upon stacks of pesos. His happiness returned.

"What on Earth did I get up to?!" shouted Zander. He quickly pulled the hat off. It all vanished in a flash. "Cheryl, I think I might be living a double life." He turned to face her, but she was no longer standing in the doorway.

She stood in the entry hallway, gazing at the pictures on the wall. The red frames had also attracted her attention, especially the one surrounding the map. "Senegal," he said softly. "Bird mentioned Senegal after you left to get his milk tea, and now… here it is in your home." She pulled the map off the wall. "This can't be a coincidence."

"Roll it up and take it with us," commanded Zander. "I think it might be related to some sort of smuggling I've been up to. When I put on the hat, I'm driving proceeds connected to… some abysmal things."

Cheryl shook her head. "Zander, the hat looks like it's from forever ago. I'm sure it's far in your past. Something dumb you did in your twenties."

"I wanted to warn you in case things get ugly."

"Oh, I'm not worried about it. We all have a bad past!" laughed Cheryl. "Zanny, you know I've been to jail. I'm no prude…."

"You have?"

Cheryl nodded and gave a sweet, little shrug. "Nobody's perfect, honey."

"What for, might I ask?"

"I'm a pretty *cool* HR lady," she explained. "I used to rob liquor stores."

"...I had no idea," exclaimed Zander.

"Oh yeah, lots of HR ladies are felons, actually," explained Cheryl. "It's a popular choice after rehabilitation. Oregon State Penitentiary will certify you while you're incarcerated. You just need two years of classes... I was serving a ten-piece."

Zander shook his head and looked at his feet. "Then, I'm gonna count on you to be the tough gal if we run into anyone shady... I'm not this *Big* Zander that apparently does crazy drug deals with mobsters. Right now, I'm just... *Baby Zander.*"

Cheryl nodded and led the way out of the apartment door. Zander put back on the beanie as they drove to the trailer park that he saw in his mind's eye. He could see the sign next to the front gate: Goosegroin Mobile Home Corral. It was only a half-hour away.

By the time they arrived, the sun had set, and the stars appeared through the deepening blue. The many sounds of the trailer park echoed through the crisp autumn air: the low gurgle of a tallboy opening, the cry of a baby wavering on a porch swing, the mutant growl of an engine-swapped jalopy.

They came up the steps of a granite-blue deck and walked up to a sandy-white door. Cheryl kept staring at Zander, waiting for him to decide the next move.

"Do you own this place?" asked Cheryl.

Zander nodded. "That's what it feels like."

"Then can't you just… open it?"

Zander nodded. He twisted the knob, and it moved without resistance. He gave the door a little pressure; then it popped open.

"Hey, what the-" A deep voice started howling inside. "Now, what the!" Heavy footsteps rushed up to the door. Someone grabbed the door from inside, then pulled it backward, yanking the knob from Zander's hand. A tall, tan man with a long hairless head stood in the doorway. "What are you doing barging into my home?" he snarled. "People 'round here carry guns, you idiot."

The tall man's face tilted downwards, pointing into Zander's eyes. Then they slowly crept back upwards, staring at his hat. Zander stared back, mainly at the white speckles sprinkled over the shoulders of the tall man's black sweater.

"Are you wearing my hat?" questioned the tall man.

"That… could make sense," Zander raised his hand to his chin. "*You* live in a trailer. Do *you* have a red-headed wife and two kids?"

"Yes!" exclaimed the man, with a look of suspicion. "They're out shopping for a grill."

"And *you* smuggled money for the mob?'

"What?!" The man's anger flipped to fright. "Oh god, are you FBI?" He looked Zander up and down. "No- you're not FBI," he relaxed for a second; then it dawned on him—only one other man might know about his past. "Get the fuck in here!"

Cheryl chased after Zander as his body was dragged inside and tossed onto a lumpy brown sofa. Cheryl took her seat beside him.

"You're the one that dropped communication with me, man!" The tall man's words were rushed, panicked.

"I'm not sure what to say…" Zander rubbed at the brush burn on his neck from when the man yanked his shirt.

"You're the Fetid Giant…" He stumbled over his words. "The Fetid Giant that sees for miles…"

"Who?"

"The man that's been blackmailing me!" The tall man reached into a phone book and pulled out a letter hidden halfway inside. He slammed it down on the glass table between them.

"I wouldn't…." Zander stared at the note in front of him. It was addressed to the tall man, Paul Smith. It detailed all the crimes Zander previously thought were his own, then followed with instructions to prevent their release. "*By the end of the day, leave three thousand dollars under the roots of the big-leaf maple in the center of Pigeon Park.*"

"I only checked my mail after work," grunted Paul. "You gave me six hours to figure out what a *big-leaf maple* is and find it in the middle of four-hundred acres."

Zander looked back down at the note. He continued, "*Check your mail daily and await further instructions. Your secret is still in jeopardy.* Signed: *The Fetid Giant.*"

"Only you never followed up!" shouted Paul. He plopped down in his recliner. "Which left me wondering, is this fucker just gonna turn me in? But now you're here, right in front of me, wearing *my* hat. What's that supposed to mean anyways? That you've been snooping through my garbage? Is that how you know so much about me?"

"That's a lot of questions," replied Zander, sitting up on the couch. He took off the hat and handed it over. "Paul, I have a form of psychometry. I can read the dirt contacting my skin. Wearing your hat, I read your dandruff and… I saw your crimes."

Paul held his face in amazement. "Of course, it'd be something I could never have controlled for… otherwise, I've been so careful. It seemed impossible for somebody to know! It's driven me mad."

"Paul, I do not intend to use this information against you. I'm-not the same person as I was."

"What's that supposed to mean?"

"He's lost his memory," called out Cheryl. "He's been miraculously returned to innocence."

"If I've threatened you in the past, I was in a bad place," explained Zander. "It seems I've put all that bad stuff behind me. I washed it away."

"So had I!" Paul snarled through gritted teeth. "It takes some nerve to bring up my past when I've got a family to care for now." He stood up out of his chair. "I was terrified of losing my kids."

"I'm sorry."

"Sorry?" Paul shook his head and grabbed the letter off the table. He tore it to pieces. "I don't know how I was so scared of you… you're no giant! Fuck, I'm twice as tall as you…" He took a long step over his table and cocked his fist. "I'm gonna kick your ass."

Cheryl suddenly leaped up from her chair and reached for a nearby shelf she'd been eyeing in case things got messy. She grabbed a green bottle potting a rose. She threw away the flower and smashed the bottle's bottom on the windowsill. "Have you ever threatened an ex-con before?" She swung the jagged edge around in the air. "'Cause it's a pretty stupid idea."

"Jesus Christ!" Paul retracted his leg and hobbled backward. He fell back in his seat and covered his face with his arms.

"Come on!" she pulled him up off the sofa. "Get out! Get out!" Zander followed her instructions and dashed out the door. Cheryl screamed a few more threats toward Paul before tossing the rest of the bottle at the wall and bolting to their car.

"What was that?" she scolded. "Blackmailing people? That's how you afford your Kowloon squall?!"

"I'm as surprised as you are."

"Listen, criminal to criminal, that's despicable."

"You robbed people, too," replied Zander.

"I stole one hundred dollars from a cashier. You threatened to take away a man's family," replied Cheryl. "I can't help but imagine, what if someone used my past against me like that?"

"But as you said, it's in the past."

"A few days ago," sighed Cheryl. "I can't be associated with an active criminal. I already have a record; they'll think I'm helping you."

"He was a bad guy. He knew what types of activities that money paid for," figured Zander. "If I'm only picking on bad folks, that's like an anti-hero."

"I'm sorry, but any way you explain it, it's extortion," Cheryl stopped the car. "I'm afraid I'm gonna have to ask you to get out here." Her knuckles tightened around her steering wheel. "Please tell people this was all just training. We confronted our prejudices with sex workers, homelessness, and trailer occupancies."

Zander thought he'd get dropped off at the office, but they were in a parking lot next to the woods. "Where is this?"

"Pigeon Park," said Cheryl. "This is where you belong." She unlocked the doors. "Go check the tree. I'm sure you've got money waiting for you."

Zander tilted his jaw, then stepped out of the car. "I'll see you at work tomorrow." Cheryl didn't reply. Zander shut the door, and she quickly drove off.

Zander followed his instructions and crossed the trail surrounding the forest. He pushed further and further into the dense, green interior. As he went further, his instincts took control, directing him through the gaps in the trees. It took him twenty-five minutes to reach the center.

There it stood, the big-leaf maple. It drew Zander in and brought him to his knees. He reached behind its exposed roots and found the money—lots more money. Zander's first reaction was to stuff it in his pockets, but slowly he realized what he was doing and stopped. He tossed it all back out onto the dirt.

He touched his face and shook his head. He couldn't believe he resorted to blackmailing. He didn't *need* the money. He did it out of spite. Big Zander wasn't just bitter; he was sadistic.

He spun around and leaned his back against the tree. He breathed deeply and slowly opened his eyes. The night was dark, but he could see the shape of a rock sitting atop a nearby ledge. On its face grew a thick layer of moss with a barren streak surrounding a crack in the stone. The shape of the moss looked just like Senegal.

Zander's body tensed up. His breathing spiked as he approached the moss and laid his hands upon the fur. It tickled his palms as they lowered down to the soil. It was loose, so he began digging.

His hand hit something hard while grasping at the earth. He squinted his eyes; it was blue plastic. He swiped away the dirt and found the top of a rolling briefcase. He yanked it out of the hole. He cringed and undid the zipper around the edge. He flung open the flap.

Inside were files, huge stacks of them. He wasted no time gawking and tore into the first one on top. *"Linda Coutheright, Sweater,"* it read along the edge. It detailed her life in three short paragraphs; she was a baker with a short temper living with her mother. Then it described her crime: threatening an assistant with a knife. It followed with a checkmark next to the word "Payment," then ended with a blank section, "Further Ideas."

Zander plucked more files. They each had a name followed by a garment, most being hats, others being sweaters, a few being scarves, and one being a pair of earmuffs. He stopped pulling them out when he recognized one of the names: *"Paul Smith, Winter Hat."* Zander froze for a second, then flipped open the folder. Inside, the "Further Ideas" section was not just filled in but took up three whole pages. It was a plan; a big, disgusting plan; all designed by Big Zander.

Baby Zander's face tightened. All this anger he felt when near the rock and seeing the files had to come from something *significant*. Something made Big Zander want to dirty the entire world, or at least most of Portland. Zander knew only one man could shed some light on this. He needed Stink Bird to tell him the truth this time.

It took him two hours to leave the woods and get a taxi back to Argay, where he could confront his supposed friend. When he arrived at the tent, strange noises bounced off the alley's walls: two breaths overlapping each other, their paces slowly converging into synchronicity. Zander walked up to the flap and tore the zipper downwards.

"Hey- ay!" shouted Stink Bird. He quickly flung his body off a woman beneath him and simultaneously pulled a sleeping bag over both their bodies. "Jesus, Baby Zander, do you not even remember what sex sounds like? Knock first!"

"Cheryl!" exclaimed Zander peeking at the woman inside. "What the Hell are you doing with Stink Bird?"

"Honestly, I came here to get answers, much like you are," she explained, feeling around Stink Bird's garbage for her top. "It seems I was seduced."

"It's the androstenone, man," laughed Stink Bird. "Stop denying its powers."

"I have questions, but I have no patience to sleep with you, Stink Bird. I need you to fess up to what you've done." Zander threw Paul's file into the tent. "You knew about this, didn't you?"

Stink Bird stared at the file in disbelief. "You found your cache... how'd you get to and from Senegal in under a few hours?"

"There's no Senegal involved, you idiot. It's a Senegal-shaped landmark."

"Don't call me an idiot!" Stink Bird snarled. "I didn't fail the system. The school system failed me. I didn't get a *doctor's note*, like your privileged ass. Back then, when you didn't shower before school, they slapped you with a paddle and turned you away."

"You didn't have a disease," argued Zander. "You could have showered."

"Ablutophobia *is* a disease!" growled Stink Bird. "My mind is scarred by Tyler Vanosos."

"I've never heard of him."

"He's my Norman Bates... the man that robbed my house when I was a kid. I was in the shower; he pulled back the curtain and held me at gunpoint." Stink Bird shivered and wrapped his arms around his body. "He kept asking if I knew where my parents kept their money. I didn't... but I couldn't... make... words." Stink Bird's jaw tightened up as he remembered. Cheryl came up behind Stink Bird and held him tightly, trying her best to settle his convulsions.

Zander felt guilty. "I'm... sorry." He relaxed and fell out of his accusatory stance. He sat down on the pavement in front of the tent and looked at Stink Bird eye to eye. "It's just... you saw my doctor's note... and you know about Senegal, so you've clearly been to my apartment."

"So what?" Stink Bird grumbled. He threw Cheryl off his shoulders.

"Then, did *you* bathe me?!"

"No!" argued Stink Bird. "Nobody bathed you… *you idiot!*" He flung about his finger. "You got caught in the rain!" He pointed to the start of the alley. "I found you drooling only a few feet away from my tent. I took you home."

"And you made it seem like I bathed myself!"

"Yes…" sighed Stink Bird. "I tried to get rid of Big Zander. Remove all traces of Operation Snowflakes."

"Operation Snowflakes?"

"You followed people home from the dandruff shampoo aisle," explained Stink Bird. "You'd rummage through their garbage and find their old clothes laced with their flakes. You'd try it on and use their memories to blackmail them."

"You wanted the money, didn't you?" questioned Zander. "You thought you could find it before I could remember it existed."

"Yes, but there *is* more to it," said Stink Bird earnestly. "You see, you… had this plan."

"I know the plan," said Zander sullenly. "It's in that file… I was going to blackmail Paul into driving a truck full of metam sodium into Bull Run."

"Why on Earth…" called out Cheryl.

"If I contaminated our water supply… nobody showers." Zander's head dropped. "I'd make everyone *like me.*"

"You were pushed to the brink," explained Stink Bird. He looked at his friend with pity. "Driven to madness. They… they made a mockery of you."

"You can't tell me," said Zander.

"I'd thought you were begging me to know…"

"Stink Bird, I should thank you," replied Zander. "You stopped me from making a huge mistake. I don't want to know what they did to me that made me so angry. I don't want to be angry like that ever again."

"You just wait; Big Zander will still find his way out," frowned Stink Bird. "As long as the world treats the dirty like dirt, you'll eventually seek justice."

"I think there's a way I can take the abuse… and not want to poison a lake," explained Zander. "But I'm going to need both of your help."

"What other way?" questioned Cheryl.

Stink Bird nodded; he had the same question.

As the dawn rose in Portland, Cheryl and Stink Bird waited outside Zander's bathroom door as he began to undress. Zander never liked the feeling of being dirty. Even after just one day without showering, his body felt heavy with scum. Due to his condition, he could never recall that glorious feeling of stepping into a hot shower and having the weight of all that dirt lifted from your head. Zander looked forward to it.

Zander pulled off his socks and threw them into a pile of clothes for Stink Bird to burn. He stepped under the steaming water and let the droplets prick at his skin. It felt luxurious, like stepping into a warm embrace. Slowly, the sludge of life melted away and circled his drain. The feeling of being washed was like a weight being lifted when someone finally forgives themselves.

Zander slowly became woozy, and his head was enveloped in numbness. He lowered himself down to the floor of his bathtub and curled up into a ball. He rested the side of his head on the acrylic and went into a deep sleep.

When Zander woke up, he would be completely dried off, re-clothed, and carried far away from his apartment. He was now lying in a tent in an alley in the middle of Argay, convinced that's where he's been living for over a decade. He felt the clothes placed on his body: a browning Blazers sweatshirt and starchy pajama bottoms covered in dogs.

Zander was wearing Stink Bird's clothes and, with that, his grime, the same grime that had accumulated over the fifty-five years of Stink Bird's existence. Wearing Stink Bird's clothes, Zander held his memories as his own. The memory of a life he didn't live, but one he thought he might prefer.

Zander willingly took on Stink Bird's identity. He acquired his better luck with women, his propensity to milk tea, and his superior outlook on their stinky situation. While Big Zander longed for vengeance, Stink Bird had long ago "found his peace." Wearing his clothes, Zander took on his immunity to "shoving off."

Meanwhile, Stink Bird abandoned his whole life as a gift to his friend. In exchange, he became Cheryl's next project. They cut his hair and began to challenge his fear of bathing using Cheryl's genius strategy.

"You promise you won't leave?" he asked Cheryl. He was standing naked in the bathroom of her apartment.

"I promise," smiled Cheryl. She held back the shower curtain and beckoned Stink Bird to follow her inside. "Come on in…"

Stink Bird took a deep breath and stepped inside the tub. Cheryl's cool, naked body immediately embraced him. Then, she reached behind Stink Bird's back and started the water. Stink Bird felt the shower stream mixing in with the tears running down his face. He wiped his hands over his face and cleared his vision. He saw Cheryl smiling back at him. Showering was much less scary when he wasn't doing it alone.

A Reason to Burn: Washed

There are many meanings behind burnings. The noblest is the elimination of the past. It is our right as human beings to start anew, given we make amends with anyone we've wronged. In my case, the first person I cheated was my former self.

From eighteen to twenty-five, I cheated a young Evan Witmer out of a life of normality by shirking my responsibilities to keep my temple clean. I would brush my teeth only once a week and shower every three days or so. I'd never wash my clothes, and my sheets were covered in dried blood, vomit, and cum. My roommates throughout undergrad were silent witnesses to my horror show, clearly dismayed but unable to muster the courage to call me out. In college, there are much bigger stressors to handle than a dirty roommate. Still, I owe them my gratitude for enduring my clear deficiencies, especially the young Pakistani man who found a pair of my jeans coated in feces between our beds and still decided to be my roommate the following year.

Averse to deodorant, my body odor fouled during large, crowded parties. It was embarrassing to my initial set of friends, and I would stop being invited to their gatherings. This abandonment contributed significantly to the loneliness I felt during college. I was lucky enough to find a different friend group that was less concerned about looks and smells, and they saved me from complete isolation. I thank them.

Dating was hard but not impossible, especially during a small streak of cleanliness I mustered during my first year of graduate school. The feeling of maturity that came with post-grad, combined with an exceptionally motivating new roommate, turned me into the best version of myself. I met the first love of my life and later ruined it over a three-year decline back into foulness.

This girlfriend expected the bare minimum, which I could not achieve. I was a terrible partner. I left the kitchen sink full of dirty dishes, and the dishes that I did wash were half-assed and blotchy. Additionally, the vacuum wasn't used, and the refrigerator's walls were caked in spilled food. Things were made even worse by an enormous pet rabbit who could swallow a house cat. I allowed him to move freely throughout my apartment. He refused to use his litter box and would leave small, dry droppings all over the carpet that I would pick up with my bare hands to dispose of. I wouldn't wash my hands afterward, and then I'd go and handle food. My friends were terrified to try my cooking, and to those who did try it—I'm lucky I didn't poison you.

My girlfriend asked me to shave, shower, and deodorize. When I didn't, she lost attraction and fell out of love with me. Near the end of our relationship, I began taking medication for my bipolar disorder, and things were just starting to get better. I found the energy to clean myself and the apartment, still half-assed, but there was finally an active effort again. It was too little too late, however. There were many contributing factors to our breakup, but there's no denying the connection to my slothfulness.

I've had two girlfriends since the first love of my life, one of which I lived with. She was highly OCD, and so I learned the skill of "deep cleaning," as she called it. I was slightly resistant to her extreme ways (cleaning doorknobs seemed a little excessive). Still, our relationship had a lasting effect on me and seemed to push me into "clean enough" territory.

I am not cured. I still have days when the scum builds up in my bathroom sink, my toilet turns brown, or my hamper overflows. However, this only lasts a day or two before I have a big "clean day meltdown" and reset my apartment into pristine condition. I encourage myself through the thought of a new girlfriend coming over and saying those instantly gratifying terms, "You're pretty clean for someone your age."

By burning "Washed" and encouraging others to do the same, I am fulfilling a destiny of sorts. Zander Xenarthra is the old Evan Witmer. Therefore, by destroying this manuscript, I am symbolically disintegrating my previous abnormalities in favor of a cleaner, healthier life. My skin is less spotted; I don't offend when I lift my arms, and my teeth have returned to eggshell white. May this great cleansing fire wash away the past.

- Auteur Aromatique, Evan Witmer

An American Weekend

For some, Friday starts the moment they walk out of the office, but not everyone is privileged with a ten-minute commute. For people like Austin, it's an additional forty-minute drive home before the feeling of Friday washes over him. He does his best to shorten the trip mentally by playing something fun on the radio.

"Take your medicine, Austin!" shouted the agile voice of a late millennial, putting on fake Texas gruffness. "It's four o'clock, which means we've got happy hour starting at Pour Hole, Batty's Pub, and The Yes & When..."

Austin was named Austin long before Austin moved to Austin. He was a transplant from Phoenix, and his parents were originally from Senegal. Before he got the job at Dell Headquarters, he didn't realize there were such populated places bearing his name. Since he arrived, he's enjoyed hearing people address the whole city and imagining they were just talking to him.

"Plenty of people are dining outside... seventh straight day of sunshine..." continued the show's host. "Considering it's May, Austin is unusually dry..."

Austin frowned. He shook his head, then cracked open a Dr. Pepper he took from the vending machine outside his cubicle. "I'm working on it..." he said to himself. He took a sip.

By the time the drink was finished, Austin's ride home was completed. He parked along the street outside his apartment in

Clarksville. He went inside and immediately began to strip. It was casual Friday, so his shirt was a comfy short sleeve, but he was still required to wear khakis and loafers, neither of which breathed well enough for this heat. He leaned against the arm of his sofa and pulled off his left shoe.

"Oh," grumbled a voice from the other side of the couch. "How was work, Austin? Any better?" Austin's leaning had jostled awake one of his roommates, Benny. The apartment only had two bedrooms, so Benny slept on the couch and kept his belongings in the hollow of the footrest. Benny's workday started at six-thirty and ended at three; this gave him an hour and forty minutes to nap before his roommates made it home. At that point, he'd have to exert himself keeping up with their dissipation.

"My day…" sighed Austin. "This whole week was…"

"A Fat Cock in the Hole," Antonio, the other roommate, appeared in the kitchen and slid three martini glasses forward on the granite of the serving window. Each cordial consisted of a beige cream with an orange splatter spreading outwards from its center. "It's donut-flavored liqueur with a splash of orange chicken sauce."

"That sounds terrible," said Austin, staring at the drink.

"I'm still coming out of my stupor," mumbled Benny, rubbing his eyes. "Did you say orange chicken?"

"It's from Weird City Bartender," said Antonio, holding up a picture of a brightly dressed man on his Instagram. "Don't be so stiff. It tastes like an orange Tootsie-Roll pop."

"I'm not stiff," rejoined Austin. He quickly snatched the drink and sipped long and loudly on the brim. His eyes opened in surprise as the drink left his lips. "It's like a chocolate-flavored screwdriver." Impressed with the drink's surprising quality, Austin downed the whole glass and asked for another.

"It's not *that* good…" Antonio's eyes pinched. "Trying to get drunk? I suspect someone's feeling lonely."

"I don't need to get drunk to talk to a woman."

"Austin had a hot date just last night," chimed in Benny.

"Really? You should invite her out…" suggested Antonio.

"No, no," chuckled Austin. "It didn't go well…"

Antonio and Benny waited for him to continue. Austin's forced smile just vanished, then he went quiet and still.

"You want to follow up on that?" questioned Antonio.

Austin shook his head and mouthed the word "Nah," but the only sound to make it out was the snap of his lips and an inaudible whisper.

Antonio was worried for his friend. He grabbed some shot glasses and poured out more donut liqueur, topping each off with a splash of plain vodka. He figured he might be able to loosen the clasp on his friend's jaw with a couple of strong drinks and a few friendly faces. They took their shots, then got a rideshare to meet their friends at The Yes & When. Cassie and Jessie were waiting at the table, talking about their recent decision to move in together while Ari fetched them all some drinks.

"*I'm* not moving your bed all the way to my place," said Cassie with a sly grin.

"We both can't fit on yours," countered Jessie.

"*I* can fit on the mattress," said Cassie, patting the rounds of his chest. "And *you* can fit on top of *me*... I'm very soft."

"Stop with the PDA, Austin's having lady problems," shouted Antonio over the crowd's roar. "No need to rub it in."

"I'll speak for myself, Tony," said Austin.

"But that's just it—you *haven't* spoken on it at all," complained Antonio. "Please, how was your week?"

"Absolute Dogshit," said Ari, returning from the bar. Their hand carried a plastic platter with a dozen shooters spread out across the surface. Each shot had a brown swirl floating at the top. "Absolut vodka, Bird Dog Whiskey, and a dollop of chocolate mousse," Ari listed the ingredients.

"Is this housemade mousse?" asked Cassie, eyeing it excitedly.

"Guys, quiet," barked Antonio. "He's finally going to speak."

Austin threw back his dogshit and let it lead the way forward. "The date yesterday went horrible, but I already know it's my fault. I'm just trying to move past it."

"But what made it horrible?" asked Ari, taking their seat.

"I took an edible beforehand. She got to know an exceedingly rare side of me," explained Austin, "It completely backfired. We started talking about our favorite movies. I walked her through the entire plot of Run Lola Run. It took me two hours to finish— it's only an eighty-minute movie!"

"You have a date every other week," said Cassie. "It's not the end of the world."

Austin shrugged. He still looked miserable.

"Well, it must feel good to have that out in the open," said Antonio with a warm grin.

"No," said Austin bluntly. "It's actually really hard to get my thoughts to stop cycling, and when I say it out loud, it just picks up faster and louder."

"Or maybe there's just more bothering you?" questioned Jessie.

Austin huffed. "Well, I had this mix-up with my prescriptions on Wednesday. Then on Tuesday, I got slimed."

The friend circle tightened. Everyone stared. Some looked genuinely concerned. Others looked with morbid curiosity.

Austin seemed visibly uncomfortable. He was reliving that disastrous week all over again. His head dropped. "And then on Monday…"

Suddenly Austin stopped as a strange sensation bubbled near his naval. The orange chicken sauce had mixed poorly with the cream of the liqueur, curdling into something sharp and putrid. It stung his lower intestine.

Austin quickly excused himself and headed towards the bathroom, only to find the line was eight people out the door. Feeling he might not be able to hold it, he decided to exit the premises and find a shorter line to deal with.

Outside, there were lines of young people lining up at the front doors of the adjoining bars. Even the dives were unusually popular that night. Austin looked to the restaurants instead. Most were closed for the evening, but he saw a light on at the end of the block. As he hobbled down the street, stomach trembling, his hopes were raised as he got closer. It was a bagel joint, Friggin' Good, opened unusually late. Without many people craving egg sandwiches at this hour, the line was non-existent. Austin hurried inside with ease.

"Bathroom?" he said, trying to stand up straight and look normal.

The woman behind the counter raised her head from her phone. "ID."

"ID?" Austin griped.

"ID…" repeated the girl. She held out her hand and snapped her finger.

Impatiently, Austin reached into his pocket and pulled out his wallet. He slid the license out of its slit and placed it in the girl's hand.

The woman nodded, then handed it back. "Right this way." She pointed to a steel door behind her. It looked like the gateway to the kitchen area.

"I can go behind the counter?"

The woman's face remained stagnant. She nodded. She pulled a lever underneath the counter, and a section of the counterwall folded backward.

Austin went through the gap, then hurried through the metal door behind the cashier. He ran inside expecting to find ovens, grills, and a glorious staff bathroom somewhere along the wall, but instead, the world inside was unexpectedly chaotic.

It seemed he'd wandered into a speakeasy, not that there have been any real legal limits on alcohol since 1933. The "fun" of these speakeasies lies in their secrecy from the general public. The appeal being if you're lucky enough to find one, you feel as though you are part of a clever elite.

Lucky for Austin, because the *real* Friggin' Good was well hidden, its capacity was nowhere near full. Austin was, therefore, able to use the latrine in the back instantaneously. His business inside was a long endeavor, however, and by the time he emerged, the population inside the bar had doubled, making escape more difficult.

Austin stood still for a second unable to find a route penetrating the crowd. His anxiety began to soar again.

"Take your medicine Austin!" said a cheery voice behind the bar. Austin turned to see a bartender place a glass horn in front of an empty seat to his left. The horn stood up straight with the help of a wooden stand wrapped around its midsection. Inside the horn were amber liquids, too flat to be beer. "It's mead," said the bartender, enticing Austin to sit down and have a sip. "Come on, try it. It's nice and basic compared to the other junk you've had tonight."

Austin couldn't fight her logic, even though her logic seemed to rely on events she couldn't possibly know. Austin took the seat, then gazed the bartender in the eye. She looked unfamiliar; her wispy curls were bleached and dyed silver. It looked like a soft cloud was resting on her head and flowing down onto her shoulders. She wore a long, gold apron over a white blouse and pants.

"Have we met?" asked Austin.

"Do you know a girl named Friday?"

Austin pursed his lips and shook his head.

"Then we haven't met formally," she said with a smile. She reached over the counter and snatched up Austin's fingertips. She greeted him gracefully. *"I'm* Friday."

"And I thought *my* name was renowned... you must feel flattered every time you hear TGIF."

"Well, yes!" laughed Friday. "I've earned my praise. I'm the best bartender in this city. I deliver peace of mind." Friday tapped the tip of the glass horn's curl.

Austin acknowledged the suggestion and held up the glass to his lips. He hadn't had mead before, so he didn't know whether to chug it like beer or sip it like liquor. He took a little bit too much, and it burned his throat.

"Woof!" exclaimed Austin. "That's very strong... Are you trying to loosen me up, too?"

"Pardon?"

"You know, get me drunk so that you can yank the life story out of me. Isn't that what good bartenders do? Listen to us drunks ramble?"

"Not the good ones, no," said Friday with a sullen glance. "I'm afraid my field's become infested with selfish ears, looking to speed up their time at work by digging into other people's business... but that's not how *Friday* works."

"No?"

"No! If your week was horrible, then I'm the hard stop!" explained the barkeep. "We all need a break from the madness; it's the first step in letting it go. You need to feel free of its effects to see how little it really matters. Tonight, I want you to forget." Friday tapped the horn again. "This should help—so should a good distraction—you like darts?"

"Oh," Austin chuckled shyly. "I've got no aim."

"Then how about a soothing conversation?" asked Friday. "Have you met Grace?"

Friday reached over the bar and grabbed the stool cushion beside Austin. She spun it around with a quick whip of her wrist. The person beside Austin was suddenly face-to-face with him. It was a cute girl, short, broad, and blonde, dressed in a tight denim jacket. She was a little bit younger than he'd normally date. Not that he'd have to date her to engage in some light-hearted discussion.

"So, what's the wackiest thing you've ever seen on the Metro?!" asked Grace, trying to break the ice. She spoke with bombastic hand gestures to highlight her words.

"I've actually never taken the bus," shrugged Austin. "I take my car."

"Cars, huh?" Grace's enthusiasm was unwavering. "I can do cars too! What's your dream car?"

"A red 1984 Audi Quattro," responded Austin.

"And what car do you drive now?"

"A red 1984 Audi Quattro."

"Oh… so you've got your dream car?" exclaimed Grace. "That's exciting!"

"It's actually in the shop."

"Oh?"

"I honked at some drunk bitch on Thursday blocking the lane. She smashed my headlight with her heel."

"Oh… I'm- I'm so sorry."

"I was driving while high, so I couldn't call the cops either…."

"Y-you know what, I don't think Grace is working," interrupted Friday. She quickly grabbed Grace's seat and spun it around until she faced the other direction. "Goodbye, Grace… hello Aeneas!" When Friday turned the stool around again, the jean jacket was now filled with a fashionable older male of relatively the same proportions.

Aeneas snapped his fingers beside his ears. "Who likes to talk about old cartoons?" he said with a carefree, Bushian twang.

"Like, are we talking favorite characters or deep headcanon?"

"I was actually wondering which Scooby-Doo villains you think you could take in a fight?"

"Is this assuming they're actual monsters or still just dudes in masks?"

"Actual monsters."

"Okay then," Austin sipped his drink and nodded with a legitimate interest. "Aeneas'll do."

The two made the most of this riveting conversation over the next two hours. As they downed their honey wine, they discussed how the Creeper, like most hunchbacks, would have terrible athletic abilities and could be quickly incapacitated. Meanwhile, they agreed that Charlie the Robot could probably tear their limbs off and that the Ghost Clown could hypnotize them into suicide.

Austin and Aeneas became best friends for the night. Their conversation only ended when midnight rolled around, and Friday needed her herald to calm the qualms of some other poor soul who had just sat down to Aeneas' right. Friday grabbed Aeneas' stool and flipped him around. He changed into a tall redhead mid-turn and greeted the girl now in front of her. "You come here often?"

The girl shook her head. "I was just looking for a night bagel…."

Meanwhile, Friday leaned over the counter and asked Austin. "How are you feeling now?"

Austin's eyes flickered. "Relaxed… and a little drunk- like one of those cows in Kobe beef!" His face looked noticeably different from the last time they spoke. The little crinkles in his brow were gone.

"Good. Looks like we got to you before they reached the core."

"What's a-," stuttered Austin, drunkenly, "a core is…?"

"It's the central disaster that cracked the foundation. Its aura shakes the rest of the surrounding week," explained Friday. "If you were to repeat that in your head, its effects could last the rest of the month."

"So, I just… bottle it up?"

"Until tomorrow, sacred cow," said Friday, sliding a check under Austin's nose. "That's when your *adventure* begins."

"What adventure?" asked Austin, signing his name on the bill.

"Saturday."

After leaving Friggin' Good behind, Austin checked the window outside The Yes & When and didn't see his friends sitting inside. They never stayed out past midnight anymore, and so he imagined they all headed home. Austin figured he'd do the same.

His rideshare took him back to Clarksville. Entering his apartment, it seemed he'd missed a hell of an afterparty. Everyone from the bar had passed out; except Benny, who was nowhere to be seen. Jessie and Cassie were snuggling on his couch, fully clothed, while Ari lay naked under their Flokati rug with a large human-sized lump between their knees.

Austin tried his best to keep quiet and walked into his bedroom to pass out. All the sugar and alcohol in his veins added turbulence to his sleep, which inspired him to dream. He saw himself in a dark rainforest; it started pouring. He needed to cross the river before him, but the bridge was out. A black whip suddenly flew over his head and wrapped around a branch above the river. Someone grasped Austin from behind, and the earth slid out from under his feet. He swung over the river and felt his face cutting the dense, humid air. He landed hard on the other side. He looked up to see his hero.

"Hey, do you want some breakfast?" Antonio's head peaked into Austin's room. "Also, do you hate us?"

"*I want food, yes*," mumbled Austin with his face stuffed in his sheets.

"But do you hate us?"

Austin groaned angrily. "I certainly don't."

"Then why'd you get up and disappear… Did you find a girl?"

"Sort of, I got trapped in a speakeasy, but the people inside turned out to be really cool."

"Cooler than us?"

"Kind of, yeah."

"Oh," Antonio withdrew his head. "Well, come outside, and I'll pour you some coffee."

Austin climbed out of bed and changed out of last night's clothes. He slid on something more comfortable. He walked out of his room and sat at the serving window. He waited quietly for his drink.

A ceramic scrape sounded as a mug was slid under his nose full of warm, brown coffee with a thin slice of ghee melting on the surface. A sprinkle of cinnamon freckled the butter. That's how Austin liked it; only Antonio knew that.

Austin looked up at Antonio; he was leaning on his elbow and staring at him with a smile. He brought a pipe to his lips, popped his thumb off the carb, then took a drag. He reached out to pass it to Austin.

Austin rebuffed the offer.

"How come?"

"I still feel weird about Thursday," said Austin. "No more weed, not for a while."

"But don't you want a bowl with your bowl?" Antonio frowned as he stuck a bowl of Choco Donuts beside Austin's mug.

"No, no, don't fight it. He'll serve his purpose…."

Austin looked up from his cereal and glared strangely at Antonio. He didn't recognize the voice that just spoke. He turned to his right and faced Cassie's ear. He leaned backward and looked beside Cassie. He saw the back of Jessie's head. He leaned back further and looked next to Jessie. There was a man wearing their Flokati rug like a toga.

"Who's that…" asked Austin. "How'd he get in here?"

The man turned to face Austin. He smiled through a big curly blonde beard. "I slept with that juicy enby," said the bearded man. "Thought they lived here?"

Austin shook his head. "Ari lives in Riverside."

"Then they won't be joining us?"

Austin had no idea what he was referring to. Cassie's mouth quickly shot open to explain. He turned to Austin, then flipped back to the bearded man. "Me and Jess are down to clown still, man, but I'm not sure about everybody else."

"I might be. What was your plan?" asked Antonio.

"The ultimate Christian Slater movie marathon," explained Jessie. "We came up with it last night at the bar. They had Mr. Robot on tv, but right around 1990, *that* was peak Slater—are you in?"

"They've got to be! We'll need all hands…" commanded the bearded man. "I hope you all understand the seriousness of this challenge. We need a coordinated effort. Currently, Austin's all we have in terms of safe drivers. He and I can fetch our favorite snacks. Jessie can pirate the movie because her dad's in the FBI, and he lets everything slide. Cassie can then set up Antonio's new projector because Antonio lacks technical skills, while Antonio uses those beefy arms to move the furniture away from the wall- then we'll have our screen."

Austin was surprised this stranger knew his name. "I'd love to drive, man," said Austin, "but my car is in the shop."

"No problem. We can take *my* whip." The bearded man suddenly tossed his car keys in Austin's face. Austin reacted fast and caught them mid-air. "We need to leave now if we're gonna start before one. And we gotta start before one if we're gonna finish before six."

"What's at six?" questioned Austin, staring at the key chain. There were seven signet rings attached to the main loop. They looked expensive, but the car brand on the key was certainly not.

"Private party," the bearded man stood and approached the front door. "Y'all can't come." He motioned for Austin to follow him. The bearded man led Austin outside to his car, parked against the curb. It was a black Astra with a grim reaper decal on the door. Austin undid the lock and hopped into the driver's seat.

"So, I was thinking we should go to Central Market," explained Austin, starting the car.

"Man, there's no need to get on the highway! We're trying to save time," griped the bearded man. "Just go to a gas station; we don't need no fancy candy."

"I thought we were getting our *favorite* snacks," asked Austin, "'cause then *I* need chocolate-covered blueberry chips, and Jessie likes her spicy prunes."

"Oh… I'm sorry," apologized the bearded man. "I guess I'm surprisingly low maintenance in this case. I just like Sour Patch Kids."

"Central's got sour peach rings."

"Ew, no," gagged the bearded man. "They've got to be kid-shaped."

Austin frowned; he stared at the man with repugnance. "What *is* your name? In case I should inform the police…"

"Saturday," said the bearded man.

"Hmph," exhaled Austin. "Yesterday, I met a Friday."

"And tomorrow you'll meet Sunday," explained Saturday. "That's the nature of time…"

Austin thought about what the man was saying. "Is there a reason you're each visiting me?" questioned Austin.

"To delicately end this horrible week," answered Saturday, "and prepare you for the next."

"There had to be people with worse weeks than me...."

"You got spit on!" exclaimed Saturday, raising his brows.

"That's not exactly how it went down," grimaced Austin. "Look, I thought I wasn't supposed to be talking about last week."

"That's Friday. You never set sail on Friday; it's bad luck. But Saturday's the adventure, and this is all part of the exploration phase."

"Well, I didn't get spit on; I got slimed," explored Austin. "I was told never to go to Montopolis after dark, but that's where Renel's is, and I wanted fried yams. I figured maybe I was being prejudiced, so I traveled outside my comfort zone."

"Challenging your whiteness to get hip food. That's very millennial of you."

"Thank you," said Austin. "So, I got there at about midnight. I walk outside with my yams, and there's this homeless man waiting for me. He begs me for a yam. I was just gonna give him one, but the owner comes out with a box hatchet. 'Don't talk to my customers, Richard!' Richard freaks out. He's got an empty can of Dr. Pepper he's been using as a spittoon. He tosses it at me in anger—I get chew in my eyes and an old cigarette stuck to my lip."

"Oh, Austin," frowned Saturday. "Big reveal, Tuesday's horrible. He's a big fat war criminal."

"So seems the rest of the work week…."

"No, no. Monday's stern, but he's refreshing. *You* only think Monday is the worst because that's when your boss scheduled your biweekly meetings. And you hate your boss!"

"I'm uncomfortable with criticism…."

"We all are… that never goes away," shrugged Saturday. The car stopped; they'd arrived at Central Market.

"This Monday was different though," sighed Austin. "It was so much worse…"

Saturday held up his hand. "Save it for later, Austin; we've got candy to grab… and your friends should be with you when we reach… *the core*." Saturday opened his door and stood up out of his seat. "Quick suggestion: you're not gonna ask for any money back on this candy, okay?"

Austin pulled open his door and took a step out. "Why's that important?"

"The first part of an adventure is bringing the team together," explained Saturday. "We'll use free candy to solidify that bond."

By the time the boys returned from the store, the projector hung firmly from the ceiling. A beam of light ran from its lens and collided with a white wall beside the front door. The seats and couch had been assembled into a single row behind the projector.

Jessie was behind the laptop loading the torrent on VLC. Austin passed her the dried fruit; she smiled and reached into her pocket for her wallet. Austin told her to put it away. It was all on him.

"Thank you, Austin," said Jessie. "I think you'll like *Heathers* if you like *Run Lola Run*. It has that dream quality."

"I thought we'd do *True Romance* first," called out Cassie. He looked annoyed. "Go in descending order from most unhinged Christian Slater."

"I agree, but Jason Dean is clearly more unhinged than Clarence Worley," argued Jessie.

"Wait, wait, wait," exclaimed Antonio. "I think the *second* movie should be the darkest Slater," he suggested, "to contrast with how silly *Ferngully* is at the end."

"Austin, hurry, the tension is rising! Finish snack duties," Saturday commanded.

Austin tossed some Fritos to Cassie and Bugles to Antonio. As each took a bite of their favorite textures and flavors, they all became more open to compromise.

"Antonio's right; the climax should be the darkest Slater," decreed Saturday. "But also, Cassie's right, Jason's far darker than Clarence. But this amounts to the exact same order Jessie originally picked, so we should all be satisfied—right?"

Cassie looked at Jessie. Jessie looked at Antonio. Antonio looked at Saturday. Everyone nodded. The order was agreed upon. "I think we just might be able to pull this off," smiled Saturday.

"It's just three movies," shrugged Austin. "How hard could this be?"

"No adventure comes without obstacles," warned Saturday, "but you've got an expert at the wheel." He sat in one of the recliners and opened his Sour Patch Kids. Something irked Austin, the way the kids gnashed in his teeth. He averted his gaze and took the other recliner. Jessie and Cassie cuddled up on the couch. Antonio laid out on the floor. With everyone in place, Jessie started *Heathers*.

It was just around the time Christian Slater took his first victim when the door to their apartment slammed open, and the whole movie was interrupted. Benny came scrambling in with a girl under his arm. Austin was the only one not to recognize her.

"Oh my gosh, you two never stopped drinking?" Antonio called out. He realized they were wearing the same clothes they had on when they left the bar on Friday night.

"We went to the canteen at the VFW… turns out they never close!" said Benny. His eyes had long shadows underneath them.

"Stacey, you didn't mention you were a veteran?" questioned Jessie.

The girl with Benny shook her head. "I'm not, but they don't care. I've slept with most of them."

Benny looked concerned, realizing his bed had been commandeered for a higher purpose. "Hey, since you guys are on the couch, can I borrow one of your rooms?"

Austin swallowed the blueberry chip in his mouth and hung open his jaw. He turned around and looked at Antonio. Antonio stared back, equally uninterested in sharing. Antonio was gay, so it did seem more unnatural to pollute his bed with the essence of straight sex. Antonio and Austin reached the same conclusion quickly; the choice was obvious.

"It's all yours," said Austin, pointing his thumb toward his room. Benny and Stacey were ecstatic and charged on in.

"Thanks for that," said Antonio with a surprised look. "I mean, I just washed my sheets."

"Oh, it's really no big deal," repeated Austin. "Besides, did you see those bags under their eyes? They're just going to go in there and sl-"

Suddenly, a one-man clap echoed from Austin's bedroom.

"Seriously, thank you," repeated Antonio. "I'm sorry if I've gotten on your nerves lately with prying."

"No, it wasn't-" Austin shook his head. "I just wasn't ready..." He listened to the loud smacks echoing about the walls. "I guess we've got time now, though… until the noise dies down and we can hear the movie."

The clapping began to pick up pace.

"What happened on Monday?" questioned Antonio.

"I got a warning letter at work," said Austin with a large release. "A *real* warning letter. I need to shape up!" He smacked his hands up into his face.

"You coming in late?" asked Antonio. "It's not sexual harassment, is it?"

"No, no! I'm a good worker- and a good human being. I just- have a slight problem with socializing at work. It doesn't come naturally to me."

"So basically, your boss reprimanded you for working *too* hard?"

"That's how I see it, too!" exclaimed Austin. "I skipped a going-away party for Karen. He says I'm too stiff, and it's affecting the team's synergy. I just think office culture is kind of corny. I'd rather just do my job. Hearing the fun-suckers call *me* the fun-sucker—it crushed my soul a little. I started questioning everything. Are all the problems in my life because I'm afraid to let go?"

"Austin, work culture *is* corny. You're not crazy," chuckled Antonio.

Bed springs began squeaking to the rhythm of the claps.

"Well, everything this week ended up with me overcompensating for being too uptight," continued Austin. "I messed up my date because I thought a hit beforehand would lighten me up for her. I went where I didn't belong because I was sick of being so uncomfortable with everything. And on Wednesday, I was so frustrated, I thought I might as well skip my ADHD meds in the morning to see if that would loosen me up a bit, and that was just…"

Austin sniffled, and everyone turned to face him. They could see he was now crying.

"I'm sorry," he apologized. "I shouldn't cry on the weekend."

"No, no," called out Saturday. "There is no better time."

Austin took a moment to collect himself. He wiped his tears on his wrists. The sounds of his sobs slowly faded in unison with the sounds of the shouting in Austin's bedroom. Everything crescendoed, then went to silence.

"I think we can continue the movie again," said Saturday, pointing at Jessie. She nodded, then clicked the play button.

Christian Slater continued his killing spree over the entirety of the two movies. By the end of *True Romance*, Austin was feeling much better. The gang paused for bathroom breaks. Austin saw Saturday stand up, look at the clock on the wall, and hurry to the front door. Austin quickly followed him.

"Leaving without saying goodbye?" called out Austin. "You won't be finishing it out with us?"

Saturday shook his head. "Benny's interruption cost us a half hour," explained Saturday. "It's five-thirty. I've got to be there at six."

"Where?"

"A beer pong tournament," said Saturday with a profoundly serious gaze. "My partner just got his grant rejected on Thursday… he needs me. *You* can take the wheel from here."

"*I* can?"

"Austin, you've led your own adventure every weekend up until now," explained Saturday. "You only lost your confidence, not your talent. You're not stiff, Austin. Dull people don't have weekends like this." Saturday held out his arms, signaling to the many moving parts in the apartment. Jessie and Cassie feeding each other snacks on the couch. Antonio swiping on Tinder for boys that look like Christian Slater. Stacey and Benny chugging water straight from their Brita.

"It doesn't seem like much," frowned Austin.

"You don't need to leave your house to have an adventure. You just grab a few friends and complete some wacky mission," said Saturday. "It's astounding what the human mind can accomplish with absolute freedom between sunrise and sunset." He stepped out of the apartment. "I'll see you next week."

Austin nodded, then shut the door. He turned back towards his friends, watching as they all seemed to enjoy themselves. There was a sudden rush of pride.

"Hey, Austin," came the voice of Antonio. "Do you- do you want to smoke, now?"

"Oh, he's got to!' called out Cassie. "These first two were *good* movies. But by God, you're gonna wanna smoke for *Ferngully*."

"Don't push him!" griped Jessie. "He just got done telling us he's upset."

Austin smiled and walked up to Antonio. He took the bowl from his friend's hand. "No, no, I think I'm fine now," he said, taking a huge puff. "Long as I don't have to drive."

He wouldn't. By the time the fairies defeated the smoke monster, all parties enjoying the film had grown incredibly tired, far too tired to repeat a night out like Friday. By seven, they found themselves respectfully separating. Cassie and Jessie returned to their own home, as did Stacey, after sobering up. Benny plopped back down on his couch, giving Austin access to his bedroom again. Antonio then disappeared to meet up with the closest thing to Christian Slater in Travis County.

Austin finished out his adventure with a smooth landing. After a quarter-hour of video games tucked under his sheets, Austin fell asleep with his console flashing "Game Over" beside his face. Austin dreamt that night of sailing on a ship. A loud revelry cheered and sang below deck while he faced the sunset, leaning over the galver.

Austin was the only one still in the apartment when he woke up the following day. Benny had gone off for a brunch date with Stacey, and Antonio was still out playing Wynonna Rider.

Austin felt brunch was only earned if someone spent Saturday night intoxicated. He wasn't very hungry, but he had weird amounts of energy. He decided to make a healthy choice and go for a walk. There was an untouched stretch of Colorado River hidden underneath the highway where Austin could feel alone.

He walked along the side of the river, letting the heat bake him. It felt nice to get outside after spending yesterday all cooped up. Sunday didn't live up to its name, however, and the sky turned dark when he turned around to head back home. As the first raindrops hit his skin, he was passing by a park bench hidden behind a tree along the water's edge. He quickly sat down to rest and opened an umbrella over his head.

"Feeling better?" A voice suddenly sounded off to Austin's right. He shuddered and jostled for his umbrella. He turned to see an old man in a gown sitting beside him. Austin quickly realized it was religious garb. He panicked and moved the umbrella over the old man's hairless head.

"I'm so sorry!" shouted Austin.

"Why are you sorry?" questioned the old man.

"I didn't see you praying! I hate to intrude."

"I wasn't praying," said the old man. "Squeeze in, or you'll get wet."

Austin scooched over to the right until his head was uncomfortably close to the stranger's. At least they were both dry. "I've been exercising," explained Austin. "I'm so sorry if I get any sweat on your nice robes."

"Feel free," said the old man. "It was hot today." He pointed to the black stains under his arms. "This robe's going straight to the dry cleaners."

"It's kind of a warm day to wear that," said Austin.

"Well, it's required," explained the old man.

"Oh, I didn't know," replied Austin. "Is that a Methodist thing?"

"Yes," said the old man, nodding.

"But hang on, that rosary looks Catholic," said Austin, staring at the beads around the man's wrist.

"Yes."

"And those gaiters are straight Episcopal." Austin pointed at the coverings on the man's shoes.

"Yes."

"Well, which is it, man?"

"Whichever you find least antiquated," laughed the old man.

"Are you trying to sell me something?"

"No… Sunday's not a shopping day," said the old man. "Tell me, Austin, why do people attend church on Sunday?"

Austin dipped his head down and pondered. The old man knew his name. Austin figured he knew the old man's name, too.

"Because they're Christian," answered Austin bluntly.

"Tons of Christians don't go to church on Sunday," replied the old man.

"Well… they're supposed to."

"Are they?" questioned the old man. "The Bible says the Sabbath is on Saturday, so it would seem no one's going when they're 'supposed to.' So then, why do they go on Sunday?"

"Well, I'm guessing *your* Sunday," suggested Austin. "So why don't you just tell me."

The old man shook his head.

"Is it bad that *I* don't go to church on Sunday?" asked Austin.

"*This* is close enough," replied the old man. "Maybe even better. It's an empty path. Somewhere you can hear your own thoughts."

"But I'm hardly thinking anything devout or spiritual," explained Austin. "I just think about next week."

"We all are," sighed Sunday. "By sunset, our minds will be riddled with anxiety as we anticipate what comes… *next.*"

"The peace you find on the weekend is so short-lived," frowned Austin. "It's not fair."

"The new week is inevitable; you gotta clear the board before you start a new game," explained the old man. "Sunday's your last opportunity… So, what are you still holding onto?"

"Guilt," answered Austin. "I'm scared to let it go. What if I repeat the same mistakes? I could get fired…"

"People think there's some strainful process to extract the experience from our mistakes." Sunday shook his head. "Unless you're in an exceptionally small minority, your body learns from error quite naturally. Like mice in a maze. It's an unconscious ability."

"I have my meeting with my boss tomorrow. I did casual Friday for the first time, and my coworkers liked my Hawaiian shirt. I hope my boss sees that I'm trying," sighed Austin. "Mondays scare me so much nowadays."

"Sunday and Monday. The Sun and the Moon. Polar opposites, but they each serve their purpose. Try not to fear the dark, Austin. Without the work week, we wouldn't appreciate the weekend."

Suddenly the rain let up, and the pitter-patter on Austin's umbrella went silent. Sunday stepped out from underneath its shade and stood in front of the park bench. He approached the river before them and stood at the stony edge. Austin closed his umbrella and walked to the old man's side.

"You know, Austin, people used to be so strict about their Sundays," said the old man with wide eyes and a soft smile, "but there's no right or wrong way to forgive ourselves." The old man leaped into the water with a quick skip. There was no splash, just a circle of ripples where he entered. When the waves flattened, the sun itself was reflected on the water, like a mirror held under the sky.

Austin walked home with his umbrella tucked under his arm. He couldn't feel the previous week following him around anymore. The space around him was incredibly quiet. He saw something in the distance but wouldn't let it frighten him. He breathed deeply and looked up at the clear, blue sky.

A Reason to Burn: An American Weekend

"An American Weekend". It's Friday night, and I arrive at my shift at 10 p.m. Something smells like shots. It's just the sourdough. I have eight hours to bake twenty-five baguettes, one-hundred-twenty bagels, eighty-five bread bowls, and sixty-five muffins before Panera Bread opens at 6 a.m. There're no customers. No need to fake politeness. My manager can be as mean as she wants. We're understaffed and I have to go faster. I chug an iced coffee. Things get burnt. We're running behind. I chug an iced coffee. That's my lunch; it's 2 a.m. There're kids in the parking lot. We lock eyes through the glass. They make a joke. I chug an iced coffee—this time, no cream or sugar.

"An American Weekend". It's Saturday and I sleep till noon. That's all the sleep I'm allowed. I'm the manager now. I have off, but I can't take off. Bills to pay. Can this car pay for itself? It used to be two stickers—one Uber, one Lyft. I pick people up. Day-drinking looks fun. I drop people off. I've never been downtown. A bunch more stickers. I deliver their food now. I'm back at Panera picking up salads, dropping off salads. People and salads. Another damn sticker. I do groceries now. These bags are heavy. My arms are tired. They live on the third floor. My legs are tired. It's 8 p.m.; I let myself rest. Go see your friends? I can't move anymore.

"An American Weekend". It's Sunday morning and there's no blue laws left to protect me. I am not a teenager working at Chick-fil-A. I am an adult and I work at Panera and I need to be there thirty minutes before 6 a.m. My brother lives in Germany; they have sonntagsruhe. I think I smell Düsseldorf—no, it's just the turkey sausage. Slap an egg on top. Put it in a bagel. That's somebody's brunch. I've never had brunch. Sometimes I don't have breakfast. Sometimes I skip lunch. I'm done at 4; it's back to Uber; it's back to Lyft. People and salads. People and salads. It never ends.

"An American Weekend". What *real* American has a weekend?

- Bloodshot Bread Maker, Lenna Hart

Roadwork

You see it on the side of the road all the time, but you rarely pick up on what it means. Between the lines of the shoulder lies a bent piece of plastic atop a bed of red and orange glass, or a curl of rubber surrounded by chips of metal and paint, or a skid mark arching like a rainbow and ending in a severed spoiler. This is the subtle detritus left behind by the unintended car accident.

It's the tow truck driver's responsibility to sweep up after a crash, but they're only required to clean the debris blocking the actual road. Then, volunteer beautification projects and tax-funded street sweepers remove anything else left to the side. Either might take months before passing over a particularly cluttered area. An extended interval between accident and cleanup is not proper, however, for we lemurtologists. Mere hours after a crash, I'm on the scene with a weatherproof notebook and my folding chair.

"Hunter Barcia. Hunter Barcia. Hunter Barcia." I repeated the victim's name as I sat back comfortably in my seat. I cracked open my can of coffee and placed it in the felt cup holder. It's only 5 a.m. The accident occurred around midnight. "Hunter Barcia. Hunter Barcia." Gradually, his spirit rose from the prismatic stain left by his crumpled gas tank.

Hunter was a grisly sight. His head looked like the jaws of a wrench, with a massive dent in the center that pushed his eyes and nose down into his chin. "I'm going- to get- fusilli salad. I'm going- to get- fusilli salad." He said the words slowly and rhythmically. "I'm going- to get- fusilli salad. I'm going- to get- fusilli salad."

Surface-level ghost dialogue is reminiscent of their last thoughts before dying. It's typically useless to lemurtologists whose ultimate goal is to get the ghost to fade away. To do so, we must deepen the conversation to reach the root of their problems. At the moment of their death, some troubling thought was looping in the background of their mind. For them to pass on, I must clear this trouble.

"Hunter Barcia is a nineteen-year-old honors student set to graduate from Windham High School this Spring." I found an article related to Hunter in his local newspaper. Hearing the details of his former life can easily stimulate a response. "His interests include... soccer... card games... and training his dogs Bono and Albie."

The ghost's demeanor suddenly changed. Warped by his injuries, it was hard to categorize his facial expression. "Little man- get out the road! Little man- get out the road!" This was telling but not particularly valuable. I tried a different statement.

"Hunter's scored more goals in a single season than anyone in Rockingham County history, garnering their team national attention from USA Today and the NFHS."

No response. The ghost returned to a dreary, neutral state.

"Hunter's father, an elementary school principal, cites gentle discipline and consistent attention as his family's secret to success. His mother, a child psychologist, stated that she 'couldn't be prouder'."

"Proud of me?" The ghost whimpered. His eyes closed. I opened my notepad. "Proud- of... of *me*?!"

With a reaction like that, I struck an incorporeal nerve. I copied down what I said and the ghost's response then pressed further. I folded up the article from the news and began to freestyle.

"Were your parents hard on you, Hunter?"

The ghost tilted its head. "Proud of- *me*?" he repeated.

I sighed in frustration and pinched the skin between my eyebrows. "Are your parents verbally abusive, Hunter?" I asked, louder, more irate. It was early, and I was losing patience.

Hunter straightened his neck, then lost his look of confusion. He'd returned to neutral.

I stomped my foot and took a big gulp of coffee. As quickly as I'd picked up on something, I'd lost it.

"Drivers are staring at you, honey," came the voice of a short girl approaching in a bright yellow vest. She had a sign in her hand that read 'Stop' on one side and 'Slow' on the other. She was the functional replacement for the traffic light Hunter had knocked over.

"I'm sure they're just *rubbernecking* at the ghost," I replied.

"Honey, you look like a drunk parent snarling at his kid's soccer match."

I looked down at my seat. It *was* the type you'd bring to a sporting event. "I'm not having any luck with my patient."

"My therapist, Paul, he wouldn't lose his temper like this, and I *never* take his advice," explained the young girl. "It's unprofessional of you to get mad."

"My job isn't therapy," I took a deep breath. I didn't want to lose my temper again, especially at someone who wasn't dead. "That's my fault for the confusion. I shouldn't call them patients. That humanizes them."

"Well, they *are* human, aren't they?" questioned the girl. "They're just missing all the parts."

"No." I stood up out of my chair and then pinched its corners together. It collapsed into a compact column that I could stuff under my arm. "It's more like a human-shaped dent."

I could have stayed longer and tried further stimulus, but I hated feeling gawked at, and the morning rush hour was just beginning. I'd learned enough, anyways, to know that Hunter's parents may have the key to exorcizing their son. The trick was getting them to pick up the phone. After a week without an answer, I grew too impatient, and I decided to visit their address in person.

I traveled to their suburbs and found their house — an almond single-story with farmhouse flair. I rang the doorbell at their front door. I heard a computerized voice echo, "Visitor- front entry." A pair of dogs started barking. A man yelled at them to cool down, then opened the door.

"Yes?" said the man; this was Hunter's father.

"Jack Doll, lemurtologist for the Rockingham County DMV," I said, holding out my hand. "You seemed to have missed my calls."

"*Ignored*," said the father sharply. He kept his hand pressed to his doorframe. "We're in mourning."

"I apologize for what must seem like an inconvenience," I reasoned, "but if you allow me to ask a few short questions, I'll be out of your hair in a half hour, and you'll *never* see me again."

Mr. Barcia hummed suspiciously. "Come on in." He lifted his arm and allowed me to enter. I sat in a leather recliner in his living room while he fetched his wife. The two sat down on a loveseat across from me.

"When I heard your messages, I thought it was a joke," said the mother. "What does a lemur have to do with any of this?"

"Oh miss, lemurtology comes from the Latin word 'lemur,' meaning spirit or ghost," I explained. "Our profession has existed since the early 20th century for curing haunted highways and public property."

"So, you're with the state?" questioned Mr. Barcia. His face turned bleak. "You're pressing charges, aren't you?"

"Charges?'

"The boy's dead," he puffed. "What good does it do him to give him the DUI?"

"Oh! There will certainly be no DUI charge," I replied. "If your son is casting a specter, then there was little alcohol in his system," I explained to the couple.

"You can tell that?" questioned Mr. Barcia.

"Yes. From what we know of how ghosts come to be," I answered, "there needs to be a sudden absence of consciousness. The elderly rarely leave behind apparitions since their brain function has slowly dwindled before their death. Basically, their mind tapers off. Same goes for people in comas and people with degenerative diseases. A ghost requires a mental decline with a nearly infinite slope. 'On' one second, 'off' the next. Alcohol use, however, leads to something more like that of gradual senility."

"That's good, isn't it?" questioned Mrs. Barcia. "Our boy was a good boy, then."

"I'm not part of the justice system, in case I haven't made that clear. I don't have any duty to speak on behalf of your son's qualities," I explained. "I'm simply trying to clean him off the side of the road."

"Oh, God!" Mrs. Barcia buried her face in her husband's shoulder.

"You couldn't have worded that a little nicer?" he griped.

"Mr. Barcia, your son has cost the city of Ellensburg roughly $10,000 by destroying its traffic controller. The city opted not to make the victim's family pay for these damages, but the option still exists. Every day, your son's ghost scares off an estimated three to six hundred potential tourists arriving at-"

"Now, where did you get that number?!"

"These are calculated from the decline of ticket sales at Canobie Family Fun Center since the accident," I explained hastily.

"Six hundred people are scared to drive past my son?!"

I let out a low sigh. "Phasmophobia is extremely common in small children, those of which Canobie Family Fun Center primarily caters to."

Mrs. Barcia let out a whimper and wiped her nose on her husband's shirt. Mr. Barcia looked at her and expressed his worries. "You need to be more sensitive."

My temper flared. "I can't be nice right now because I'm desperate to keep you two from losing money that should be spent on flying your family out here for a decent funeral!" I explained. "Now, let's cut the crap and start telling me all the ways in which Hunter could have failed you."

"Failed us?" His mother sniffled. "Hunter's ghost is saying he *failed us?*"

"Well, all I can say for certain is he finds it hard to believe when I tell him you're *proud* of him."

"We are proud of him!" whimpered Mrs. Barcia. She turned to her husband and patted his chest. "Aren't we, Rod?"

"I might know," said the father softly.

"What?" questioned the mother.

"I think I might know the -" His father stuttered, "the reason he might feel like... we aren't supportive."

"What did *you* do?" questioned Mrs. Barcia with wide, angry eyes.

"I told him I'd pay his whole way if he got into Dartmouth," he explained, "then he didn't, so I told him we wouldn't pay for UNH."

"Roddy!" She slapped her husband's ribs.

"It's cheaper. He can afford it on his own!"

"You drove our boy to suicide!" hollered Mrs. Barcia.

"Hold on; there's no evidence this was a suicide," I interjected. "Unresolved feelings don't have to relate to the cause of death."

"Then what made our son swerve into a pole?" shouted Mrs. Barcia.

"Probably... a squirrel," I explained.

"A squirrel in the road?" She looked confused.

"Why wouldn't he just hit it?" growled Mr. Barcia.

"Do you have pets?" I responded.

The couple nodded.

"You don't hunt?"

The couple nodded again.

"Younger generations have such a soft spot for animals. They're five times more likely to try and miss potential roadkill," I explained. "Your son couldn't take the life of even a *small, stupid* creature."

"Oh God!" cried his mother. "He traded his life for a tree rat!"

"Let's not have a meltdown," I sighed. "It's like you said, your son was… a good boy."

With the issue out in the open, the only thing left for me to do was get the father to apologize to the ghost. The easiest way is a direct confrontation, but some people take issue with that.

"Does it look like Hunter before or after a pole crushed his head?" asked the father.

"After," I replied honestly.

"I can't look at him, man," the father was tearing up too. "I don't wanna see him that way."

I nodded. "There is another way. Our profession has modernized."

That afternoon, I returned to the crash site to prepare for the exorcism. Ghosts are not fully cognizant, and so they are easy to fool. This prompted me to use what we call a 'scarecrow,' a plastic body dressed in the clothes of the apologizing party. I have a specialized model head with an iPad attached to the face. I Facetimed with Mr. Barcia and set him up before his son. I put a piece of tape over the iPad's lens so Mr. Barcia wouldn't need to see his son in return.

"H- how are you doing, Hunter?" he stuttered. It was awkward for him to acknowledge this *thing* as his son. "Is there- what can- what can I do for you?"

"Dad?" whispered the ghost. "Dad!"

"Yes, son, I'm here."

"Dad, aren't you proud of me anymore?"

"Son, yes! Yes, I'm so proud of you!"

"But the money…."

"Forget the money! Fuck it all, son, I'm paying for you no matter what I -" Mr. Barcia shook his head. "I didn't think when I said that. I thought I was teaching you a lesson- something about holding people to promises- but I had no time to flesh it out. I should have talked to you while I had the chance."

"Dad." As soon as the ghost felt the relief it needed, it simply disappeared, fading quickly like the end of a firecracker.

"Mr. Barcia, that was great. He's all gone now," I said after tearing the tape off the lens. "Really, really great stuff; I can't thank you enough for this."

"Just like that?" He sounded disappointed. "He didn't give much of a response afterward."

"Yeah, it's always like that," I explained. "A ghost gets what he needs and dips. It doesn't stick around to return the favor."

Mr. Barcia coughed. He shifted uncomfortably. "Well, I've- I've got to go."

"Mr. Barcia, thanks again; you seriously were a huge-"

Bloop. He ended Facetime.

"Quite a boring ending to an otherwise touching show," came the sweet young voice of the crossing guard. It was midday, and there was barely any traffic to stop.

"Disappointment is a part of life," I said dryly, taking apart my scarecrow.

"So, when it's leaving, there's no flash? Not even a poof? Just... gone."

"Yeppers, that's it," I replied quaintly. "What did you expect?"

"Well, I, uh, I don't know."

"I'm not judging at all. I actually agree; it's surprising how anticlimactic their departure is," I explained. "Before I got into this, I thought they would glow, collapse into a singular point, and then *flyyy* up into the air."

"I thought maybe they'd lie back and cross their arms. Then slowly descend into the earth like how they were buried."

I nodded. "All that work deserves a better reward."

"Would you call this case particularly *hard* work?"

"Mmm- nah!" I exclaimed. "This one was a simple one. A family quarrel solved with love."

"Well, *I* have a not-so-simple one."

It took me a moment to realize she hadn't just said a fluffy nicety. She took a sharp turn into self-interest, and it surprised me. "What do you mean you *have* one?" I asked. "You found one that hasn't been reported?"

"Oh, I've reported it," she replied. "It's not on a major highway, so they don't care."

"It's a backroad, isn't it?"

"Dirt road, surrounded by trees."

I turned to face the girl. I stared into her tired eyes. They stuck out on an otherwise youthful face. There had to have been an age difference of twenty years between us.

"Could you fix it for me?" she asked.

I shrugged. "I mean, I *could maybe* when I'm off the clock. Where exactly do you live?"

"Lane 3, Zelly's Woods," she answered excitedly. "You turn off of 441, then it's two miles of dirt path, and my brother's house is at the end of it."

"That's certainly off the beaten path," I replied, thinking about the distance from my house in Salem. "So, then, where's the ghost?"

"Halfway up Lane 3," she said. "There's two of 'em."

"You know them?"

She nodded solemnly. "I know them. One's my brother. The other one's his kid."

It's near impossible to have the focus to handle two ghosts at once, let alone three, so I decided I wouldn't take anything big at work while I spent my after-hours in Zelly's Woods. I could temporarily reduce my effort to paperwork, which was easy after the big win I got with Hunter. During my shift, I filed Hunter's Confirmation of Exorcism, reported on the procedure used, and began running social media scans for my next professional case. Then, I went to the crossing guard's house in the evenings. I would learn her name is Cyreen.

I arrived at Lane 3 around dinnertime. The sun was going down. I turned on my high beams and went ahead down the long, unlit road. The terrain was brutal, rumbling hard under the tires of my frail little Grand Am. We came to a bumpy stop as the ghosts suddenly appeared in my headlights.

There they were: a seven-year-old boy and a thirty-five-year-old man. The former wore gym shorts and an outer space t-shirt. The latter wore a tight polo tucked in and belted into his khakis. Both their abdomens were caved in and flattened against their spines. It almost looked like they'd been starved.

It's not only awkward driving through a pair of apparitions; it's borderline disrespectful to the dead. Even with all my years of experience, I try to avoid it. It feels like you're going to get cursed. I would have driven around them, but the road was too narrow. I shut my eyes and pressed the gas pedal. I opened them again when I was sure they'd passed. You can't *really* feel them go through you, but your body still gives you a chill.

When I arrived at Cyreen's, she had a plate of sliced turkey and mashed potatoes waiting for me at her kitchen countertop. "Sit down," she said, smiling. She patted the seat beside her.

"I already ate," I told her.

"Well, don't do that anymore," she chuckled. "If you're gonna help me, I'm gonna feed you, okay?"

I nodded and dropped my belongings. "Alright."

"Did you see the boys?" She quickly touched her mouth. "Oh, I'm sorry, I shouldn't say boys, should I? They're dents."

"No! No!" I exclaimed. "Call them whatever you feel. *I'm* the only one who has to be formal. *You're* the grieving sister and aunt."

"Oh, I'm not grieving," she replied. "They've been there for two years, Jack."

"The DMV didn't help you for *two years*?!" I exclaimed. "They made you drive back and forth through your loved ones for two years?"

Cyreen looked surprised at how emotional I got. She nodded.

"Cyreen," I sighed. "How did your brother crash?"

She once again patted the seat beside her. This time I followed her instructions and sat down.

"This road has no one on it besides my brother and me, and we only have one car," she explained, "which means you get relatively used to not having to slow down for anyone coming up and down Lane 3." She pointed outside. "But someone looking for their glamping sight took a wrong turn and came down our road. They *sped* down our road. Much faster than Arnold. It was just about this time of day and neither made the call to put their lights on yet. Arnold was taking Ryan and Duncan for ice cream when they collided."

"Which of the boys is out there?"

"Ryan," she said sullenly. "The older of the two. He was in the front seat with his daddy. Duncan stayed in the back. It doesn't make any difference without a seatbelt on."

"Was Duncan asleep in the back?"

"How'd you know?" she asked.

"Sleeping people don't leave ghosts," I answered. "That's why people are relieved when you die in your sleep." Suddenly, this prompted a memory to flash before my eyes. I winced uncontrollably. I realized my expression was exposed, so I hid my face.

"Does that bother you, Jack?" asked Cyreen. "Little kids dying?"

"On the contrary, it's familiar territory," I replied. "I'll be honest, though, they're tougher than adults. Kids are bad at communication when they're alive. In death, it gets extremely abstract."

"Then how do we deal with them?" she asked. "'Cause I can get used to seeing my brother like that every day, but the sight of that kid..." She shook her head. "If you could just get rid of that one."

"I'll take care of them both," I guaranteed her. "Come with me."

Cyreen put my plate in the fridge and followed me to the car, where we drove back to Ryan and Arnold's haunting ground. A slight curve in the road marked the spot. It was just enough to block the sight of another car ahead.

When we arrived, the ghosts weren't appearing. "Arnold," called out Cyreen. "Arnold. Arnold. Arnold." Suddenly, he rose from the earth. Ryan followed soon after.

I was surprised. "You figured out how to raise them."

"It's their names," she laughed shyly. "How else do you call out to someone?"

I nodded. "Cyreen, I take you've talked to them already?"

"Oh, every Sunday!" she replied. "I say a little prayer with the two of 'em. Sometimes mom comes out and joins me too."

"Your mom or Ryan's mom?"

"No, Ryan's mom is in jail," replied Cyreen bluntly. "It's me and Arnold's momma." Cyreen started to cry just a little. "She misses her kid. And her grandkids." She wiped the wet makeup out of her eye.

"When you talk to ghosts, do they talk back?" I asked.

"Sometimes." She had to think about it. "Arnold especially. He says my name and gets all excited."

"Excited *happy*? Or excited *angry*?"

"I think it's best just to show you," she walked up to her brother's ghost and greeted him sweetly. "Hello, Arny," she said. "Some of the nurses and I are starting a bowling team. They weren't gonna let any aides on the team, but apparently, my name precedes me down at Tim's Pins." Cyreen laughed modestly.

We waited for a second. Arnold didn't move. He stood idly, besides little trembles in his arms and legs.

"I'm sorry," frowned Cyreen. "I swear I was able to get him to do it."

"I believe you can, dear," I encouraged her. "Really think about what specific topics trigger."

"Uhm, I thought it was hearing about my day," Cyreen's head dipped, and she lost some enthusiasm, "on second thought, maybe it's just the sound of me complaining." Cyreen sighed. She looked back up at her brother. "There's still a lot of talk about layoffs at work. You wouldn't think that with how they've expanded things, but something has to be traded. 'More nurses, less aides.'"

"Cyreen," he suddenly broke his silence. "Cyreen," he said softly. His lower eyelids tensed up. His brow folded.

"See, I knew I could do it," said Cyreen. "I guess I only come here to tell 'em my problems."

I stepped up to the ghost and ran my finger through the air over creases in the forehead. Then I ran it under Arnold's eyes. "That's anxiety," I said. "That's worry and woe."

"What's he worried about?"

"*You*," I said assuredly. "The stimulus is definitely you."

"I won't necessarily get laid off," she told her brother. "It's probably a rumor!"

"I don't think that's what he needs to hear," I explained. "The anxieties run deeper than that… Cyreen," I called out. "Cyreen, why would he have to worry about you?"

"I was a junkie kid," she replied. "I guess he's always been worried about me."

"Are you sober?"

"Oh yes! For three-and-a-half years," she replied. "My mom had me move out here with Arnold. It's so isolated, so it cuts me off from my bad influences. My boyfriend liked crack, and my best friend liked heroin. I would flip-flop between the two."

"Why did Arnold come out here?"

"He likes the woods."

"Cyreen, tell your brother that you're safe… or that you're better now."

"I'm better now, Arny; you don't have to worry anymore," she said sweetly and sincerely. She reached out and intersected her fingertips with the back of her brother's wrist.

I spun my finger. "Give it some detail," I encouraged.

"If something ever happens to this job, I have a backup plan. I know about an opening at Dollar General," she stared straight into his eyes. "I'm not gonna go back to Jenny or Jason. You can trust me."

"I can trust you," he replied. "I can trust you." He broke out into a smile.

Cyreen stood there for a second, her hand still touching her brother's. She was waiting for it all to disappear, but Arnold still stood there for some reason.

"What gives?" questioned Cyreen. She seemed upset.

"It's not a failure. It's just one piece of the puzzle," I tried to keep her calm. Emotions were undoubtedly getting high. It's tough to avoid that. "It's like a code on a safe. We've turned the knob and heard the first 'clink,' but now we gotta turn the other way."

"Should I keep talking to him?"

"No. No more talking," I suggested. "Sometimes it's hearing the right words; other times you have to show something to them. Something they wanted."

"Well, my brother was not a greedy man."

"Doesn't have to be something valuable," I explained. "Was there something he would have wanted you to have when you got your life together?"

"Oh yeah! Kids!"

"Uhm… no. It's gonna need to be something else," I replied grimly. "We can't knock you up just to appease your brother." I rubbed my chin and stared at her midriff. "We could stuff a pillow under your shirt and see if that does it." I caught sight of her arm hanging next to her stomach. It had a clean streak of skin going down the forearm. "How about your track marks healing? That could be a visual stimulus."

"Oh, I didn't use that arm," she said, pointing at her other wrist. A large network of black tattoos covered the arm. "There's actually still a lot of scarring. It's hidden under the art." Cyreen rolled up her sleeve so I could see the full length of the collage.

"That's quite an interesting collection," I said, examining all the minute details. There was a syringe at the very top of the shoulder. Every number on every tick mark was clear. It even had the threading where the tip is attached and 'BD Epilor™' along the side.

"That's the last needle I ever used," she said, pointing at her shoulder. She ran her finger down over the length of her arm. It passed over a box of crackers on her bicep. "These got me through withdrawal."

"Wheat Thins?"

"Fiber helps with… certain symptoms." She dragged her finger further down, passing over a headshot of Nurse Joy on her elbow pit. "*She* got me interested in the field of medicine to begin with." Then she twisted around to show a bowling alley on the back of her forearm. "And that's my healthy alternative." A little bit further down, '1 YEAR SOBER' circled her wrist in block letters. "It's my road to recovery. Every image tells more of the story."

"Except the back of your hand?" I pointed out.

"Pardon?"

"It's still blank." I began to concoct a plan. "How fast can you make an appointment?"

By the next afternoon, we were both sitting at a small, dingy tattoo parlor in downtown Deerfield: Cowbird Ink. Cyreen leaned back in the adjustable chair while the artist nipped her skin. Meanwhile, I sat back and watched from a squeaky stool.

The artist was a tough-looking man named Joshua with huge arms and a large gray beard. Every few seconds, he took a break from staring at the back of her hand and looked up at me. He looked dismayed.

"Shouldn't you be watching what you're doing?" I asked him as he shot me another gaze.

"Cyreen, honey, why is this guy paying for your tattoo?" asked Joshua. "Has he been paying for a lot of things for you?"

"Hang on," I held out my palm. "Don't misunderstand me."

"He's an exorcist. He's helping me with Arnold."

"You have money to afford a personal exorcist?"

"No," sighed Cyreen. She winced as the needle hit a particularly sensitive area. "He's doing it for free," she cringed.

"Well, surely he expects *something* in return," he said suspiciously. He took a break from his inking and dropped his arms to his sides. His massive chest expanded outwards. "I figure, what could an old man have to gain from a young girl?"

Cyreen didn't answer. She looked down at the progress on her hand.

"I'm not creepin' on her, man," I told the guy.

"Well, there has to be something in it for you," Joshua looked disgusted. "I know the way you think, man. Her brother's gone. Now, she's easy prey."

"That's not why I'm helping her."

"Cyreen, aren't *you* curious why this man's giving you services for free?" asked Joshua to his client.

Cyreen sighed. "To be honest, I *was* surprised you agreed to this. I figured there might be some nasty thing you wanted in return." She faced Joshua. "But so far, he's done nothing like it."

"I find helping people gratifying."

"You work for the DMV," replied Cyreen glumly. "We both know that's a lie."

"I... see a familiarity between Cyreen and me." I didn't want to get into it; not with people I barely knew.

"You a recovering addict?" shot Joshua.

"No..."

"Then where's the connection?"

"I couldn't get..." I paused and tried to relax. "My home insurance wouldn't cover a lemurtologist. It was cheaper to DIY it. That's how I got started in this craft. Self-taught with YouTube videos."

"So, he helps others that can't afford it," said Cyreen. "See Josh; he's a good guy."

"Oh, he's a friggin' superhero," grumbled Joshua sarcastically. He put the last few touches on Cyreen and patched it with a bandage. Then he approached me. "That'll be a-hundred-fifty... *Venkman*." He stretched out his hand. I tossed out my credit card.

By the time we returned to Cyreen's home, the sun was ready to go down. "Stop here," said Cyreen as we reached halfway down Lane 3. "We don't have time to go back to the house first." I pumped the breaks. She dashed out of the car, determined to use the last few minutes of daylight to our advantage.

Cyreen ran up to where her brother's ghost projects. She said his name a few times before he and Ryan appeared side by side in the middle of the road. I put the car in park and hurried after her. "Do I just show him?" she asked, fiddling with her bandage. "Does there have to be some sort of prelude?"

"You could say, uh, a few words if you want to add some context," I explained. "Ghosts *can* be a little slow."

"So can Arnold," laughed Cyreen. She peeled back her bandage until just the edge clung on. She revealed the black outline of their house on Lane 3. "Arnold, you left me the house in your will, and I… think it makes a fitting end to my journey." She held it up closer to Arnold's face. His eyes seemed to be drifting over the details. "It's not a kid, but it's my responsibility now, and I've taken good care of it. It looks like how it did when you left it." I saw tears welling up in Cyreen's eyes.

Arnold's lips began to purse. "Cyreen," he said again, but the tone was different this time. His eyes weren't so strained. They were wide and full of surprise.

"Mom spends the night sometimes," whimpered Cyreen, "she says she's proud of me."

Arnold smiled. It was a pleasant surprise. "Cyreen's… Cyreen's alright." Suddenly, the air in front of Cyreen grew dull. She was left holding up her tattoo to no one. She let her arm drop.

Cyreen wiped her tears and stared down at the remaining ghost. Ryan's head looked up at where Arnold used to be. He stood silently gazing into nothing. "Should I…" sniffled Cyreen. "Should I try it on the kid too-"

A blast of sonic energy suddenly disrupted the still air. Ryan's ghost suddenly became further warped. His head stretched vertically as his jaw hung open wide.

"Jack, do something!" called out Cyreen.

Ryan's lips peeled back, and his teeth reached out from his gums.

Cyreen fell to the ground and covered her ears. "Make him stop!"

The sound that emanated from the little boy was inhuman; a mosquito's whine amped up to an impossible degree. It stung my ears, but I powered through and hurried into my car. I drove up to Cyreen and opened the passenger side. I flung myself over the center console and reached over the passenger seat. I pulled her off the ground into the car, then helped her shut the door. Everyone was safely inside, so I drove off toward the house.

Inside the walls of my car, the screech could still be heard. It was just duller. It was deadened enough that at least Cyreen and I could hear each other when we spoke. "What's Ryan doing?!" shouted Cyreen. "I've never gotten him to speak before... and now he's a siren!"

I shook my head with a look of doubt. "It's not unheard of for two ghosts to be intertwined. Ryan clearly shared some connection to his father's spirit that we robbed him of. We disrupted the balance of energy, and now... like I said, kids are abstract."

"But you've handled kids before, right?" questioned Cyreen. "You're no greenhorn."

"Yeah..." I nodded slowly. "I've handled a kid before."

"*A* kid?" exclaimed Cyreen. "Like one?"

"It was the first ghost I ever exorcized," I replied. "If I could do it back then… well, now I have so much more experience."

"The first?" said Cyreen. "The one you DIYed?"

I nodded hesitantly.

Cyreen put the pieces together. "Jack… was that *your* kid?"

I sighed. I didn't want to talk about it.

"Jack, have you lost your son?"

"A little girl," I corrected her. "Mauricia. She was crushed."

"By what?"

"Uhm…" The words struggled to come out. "Me. Me and my bed. We were living in an old townhouse in San Fran. A leak had been rotting the wood between our floors. We would have caught it had it happened more gradually, but there was an earthquake, which helped move things forward in a single night."

"Oh my gosh, Jack!"

"I crushed my daughter, Cyreen," I'm not a crier, but my body couldn't help but shiver, "and my insurer left me to take care of the ghost. She was flat like a pancake."

"Jack…" Cyreen shook her head.

"And it was *my fault* she left a ghost!" I was yelling now. "I didn't read to her that night. I skipped the bedtime story and tucked her under the covers. I was so tired that day." I could feel my breathing speeding up. "She must have been up for hours because I got lazy."

"Jack, I don't want you torturing yourself. Seeing Ryan must… bring back memories."

"It does," I admitted, "but leaving now would leave those feelings unresolved. On the other hand, if Ryan goes away, it could really do me some good."

"What's the plan then?" questioned Cyreen.

I parked my car in her driveway. I stopped the engine. "We need to understand how Ryan viewed the world."

"I know what can help with that." Cyreen got out of the car and led the way. She took me upstairs to Ryan's room.

The walls themselves were a soothing shade of lavender. Decorating them were posters of spacemen in smooth, metal spacesuits holding smooth, metal space guns. These soldiers had enemies, action figures on Ryan's shelves of green and blue aliens vaguely shaped like roaches and spiders.

I walked up to the boy's bed and stared at the graphic on his sheets. An epic scene played out where the player characters drove a hover car through a crowd of armored beetles. "One day in the future," I said, touching the fabric, "all the cars will be self-driving. Then there won't be any more accidents."

"But there'll be new ways to die," sighed Cyreen. "I bet spaceships will blow up all the time."

"Oh my gosh, we'll have to find a way to send lemurtologists into space, or we'll just leave all these ghosts hangin' around our upper atmosphere. That *could* scare the aliens."

"And that could be a good thing," said Cyreen, touching one of the villainous action figures.

I nodded. "It really could."

"What can we learn from all this?" asked Cyreen, waving about her arms.

"Well, drawing from my own experience, my daughter liked this book series called *Princess Pyroraptor*. It's about a beautiful, wealthy dinosaur that rules over all the other smaller, less fortunate dinosaurs. I thought if I read it to her ghost, I could *finally get her to sleep*." I exhaled sullenly. "It's not that simple, I'm afraid. It got her attention though, but the real key is to use the world of imagination to tackle whatever's really bothering the child."

"But what bothers a child?" questioned Cyreen. "What bothers a child the same way an adult is concerned with protecting their family or preserving their self-worth?"

"You'd be surprised what they pick up on," I replied. "Mauricia could tell we weren't as wealthy as her other friends, and because of that, she felt a disconnection from Princess Pyroraptor. To show her we could still be royalty without all the money, I… dressed up as a princess. I wore a dress, and it worked."

"*It worked?*" exclaimed Cyreen. "All you had to do was wear a dress?"

I nodded with a look of shame.

"Jack, that's adorable," smiled Cyreen. "Does that mean I need to make us some alien costumes, then?"

"I don't know." I looked around the room. "That's certainly where his imagination is, but we need to determine what makes Ryan insecure?" I stared at a photo balanced on his dresser of his family. His father held his baby brother while Ryan sat beside them, laughing. "I was always surprised Mauricia never once asked about her mother. Is Ryan the same?"

Cyreen shook her head. "He remembers her from before she was arrested. He asked about her a lot. We told him she... left for a business trip to the moon. That he could see her every night if he just looked up at the stars."

I nodded. "Then I think it's time for mom to come home."

The costume selection for starship warriors ranged from twenty bucks to half a G. The beautiful thing about a child's imagination is how little we need to spend to impress. The suit we found was elastic and form-fitting, with all the armor painted on. The helmet that came with it was a thin, plastic mask with a narrow strap in the back.

We used the money we saved on some other props—a couple of smoke bombs and a strobe light. We set them off beside Ryan's projection at the edge of the woods. By the time we returned, he had still not stopped his screaming. It took the sight of his favorite video game hero emerging from an orb of flashing light to get him to calm down finally.

The star soldier approached Ryan's ghost and knelt at his side. The costume mesmerized Ryan. "M-m-mommy?" he questioned. "Are you home?"

Slowly, the soldier slipped off the mask, revealing Cyreen underneath. "Ryan," she exclaimed. "Ryan, I want you to understand I'm here for you."

"You're not Mom." His eyes turned to anger. They rolled back in his head. Slowly, his face started to elongate.

"Ryan, your mother can't come home!" shouted Cyreen. "She was never in outer space!"

Ryan's anger stopped growing. His eyes returned, and he stared at Cyreen with confusion.

"Ryan, we shouldn't have said she was coming back," explained Cyreen. "It left you hoping for something unrealistic, which wasn't honest."

"No- Mommy?"

Cyreen reached out to grab Ryan's little arms. Her hands went straight through. She grasped at the air and shook. "Ryan, your mom was a good person, but she did something bad. So bad, they had to put her in jail."

"Mom's… bad."

"I can't replace her," continued Cyreen, "but I can be someone you can rely on. If you need a chaperone on a field trip, I'll be there. Or someone to talk to about how girls work; I'll be there."

"Auntie," murmured Ryan. "Auntie Cy-"

"I'll make you lunches and take you to choir practice." Cyreen looked down at the ground. "Anything you see your friend's moms do… I can do it too."

"Auntie Cy-" Ryan's voice suddenly had a touch of joy. Cyreen raised her head to see her nephew smile again, but he was already gone. The shimmering mirage in front of her had disappeared. Her road was left empty.

I cleaned up the smoke bombs and shut off the strobe light. I then joined Cyreen in the center of Lane 3. I knelt beside her and put my hand on her back. "You're good," I said. "You could do this for a living."

Cyreen shook her head. "No," she sighed. "I wouldn't want to do this for anyone else."

That night, I let Cyreen cook for me, and we sat and ate dinner together at her kitchen table. We were silent for quite some time. She had a lot to process.

"Jack," said Cyreen as she finished her potatoes. "It's weird now that they're gone."

I shook my head. "They were gone two years ago," I said. "I, too, was left with a bit of guilt when Mauricia's ghost finally vanished. I felt like I destroyed a precious photograph. But Cyreen, we don't keep photos of our loved ones after they're killed. That's just… torturing ourselves."

I stood up and walked into the adjacent hallway; I plucked a family portrait off the wall. Arnold and his wife stood in the center. At their legs were the kids, Ryan and Duncan. Over to the left was Cyreen, her arm around her mother. I placed the photo down on the kitchen table.

"Here's where you talk to them," I said, running my fingers over their expressions. "This is where they're confident. A time when they felt loved." Cyreen took the portrait in her hands and smiled. "*This* is not a dent. *This* is being human."

A Reason to Burn: Roadwork

The demonization of the DMV does not begin with Evan Witmer's "Roadwork," but it certainly perpetuates the misconception that we are lazy, unmotivated, and apathetic. After a single read, I did not feel compelled in the slightest to burn his story, but instead, I wanted to open an informative dialogue with the author and present to him a counterpoint. To do this, I contacted him via email, which he has publicly disclosed multiple times through his social media postings and profile descriptions.

"Dear Evan," I wrote to him, "I understand writers use tropes as a means of adding new twists on concepts that already feel familiar to the reader, but I believe you erroneously exaggerated negative feelings towards DMV personnel. We not only *do* care about our jobs, but most of us are extremely satisfied helping a citizen of our fine state get back on the road. We think of ourselves as a liaison between the common man and his right to drive. We're proud, nay, excited to steer people away from the horrors of public transportation and back into the freedom of a personal motor vehicle. Any delay people may have experienced in our line of work is simply due to the sheer volume of Americans who wish to participate in vehicular handling. We cannot put one life above another, so we must all wait patiently."

Evan was kind enough to respond within the hour. These are his exact words: "Dear Road Reich if you think you're on the side of freedom with us REAL AMERICANS, I suggest you look in the mirror. The DMV was originally created during the Nixon era to prevent minorities and cool people from getting to work on time, thereby costing them their jobs and subsequently killing them. I am a strong leader in a community of self-proclaimed automotive anarchists who believe that parking lots and roadways should be treated with the same respect as international waters. The only time you can tell me how to drive my car is if I ram it through the wall of somebody else's property line."

"Dear Evan," I replied to him, "I understand that every state has independently created its own DMV. Therefore, each has its own unique history of origin. For most states, however, the creation of a DMV was to consolidate the duties of various other state departments into a single unit in order to quell the jaw-dropping incline of vehicular deaths during the 1970s. In other words, we're here to save lives, not to squash some liberal ideal. A lawless road system would surely account for tens of thousands of deaths in a single year. Would you really want that? Would you really want sixteen-year-old children to feel like they might die if they get behind the wheel?"

Evan responded within twenty minutes. "Dear Check-Engine Cheka, I do not subscribe to the theory that cars take lives. *People do.* I've driven drunk out of my gourd, going sixty miles over the speed limit hundreds of times, and I've never killed so much as a bird in the road. That's because it is actually impossibly difficult to hit another person or car while driving. Roads are huge. There's even an extra bit of road next to the road in case you need to do a little dodge-and-sneak. The only people who get in car accidents and pile ups are purposely trying to cause damage or kill people. Take away their cars, as you so propose, and they will simply find another means to enact carnage. For example, they may buy a gun, or roll a large rock onto a highway."

"Evan," I responded. "I'm beginning to believe you're not just a perpetuator of boilerplate DMV attitudes. You're actually some sort of anti-DMV extremist, the likes of which I've never encountered before. Most of the ideas you're spewing do not deserve a rebuttal, as they can be easily disputed with public resources and common sense. Still, these statements are hurtful and derogatory, and I believe they were made with that intention. For that, and I hate that it has come to this, I believe the best course of action is to burn your "Roadwork" during my company's next barbeque-and-family-meet-and-greet. I realize now I'm not just protecting a docile piece of bureaucracy. I'm putting up a noble fight against hit-and-runs, vehicular homicide, and, as you call it, *automotive anarchy*."

"Dear I-95 Inquisitor," sent Evan, "I am writing to you from the seat of a modified Toyota Supra with a spark plug built into my tailpipe. As I rev my engine, I am spewing flames from the back of my car onto a pile of legal documents. In retaliation for burning my short story, I'm burning my license, registration, and proof of insurance. As you have desecrated my art, I have now desecrated your own. I'd say we're even…."

"Evan," I gave up. "I'd say you're right."

- Lifesaving License-Examiner, Andrew Spadden

Appendix: Help, I've Purchased an eBook

As mentioned in the prologue, the wide distribution of electronic literature has absolutely put a damper on book burnings. With books existing in a digital format, it feels kind of helpless burning physical copies. After all, as long as these digital copies exist, the book can be reprinted. It's harder than ever to wipe an idea off the face of the earth, and it's easier than ever to spread new ideas rapidly and anonymously. That said, all hope is not lost. To repeat myself, book burnings have never been 100% effective at deleting disagreeable premises from history. If that's your end goal, you're going to be disappointed. The spirit of book burning is in the symbolic nature of defiance against the idea that's been lit aflame. It's basically viral marketing—fires spread, and as more and more people copy your book burning, it will raise awareness. Soon you have an entire movement of people standing in solidarity against a book of your choosing.

In other words, it doesn't matter if a copy is technically being destroyed when you're burning your ebook. All that matters is the show. To achieve the best effect, I would bring the book up on an electronic tablet. Tablets are pretty book-shaped, and you can set it up so it's showing the book's cover on the front. Now, tablets are a bit harder to burn than book materials. You should still start by finding a patch of gravel far from any vehicles or powerlines but then throw the tablet directly into the center of the pit before doing any lighting. Then, you'll want to put on full facepiece respirators. After that, stack some paper towel rolls filled with dryer lint on top of the tablet. Next, find an old piece of mail, hold it by its edge, and light the corner. Toss this on top of the paper towel rolls, and that should be enough to get you started.

Now it may take a much longer time to burn through an electronic device than it does a paper copy. You're going to have to be patient. In the meantime, prepare more paper towel rolls stuffed with lint in case the fire gets too weak. You'll want to keep it hot until the battery inside the tablet explodes. With that pop, you'll have made your point.

If you enjoyed this book... it's part of a series! The Odd Fiction series also includes *Pages from the Pizza Crows* and *Digest: Ten Short Stories by Convicted & Plausible People-Eaters.* Each short story collection contains ten really weird short stories contained in an equally weird framing device. Also, my first full-length novel, *Tall People,* is up for pre-order due out February 2025.

If you enjoyed this book... write a review on Amazon and Goodreads. Seriously. Do it now before you forget. People put it off till later and then never do it. Do it. Make an account and add a review. Don't have an account? Get an account. It's not a contract with Satan; it's a ten-minute process to help struggling artists.

If you enjoyed this book... follow me on social media. @authorevanwitmer is the hottest thing on TikTok and Instagram—make a short video reviewing my book and tag me in it (you might receive treasure). The Odd Fiction Facebook page is constantly posting free short stories before they're published in print. Send me an email to oddfiction528@gmail.com to be added to our mailing list. The people who did that already just got this book for free. I'm just saying a fourth book is definitely in the works.

If you enjoyed this book... force people to read it. Yell at them. Get scary and obsessive. Tie the book to a tree in your neighbor's yard. Read it out loud in a Taco Bell bathroom. I don't know. I'm not selling as much as I should be. I need help. Please. I'm so fucking poor. My cat needs milk. I can't afford gas for my car, so I have to take my push-bike to work. It's getting real bad. I might have to sell my laptop for food. Then I'll be forced to write on the walls, and we all know how that ends.